THE GHOST OF GOLD CREEK

Lisa Michelle Hess

Praise for *The Ghost of Gold Creek*

"Lisa Michelle Hess sculpts characters in *The Ghost of Gold Creek* that stand the test of many readings. But to say Misty, Lou, and Ford are compelling is like saying their relationships and adventures are only side-notes. Instead, the masterful combination of mystery, action, actors, and fresh writing style mix to make a lasting impression. I've just added Hess to the top of my Authors to Watch list."
~ Peter Leavell, author of the award-winning
***Dakota Sunrise* series**

"A sleuthing adventure that delights the senses. Beautiful, romantic, and suspenseful, a memorable YA debut readers are sure to love."
~ Heather Woodhaven, author of *Protected Secrets*

"I love this book! Beautifully written with insight as well as humor, *Ghost of Gold Creek* has it all—adventure, mystery, danger, heartbreak and romance, plus an archeology dig. Young Adult readers as well as the young at heart will sink deep into Misty's world and not come up for air until the final word."
~ Rebecca Carey Lyles, author of the *Kate Neilson* Series

"*The Ghost of Gold Creek* is a coming of age novel like a memorable summer, exciting, introspective and hinting at first love."
~ Hilarey Johnson, author of the award-winning
***Breaking Bonds* series**

"I like mysteries, I like adventures, I like ghost stories… I especially like really good writing. Lisa Michelle Hess gets an "A" in every one of my categories with *The Ghost of Gold Creek*, along with emotional twists and turns that kept me riveted right to the end of the book."
~ Patrick E. Craig, best-selling author of
The Mystery of Ghost Dancer Ranch

A Note to Readers

Some friends and I got together and filmed a few scenes from *The Ghost of Gold Creek*—a little bit cosplay, a little bit movie trailer—a whole lot of fun. If you're reading this novel electronically, you can click on the links you'll find three times in this book, to see a short preview of what's coming up next in the story. Real book readers can type the links into their browsers to see these scenes, as well. See the full book trailer at https://youtu.be/JYLu3Nkijr0 Or, if you prefer your own imagination, ignore the links, and just keep reading. Either way, enjoy, and thanks for reading!

Best,

LMH

For my sister, who said,
"This would make a great novel, Lis. You should write it."

"I will not leave you as orphans.
I will come to you."

THE DREAM

UNSEEN, I STAND ON the edge of a mountain and observe the events that transformed my life. I ache with futility and my desire to change the past. But there is no going back, only forward.

This dream always begins with a woman, illuminated by the light of a full moon. Kneeling on snowshoes, she comforts a lucky tourist—lucky, because he won't die this night. The man is waist-deep in the snow, victim of a common mistake among tourists during the mountain's spring thaw. He's fallen into a snowy sinkhole at the base of a tree. He has a broken leg and cracked ribs, and his face is twisted in pain.

By some trick of the airwaves, his family managed to make cell contact with the woman, at a U.S. Forest Service station, in a little mountain town called Alton, Washington. She tells him to hang on. She reassures him with a confident grin that he'll be okay, and I see the agony and stress flow out of him.

He believes her, because no one can resist Mom's smile.

The tourist's wife and kids gather nearby, refusing to leave his side, and the rescue helicopter has only so much room. Mom, who is muffled in her thick Forest Service parka and fur-lined hood, volunteers to stay behind. She tells them she'll enjoy the hike back down, jokes around with the crew, and they don't worry. My mother is soft on the inside but mountain-tough on the outside and intrepid. She has years of mountaineering experience. When the others leave her, she is less than a mile from the trailhead.

She waves, and the helicopter roars away. Their lights turn, point toward Alton, and in minutes, the silence settles around her. She switches on a head lamp and begins the journey home, weaving her expert way through the trees and down the steep slope.

Tackling a snowy mountain is Mom in her element. I'm aware that she's anxious to get home to us—she knows she shouldn't be up there alone. I also know she loves this moment: The polar sting of crystal night air in her lungs. The way the frosted mountainside glows in the rising moon's light.

But the warmth of the day has begun an early thaw. When the sun went down, the temperature dipped, and the trickling slope turned into a sheet of ice. Slippery, no-way-to-stop-yourself ice.

All it takes is one wrong step.

She slips in silence over the edge of the ravine. I go with her, and for a moment we're floating together. Sometimes those few seconds are long enough for her to speak to me, and she always says the same thing, "You're just like him."

Our bond ends with an abrupt thud against the tree where her body comes to rest, and here is where I usually wake up, tears on my cheeks. Tonight, as never before, I can feel her pain in every bone of my own broken body. This is new, and so is what comes next.

ONE

"MY NAME IS MISTY Stevens." I tried to catch my breath between words. "Is my mom… Are my mom and dad here? Karen and Paul Stevens?"

The receptionist pushed a button and said my name into the mouthpiece of her headset. She listened, nodding, then raised solemn eyes to mine. "Someone is coming for you, Misty. You can wait right here."

I had the impression she'd been expecting me. I wasn't sure if that was good or bad, and my faith that everything would be okay began to waiver. After a few minutes, a nurse appeared from around a corner and approached me with a practiced half-smile that fit every scenario I could imagine.

She said my name and I nodded, trying to interpret her expression. Before I could manage a question, she asked me to follow her. With brisk steps, she led me down a bright hospital corridor. She seemed kind. Why did it feel like there was a band around my heart, squeezing tighter and tighter?

We entered something like a small waiting room, only it had a door you could close, and no one else was waiting. The nurse said, "You can have a seat here," as she scooped a pile of magazines off a stiff-looking sofa. "Your father's on his way."

I didn't sit. I stood in the middle of that room as if I'd lost the will to move.

Dad's husky frame filled the doorway. He made his way toward me unsteadily, exchanging a glance and nod with the nurse as they passed each other. I scanned his face, once again searching for clues. He looked like any archaeologist coming off a site—like he'd dug himself up. Only, in the grime on his cheeks, clean streaks ran from his eyes to his beard. Never in my fifteen years of life had I seen my father cry.

I collapsed onto the hard sofa and waited. Dad pulled up a chair across from me. He sat, unspeaking and hunched over, fingers laced so tightly his knuckles turned white. His lips parted, but no sound came out. Silence filled the room, and I was okay with that. As long as he didn't say the words, I could pretend Mom was alive and well.

Finally, from that bowed head, came a raspy whisper. "The emergency team did everything humanly possible, Misty." His voice caught and he shook his head. "Your mom is gone."

"I'm so sorry." The words tumbled from my lips before I could even think. I wanted to make him feel better. I was desperate for him to turn back into the strong, confident Dad I'd always known and make everything right. But I'd said I was sorry as if it was my fault. As if he'd lost more than I had.

His head shot up and his startled eyes locked onto mine. There was the hospital buzz all around us, the concerned-looking doctor hovering outside the open doorway. None of that mattered. Inside our bubble, the world stopped.

I didn't know what Dad was thinking, but I was willing him with everything in me to say I'd heard him wrong. He would reassure me, tell me this was all a mistake and there was still hope.

Instead, his face crumpled and tears seeped from his closed lids. For the first time, I watched my dad cry, and his tears washed away the world I'd always known.

I expected him to put his arms around me and pull me close—like Mom would have done. But he didn't know how to comfort me any more than I knew how to help him. Comforting was Mom's role in both our lives, and she was gone. *She was gone.*

I was on my own.

Dad opened his eyes, but he looked at the ceiling, not me. In halting words, he explained what happened, as if he was still trying to understand. I thought I should be crying, but I wasn't. My hands were cold and clammy. My entire body was covered in goose bumps. A shudder ran up my spine that left me weak and lightheaded. But no tears.

"She survived long enough in the ravine to make contact with the rescue crew," he said. "By the time they got down to her, it was too late."

Beyond numb, I didn't startle when Mom's friend, June Phillips, burst into the room, her daughter, Lou, close behind. "Paul, I'm sorry it took us so long to get here…"

Dad stood and turned. June took in both our faces and pulled up short.

My best friend dodged around her mom and threw herself on the couch next to me, practically in my lap. "Misty, this is so awful. Your poor mom." I barely registered that she was in her workout clothes. June must have picked her up at the dance studio. Despite her nickname, Lou was all girl, and she was in full drama mode. She put her arms around my neck and laid her head on my shoulder, unaware of how bad the news really was.

I said nothing, finding it harder and harder to swallow past the lump in my throat.

I could see them both in profile, and all Dad had to do was shake his head at June. Her mouth opened and her whole body slumped. "Oh, no." She took in a sharp breath, reached out and touched his arm.

Lou must have been watching, because I felt the shock go through her. She pulled back and whispered, "Misty."

But I couldn't look at her. I couldn't tear my eyes from Dad. He squeezed June's hand and turned toward the waiting doctor.

June was wiping away tears with both hands by the time she turned toward me. Her gaze softened and she murmured, "Okay." She squared her shoulders, took a deep breath and let it out slowly on her way to the empty seat beside me.

Easing me close to her, she kissed the top of my head and reached across to grasp Lou's hand. Encircled in their grief and their love, my throat tightened around a rising sob.

June whispered, "I'm so sorry, Misty. I went by your house like your Dad asked me to, but you were already gone. How did you get here?"

"I heard it on the scanner." I was surprised at how normal my voice sounded. "I rode my bike."

She nodded, and we all fell silent. What else was there to say?

Outside the open door, I could see Dad talking to the doctor. He took the clipboard the doctor handed him and signed the papers attached to it. When he gave them back, the doctor said something I couldn't hear, placed a hand on Dad's shoulder and walked away. And that was it. That's all it took to transform a family from one that everybody envied, to only Dad and me.

He rubbed his face and stared at the dirt that came off on his hands. He acted surprised, like he'd forgotten he was checking sites along the river earlier that day—as if he'd forgotten everything about his life before Mom's accident. That was when I felt the first tear run down my cheek, because I understood. This moment was surreal, except for one, sharp, piercing piece of reality we couldn't shake: Mom was gone.

TWO

THE SOUND OF LOU'S whistling snore woke me, and I glanced past the back of Dad's head to see we'd driven into rain. Water poured down the windshield and faint lines on the highway glistened in the glow of our headlights. I dozed and woke and dozed again, always to the sound of our tires slashing through water and the windshield wipers' rhythmic beat.

IT SOUNDED FAR AWAY, Dad's voice. "Girls. We're here."

I opened my eyes and gently lifted Lou's head off my shoulder. She face-planted into her pillow, pulled her blanket over her head and mumbled, "Five more minutes."

Raindrops drizzled across the windows, but I could see dark trees on either side of the rutted driveway our Suburban was bucking over. Eventually, even Lou was jarred awake.

After what seemed like forever, we broke into a clearing and rattled to a stop next to a ranch house with lines I recognized—Mom's childhood home. From old photos I'd rescued out of her stuff, which Dad had mostly gotten rid of, I knew this house was cedar-sided, sitting in a clearing surrounded by evergreens.

In the headlights, the house appeared larger than in the photos, and lonelier. A few steps led to a wrap-around covered porch and a rough timber door.

Dad turned off the car and the only sound was the ticking of the old engine cooling.

He blew out a long breath and glanced back at us. "I need to find a bathroom and a bed. Why don't you girls dig out whatever you'll need for tonight. We'll unpack the rest in the morning."

I hoisted myself over the back of the bench seat and extracted a duffle bag, one I hoped held my toothbrush along with some clothes. Lou dug around for a couple of her bags, while Dad opened up the back and pulled out a suitcase.

A blast of damp, fresh air blew into the car, and I smelled…*something*. Nostalgia whispered a faint memory, which vanished before my groggy mind could grasp it. I struggled out of the back seat burdened with bags, blanket and pillow and trudged up the porch steps ahead of the others.

"Go ahead on in, Mist," Dad called. "I got a text a couple hours ago. They left it unlocked for us. Key'll be inside."

I held the wood-trimmed screen open with my body, but hesitated before turning the door's knob. After that day at the hospital three months ago, when Dad had told me mom was gone, crossing new thresholds and stepping into unfamiliar territory made my heart race and my breath scarce.

Dad sounded tired and just barely hanging on to patient when he came up behind me. "Something wrong, Mist?"

I breathed in, heart pounding, and twisted the knob. It was stiff. I had to put a shoulder against the door and lean hard to shove it open. Hinges creaked in protest as I stumbled inside to a pitch-black room and pulled up short. Lou bumped into the back of me.

"Hold up. I'll get it." In the dim porch light, I could see Dad fumble along the wall next to the door. "There it is." A click of the switch, and the room lit up.

Lou whimpered, "Ouch," and covered her eyes. Arm outstretched like a blind person, she inched forward and eased herself over the arm of an old, brown-and-tan plaid couch. Flopping backward with her pillow over her face, she mumbled, "I'm sleeping here."

Dad pushed the door shut behind me. "It's up to you, Lou." He pointed at a narrow flight of steep stairs. "But I'm guessing we can find some slightly more comfortable digs if we look around."

Despite Lou's protests, the wimpy overhead light wasn't that bright. The dull glow it shed on the large space left the room's edges in shadow. It felt creepy, as if we were sneaking into someone else's house.

On my right was the living room and Lou on the sofa. She lifted the pillow off her face and craned her neck to squint at the narrow stairway, which actually looked like it led to nothing more than a hole in the ceiling. In front of the sofa was a log coffee table on a round, threadbare rag rug. A recliner rocker sat in one corner, an ancient wood stove squatted in the other.

To my left, a chrome-trimmed table floated in a sea of bare wood floor. Its blue speckled Formica top matched the cracked blue vinyl seats of the four chrome chairs gathered around it. Through the open doorway beyond the table, I could see the corner of a refrigerator.

Dad strode across the room and opened one of the two doors in the opposite wall.

I startled when Lou leaped up. "Bathroom, yes! I call it." She slipped past Dad and shut the door behind her.

"One bathroom and two teenaged girls." Dad looked resigned. "For an entire summer. This should be fun."

He shrugged in response to my look, which held the opposite of sympathy. "I know." He moved toward the other door. "Coming here this summer wasn't your idea."

"Right?" I joined Dad at mystery door number two. "Bedroom, I presume?"

"Yep." He opened the door and switched on another dim overhead light. Most likely, the room had once been a large master bedroom. Now, it was more like a bunk house, with one double bed and two of the walls lined with bunk-beds. Hooks and shelves covered the other walls.

"Huh." Dad frowned. "They must have some large groups that come through here."

I had an awful thought. "We're not all sleeping in this room?" I stared at him, wide-eyed.

The toilet flushed and Lou wandered out of the bathroom. She glanced at us standing in the doorway of the bedroom, shrugged, and ventured up the squeaky staircase.

"What?" Dad peered over his glasses. "The idea was to spend some quality bonding time this summer, wasn't it?"

"Dad," I figured he was teasing, but I was in desperate need of reassurance. "You are joking, right?"

Before he could answer, a thud dropped above our heads, followed by the sound of creaking floor-boards. Lou's muffled

"Oh, cool," filtered down to us. "Misty! Come up here. This is gonna be great."

I whirled, leaving Dad and the bunk room behind without a backward glance.

Upstairs, Lou stood in the middle of an attic loft bedroom. Through two four-pained windows on the wall behind her, I could see out over the porch to the dark outline of woods beyond the front yard. Twin beds under the windows held bare mattresses, but someone had left thermal blankets and sheets folded on top of them.

Lou threw herself onto one of the beds and stretched out, hands behind her head, legs crossed. "This is way better than I expected, Misty. I mean, it's basic but it'll be cool. Like a summer-long slumber party in a tree house."

She pulled a bunch of bracelets off her wrists and dropped them on an apple crate between the two beds. A double dresser was pushed against the wall next to the doorway, the only other piece of furniture in the room. Here, too, hooks lined the walls.

Lou was right. There was something charming about the loft, and I tried to picture my Mom in this room—like a princess in a tower. Only, western style.

It didn't take us long to make up the beds with the donated linens and the quilts we'd brought from home. I snuggled under my blankets and lay there, listening to the creaks and groans of the old house. It smelled like most dig quarters, musty, with hints of mold, sweat, old food smells and pine-scented cleaning chemicals. Other than Lou's soft snores, it was very quiet—even compared to sleepy little Alton back home, but the house's thin walls weren't exactly sound-proof. I could hear the wind in the trees and the soft rain's patter on the porch roof.

Few people would find the place luxurious, but despite the familiar scent, this was way better than most archaeology camps. Mom had donated the land and its buildings to the Forest Service after her parents had passed away. It was the house where she'd been born and raised, picking apples, farming, and breaking horses with her father. Something about it was already beginning to feel like home.

No sign of Mom, though. I was pretty sure the thrift store furniture I'd seen so far was not the same furniture Mom's family had owned. A lot of those pieces were back home in Alton. The attic was empty of discarded possessions—no old toys or posters on the walls—not one thing to haunt me with the memory of my mother. I should have been relieved.

I WOKE WITH TEARS on my cheeks from the same recurring dream where I found myself, on the side of a mountain, watching Mom's last moments of life, night after night.

Filtered light danced across pine beams above me, and the only sound was an occasional plop, like water dripping somewhere outside.

I rubbed my eyes and peeked over at Lou, hoping I hadn't been yelling in my sleep again. A strangled snuffling erupted from the tangle of pillow, blankets and girl as she turned over, undisturbed by the tinny ping of old bed springs. I breathed a sigh of relief. She was still asleep.

Clutching the covers under my chin, I remembered my disappointment of the night before. The familiar band tightened around my chest—

I caught a glimpse of something on the log beam directly over my head. I pushed the covers back and struggled to stand in the middle of the bed. Groggy and a little off-balance, I used the wall beside the bed to steady myself. With my other hand, I traced the rough letters with my finger. K A M, crudely carved as if by a young child, but unmistakably Mom's initials—Karen Anya Murphy.

My knees hit the bed and I exhaled. After accepting the fact that we were coming here for the summer, ready or not, I'd hoped to find some sign of mom in the Juliet Mountains. And this was it—proof my mom was here, before she was my mom.

I smiled. She'd left this one signature behind. Were there others? I had all summer to search for them.

I crawled to the head of the bed and reached for the window above it. Pushing the faded curtain aside, I twisted the old bronze latch and cracked open the window. Water droplets sprinkled onto the porch roof below. I shivered in the moist morning air that seeped in.

In the distance, the whistle-warble call of a meadowlark tangled with the nearby rustle of a breeze through tall grass. I breathed in the pungent scent of wet sage and…something else. It was the scent from the night before, whispering of my childhood—sharp evergreen with undertones of warm, sweet vanilla—ponderosa pine.

I'm toddling through dry evergreen needles, placing one foot in front of the other, holding my hands out for balance. Stumbling across a rough spot, I abruptly find myself sitting. Unbothered, my gaze moves up, up, trying to see the tops of the trees. But they are too high. I put my hands out to keep from falling backward, scrunch my fingers in the pine needles, and quickly shake them when the tiny barbs prick my skin.

All around me, scraps of sunlight litter the forest floor. Though I suspect they can't be captured, my arm stretches toward the closest one. The sound of my mother's laughter stops me. I look up to see her smile, and I giggle in response.

She sits behind me, puts an arm around my waist and pulls me into her lap. With her other hand she gently turns my pudgy palm up and moves it beneath one of the beams of light. I hold the bright spot in my hand, and it feels warm, like a kiss.

I don't know how I knew, but I was certain that memory had happened here, in this place, somewhere in the Juliet Mountains.

Lou groaned, pressed her face into her pillow and burrowed farther under her covers. I let the curtain drop, climbed out of bed and dug some sweats out of my bag. The bottom of me taken care of, I tiptoed across the cold wood to where my hoodie lay in a heap in the corner. After shaking it out, because, *spiders*, I pulled it over the thin t-shirt I'd worn to bed.

Based on the mingled aromas of aftershave and freshly ground coffee that met me half-way down the stairs, I figured Dad was already up, but he was nowhere in sight. I rummaged through the grocery bags parked on the kitchen counter. Among other things, I discovered some instant hot chocolate packets, toast-makings, and homemade huckleberry jam from our favorite booth at the Alton Farmer's Market.

My breakfast balanced in one hand, I opened the front door and pushed through the unlatched screen. The seating choices were two, weathered Adirondack chairs and a swing attached to the porch roof. I gave the swing a little nudge with my knee. It creaked sleepily back and forth.

Enticed, but not quite trusting it, I set my cup on the railing and settled into one of the chairs, pulling my bare feet onto the chair and stretching the bottom of my hoodie around my knees. The morning was still and cool. This was where I was going to spend the summer, and I had to admit, it was beautiful.

In front of the house, a small patch of spindly pine grass, cropped short, was bordered by a split-log fence on the far side. Past the fence, a gravel drive ran from the back of the house and connected to the rough dirt road that led to the highway. Grassland that had probably once been pasture stretched out beyond the drive until it met a thick stand of pine and underbrush.

I stared at those trees and that feeling of familiarity crept back. I'd been here before, I was sure of it. Or not. Maybe I only recognized features from all the pictures of Mom's childhood Lou and I had been poring over and posting for weeks.

I'd managed one sip of cocoa when I heard brisk footsteps crunching through gravel from behind the house. Dad appeared on the driveway. "Morning Misty!" He took the porch steps two at a time, more cheerful than I'd seen him in weeks.

I gave him a crooked smile, still only half-awake.

He gave the swing a push. "Let me do some work on that before anyone sits on it." He gestured toward the mountain peaks that rose above the trees, blue and hazy in the early morning light.

I nodded. "Yeah."

Dad sucked in a deep breath, exhaled and dropped into the chair next to me. It felt like we were alone in the universe and that usually made me uncomfortable. But the sweetness of the cocoa on my tongue, the warmth of the cup between my hands, and the beauty of the morning—it was a near-perfect moment.

I heard a familiar snuffling sound above us, and Dad made a face. I'd left my window open and the sound of Lou snoring in her bed easily carried to the porch.

He gave my arm a nudge. "Guess what I found in the barn out back."

"Not rats or something nasty, I hope?"

"Ah, Misty, always the optimist. Nope, nothing nasty. I found all the equipment for the project that I asked for, which is good. In addition—" He paused dramatically. "I found a surprise."

"What kind of a surprise?" I was suspicious. Springing this project on me and uprooting me from my home had been enough of Dad's surprises for one summer. "A good surprise or a bad surprise?"

He squinted into the distance, as if he was seriously considering my question. "I guess that all depends on your point of view. I think she and I have come to an understanding, though."

"You and—*who*? Dad! What's in that barn?" I struggled to get out of the low chair while balancing my plate and cup so I could check out the barn for myself.

He reached for my dishes, laughing. "Need a little help, there?"

At the sound of vehicles rattling up the long, bumpy drive from the highway, we both turned. A U.S. Forest Service truck came into view, followed by a cool, faded-blue Ford F-150.

Dad jumped to his feet. "Here comes the welcome wagon. Why don't you see what you can do with the undead up there, while I get acquainted with our hosts. We'll meet you girls around back at the barn when you're dressed."

I started for the door, but turned back. "Dad?"

"What is it, Misty?"

"Have I been here before? With Mom, I mean?"

"You know," he nodded, stroking his beard with two fingers. "I'd forgotten, but you *were* here once before, right after your grandma passed away. I was stuck on a project, so I came for the memorial service and left. You and Karen stayed to clean out the house." He shook his head. "I don't know how you could remember it, though. You were, what, maybe two years old? Did she tell you about it?"

I shrugged. He studied me for another couple of seconds, turned and headed down the porch steps.

But Mom hadn't told me, and I did remember that day in the woods. It was one of the first lessons my mother ever taught me—that things aren't always what they seem, but they can still be beautiful.

For a preview of what's coming up, go to
https://youtu.be/SNz74ApSR6M

WHILE DAD WAS TALKING to the people from the local Forest Service office, I showered and dressed and, after repeated attempts, managed to drag Lou from her quilt cocoon. She mumbled something unintelligible and headed straight for the bathroom, so I decided to unpack my stuff. I pulled out jeans and shorts, a couple flannel shirts and a bunch of t-shirts. I had the flip flops I'd worn on the trip the day before. I'd also brought my hiking boots to work in, and my favorite pair of blue Chucks.

I deposited the box of Mom's photographs on the apple crate between our beds and pulled out her old orange sweater that I'd stuffed in the bag with the photo box. After I hung the sweater on one of the pegs, I stepped back. I wasn't sure why I'd thrown it in at the last minute.

I grabbed my sneakers and hit the main floor as Lou emerged from the bathroom in a cloud of steam, stunning, as always. She was wearing boots, jeans and a t-shirt with *Doesn't Need A Cowboy* emblazoned in sequins across the front. She twisted her long, dark hair into a bun and smiled. "Let's do it."

I felt like a little kid standing beside her in my blue Converse, frayed cut-offs, and a vintage Care Bear t-shirt, water still dripping off the ends of my blonde dreads. For sure, no one would ever mistake us for twins.

I raised an eyebrow. "Nice shirt."

"Yeah, go Mom. She gave it to me at the beginning of rodeo season, before I dashed all her dreams about my barrel racing star status this summer. I have to say, though, I actually love this shirt."

I elbowed her. "You're a star to me." I was only half-joking. I loved Lou, the best friend I'd ever found in all our moves and all the remote locations over the years. Always being the new kid, the new homeschooled kid, was sort of the nightmare of my childhood. It was so hard, in fact, that the years we lived in places where there were no other kids, where it was only me and my parents, those were the best years of my life.

Until Lou.

She was a year older than I was, but we'd connected the first time we met. I think she needed someone in her life who wasn't bursting with expectations for her future successes. I just needed a friend. She was beautiful and popular and her family had lived in Alton forever. When she accepted me, so did all her other friends. It wasn't going too far to say she'd changed my life.

"Thanks for coming along and keeping my summer from being a total loss."

"Are you kidding me?" She looked at me like I was crazy. "A chance to get away from my mom for a few weeks? You're doing *me* a favor. I love her, but she was driving me insane! 'You're not a little girl anymore Lou. You need to make a decision, Lou. Dancing or rodeo, Lou'—gah!"

Lou's June impression was spot on.

"It was like she kept confusing me with you. So sad." She sighed, shaking her head. "You'd think she'd know by now, you're the responsible daughter. I'm the flighty daughter, and from what I know about her teen years, I'm exactly what she deserves."

When we walked out the front door, the vehicles were all parked in front of the house, but no one was around, so we headed back to the barn. There was still moisture in the air, but the day was warming and drying fast now that the sun was up. Nothing stayed damp for long in the high desert, even this far up in the mountains. I knew that from past projects.

We were almost to the barn—another cedar-sided building with a pitched roof, weathered to gray—when the door crashed open. I stopped short, but Lou jumped back and yelled, "Whoa!" as a tall lanky guy stumbled out the door, struggling with the kind of heavy framed screen archaeologists use to sift dirt.

Dust and bits of hay swirled and settled around him and we all stared at each other in surprise. He was about seventeen, I guessed, with short black hair and equally dark eyes—eyes that sized up Lou and me in no time flat. "Uh, hi," he mumbled, moving past us with the screen.

"Hi," I responded. *So awkward.*

Lou didn't say anything at first, and we watched him walk away. But before he was out of earshot, she purred, "Hmm, that looks promising."

The guy's step faltered, and I wanted to climb under the nearest rock. My elbow made contact with her rib cage and she said, "Ow! What?" The look she threw me was completely innocent.

I heard Dad clear his throat behind us. "Girls?" We swiveled back around toward the barn and there was Dad, standing in the doorway. A stocky, friendly-looking man in a Forest Service uniform stood next to him. "I'd like you to meet Kurt Hansen, the director for the Juliet Wilderness Area. Kurt, this is my daughter Misty and her friend, Lou Phillips."

Kurt smiled. "Nice to meet you, girls." We all shook hands. "Glad you could join us." He nodded toward the place where the mysterious guy had disappeared around the house. "I guess you two already met Ford."

Lou giggled. "Not exactly, but we'd like to." This time she stepped back, out of elbow range.

I looked from Kurt to my father. "And Ford would be…?"

Kurt gave Lou a bemused look and turned to me. "Ford Tomaka is the son of a friend and colleague of mine from a forest up in Montana. He's interning with me this summer and he'll be working on the Passports in Time team with you two. Most of the volunteers are camping up at the Gold Creek campground. It's closer to the site. But Ford's folks are old family friends, so he's staying with me in town."

Kurt's gaze moved past us and he called, "Ford, come on over and I'll introduce you to a couple more members of your Passports team."

Lou and I turned back around—I was getting dizzy—and there was the guy, Ford, striding toward us, minus the screen. He smiled only the slightest of smiles when we were introduced, but he seemed nice. Secretly, I agreed with Lou. This project seemed a lot more interesting than it had a few minutes ago.

"Kurt was telling us you're from Montana," Dad said.

"Yeah," Ford said. "We've been all over the West, though. Lived in a couple places in Washington, and northern Idaho, before my family landed in Montana." His eyes met mine. "You know how it is."

I did know. When he said that, though, I realized how few kids had career Forest Service parents like mine. This was one aspect of who I was that Lou, an Alton girl born and bred, really didn't get. But Ford would.

I barely had a chance to nod agreement before he turned back to Dad. "This is the first time I've been to the Juliets. My grandma and grandpa live up near Pendleton, though, and I've spent summers with them."

"Your mom said you have some people down near here, too," Kurt said.

Ford nodded, but I watched his smile fade. He looked down and kicked a boot in the dirt. For whatever reason, he didn't want to talk about that side of his family.

"So, Dad," I dove in, breaking the awkward silence. "What was the 'surprise' you found in the barn this morning?"

Lou started for the barn door. "Oh, yeah! Misty was telling me the barn has secrets."

"Come and see." He ushered the two of us into the barn and the others followed. It took my eyes a minute to adjust to the dim light, so I heard a nicker before I saw the horse.

"Oooh," Lou squealed. "Adorable!"

With complete confidence, like she owned the barn, Lou strode straight for the stall in front of us and the short, stocky, red roan horse it contained. "She's a mare?" Lou asked, looking back at Kurt, who nodded.

The mare's head looked too large for her small body, and her huge ears flicked back and forth, alert to the racket we strange creatures were making in her barn. Her eyes widened and her nostrils flared. As Lou moved toward the roan, she snorted and backed away.

"Oh, stop," Lou half-scolded. "It's all right." She scanned the barn and pointed to a box of horse cookies. "Ford, help me out here."

He grabbed a cookie and tossed it to Lou, who caught it in mid-air. The movement caused the horse to startle slightly, but she couldn't back any farther into her stall.

"Look what I've got," Lou sang softly. She extended her arm and held the treat close enough for the horse to reach by stretching her neck over the stall's gate. "Come on," she coaxed, "you know you want it."

The mare stepped forward, eyed the treat and breathed a loud snort. Her eyes rolled back to Lou, who gave the cookie a little wiggle. After a few more seconds, shuffling hooves and more snorts, she moved closer and stretched her head toward the cookie. She nosed it, then wrapped her lips around the treat.

Lou let go and brushed her hands together. "There now."

The horse munched the treat, her eyes on Lou, who was smiling. "See what you get for being so brave?" She reached over the gate and patted the horse's side. The mare's muscles twitched nervously under Lou's hand.

"Who does she belong to?" I wondered out loud.

"Cool, huh?" Dad said. "Kurt says she's a rescue horse."

Ford walked over and joined Lou at the stall. Kurt was leaning in the open doorway, and as he watched Ford and Lou with the horse, he smiled. He glanced at Dad. "Looks like everyone's getting along great."

"I told you they'd be fine," Dad said. He turned to me. "One of Kurt's assistants owns Rosa. She's gone for the summer, studying wild horses on an island off the Japanese coast."

"Always been a dream of hers, apparently," Kurt said. "We were hoping you young ladies wouldn't mind helping out with Rosa while you're here."

Ford rubbed a hand down Rosa's neck. "Does being a rescue horse mean she was abused? She looks okay to me."

"She was abused," Kurt said, "but she's doing great now. Susan's done wonders with her. That horse was nothing but a scared bag of bones when she first came here, but she was always sweet. You can see she's shy, though, and if she finds a situation uncomfortable, Susan says she shuts down."

"Come say hi, Misty," Lou called.

I shook my head. "I think she's met enough new people for this morning. We'll get acquainted later." The fact was, Ford acted as comfortable, and experienced, with horses as Lou was. I wanted to pet Rosa, but I didn't want an audience.

"Kurt and I are going to head over to the office," Dad said, "and pick up the rig we'll be using to drive everyone out to the work site. Ford, Lou, we'll have plenty of chances to get to know Rosa later. Let's get over to the campground and meet the rest of the crew."

Kurt led the way as we all tramped out of the barn and toward the cars. He turned to Ford. "Why don't you and the girls head over to the campground in your truck. Dr. Stevens and I will meet you there. Hey, Paul—" He motioned to Dad. "You can look over our GPS and surveying equipment at the shop if you want, and we'll get the stuff you need signed out to you."

I watched Dad eyeing Ford. I was pretty sure he was wondering if he could trust this guy with Lou and me. I crossed my fingers and prayed this wouldn't be one of those extremely embarrassing, over-protective parent moments.

Finally, he nodded. "Shouldn't take us long. We'll be right behind you."

I exhaled. *Disaster averted, at least for now.*

Kurt told Ford they'd meet us at the front gate, and we parted ways.

Lou swung into the truck and scooted across the bench seat to the middle, next to Ford, and I climbed in after her. Ford waited a minute to give the dust from Kurt's truck a chance to settle, rolled onto the dirt road, and we made our bumpy way to the highway.

Lou looked up at Ford. "I'm loving this truck."

Ford gave a proud nod. "Thanks. Dad and I have done a lot of work on it."

"I can see that. So, you've met the other people on the Passports team? How many are there?"

"Three others and—" He glanced at us. "You two are definitely the youngest people on the team."

She shrugged. "We figured."

"No, I mean, if you don't count me, the next youngest person is about fifty years old. And one woman has got to be pushing eighty." Ford smiled when he mentioned the eighty-year-old.

"Really?" I said. "Eighty?"

"Yeah, but she's cool."

An eighty-year-old woman who a guy thought was cool? Either there was something special about that woman, or maybe, something unique about this guy?

Ford was looking over Lou's head at me, and I was fighting the dork urge to tell him to keep his eyes on the road, when he said, "Cool hair—" and turned his attention back to the pavement in front of him.

"Oh, uh, yeah," I stuttered. "Thanks."

Lou did a double-take and winked at me with an impish grin.

I rolled my eyes, and turned away, feigning interest in the landscape outside my window. Ford's comment *had* surprised me. Up to that point, he'd seemed like a guy who didn't give a lot away.

The dreadlocks envy wasn't new to me, though. I got that from all kinds of people—except Dad, of course, who hated them. But Lou'd convinced my mom, who handled what my dad called *the girl stuff,* that my freakishly long, strawberry-blond hair would look great in dreads. I wondered, briefly, how stuff like that would work now, with Mom gone. Dad wasn't completely immune to Lou's puppy eyes, but more so than anyone else on the planet.

"Ford, where in Montana do you live?" Lou asked.

When he turned to her, their noses almost touched, which as far as I could tell, neither of them seemed to mind. He grinned. "Not too far from Missoula. You been there?"

I started to shake my head, then realized he was talking to Lou. "Oh, yeah," she answered, "rodeo every year there, at least once. Missoula's kind of a cool town."

He lifted a shoulder. "It's all right. So, you're a rodeo girl, huh? I have a lot of friends who rodeo."

For the next twenty minutes, Lou and Ford settled into a comfortable conversation about rodeoing and acquaintances they had in common. I just sat there and watched Lou deploy her awesome powers of flirtation.

The sun through the windshield warmed the cab of the truck while we rolled through a green corridor of evergreens, leafy trees and rippling, dappled shadows. I cracked open the window and leaned back in the breeze, half-listening to Ford and Lou. "Oh yeah! I know him—he's an amazing roper…" I fought the desire to close my eyes and zone out.

After about ten minutes, we came to the outskirts of a town, and Ford slowed the truck. "Welcome to thriving Ponder, Oregon."

I sat up to look around, but it didn't take us more than five minutes to drive from one end of Ponder to the other. When we passed a large grocery store with that familiar green coffee-mermaid sign, Lou yelled, "We're saved!" A city hall and a tiny library came next. I noticed a lot of empty storefronts, but I also caught a glimpse of a feed store and an auto parts store that looked like they did some business. Then, we were back into forested highway.

After another fifteen minutes, during which Ford and Lou realized they had actually met each other in Missoula two summers ago, we turned off the highway and into the campground. "Wow!" Lou was saying, "I can't believe we've met before. What a small wor—"

She stopped mid-word because the scene through the windshield in front of us was incomprehensible. Maybe I *had* fallen asleep and I was still dreaming.

A cow ran in front of the truck and Ford slammed on his brakes. Lou screamed and grabbed my arm. I gripped the door handle. The frightened animal swerved around the truck and disappeared into the trees on the side of the road.

"Whoa, *what* happened here?" Ford sounded as confused as I felt.

I'd never been in a war zone, but I imagined it would look a lot like the scene we'd just driven into. Trampled clothing, boots and backpacks littered the landscape. Downed tents lay in jumbled heaps and overturned coolers spilled their contents onto the ground. Two people dashed past, their eyes wide. Others wandered in circles as if they were in shock. Some gestured wildly and talked at full volume in a language I didn't recognize.

Weirdest of all was a mangled covered wagon that lay on its side beside cinderblock restrooms, one spinning wheel wobbling slowly to a stop.

THREE

THE MINUTE WE OPENED the pickup doors, we were accosted by an older bowlegged man in a snap-front shirt and denim jeans tucked into short boots. His gnarled hand brandished a clipboard at Ford. "You—what's your name?"

Ford took a step back.

"I'm Ford Tomaka, sir, and this is—"

"Tomaka…Toma…" The man scanned his clipboard. "You're not on my list. How do you spell that?"

Ford started to spell, "T-o-m…" His forehead wrinkled. "Um, what list is that?"

"No matter." The man waived away his question. "Sounds like you speak pretty good English for a Japanese. Can you ask one of the other delegates what happened here? I can't get anyone to give me a straight answer."

Ford glanced down at his boots and shook his head. "I'm not part of the Japanese delegation staying at your ranch. We just got here a few minutes ago. I'm sorry, but I don't know any more than you do."

The man squinted up at Ford and flipped through the pages on his clipboard once more. "I'll be durned…" Without another word, he turned and strode toward one of the many campers stumbling about the site.

Lou giggled. "He thought you were one of the tourists?"

"Yeah," he said. "Wouldn't be the first time I was mistaken for something I'm not."

I could imagine. Between his dark hair and eyes, and that last name, this probably happened to Ford all the time. "Do you know who that was?" I asked.

"Robert Blackwell." He nodded toward the man. "We've actually met, but he obviously doesn't remember me. I know his wife better—I see her in town every once in a while.

"The Blackwells own a ranch that borders the wilderness area. They take in tourists from the city and give them the 'cowboy' experience. I guess it's kind of a new operation for them, though. He has a bunch of different stuff people can sign on for, like—" he aimed a thumb at the covered wagon. "An Oregon Trail pioneer thing."

Mr. Blackwell was by now deep in conversation with a small sturdy woman who I guessed was even older than the rancher. She smiled sympathetically.

"That's Beatrice Grant he's talking to. She'll tell you she's 'Bea to her friends' when you meet her. She's part of our group—" He looked down at me. "Remember the eighty-year-old woman I was talking about?"

I nodded, watching the woman attempt to calm the old man, without much success

People passed by us, gathering clothing and gear strewn across the campground. They were still excited about the stampede, talking and making dramatic, excited gestures. A few were taking pictures with their devices and obviously posting them.

"These tourists are from Japan?" I asked.

"Yeah," Ford said. "You know how Rosa's owner, Susan, is studying that wild horse herd in Japan? She's there on an exchange program. A whole bunch of researchers from here went over there, and these guys are the researchers from Japan. Some of them are staying at Blackwell's ranch for a few days to get the pioneer experience. Some are camping here."

Blackwell shook his head at Beatrice Grant and turned, red-faced and perspiring, back toward us. I started to inch behind Ford.

A humongous white van drove through the camp's entrance and stopped. I could see Dad and Kurt through the window and gave them a panicked wave. Kurt left the van and headed off the irate rancher.

"Bob, looks like you all had some excitement out here."

"You know I've always had good relations with you people." Blackwell was so agitated he was trembling. "I do what I can to keep the peace, and I've defended what the Forest Service does in the wilderness area more than once to the other landowners. But that horse." Blackwell shook his head, jaw clenched.

Lou nudged me and whispered, "That stallion your dad told us about."

We'd heard about one of the wild stallions that roamed the area, a weird-looking rogue with deformed ears that had run-in after run-in with ranchers, visitors and other wild horses. Everyone was trying to catch him, with no luck so far.

"Look, Kurt—" Blackwell tapped a pen violently against his clipboard. "That stallion is a rogue and a danger to people and other stock. You know I don't mind the feral horses. A wild stallion sired one of my best mares and that's fine by me. But if you can't manage these herds—"

Kurt held up a hand. "You know as well as I do, we're on alert to capture that horse. I'm sorry this happened, but you can be sure we'll take care of it."

"You've always done right by me in the past, but that horse better not steal any of the private herds from the ranchers around here." He took a step closer to Kurt. "There's a lot of talk among folks about too many wild horses for the grasslands to handle. Some say they're using up your grasslands and looking for greener pastures on ours."

"That is not accurate." Kurt's mouth set in a firm line. He didn't look like someone easily bullied. "True, the herd has gotten bigger. We're planning a round-up later in the summer. But there's still plenty of forage for all the animals within the boundary."

"I'm telling you what I hear. People are upset and we're all watching to see if you can handle this rogue." He leaned closer, peered up into Kurt's eyes and growled, "So handle it." Without giving him a chance to respond, Blackwell stalked away.

Once he was out of earshot, Dad said, "That is one tough old hombre. You deal with this a lot around here?"

"More than I'd like. Blackwell's not so bad, really. But that stallion has been causing a fair amount of trouble." Kurt waved a hand that took in the carnage at the campsite and included the overturned wagon. "I'd be angry, too. Bob's right. We do need to do something about that particular mustang, at least."

Beatrice Grant, who'd been hanging back, joined our group after Blackwell left. She was chuckling and shaking her head.

"Old boy is madder than a sack full of ferrets. I sure am glad you showed up when you did, Kurt."

Kurt offered her a wry smile. "I hear we've had another stallion sighting."

"Yep! It was Lookout, mule-head and all, and he wasn't alone. He was with about five head of cattle, urging them on. The whole crew stampeded through here, and I swear—" Her face creased into a smile. "That horse had a grin on his big funny face."

"The stallion's real then," Dad said. "We thought maybe it was one of those Big Foot stories that gets passed around among the tourists."

"Lookout's real, all right, and he's getting more aggressive. I hope those cattle weren't Blackwell's." Kurt blew out a frustrated puff of air, raked his hands through his short hair and resettled his cap on his head. "I'm afraid, one way or the other, that horse has got to go."

Lou shot me a worried look.

"Is he really so dangerous?" I asked Kurt. "You could end up taking him out?"

Kurt shrugged, surveying the disaster surrounding us, and turned to Bea. "I've got to call this in Bea, take an inventory of the damage and make sure nobody was hurt." He frowned. "I'll be doing paperwork for days."

Ford asked, "Anything we can do to help?"

"Thanks," Kurt said, "but I'll call it in to the office and get some help out here immediately. It's better if my staff helps clean up, and that way we can review the damage and write up reports at the same time."

I realized Kurt had been asking Bea to take over the task of bringing all the team members together, and she seemed pleased to do it. She gave him a motherly pat. "I've got this. You go on and do your job." She turned to the rest of us with a bright smile. "Follow me, troops. I'll introduce you to the other two members of the team."

Dad tucked a map under one arm and we followed Bea, introducing ourselves to her along the way. We weaved through the campers collecting their belongings to a cozy grouping of tents in the back corner of the campground. Apparently, our fellow crew-members' campsite had been outside the path of the horse and cattle rampage.

Bea called to a couple who looked a little older than Dad. They were helping some other campers reassemble a nearby campsite. "Frank, Donna. Dr. Stevens and the others are here. Come on over when you're done."

She pointed to a large picnic table. "Can I get you folks anything? We have water. I can make coffee and I'm heating water for some tea, so either one's no trouble."

I was pretty sure Bea was one of those women you could stumble across on a desert island, and she'd rustle up a tasty lunch with nothing but a machete, a coconut and three bananas. We all opted for water, and she pointed to some icy bottles in a nearby cooler.

Lou sat down right in the middle of a bench on one side of the picnic table. I chose to walk around the table and sit next to Bea, leaving the spot on the other side, next to Lou, for Ford.

I had spent more than a few hours being Lou's ally in guy conquests. It was habit, at this point, and I'd learned a few things from her that made me appear, if not actually feel, more confident around guys.

Ford surprised me when he came around and sat on the other side of Bea, and I suppressed a smile at Lou's brief look of confusion. This boy was no pushover, I could see that already. But I was pretty sure she'd have his complete attention by the end of the afternoon, and for the rest of the summer, if she wanted it. That was fine with me. It was just sort of fascinating to watch her have to work for it.

The couple Bea had called were making their way toward us through the scattered debris. The gray-haired man's face was lined and leathery, punctuated by a bushy mustache. He and the woman, who seemed strangely familiar, shared each other's space comfortably.

"This is Frank Adams and his wife, Donna." Bea smiled up at Donna as she came and sat next to Lou, across from the older woman. "And—" Bea pointed at Donna and looked from me to Dad. "Donna also happens to be *my* daughter."

No wonder Donna seemed familiar, she was a younger version of Bea.

We exchanged names and heard about the stampede from Frank and Donna. "We've done it all!" Donna laughed. "Climbed to the top of pyramids in Mexico and had our picture taken in front of the Great Sphinx in Egypt. Swam with the dolphins and cruised the Inside Passage. But this is the first archaeological project we've ever done and the first stampede we've ever experienced."

"And," Frank said cheerfully, "we've never spent our vacation with three teenagers." He winked at me sitting across from him, but not in a creepy way. I liked all three of them already.

"Speaking of that—" Dad broke in. "I'm planning to start first thing tomorrow morning, so I'd like to fill you all in on our project."

"Oh, yes, please," Bea said. "We're excited to get started."

Dad, standing at the head of the table, pointed to the map that now lay in front of us. "We'll be driving up this Forest Service road all the way to here, right beside Gold Creek. This has become a popular spot for tourists to play at panning for gold."

"There's actually gold in Gold Creek?" Frank elbowed Donna. "Honey, we've finally struck it rich. I told you this vacation would have its own rewards!"

She laughed. "He did actually say that."

"There used to be gold in the creek," Dad said. "And veins in the mountain, in the 1860s. Every once in a while, a tourist will find a fleck or two of gold in the stream, which keeps them coming back. The area's become so popular, the Forest Service plans to put a pit toilet—" He pointed to a spot on the map next to a dirt road. "Right about here."

Lou frowned and whispered, "A *what?*"

"An outhouse," I whispered back. She gave me a weird look. I shrugged. Most Pacific Northwest archeology had to do with the effects of construction or road work—I was used to how unromantic the reality was.

"Our job," Dad continued, "is to sift through the dirt in this area and make sure the pit toilet construction isn't going to run into anything of historical significance because, and here's the kicker—one of the earliest homestead sites in Oregon is supposed to be somewhere in this area."

He circled the spot on the map where we would be working. "But it's never been pinpointed and recorded. I wouldn't mind if our team got to be the one to unearth that cabin site."

I watched Dad out of the corner of my eye. Nobody else at the table realized the significance of the kind of find he was talking about. But I could tell by the way his grin made it all the way to his eyes that in the archaeology world, finding the homestead site would be considered a huge accomplishment.

So maybe this was it—maybe this summer had nothing at all to do with Mom, or me. At least as far as Dad was concerned, it was about the itch to record a site no one else had been able to locate. This was about another accolade, another cool site he could lecture people about at another conference.

Dad spoke on, about history and archaeology, but I'd heard it all before. After a while, I elbowed Lou and we got up and slowly moved away. Ford followed us, but he seemed kind of reluctant, as if he was into the history lecture.

We wandered the campsite and passed by Kurt, who'd been joined by his crew. They were deep into cleanup and damage assessment. He gave us a distracted wave. We ended up at the campsite of some Japanese tourists Ford had met earlier in the week. They seemed fun and asked us to join them, so we ended up playing a hilarious English-as-a-second-language version of poker, with tiny pine cones for chips.

As our new friends discussed the morning's adventure in broken English, one woman asked us, "You saw the phantom?"

There was a dramatic pause, and she had the proud eyes of someone who'd just figured out how to use a new word in a sentence. We looked at each other and back to her.

Lou asked, "What do you mean?"

"You see the…" She got up and took a few galloping steps.

"Oh, the *horse*," I said.

She gave an excited nod. "Yes, yes."

Ford, Lou and I shook our heads.

"We missed him—got here too late," Ford said.

I glanced at the cards I'd been dealt, but now I wasn't really paying attention to the game.

"You lucky," she said, adding an exaggerated shudder. "I do not want to see again."

"Why did you call it *the phantom?*" I asked.

"You not know?" She raised her eyebrows. "Is…" She said something in Japanese to the man sitting next to her.

"Ghost," the man responded. He pointed to her cards. "You in?"

She leaned toward me and whispered, "Is ghost." With another little shiver she turned to the man and added, "I'm out."

Ford and Lou seemed as confused as I was.

"What do you mean?" Lou asked. "Nobody said anything about these woods being haunted."

"There you are." Dad's voice right behind us made me jump. "Let's get going, you two." I turned to see him taking in the group, the poker game. "Ford, Kurt's looking for you. He's over near Bea's camp. I think they're about ready to wrap things up."

"You okay, Mist?" Dad peered at me. "You look a little pale."

"Uh, yeah, uh huh," I stuttered. "I'm fine."

I pulled myself together and introduced Dad to our new friends. He waved and said, "I'll meet you girls at the van."

Dad took off toward the camp entrance and I turned back around to get more information about the so-called ghost, but the woman excused herself and headed toward the restrooms.

We three got up, waved goodbye and started to go our different ways. Lou said, "What do you think she meant by that? About the ghost?"

"Oh, these woods are haunted, didn't you guys hear?" Ford cracked a grin. "I don't know what she was talking about. Probably some superstitious thing." He half-saluted. "I'll see you later."

After we split up, Lou couldn't stop talking about the day and how cool Ford was as we made our way back to the camp gate. I nodded and laughed at the appropriate moments. But inside, I was thinking about what Ford had said, about the woman being superstitious. Maybe he was right, but that woman had seemed seriously spooked. Today was the first time I'd heard about the homestead site Dad was interested in, and the first anyone had mentioned ghosts. I wondered what else Dad wasn't telling me.

FOUR

A RESTLESS NIGHT'S SLEEP did nothing for my mood. The idea of Dad bringing us to the Juliets for reasons he was only now revealing left me irritated, and I was still out of sorts when we met up with Ford and the rest of the crew at the entrance to the campground.

We piled into the van and backtracked, looking for the primitive road to the project site, somewhere between Ponder and Mom's old house. The van bounced over the pitted road—barely more than a wide path—and Dad finally braked to a stop at a meadow on the banks of a gurgling little stream—Gold Creek.

The thermometer in the van read forty-eight degrees, but a breeze strong enough to make the tree branches bounce and wave blasted us when we climbed out of the van. We huddled around Dad, shivering, gloved hands stuffed in our pockets, fleece hats pulled low.

Dad walked a few steps from the group and turned. I knew he was preparing for his "Why Cultural Resource Management?" speech. I could recite it in my sleep: "Archaeology is the story of us, human beings, through time.

The official version is that archeology is the study of past ways of life through analysis of surviving physical remains."

Little puffs of fog erupted from Dad's mouth as he talked. "One of the methods we use to extract information from those remains is an archaeological survey like the one you'll be participating in. It consists of a three-phase approach to locate, evaluate, and treat significant archaeological resources or sites."

"So, what we're doing today is Phase I?" Lou asked.

Dad nodded. "That's correct."

Out of the corner of his mouth, Ford muttered, "And, wasting no time, Lou snags the teacher's pet award her first morning on the job."

"Oh, you know it," she sassed back.

Ignoring the whispers, Dad continued. "While not every construction project merits a survey or archaeological monitoring, the assessment for this area turned up information that pointed to historical significance for this site—"

"Like its proximity to the old homestead site?" Frank asked.

"Yep, and all the Euro and Native American contact that took place during the Gold Creek mining project."

Frank smirked at us and said, "Look who's the teacher's pet, now?"

I made a mental note that Frank had better hearing than most old guys, as well as a decent sense of humor.

"We may not find anything of great historical significance at this site." Dad pointed at the dirt. "But we might find some clues to lead us in the direction of the homestead site, or clues to the way the miners lived. Not a lot is written about either, so the historical record for both is here, in the ground.

"People don't really change that much. If we can understand how individuals and groups made choices in the past that led us to this moment in time, such knowledge can help us understand how our choices today might affect those standing here a thousand years from now."

I'd been starting to zone out, but Dad's last statement caught my attention. I'd heard him say it dozens of times during other projects, but it felt relevant to me for the first time. *Understanding the past can help lead us into the future.* That could be my dad's life theme. Understanding the past was crucial to his method for solving the problems of life. Why had Dad brought us here, to Mom's past? What did this summer have to do with losing her, if anything?

Lou bumping against me brought me out of myself, and I noticed she wasn't the only one starting to fidget. Bea clapped her gloved hands softly together to stay warm. Donna was bouncing up and down. Dad was losing them. But he'd been doing this a long time. He knew how to handle an audience. He shifted, ever so slightly and lowered his voice, which brought everyone's eyes back to him.

"Everything I've told you today is important to remember. But…" his gaze passed over our little huddle and one corner of his mouth tipped up. He leaned in, as if he was telling us a secret. "The reason archaeology is important, and exciting, and *downright fun*, is the possibility that you might be the one to find…*that one thing*."

He held his hands in front of him like he was clutching a treasure chest. "That thing no one else has set eyes on for five hundred, maybe more than a thousand years. The arrowhead fashioned with care by a young boy before his first hunt. The spear point refined by an ancient craftsman for the perfect kill. The beads in a row as if they were still attached to the string a husband gave his favorite wife on their wedding day."

"They had more than one?" Lou whispered.

Dad held up one of his hands, fisted it and made a quick thrust. "Or the bison head with a spear in its eye socket."

Ford said, "Cool," and Donna said, "Oh, my," and Dad stopped, letting the pictures expand in people's heads. I had to hold my lips tight to keep from smiling. He had them in the palm of his hand.

"Or maybe…" Dad caught each of our eyes in turn. "Maybe, we find one of the earliest homestead sites in the Pacific Northwest and solve the mystery of the Ghost of Gold Creek."

Wait. This wasn't part of the script. The *Ghost* of Gold Creek? The words of our new Japanese friend from last night echoed in my mind. *The horse… is ghost.*

"Now, Frank—" Dad pulled out a couple folded pieces of paper. "I heard you have some experience with cartography?"

By now, we were all exchanging puzzled looks, especially Bea, who'd been listening to Dad with the intensity of someone whose hearing wasn't what it used to be.

"Uh, yes. Yes, Dr. Stevens." Frank blinked. "I was a cartographer in the war."

"I remember reading that in the profile you provided. I was wondering if you could take a look at these plans and help me decide where to start."

"I'd be honored."

I was about to break in, but Ford beat me to it. "Um, Dr. Stevens? The ghost of Gold Creek? You didn't mention anything like that yesterday?"

"That's because my father taught me to save the best for last. There's more story here than meets the eye. But let's get started. The story of the ghost of Gold Creek deserves to be told around the campfire tonight."

"But—" Lou protested.

"Yeah, good luck with that," I whispered. "That's all we're getting until tonight." I pulled her away from the group. "C'mon, let's explore."

Dad pulled out the project map and began sizing up the landscape. He and Frank bent over the map together and I heard Frank say, "I think this leaning ponderosa is the same one that's indicated here." All the others were gathering around Frank and Dad. Ford, especially, acted interested.

I could remember a time when I had feeling in my toes, but just barely. I needed to keep moving to stay warm, so I steered Lou toward the creek. The drooping heads of long grass trailed in the water's edge, and I approached the bank cautiously, because I couldn't tell where the land ended and the water began. But Gold Creek was definitely more creek than river. I didn't think I could jump from one side to the other, but it didn't appear deeper than about mid-thigh as far as I could see.

Lou leaned against my shoulder. "I'm freezing."

I wrapped my arms around her, trying to share what little warmth we both had.

"I can't wait to start digging a hole and work up a sweat." She snorted. "I never thought I'd hear myself say that."

I'd done projects in the high desert before, and I knew she didn't need to worry. "Enjoy it while you can. As soon as the sun gets above those peaks over there, it'll heat up fast."

A few minutes later, Dad called us back and sure enough, the air started to warm while we were unloading the van. By the time Dad had us divided into teams, we'd stripped off our coats and hats.

First, Dad had us measure and stake out the one-meter by one-meter test pits, called *units*. Next, he showed us how to excavate about a centimeter deep at a time, scraping the soft loamy earth with flat shovels.

Once we'd accumulated half a bucketful, Dad grabbed a screen and said, "Come over here, Misty, and we'll show these guys how this is done."

Dad stood the screen on its two legs and grabbed the handles, which stuck out at about hip height. He planted his feet wide apart and nodded to me. That was my signal to dump the bucket of dirt into the screen while he pushed it gently back and forth. The dirt sifted to the ground, leaving bits and pieces of "treasure" behind.

Everyone gathered around Dad when he said, "Let's see what we have."

Ford was the first to dive in, running his fingers through the items in the screen. "There are lots of little bits of bone…and what's this?" He held up a large triangular shard.

Bea said, "That looks like pottery to me, or stoneware."

Dad signaled to Ford. He handed it over. "You know—" Dad peered closely at the piece, which had a pattern on one edge. "This isn't stoneware, it's china. What's good about this find is that, if we can match the pattern, we can date it." Dad smiled. "This is a great start."

Lou threw me a questioning look and turned to Dad. "Really? This is a 'great' find?" She was skeptical.

"Significance can be relative. It would be different if we were working in the Southwest or the base of an Incan temple." He eyed the little shard of china. "Of course, when most people think of archaeology, they think of Indiana Jones, gold, buried treasure. In fact, the first thing out of the mouth of most visitors to a dig is, 'Did you strike gold yet?' When that happens, and it will, you smile and say, 'Here's hoping,' or something like that."

He held up the piece between his thumb and forefinger. "The fact is, in Pacific Northwest and Great Basin archaeology—yes, a piece of china that points to a historically significant homestead site, is a great find."

Dad handed Ford and me the shovels and set up Donna and Frank with one screen, Lou and Bea with another one. Ford and I were supposed to throw buckets of dirt onto the screens and Frank or Lou would push them back and forth. The sifting action would leave anything larger than dust in the screens and a pile of dirt at their feet. Dad played back-up, showing Bea and Donna how to pick through what was left behind and spot anything significant.

Like Ford, I spent the morning filling my five-gallon bucket with dirt, which I hoisted and dumped onto the quarter-inch mesh screens—again and again. The work was hard, hot and dusty, and by noon we were soaked in sweat. I envied Lou, who at some point had pulled off her hiking boots and thick socks and had her bare feet and ankles sunk into the cool pile of screened dirt at her feet.

What was left in the screen after the dirt sifted was…not much. Dad said the piece of hand-painted china might date to the 1850s. We also found a few square nails, a bunch of small animal bones, and one ox shoe. We dutifully collected and bagged all these things and recorded our progress in little yellow rainproof notebooks, even though the sky "was as blue as the blood of Queen Elizabeth II," according to Bea.

By two in the afternoon, we were down to t-shirts. The sun felt like it was two inches away, and the heat bugs were buzzing. Dad said the temperature was in the low eighties. The worksite smelled of dust, sweat, and roasted pine needles. Heat waves rippled in the haze down the road.

No one was talking much by the time Dad called it a day. We'd gotten into a rhythm—dig, dump, shake, shake, shake. Frank christened it the archaeology mamba, but by four o'clock we were all more than ready to stop dancing. The last thing I did was bag up the ox shoe, and by that time I felt like I could eat a whole ox. I'd never been so happy to have a workday done. I wasn't alone.

Frank pulled off his hat and wiped the sweat from his forehead with a bandanna. "This Marine's been involved in forced marches that weren't this hard." He sounded only half-joking, gratefully lowering himself to the base of a ponderosa.

"You all did great today." Dad clapped his hands together once, and the dust puffed from his gloves. "Archaeology is hard work—not one of those branches of science for skinny-armed guys in lab coats. One of the many things I love about my profession. We use our brawn as well as our brains."

"My brawn's all gone," Bea said in an exhausted huff. She leaned against the tree trunk where Frank sat. "In fact, I think it left in 1989, so I appreciate you youngsters doing the heavy lifting."

"No problem," Ford said. "It was fun."

Lou and I turned simultaneous incredulous looks his way, and he started laughing.

"Well, I mean, I'm tired," he said. "But it was a good day. We found some stuff, and who knows what we might find tomorrow?"

That brought a rare (at least lately) smile to Dad's face. "I sense an archaeologist in the making."

"I've thought about it." Ford was completely serious.

Dad said, "We'll have to talk," and his eyes were thoughtful, assessing.

They walked back to the test pits we'd dug that day, Ford pointing out things and Dad nodding enthusiastically. So much for Dad and me bonding this summer. I'd always wondered if he wouldn't rather have a son than daughter, and right then all my doubts were being confirmed. Dad had known Ford for just shy of twenty-four hours, and he was already shaping up to be the son my father probably wished he'd had.

I felt a little jealous, but part of me understood. I barely knew Ford myself, and I already wished he was my brother…or something.

FIVE

WE'D DECIDED THE DAY before to camp at the site that first night. Then, camping had sounded like a great adventure. Now, I wondered if anyone else was regretting that decision and longing for a shower and a bed as much as I was.

Dinner consisted of sausage, cheese, bread and water, with energy bars for dessert. Everyone agreed it was one of the best meals they'd ever eaten, and we were all more energized after we ate. Lou, Ford and I decided to hike up Gold Creek Canyon to search for wild horses.

Dad wandered off to the van to check over the equipment and do some record-keeping. We three got up to go hiking, and Donna nudged Frank with her elbow. "We'd better look for some firewood. If this morning's any indication, when that sun goes down, we'll all be thankful for a fire."

"You guys want us to help?" I asked. "We could find some before we go."

Donna waved us off. "No, you kids go on."

Frank pushed himself slowly up and away from the base of his tree. "Yeah, the old lady and I can handle this job."

Donna gave him a push, then grabbed his arm to keep him from toppling over.

When we left, Bea was napping peacefully on a sleeping bag she'd thrown in the pine grass beneath the ponderosa. Donna and Frank walked side by side, competing to see who could spot the best kindling and insulting each other's efforts affectionately.

Dad's map showed there was another clearing farther up the trail called the Opal Creek Meadow, so we forged up and into the trees.

Lou was eager to see some horses and pelted Ford with questions. "Do you think we'll actually see any? Have you seen them?"

"Not yet. Kurt says the horse bands here are made up of a stallion, three or four mares and their colts. When the males are about two years old, the lead mare and stallion push them out of the herd." He paused while we scrambled over a fallen tree blocking the trail. "The young males run around alone for a few years, bachin' it, until they become strong or dominant enough to attract mares and form their own bands."

"What do you know about Lookout?" I pointed to one of the closer peaks in the Juliet Range. "He's named after Lookout Peak, I guess?"

"Yeah, and also because you have to look out when you see him coming. Careful!" He grabbed my arm to keep me from stumbling over a sapling in the middle of the trail.

"Thanks for that." I hoped he couldn't see me blushing in the shade of the trees.

He shrugged. "No problem. I promised your Dad I'd bring you both back in one piece."

"Awesome!" Lou grabbed Ford's arm. "Budding archaeologist *and* our bodyguard."

Ford smiled at her, withdrew his arm from her grasp and gave her a pat on the top of her head. She narrowed her eyes at him, then shrugged it off. "So, Lookout is one of those bachelor horses?" she asked.

"Kind of. Kurt says he's been on his own since way before he should've been separated from a mother. His theory is, she got caught in one of the roundups the Forest Service did a couple years back, and Lookout was left behind."

I kicked a pine cone to the side of the path. *Poor little guy.* But I remembered the stallion was about three years old now—not so little—and not so weak, judging from the damage he'd done to the campground. Part of me really hoped we would see him, but only from a distance.

I glanced at Ford. He was looking at me. We both turned away, then Ford turned back and so did I. He gave me a questioning look.

"What?" I asked.

"I just thought you were going to ask me something."

"Uh, yeah. So, we heard Lookout's deformed?"

"Not exactly. They say he has this perfect stallion body, beautiful, until you get to his head. I've heard descriptions like 'big, long, crooked nose and jaw and really strange ears.' The ears are supposedly set low on the sides of his head and hang down. In fact, early reports described him as a big mule."

Lou shook her head. "That sounds wild. I'd love to see him."

We broke through the trees into a clearing where pine-covered hills on either side of us sloped gently down into a hollow of grass and wildflowers. It was a miniature version of the Gold Creek canyon we'd come from. Opal Creek—more of a brook, really—wound through the tangled grassy reeds off to the side, and we decided to follow it.

We had been talking and laughing while we were on the trail, but something about the lonely quiet of the hollow encouraged silence. No one was talking when I caught movement in the trees at the edge of the meadow. I held my breath and pointed.

We crouched in the long grass and watched a huge, shadowy form separate into four creatures that moved together into the sunlight—a stallion and three mares. The dark stallion shook his head, massive and perfect. He was obviously not the rogue stallion we'd been hoping to see. The three mares cautiously moved forward into the meadow, while the stallion hung back, upslope and in the trees, as if he was keeping watch. The three mares munched their way down slope, stopping occasionally to paw the ground and lowering their noses toward the earth. They seemed content, satisfied—yet they never stopped moving. Tails swished, manes shook, patchy hides wrinkled and shimmered across strong muscles.

I forgot all about the rogue stallion. The creatures in front of us were works of art.

The mares moved nearer and spread out, revealing a tiny colt between them. Judging by his size, he couldn't have been more than a few days old, and he kept especially close to the larger mare. He was so new and tiny, he could dart back and forth beneath his mother's belly on wobbly legs.

The three of us were scrunched together, our shoulders almost touching. Lou leaned around Ford, her hand to her mouth, eyes wide. I whispered, "Have you ever seen anything like this?" Ford shook his head, his gaze never leaving the horses.

Suddenly, the colt dropped to the ground and rolled in the cool grass, little hooves in the air. Then, he hopped up, pranced to his mother, and began to nurse.

I elbowed Lou and whispered in her ear, "You have to get this."

She pulled her phone out of her pocket and scrambled backward away from us. "Turn around you two, and smile." When she took the picture of the colt and mare, with Ford and me in the foreground, her phone made a clicking sound. It wasn't loud. But that sound, or Lou's movement, caught the horses' attention.

When we turned back, the horses were motionless, perfect statues in an idyllic landscape. Every head was lifted and every pair of ears swiveled our direction. For a second, everything went still. I wasn't breathing, and neither were the two people with me—I wasn't sure about the horses. The mares seemed to size us up for a moment, assessing the possible threat to them and their baby. The stallion reared and called the mares with a nervous whinny. They turned and trotted into the trees, falling into perfect triangle formation, with one mare on either side of the colt and one behind.

We'd been cautioned by Kurt not to do anything to harass the wild horses, so we reluctantly turned back the way we had come. I looked behind me and the stallion was still watching us, his silhouette barely visible in the dark trees. He pawed the ground and uttered one more long, high cry. With a swish of his tail, he melted into the pine shadows.

"I DIDN'T THINK THERE was much chance we'd see the wild horses while we were here." Lou was still high on our encounter halfway back to camp. "And to see them our first day out…"

I didn't blame her for her excitement. I couldn't believe it, either.

"Yep, pretty cool—" Ford stopped in mid-sentence and his eyes widened when a scream echoed down from the trail above us followed by a loud crash and the sound of yelling.

He said, "Whoa!" and we froze. But the snap of twigs and other sounds reverberating down the hillside made it clear something was coming straight at us. As one, we started backing up the trail.

I don't know what Ford and Lou were thinking. I was preparing to run for my life when three people burst through the trees. They skidded down the brushy hill to the trail in front of us and pulled up short to keep from running us over.

We were confronted by two guys and a girl. They were a little older than us, dressed in strategically torn jeans and covered in about five piercings each. All three were sweaty and smudged with dirt. After the first few seconds of shock, they broke into laughter.

The girl managed a breath, and her voice was high and shaky when she squeaked, "Did you guys *see* that thing back there?"

SIX

FOR A FEW BREATHS, no one said anything. The younger-looking guy had a swirly, Celtic-looking tattoo flowing down his bicep. I realized I was staring at the same moment I noticed he was looking at my hair.

The girl said, "Hello? Where are you guys coming from, because we thought we saw—" She seemed at a loss.

"We saw some wild horses," Lou offered. "Why? What did you see?"

They exchanged looks and the bigger guy said, "Could it have been one of the horses?"

The tattoo guy shook his head. "Horses don't stalk people."

"Wait," Ford squinted up the hill behind the three, "something was stalking you?"

The guys shrugged and were beginning to look embarrassed.

The girl said, "We didn't see anything. But…" She glanced back and forth at the two guys and they all started laughing. But their laughter had a nervous edge to it.

I smelled alcohol, so their goofiness made sense. Still, I wanted to know what had scared them. "You thought something was up there with you?"

The girl's smile faded. "It's just that…" She paused and I got the impression she was weighing her words, maybe hiding something? "We all got the feeling that we were being followed…like, tracked. And then big, brave Cody here—" She tilted her head toward the tattoo guy. "He starts talking about ghosts and mountain lions and how they've actually been known to hunt people—"

"That scream—" Lou and I said it simultaneously.

"Hunt people?" Ford smirked. "Which, the ghosts or the mountain lions?"

She opened her mouth, seemed to think better of whatever she was about to say and shrugged. "Yeah, right. No, I'm sure it was nothing. Our imaginations."

"I don't think so," I said. "We did hear something—"

"It wasn't nothing, Becca." Cody scowled at her. "I heard it. It was definitely following us."

"Aww, you guys, shut up. You're freakin' the kids out." The big guy motioned down the trail. "Hey, how far to the highway from here?" His face colored. "I lost track of where we were when we started running. We parked on the shoulder and climbed to the top of that ridge." He pointed up the hill where they'd first appeared.

"Um, you've got a ways to go." I thought about how long it had taken us to get from the highway to the project site. "It's about a half-mile before you make the road that leads to the highway and then another…maybe, two and a half miles?" I glanced at Ford for confirmation.

He nodded. "Unless you really move, you won't get to your car before dark. Did you bring a flashlight?"

They looked at each other, and once again, burst out laughing.

Lou rolled her eyes at me, but I figured we were probably their only hope of making it home that night. "Why don't you hike back with us to our camp site at Gold Creek? I bet my Dad will drive you to your car."

They seemed relieved and said they'd take me up on the offer. On the hike to camp, we learned Becca and the big guy named Matt were locals. They were holding hands, so I assumed they were a couple. They were both freshmen at Southern Oregon University in Ashland, where they'd met Cody, who had a job as seasonal help at the Blackwell ranch for the summer.

The trail was only wide enough for us to walk two at a time. Matt and Becca were in back, with Lou and Ford in front of them. I took the lead and Cody came up next to me. He was a lanky guy with spiky blond hair and a hint of beard and mustache. He seemed young, though, for a college student. Turned out, he'd finished high school a year early, so he was barely eighteen—not that much older than us.

"Are you guys camping out here?" Cody asked.

I explained about the dig, a little surprised at how quickly and intensely he became interested. "Really?" he asked. "You're digging near Gold Creek? Like, where they used to do all that gold mining? Found any gold yet?"

Ford, Lou and I burst out laughing. We said, "Nope, but here's hoping," all together, like we'd practiced it.

Cody didn't laugh. If anything, he became more serious. "I've heard a lot of stories about that area. Like, about ghosts and buried—"

"Cody," Becca cut in, "those are stories that parents tell their children around here to scare them inside before dark." I glanced back at her and I was sure I glimpsed her giving Cody a pointed look before she winked at me. "Don't listen to Cody. He's full of crazy paranoia this afternoon."

Cody narrowed his eyes at Becca, but eventually shrugged and turned back to me. "Cool hair," he said. "I have a couple friends back in Portland with dreads. You look great."

The way Ford and Lou jumped on Cody's comment would have made my Dad proud.

"Yeah," Ford interrupted, "makes her look pretty mature…"

"…for a *fifteen-year-old*," Lou finished.

Mortified, I stared straight ahead. I couldn't believe this was happening to me. I'd attracted more male attention in the last twenty-four hours than in my entire life up to that point.

"Easy, man, just making conversation." Condescension dripped from Cody's every word.

An uncomfortable silence stretched into excruciating until Lou finally broke it. "You like it here, Cody? What's there to do?"

"Not much." He glanced back at Lou. "There's a coffee shop at the grocery store, and a couple of bars and restaurants in Ponder. I work ten days on, five off. I usually head back home to Portland when I'm off, but Becca and Matt talked me into staying around this week. Then there's hiking in the woods." He nudged Becca. "Which Becca *loves*—"

"Oh, you are so full of it." She shuddered. "I've lived here my whole life and these woods creep me out."

I wanted to ask her why, but they seemed tight-lipped about what had happened to them. My curiosity battled with my desire to avoid acting like a little geek who asked a million questions.

By the time we arrived at camp and handed the three off to Dad, they were completely sober and surprisingly polite. They apologized to Dad for putting him out and thanked him profusely for the offer of a ride to their car. They also thanked Ford, Lou, and me for helping them, and Cody invited us to visit him at the Blackwell Ranch.

"Speaking of Blackwell," Dad said, "he and his guests showed up while you were gone." He pointed to the upper meadow where people were erecting large canvas tents along the banks of the creek. Campers squatted in the creek, dipping metal pans into the water. After a few seconds, I realized they were panning for gold. Others were setting up long tables. The wind carried good food smells from somewhere near the covered wagon, which appeared to have survived being overturned without much damage.

Lou frowned. "I hope they stay on their side of the meadow, at least, that Blackwell man. He was not a nice person."

I couldn't have agreed more.

By the time Dad returned to camp, we had the fire blazing. Lou and I sat next to each other, our backs against a log. While we roasted marshmallows, we told the others about our encounters with the wild horse band and how we met Cody and company. Lou and Ford did most of the talking. I was content to sit back and watch the clouds flame from rose to deep crimson.

This was my favorite time of a camp day. I loved the way people who share a fire bonded with each other, even if they'd just met. The logs popped and sizzled and the smoke deterred the man-eating mosquitoes.

Slowly, the darkness rose up the trees as the sky spun itself into gold. The light faded and we were left with only each other, faces dim and shifting in the fire's glow. We wrapped ourselves in layers of fleece and moved closer to the fire, passing around graham crackers and chocolate bars.

Out in the darkness, at Blackwell's pioneer camp, someone started strumming a guitar. Frank and Donna sat across from us. He had his arm around her, and she was leaning on his shoulder. Bea sat next to them. Lou snuggled beside me, and Ford sat on the other side of her, and it felt comfortable, like somewhere during the day we'd all become friends.

After making sure the van and equipment were secure and locked, Dad joined us. Not long after that, we were surprised when Bob Blackwell stepped into our circle of firelight. Lou scooted closer to me at Blackwell's approach, but the firelight revealed a much happier face than the last time we'd seen him. While I was relieved to see his mood had improved, I was still glad my father was between us and him.

Dad rose to greet the rancher and Blackwell held out his hand to him. "How's everybody doin' this evening?" He took in our group. "Staying warm, I hope. It's s'posed to dip into the forties again tonight."

"I think we'll be all right," Dad said. We were all exuding wariness. The smiles I saw across from me were tense, and Blackwell seemed to sense it.

"I'm sorry we didn't get a chance to be properly introduced before," Blackwell told Dad. "Bad business, all that. As you could probably tell, I was mighty upset."

"I would have felt the same way. I'm sorry you've been having so much trouble." He lifted a chin toward Blackwell's camp. "All's well this evening, though?"

"I show 'em a good time." He flashed a toothy grin. "We'll be panning the creek some more come mornin', but mostly I bring guests out because they always get a kick and a shiver out of spending the night with the ghost of Gold Creek."

There it was again. I sat up straighter. "The what?"

Blackwell widened his eyes in mock surprise, then squinted at Dad. "You brought these kids out here without warning them about the ghost of Gold Creek?"

"Well, he did say he was going to tell us a story about that tonight," I said, moving even closer to Lou, who seemed happy to have me.

Dad peered over his glasses at Blackwell, like he'd given away a surprise, and turned to us. "The story goes that in the 1800s, a wild stallion was hunted down by the settlers and miners who lived in this area. The horse was stealing mares from the homesteaders and knocking down fences. So, the settlers took it upon themselves to go after him. They killed him right around here, but some of the locals swear the horse's ghost and his ghost band still wander the banks of Gold Creek, stealing people's horses, stampeding cattle, stalking hikers and campers, and generally searching for bloody revenge."

Dad stroked his beard. "It's an interesting and unique horse legend. As an anthropologist, I find it fascinating. I've never really heard anything else like it."

Lou's voice sounded small when she said, "Maybe those guys really were being stalked by something. Cody even used the word *ghosts…*"

"I don't know, Dr. Stevens." Bea sounded skeptical. "It doesn't sound that unique. Kind of reminds me of the headless horseman." She pointed across the fire at us. "You kids still have to read that in school, right?"

"No." Ford shook his head. "I've seen the movie, though."

I couldn't see Bea roll her eyes, but I was pretty sure it happened.

I don't think Ford noticed. "But this legend's not only missing a head," he said. "It's missing the horseman."

"Oh, it isn't just a story." Blackwell's voice, from the other side of the fire, held a hint of intrigue. "Percival Blackwell, my ancestor, was the one who shot that horse. And I'll tell you something else. The stallion that's been bothering us lately is a carbon copy, right down to that deformed head and those weird ears."

Frank, who was pulling a perfectly done marshmallow off the stick Donna held out to him, looked up in surprise.

"Seriously?" The tone of Dad's voice brought the quiver of an excited puppy to mind. "Your grandfather was the one who shot the stallion?"

Blackwell took a step back and put a hand over his heart. "I'm old, Dr. Stevens, but I'm not dead yet. Percival was my *great*-grandfather." He smiled. "And I hear you're lookin' for his old cabin."

Frank grunted. "News travels fast."

"Small town." Blackwell was matter-of-fact. "And despite appearances yesterday, Kurt and I get along fine. I think I might be able to help you out."

This was pay-dirt better than gold to an archaeologist. Dad's grin left no doubt about that.

"I figured you'd be interested. When I was a little tot, Granddad showed me the spot his dad showed him. Don't know that I can find the exact site—it's crazy how fast the forest reclaims places—but I think I can point you in the right direction."

Blackwell was looking around the fire at each of us, but when he got to me, he squinted and moved closer. I seized the opportunity to ask the question bothering me since I'd first heard about the "ghost" from the Japanese woman. "Mr. Blackwell, did you know your guests think Lookout *is* the ghost of Gold Creek?"

He peered at me with a strange look on his face. "Well, I'll be." I could see his features soften in the flickering light. "You must be Karen's little girl. Kurt told me about you two being family. Heck, that practically makes you locals. I knew your mom, and I was real sorry to hear about what happened."

Dad acknowledged his sympathy with a nod.

Everyone else in our group, except Lou, looked mystified and a little uncomfortable, but Blackwell smiled. "I always did like your mom. She was tough and she was kind—a rare combination. And nobody in these mountains was better at breaking horses than your mom and your grandpa. It was a real loss to the community when she went off to that college and your grandpa retired. And you know," he nodded, "you're going to be a beauty, too, like her."

Lou nudged me. I was trying to avoid the eyes of the people around me, especially Ford's.

"Only…" Blackwell took another step closer, "W*hat* have you done to your hair, child?"

Dad, standing behind Blackwell, shook his head sadly. If I could have shaved my head at that moment, I would have. I was starting to feel like the neighborhood freak. But I forced a smile, shrugged it off, and changed the subject. My hair had been mentioned so many times in the last twenty-four hours, I wasn't even blushing anymore. "About the tourists thinking Lookout is the ghost?"

"Who said he isn't?"

Lou and I turned to each other, then back to the rancher. Blackwell broke into a grin and winked. "I wouldn't worry too much about the ghost, though. Hasn't harmed a young lady…yet."

He chuckled, I assumed at the look on our faces. "Naw, seriously. What I really came over here to warn you about was that corral over there." He pointed to his group's horses, bunched together and surrounded by what appeared to be flimsy white posts and vinyl tape. "I know it doesn't look like much, but that corral is electrified. Watch out for it if you wander over that way. I'm not too worried about ghosts, truth be told, but that tape will give you a shock you won't soon forget."

Dad offered to walk with the rancher back to his camp, and I was sure it was so he could pump him for information about the homestead site and the ghost legend. Before they were out of earshot, Blackwell said, "If we find that old cabin, do you think some of my guests could help with the excavation? They're mighty interested in the Old West. I'd charge a small fee that we could split…"

Across from us, Frank, Donna and Bea's faces were obscured by the smoky haze, but I could see them exchange looks. Bea cleared her throat and shook her head. "I wonder what he's charging those poor tourists for all this silliness. That ol' boy could sell boots to a man with no legs."

MAYBE IT WAS THE LIGHT pouring through the window of the tent I shared with Lou—a bright moon. But then, no. After lying there for a minute, I realized why I was awake. The last thing I wanted to do was venture out into the cold night to pee, but I didn't want to spend the hours until dawn holding it, either.

I probably wouldn't need my flashlight to make it to the latrine we'd rigged up—nothing but a portable toilet set over a hole in a screen of trees and underbrush about fifty yards away. I grabbed the light anyway, just in case. Lou was deep in her usual sleep-of-the-dead, snoring softly. She barely stirred at the sound of me unzipping the tent.

I slipped my wool-clad feet into my hiking boots and stumbled into the night. The moon-washed scene was eerily beautiful. I breathed in the clean scent of dewy sage and pine— and shivered. The moon was low, dipping behind the mountain shadows. I passed our fire circle from the night before, now cold gray ash. I'd left my phone in one of the pockets of the tent, so I had no idea what time it was. I guessed it was the quietest and coolest part of the night—the hour before dawn.

The creaking of the tall ponderosas in the predawn breeze and the scrape of my boots were the only sounds as I crossed the packed dirt road and skirted Blackwell's corral. The horses nickered softly and shifted, acknowledging me. Careful not to touch the corral, I reached over and petted a few of their velvety noses on the way by and headed up slope.

Once in the trees, I switched on my flashlight, picking my way through the juniper and other prickly brush as quickly as possible. My teeth began to chatter and I was anxious to take care of business and burrow back into the cozy warmth of my down sleeping bag.

The last thing a girl wants when she's squatting in the woods is to hear somebody coming. At the sound of twigs crunching and the shuffle of a large body through the underbrush in front of me, I hunched down as far as possible behind my bush and held my breath. "Please," I whispered, "not Ford."

Was it a person or an animal? I wasn't anxious to encounter either one. I squinted through the breaks in the thick brush, trying to see whatever it was. No luck. Where I sat, the scant moonlight was blocked by trees and brush. I'd set my light beside me. Outside its glow, I saw only darkness.

I knew it was silly, but I couldn't help thinking of the ghost of Gold Creek. Whatever was out there sounded a lot bigger than I was. Maybe it was a deer, but what if it was a bear or a cougar? I kept still, heart pounding, legs cramping. Twigs snapped under heavy footfalls that sounded enormous in the otherwise still morning. Whatever it was kept moving, and I sighed with relief when I heard it push through the bushes away from me.

I yanked up my sweatpants, grabbed my flashlight and stumbled through the trees. Instinct told me to stay low and creep as quickly as I could in the direction of camp.

I could see the outline of things around me in the first faint light of dawn. When I emerged from the trees, the horses in the corral were alert and moving, heads raised, ears pricked. The closer I got, the more agitated they became, shaking their heads, snorting and whinnying, hopping on their front feet. Their reaction was the opposite of the first time I'd passed them, and that was my first clue that something else was there with me.

Then I heard it.

I tried to convince myself I was imagining the heavy footfalls behind me. Denial only worked for a couple of steps.

Adrenaline shot down my spine. Cold goose bumps spread across my arms and the hair prickled on the back of my neck. I poised to run and opened my mouth to yell for help.

But fresh in my mind were all the nightmares I'd been having since Mom's death. Dreams in which I tried to make some kind of sound, shout a desperate warning. It never worked in my sleep, and I wasn't sure I could make a sound in that moment, either. Part of me wondered if I *was* dreaming. Besides, I knew my stalker could easily attack before anyone came to my rescue. I kept moving, barely breathing.

The creature behind me snorted softly. Large feet clomped on the packed dirt of the trail. When I sped up, it sped up. When I slowed down, I could swear it slowed down. It seemed to be matching me movement for movement. Playing with me.

The only weapon I had against spirits or wild animals was the flashlight in my quivering fist. I swallowed past the suffocating lump in my throat, firmed my grasp on the light, and swung around.

A horse.

My stalker was a horse. I let out the breath I'd been holding. The animal in front of me didn't look safe, exactly. But at least it wasn't a cougar about to spring, and it didn't shimmer like I imagined a ghost would. He was solidly massive and terrifyingly real.

He stood there, posing in my wavering spotlight. It had to be Lookout. He was exactly as Ford had described him, yet not at all like what I had pictured. He was a huge, tawny-colored mustang with dark legs and a dark, tangled mane. A white, kite-shaped spot glowed in the middle of his massive forehead.

He had the much-talked about ears and crooked face. But there was also something noble about him. His ears weren't floppy, they were set low on his head. They stood up, then pointed down as he tilted his head, watching me.

He seemed as wary of me as I was of him.

His face didn't look deformed. It was long and expressive—a face with character. All those stories about talking animals my mother read me as a child played through my mind. At that moment, I don't think I would have been surprised if Lookout said hello.

I blinked and stepped back. We'd been standing there, considering each other, for I don't know how long. Was it seconds? Minutes?

I reminded myself that there's no such thing as ghosts, and thought back to all the times Lou said horses can sense what humans feel. Kurt had told us the stallion didn't seem upset by people on foot, so I tried to relax. After a couple tremulous breaths, I found my voice and murmured, "Hello, Lookout."

The stallion snuffled and bobbed his head, as if to return the greeting. I was shocked and relieved at the same time. At the very least, it felt safe to move. I inched backward. He followed me again, step for step. I stopped, thinking he would stop.

Instead, he stepped up to me, no hesitation, lowered his big head and took a large whiff of my hair with those wide, quivering nostrils. I scrunched my eyes. My shoulders tightened.

I heard Lou's voice in my head: *Relax. If you're chill, the horse will relax.*

I tried to loosen up, but I couldn't lift my head, and I couldn't silence my pounding heart. I could feel his warmth on my face. He smelled of evergreens and dry grass, sweat and dirt—he smelled like horse. One of his whiskers brushed against my cheek.

"It's all right," I said, as much to reassure myself as him. This close, he seemed enormous. I fought the urge to distance myself from those huge hooves that could shatter a human foot like glass.

After a couple minutes, curiosity apparently satisfied, he moved away. He dropped his head and began to sniff and paw at the dirt, like the horses we'd seen near Opal Creek.

I tried backing up again, and Lookout ignored me. He turned away, and I took a few more tentative steps. The space between us slowly widened.

Shivering and anxious to get back to my sleeping bag, I started to turn, but hesitated. I'd just survived a pretty cool wild encounter with a legend. I continued to back up, keeping Lookout in my sights, while also picturing everyone's reactions to the story I'd have to tell them. Would they think I'd dreamed it?

I felt the breeze shift and grow stronger at my back. Lookout made a sound like an audible shudder. He lifted his head and went stiff, rooted to the spot where he stood. The horses in the corral, apparently assaulted with the full scent of the wild mustang, snorted and whinnied. Some of them bucked and reared. Tails raised, they bunched and bit at each other.

Lookout swung his big head toward me and I caught flashes of white around his wide eyes. The stallion screamed and exploded into motion as the first rays of sun broke over the mountains and lit the meadow. Hooves pounding, he charged down the slope, straight at the corral.

I'll never know what would have happened had he reached the corral when it was full of Blackwell's horses, because the terrified animals broke through the makeshift fence at Lookout's thunderous approach. They scattered into the trees, the stallion in hot pursuit.

The fence sparked, buzzed, and went silent.

At almost the same moment, the camp at the creek came to life. Dad shot out of his tent and spotted me. He was at my side in what seemed like seconds, feet clad in only his thick, wool socks. "Misty, what's going on?"

I tried to say something. I opened my mouth, and shuddered, gasping, unable to catch my breath.

I could see other campers emerging from tents, groggy, blinking, unlike Bob Blackwell, who got to us with a speed that surprised me, rifle in hand. "What in the—?" he bellowed. But he was too late. His horses were gone.

Dad grabbed my shoulders and gave me a little shake. "Mist, it's okay. Just tell us what happened." His eyes darted from the ruined corral, to the trampled path left behind by the stampeding herd and back to me. "Where are the horses? Did you get tangled in the fence?" He scanned me up and down. "Are you okay?"

I realized he was asking if I'd caused all the damage.

"I'm fine, Dad." Irritation replaced the anxiety attack building inside me. "And no, I didn't trip over the horses. It was—"

I stopped when Blackwell shook his head in a bewildered way at the tangled, ruined corral—all that was left of where his horses had been. His few hairs were disheveled and standing on end. All of a sudden, he wasn't imposing at all. He seemed frail and old, as if he was having trouble comprehending what he saw.

I said, "It was…Lookout…I think."

There was a gasp from behind me—Lou. Other campers from our group and Blackwell's were gathering around, pale and shivering in the cold morning light, blankets and sleeping bags thrown over shoulders. Most of them still seemed somewhere between waking and dreaming. I could relate.

"Oh my gosh, Mist. Are you hurt?" Lou threw an arm over my quivering shoulder and wrapped us both in her blanket.

"I'm good. He didn't try to hurt me. He sort of, sniffed me, and I thought he was leaving. But instead…" I looked toward the deserted spot where the corral had been. Dad's gaze followed mine and he shook his head.

Like a sleepwalker, Blackwell shuffled to the spot where his horses had been only moments earlier. He stood quiet for a few seconds, hand tightening around his rifle. Then he hauled back and gave the corral's remains a vicious kick.

Lou and I startled in unison and took a step back. I expected Blackwell to start ranting, like he had at the campground, but he didn't. He stood in grim silence, staring up the slope where Lookout had chased his horses.

Dad came behind him and put a hand on the older man's shoulder. "I'm sorry about this, Bob. I'll call Kurt and ask him to send a van out here to transport your guests back to the ranch."

"I appreciate that, Dr. Stevens—" He drew in a sharp breath and clenched his jaw. "These days, people treat wild horses like they're sacred, part of the land. But they're not."

He rubbed his hand through his few hairs. "My great-granddad had it right. Feral horses are like thistle and cheat grass. They're weeds someone brought and left behind. But we solve our own problems around here, and solve this I will."

WE DISCOVERED WE COULD fit all of Blackwell's guests into our van. Dad was able to reach Kurt, who said he'd be out to load their gear and transport it back to the Blackwell ranch. The covered wagon, without any horses to pull it, would have to be dealt with later.

After Blackwell's guests ate breakfast and panned for gold, they broke camp and loaded into the van. Before he left, Dad motioned Frank and me over. "Frank, if you could take command for a while, I'd appreciate it."

"Be happy to help Dr. Stevens. But I don't really know what I'm doing after one day of training. I'm afraid I might miss something significant."

Dad lifted his head toward me. "That's where Misty comes in. She's been picking through screens at archeological sites since she was old enough to stand. She knows what to look for."

I was surprised at Dad's faith in me. It made me feel great…and stressed. Sure, I'd been playing in piles of archeology dirt my whole life, but I didn't think that made me a technical expert.

He caught my eye. "I'll be back before you know it. I'll check over what you've done. You're ready." He didn't give me a chance to protest, and I watched him stride away to the van and climb into the driver's seat. As he was turning the van up the road toward the highway, he leaned out the window and yelled, "Just don't screw anything up!"

I think I heard him chuckling as the van turned away from us in a cloud of dust, but I wasn't completely sure.

We set to work in the same groups as the day before, and by mid-morning we'd found more pieces of china, a few nails and some shell casings. We dug around each one, and I diagrammed their locations in my notebook. We photographed everything and bagged it.

Ford seemed to be finding a lot of large bones in his pit, maybe deer—at least that's what I thought. In the third layer of his unit, he had all different sizes of dirt pedestals with the larger bones resting on top. Dad's instructions were to note the exact location of anything we found that was larger than a fist. We had some fun trying to decide if that would be Bea's teensy fist or Frank's massive one.

As Dad was pulling up a couple hours later, Ford called, "Mist, come here. You have to see this."

That was the first time he'd called me Mist, which I found incredibly awesome for some reason. But I played it cool, hopped inside the pit he was working in, and squatted beside him.

"What do you think it is?" he asked.

He'd used a small, triangular, flat trowel to carefully dig all around a large, butterfly-shaped piece of bone.

"I don't know," I said. "Deer bone, maybe? A pelvis or something?"

While I watched, he finished dusting off the bone's top and sides with a brush. I handed him the camera so he could take a picture, while I noted its location.

He grasped its edges on each side and hauled it over to the side of the pit. "Hope you have a really big bag for it."

"Whoa." Dad's voice was right above us, and we both looked up. "That's a big…" His voice trailed off when he glanced down into the pit, at the spot where the bone had been. "What the…?" He grabbed Ford's trowel and squatted down in the pit beside the pedestal of soil.

By this time, everyone was gathering around our pit, trying to see what he was doing. He dusted the dirt off of something metallic-looking that had been directly under the large bone.

"Dad, what is it?"

"I'm not sure. I think it might be a lever closure on a really old jar…oh, sh--!" As Dad had scraped the trowel across the top of the pedestal to shave off a bit of the soil, there was a little "ping", and the lever holding the lid in place popped off.

"A jar right-side up in the ground." Dad sounded like he was talking to himself, but he turned his head and caught my eye. It took me a couple seconds to realize what he was getting at. Almost everything else we'd found in the pits was lying on its side. The fact that this jar was standing upright was really weird.

"It was intentionally buried there by someone," I guessed.

Dad nodded. "I'm thinking so."

"How old do you think it is?" Donna asked.

My father pursed his lips. "This kind of lever-seal. Maybe 1860s."

"A jar buried on purpose." Ford looked from me to Dad. "That would mean something inside was important to someone, right?"

Frank leaned over my shoulder. "Can you see what's inside, Dr. Stevens?"

Dad moved the lid farther to the side and peered into the jar for a second. He stood up and dusted off the knees of his jeans. "I hate to tell you all this, but it looks like a bunch of rocks."

The group let out a collective groan, all except the ever-tenacious Beatrice Grant. "Does that make sense?" she said. "Why would someone bury a jar filled with rocks? Can you get one out? Can we look at it?"

Dad was shaking his head. "We need to leave it intact so it can be examined in a lab." The faces around me all wore expressions as disappointed as I'm sure mine was.

Ford's shoulders slumped.

Lou let out a pathetic, "Aww."

Dad had a perfect view of our six dejected faces surrounding him like a halo. I watched him narrow his eyes. "But this is supposed to be an educational project…and it's not often we find something like this…"

I held my breath.

Dad seemed to make a decision. "Let's get the next layer dug out of this pit, and if the jar is intact—"

Ford smiled. "Yes!"

Dad held up a hand. "We'll take a look and see what's inside. But don't get too excited, it doesn't appear to be much."

It didn't matter what Dad said. We'd found buried treasure, we were sure of it. That jar was the most exciting thing I'd seen at a site since Dad's crew dug up a woolly mammoth skull in Eastern Washington. I'd only been eight years old. I could barely remember.

Good thing Dad was there to keep us honest. At that point, none of us were in the mood to be careful. We'd turned into a mob of thieving pot-hunters.

He was acting like the detached scientist, but I could tell Dad was excited too. He took over excavation in the pit and moved fast. He unearthed a lot more bone, but nothing as significant as the old, amber-colored jar that slowly emerged from the dirt. We noted and bagged up all the other finds, until the jar was the only thing left in the pit, on its own little pedestal of dirt.

Dad picked it up almost reverently. He carried it over to the long camp table we used as our impromptu lab whenever we needed to sort something or take a closer look. The rest of us trailed in a procession behind him. When we were all there, he tipped the jar on its side and carefully shook the contents onto one of the dust pans we used for scooping up soil. For a few seconds, it did look like a bunch of rocks. But then, something glinted in the sun.

"Dad—"

"Uh, Dr. Stevens," Frank said. "My eyes aren't what they once were, I'll admit. But I'm pretty sure those rocks are sparkling."

Dad picked up one of the stones between a thumb and forefinger and held it up in the light. As he turned the nugget back and forth in the sun's rays, we could all see gold sparkles peppering its surface.

A giggle bubbled up from inside me. I grinned at Dad. "Found any gold, yet?"

SEVEN

WE WERE ALL CRAZY excited about our find, but Dad tried to keep our expectations in check. "Hang on, folks. With rocks peppered over in minerals, determining the difference between real gold and something like pyrite can be difficult." He returned the rock to the jar. "We have tricks that can be used in the field to establish whether or not something *is* real gold, but those methods are all destructive in some way. Until we have this analyzed by an assayer, we won't know anything for sure."

"But," Lou's voice was hopeful, "seems like somebody would only bury something that was valuable, doesn't it?"

"That's usually the case. But, who knows?" Dad shrugged. "Could've been a child's collection of pretty rocks—kids bury stuff all the time and forget about it. There could be other explanations. However, if this site is what I think it is, this would be a clever place to hide something, a place most thieves wouldn't think to look."

I WATCHED NERVOUSLY WHILE Dad checked through the work we'd done during the time he was carting people back to the Blackwell Ranch. After examining everything closely, he patted me on the shoulder—the closest my Dad gets to an 'atta girl.

I breathed a sigh of relief.

"What I believe we have here, folks," he said, "is someone's old garbage dump."

"Ewww—" Lou wrinkled up her nose. "We're picking through somebody's trash?"

Bea frowned. "That's not much to write home about."

"Now you know why archaeologists are sometimes referred to as history's garbage collectors." Dad smiled. "Actually, we can learn a lot about someone from their garbage, a lesson identity thieves have absorbed all too well."

"Misty," he turned to me. "What knowledge have we acquired from this garbage, so far?"

I shot him my best laser-beam-eyes look. Dad knew I hated to be put on the spot, at least, he should have known. But he raised his eyebrows as if to say, *we're all waiting*, and let the silence build.

I bit down on my lower lip and thought about all the things we'd found. "The gold..." Dad raised an eyebrow. "Or whatever, is cool, but it's kind of weird. I don't know if we can make anything of that right now." I stole another glance at Dad and he was nodding. So far, so good.

"If we can find part of a maker's mark on the china, it could tell us where it came from and..." I was reaching. "And the dates, or the approximate dates it was used?"

Dad dipped his head. "What else?"

I racked my brain, trying to think what answer he was looking for. "Dad, I don't know…" Then it hit me. "Wait! What if this *was* Percival Blackwell's dump—"

"A big if," Dad said, "but go on."

"If it was his trash heap, that would mean his cabin probably wasn't too far from where we're standing."

Dad smiled and motioned to the others. "Misty is right. We're dealing with a big 'if,' but it's worth a little investigation of that area over there." He pointed behind us to a spot in the trees, on the other side of the road. "Which is also the general area Bob said his grandfather showed him. How about we eat lunch and take a break from screening, survey the area, and see what we can see?"

Donna sighed. "Wandering around in the shade sounds heavenly."

At lunch, Ford, sitting between Lou and me, wanted to know more about my encounter with Lookout. "When it came to meeting you, he didn't exactly live up to his name," he said. "He just sniffed you and wandered off?"

Lou broke in before I could answer. "Ah, but what's in a name?" Her drama teacher had gone all Shakespearean this year, and Lou never missed a chance to insert some Old English phrase into the conversation.

Ford didn't miss a beat. "What *is* in a name? L-o-u, isn't that kind of, you know, a boy's…?" He trailed off at Lou's withering look. "It has to be short for something, right?"

Lou tipped her head. "Actually, yes, it is. The full name is Lilou Rose Phillips. Lilou is French for Lily."

"Really? Wow. I kind of like it. It fits you."

"What can I say?" She sighed and shrugged. "Mom was the last of the hippies. After high school, she took her college money and hopped the first plane to Europe. Wandered all over, 'sowed her wild oats' as she would put it—" Lou rolled her eyes. "And by the time she headed home she was traveling for two, if you get my drift."

I'd heard the story of June's wild past, but everyone else suddenly turned our way. Bea said, "How bohemian and romantic." She had a bemused smile on her face and a far-off look in her eyes.

Dad didn't let us linger long on the implications of Lou's story. "From flower child to city mayor," he said. "What an amazing journey June has had." He turned to me. "Misty, tell people how you got your name."

"Dad," I said. "No way."

"C'mon—" Ford leaned toward me. "You tell me your story," his voice was intimate, "and I'll tell you mine."

I looked into those dark eyes of his… "Okay, but don't laugh."

Lou crossed her heart.

"A horse. I was named after a horse."

Lou giggled, then slapped a hand over her mouth. "I'm sorry," she mumbled from behind her fingers. Attempting a straight face, and failing, she giggled again. "I can't believe I didn't know this about you. Tell me everything."

So, I told them about Mom's love for children's literature, including horse stories like *Misty of Chincoteague*. It felt natural to talk about her. I wasn't sad or tearful, which surprised me.

"I remember that book," Lou said. "I read it when I was about ten years old—it's a great story."

"Yeah, but she could have named me after the girl. Why did it have to be the horse?"

"Misty," Lou smiled. "The horses are always the best part in a story."

I couldn't help grinning back at her before I turned to Ford. "Okay, your turn."

He was silent for a few seconds, a wry set to his lips.

He said, "We did have a deal." Straightening up, he took a deep breath and spoke three words very slowly: "I am Polish."

Frank perked up. "Tomaka is Polish? I thought it was…"

"I know." Ford held up a hand. "It sounds Japanese. But Dad's ancestry is Polish and my Mom is Native American, thus…" he pointed to his face and shrugged.

"Interesting!" Donna sounded delighted. At that point, I was loving how Frank, Bea and Donna made everything we said sound fascinating.

I'd found out Frank and Donna never had children of their own. I'd also noticed, over the years, that childless couples fell into two camps: they were either annoyed by other people's kids or deeply interested in how kids work. Frank and Donna definitely fell into the latter camp, which seemed to encourage Ford.

"In my parents' minds, before nationality, before tradition, before heritage, there is their love of the land, and specifically our nation's national forests." His voice was taking on the quality of a public-service announcement.

"Then, comes the child." Ford pointed to himself. "And the desire to bring their love of the child, and their love of the forest together. Plus, as the child arrives, a job transfer sends the family to a new location in…" He paused. "The *Gifford Pinchot National Forest.*"

There was a moment of puzzled silence. *Gifford…Ford.* Laughter rippled through the group. "Finally," Ford continued, "there is the naming of the child. And the circle is complete." He brought his hands together and bowed his head. The adults clapped.

"Your full name is Gifford Pinchot Tomaka?" Bea was wide-eyed. "Zowie! What a title."

Ford shook his head. "My parents are not completely without mercy. My middle name is Charles, after my grandpa."

"Gifford Charles Tomaka." Lou shook her head. "That is an astonishing name."

"Yes, it is, Lilou Rose." He threw her a wicked grin. She gave him a big shove that almost knocked him off our log.

"Nobody gets to call me that except my mother, especially not you. Don't even start." Lou was laughing, which I figured was good because Ford's expression suggested he wouldn't be yielding to her commands anytime soon.

Across from us, Frank was picking at a pinecone, like he was thinking about something else. "Dr. Stevens, where do you think the Juliets got their name? Shakespeare, perhaps?"

Lou perked up. "Shakespeare? Like the Romeo-and-Juliet kind of Shakespeare?"

"Well, yeah. I don't know any other Shakespeare, do you? What? You don't think the people who settled this area read classic literature?"

"I don't know." She shrugged. "I guess I never really thought about it."

Dad swallowed his last bit of granola bar and washed it down with a big swig of water. "I've heard different theories about who these mountains are named after, but a Shakespeare play is as good as any. When families traveled over the Oregon Trail, they likely didn't bring boxes of books. But pioneer diaries mention literature like the Bible, of course, and also works of Shakespeare, Milton, Chaucer, Donne—these mountains might as well have been named The Apostles, or the Paradise Mountains."

Dad tilted his head toward Frank. "Course, there's also precedent for the fact that 'Juliet' might have been some miner's sweetie in town."

Frank chuckled.

Bea cleared her throat and turned toward Lou and me. "You girls know the old story of what happened when the pioneers on the Oregon Trail got to the fork in the road in eastern Idaho, don't you?" She had a gleam in her eye, like it was a good story.

Lou and I shook our heads, but Ford smiled—obviously in on the joke.

"At Fort Hall, Idaho, the pioneers would come to a spot in the trail where they had to make a crucial decision about which way to go, north or south. One path had a pile of fool's gold next to it and an arrow pointing down toward California. The other direction had a sign pointing up to Oregon country that said, 'Paradise This Way.'" She paused.

I was confused, and Lou was no help. She shrugged at me.

"Okay," she said. "We don't get it."

Bea pointed at Ford.

He half-grinned and said, "Everyone who could read came north."

"Wait a minute," I said, laughing, because the story *was* funny. But I was skeptical.

Dad said, "I don't think my little skeptic's buying it."

"Smart girl." Bea's smile was encouraging. "What is it, Misty?"

"Well, didn't people come to this part of Oregon looking for gold? I pointed a thumb behind us. "*Gold Creek?*"

"The way I heard it," Dad said, "only one company mined all the gold in this area—and it was owned by a syndicate of investors back East. Most people who settled these mountain valleys were struggling farmers, enticed by fertile land, wide-open spaces, and dreams of a better future."

He stood up and stretched. "Shall we get started?"

We spent the rest of the afternoon on a visual survey of the area in the woods. It was fun, but we didn't find any clues to the location of the old homestead site. As we were stowing our gear and getting ready to head home for the night, Kurt pulled up. He leaned out the cab window and motioned to Dad. "Has Bob Blackwell been by here this afternoon?"

"Nope." Dad shook his head. "You talk to him?"

"I tried calling him to follow up on this morning's Lookout sighting. His wife told me he'd gone out 'shooting.'"

Dad grimaced. "That sounds ominous."

Kurt climbed out of his truck, and his movements had a weariness to them. "He'd better not be looking for that horse, or there's going to be hell to pay. It's against federal law to mess with the animals inside the boundary."

"Wait, what?" I didn't like the sound of that. "He wouldn't kill Lookout, would he?" I was still jumpy after my encounter with the mustang, but I didn't think he should be shot. "That horse wasn't threatening with me at all…" My voice trailed off, though, remembering Blackwell's coldly furious statement about taking care of his wild horse problem.

"Lookout doesn't usually threaten people," Kurt said. "Like the other wild horses in the area, he's used to tourists following him around. The horses are relatively calm, even curious around humans. In Lookout's case, it's other horses that seem to agitate him—which, unfortunately, includes horses with people on them."

Ford wandered around from the back side of the van. "Why do you think that is?"

"I've talked to some of the researchers here from Japan, and they have an interesting theory. They're convinced it's got something to do with those ears."

"Oh, yeah," Lou said, "horses do a lot of communicating with their ears."

"Right," Kurt said. "The researchers think that because the other horses didn't understand Lookout's ears, and because he was separated from his mother so early, he developed more aggressive ways to get his point across."

"So, he's really just misunderstood and all alone," I said. "Poor guy." I felt a weird connection to Lookout after our encounter that morning. He'd lost his mom, he was all alone and misunderstood…it didn't take a psychiatrist to understand why I felt sorry for him, but that self-knowledge didn't stop me from feeling it.

"Lookout's a puzzle," Kurt said. "Nobody's been able to figure out where he goes between sightings. I've put in a call to several volunteers who help with search-and-rescue and tracking the wild horses. They were planning a week-long count of the herd soon, anyway. I've requested that those who are able, come early to search for Lookout, and some of the Japanese researchers asked to ride along. With that many savvy riders, we shouldn't have any trouble rounding up Blackwell's runaways."

I was still worried. "What will happen to Lookout if you catch him?"

"With that one, I don't know. One of the volunteers might want to take him and try to work with him." Kurt said it like he wasn't convinced. "I hope Blackwell isn't thinking he'll find that horse on his own. How ironic would it be to have history repeat itself?"

Kurt asked us to point him to the scene of all the excitement with Lookout that morning. A couple minutes later, he called me over to where he was crouched low, examining the ground where Blackwell's corral had been. I walked toward him, but he held up a hand. "Misty, stop right there."

I froze.

"There's a partial track right in front of you, and I don't want it disturbed." When our eyes met, his mouth was set in a hard line. "Your Dad called and filled me in this morning, but would you tell me again what happened to you?"

I told him everything I could remember about my interactions with Lookout, about the other horses breaking through the pen, how Lookout chased them away.

"Are you sure it was Lookout that caused those horses to break?" Kurt was scanning the dirt at our feet.

"I don't know." I was confused. "What else could it have been?"

He stood up. "Think back. Did the other horses break before he ran toward them…or after?"

Eyes closed, I tried to picture the scene in my head. "Before, I guess. I thought they'd caught his scent or something."

"It was before? You're sure?"

"Yeah, definitely." I opened my eyes. "They broke and he ran after them. Why?"

"I think those horses caught the scent of something dangerous. But it wasn't Lookout." He bent down. With his index finger, he drew a circle around a print in the earth at my feet. But even I could see it wasn't the deep, circular gash of a horse's hoof. I'd seen that kind of print before, in the mountains back home. It was a cougar paw print—a big one.

I SANK INTO MY corner of the sofa, blankets wrapped around everything but my head. "This feels like heaven after sleeping on the ground last night."

Lou, cuddled in her corner, looked up from her laptop. "Agreed. This sofa's not half-bad."

Despite the warm days, the temperature continued to plummet as soon as the sun dropped behind the Juliets. Since the space heaters in the bedrooms and the wood-stove in the living room were the only sources of heat in the ranch house, Dad had lit a fire before heading out to the makeshift lab he'd rigged up in the barn. I knew he'd be there for a couple of hours, sorting and cataloging the finds from the dig.

We'd pulled the sofa and coffee table close to the wood stove, and the glow in the grate radiated sleep-inducing comfort. Before my eyes slammed shut, I caught sight of the box on the coffee table in front of me. I sat up, pushed my blankets aside, grabbed the box off the coffee table in front of me and started sifting through Mom's pictures.

Lou was pecking away on her laptop. "I still can't believe this place has internet. Thank you, whoever invented satellite dishes." She'd begun with the obligatory e-mail to her mom and moved on to chatting with friends, catching up on the gossip from back home.

I knew all this because she kept up a running commentary. "Mom says Too Tall misses me," and "Oh. My. Gravy. Ronnie asked Michelle out! Can you believe it? I didn't even think they liked each other." Finally, she downloaded the pictures from her phone and began clicking through them.

I scooted toward her. "I want to see."

She smiled mischievously. "Okay, what do you think of this one?" She turned her screen around. It was the picture of Ford, me, and the wild horse band. I thought it was a great picture, but I wasn't about to give Lou the satisfaction of saying so.

I gave her a sideways look. "Not bad."

She nudged me with a foot. "Yeah, right. 'Not bad' she says, all casual. You like him, don't you?"

"C'mon, I barely know him…hey, look at this." I held up a picture.

Lou smirked at me. "Nice try. I sent Ford a copy." She looked all innocent and batted her eyes. "We'll see what he thinks of it."

"I thought you were my friend."

She scooted next to me. "I am, and I'm going to do something about your abysmal social life if it kills both of us." She elbowed me. "Cheer up, little camper. If I know guys, and

I do, he'll think it's great. Bet you money he posts it by tomorrow. Now, what did you want to show me?"

She leaned over the picture in my hand. It was of my mom, when she was a teenager, standing on a ladder that leaned against a tree heavy with apples. Her dark hair was held back with a bright red bandanna. She was wearing jeans, a t-shirt and an apron around her waist with bulging pockets. One hand on a ladder rung, she held an apple in the other, and she was laughing down at the camera.

"Whoa." Lou scanned the photo. "That's your mom, right? She's like, what? Our age?"

"Uh huh. But look where she is."

Lou was silent for a second. She shrugged. "She's…picking apples?"

"Right, but I bet it's that old orchard out back."

She squinched her eyebrows. "Prob'ly. This is where she grew up, right—"

"Yeah," I interrupted her, shaking the box. "I think I can place other pictures in here." I dug through the photos. "Like this one of her and Grandpa… That's the pasture out front. You can see the woods and the trees in the background. And this one—isn't that the meadow where we saw the wild horses?"

She took the picture from me. "It could be…" She started nodding. "I think you're right. There's the creek, the draw, and the hills look the same…cool, Mist!" She handed me the photo. "You're totally walking in your mom's footsteps."

I stared at that picture of Mom in the meadow, a band of horses behind her in the distance, so like the picture Lou had taken of Ford and me. I met Lou's eyes and a slow grin spread across her face. "I know you. What plan are you hatching in that brilliant brain of yours?"

"I've been trying to figure out what to do with these old photos, and that picture you took yesterday… It looks so much like this one of Mom, and—"

"We could recreate these pictures of your Mom, only with us in them."

I'd more been thinking pictures with *me* in them, but Lou's enthusiasm had me nodding. *Us* would work. "It'd be a way to do something with the pictures and document our summer, all in one shot, so to speak."

"I love it!" She sat back. "This is gonna be great. Let's do the orchard one tomorrow when we get home."

"When we were feeding Rosa, I saw one of those little ladders in a pile of junk in the barn. I'm sure we could use that, if it's still sturdy enough to stand on."

We spent the rest of the evening laying out the photos, looking for locations we could place. At least a dozen of them had potential. As we prepared to leave the warmth of the fire and make our way up to our cold attic beds, Lou hesitated. "If we're both in the pictures, who's going to snap the shot? I don't know if I can stand an entire summer of pushing the button and diving into the frame."

We leaned back on the sofa, staring at the dying glow in the woodstove. I turned to Lou. She was grinning back at me, and we said it at the same time. "Ford."

WE TOLD THE GROUP about our plans the next day during lunch, and Bea and Donna, especially, were enthusiastic about the idea. When I asked Ford if he would take the pictures, he smiled and said, "I'm in." No hesitation. I ignored Lou's wink.

"I'd like you to make copies of the photos you want to reference," Dad told me. "I'll archive the originals." *Now* he was interested in the photos? He'd almost trashed them along with most of Mom's stuff a couple of months ago. Lou's mom, June, said he found it too painful to have all Mom's things around him, but I still had to stuff my frustration.

"Okay." I nodded like a bobble-head. "No problem." I'd already resigned myself to the prospect of never understanding my father. It was like Mom had been our universal translator.

We parted ways at the campground a little earlier than usual that afternoon. Dad drove to Ponder to go over some paperwork with Kurt. Bea, Donna and Frank made it clear they couldn't wait to swallow dinner and hit their cots. Lou and I piled into Ford's truck, and the three of us headed for the ranch house.

Lou was in full-on event-coordinator mode as we pulled up the driveway. "I was thinking, the t-shirts and jeans are easy. But I don't know where we're going to get aprons like the one your mom was wearing in that picture. And the bandannas." She rolled her eyes. "I left all my rodeo girl gear at home this trip."

"No worries," I assured her. "Wait 'til you see Dad's bandanna collection."

Ford lifted an eyebrow. "Your dad has a bandanna collection?"

"Well," I said, "as you may have noticed, he wears them on digs, and also under his motorcycle helmet when it's hot. He goes through them like a knife through butter—"

The truck came to a stop in front of the house and Lou gave me a funny look. "I think Bea's rubbing off on you."

"That'd be okay with me—Bea's great."

"Right?" Lou said, climbing out of the truck. "I hope I'm that cool when I'm ancient."

Before I followed her, some sound Ford made caused me to glance back. "What?"

He threw a look behind him. "What do you mean, what?"

"You had a weird look on your face. Is there something about Bea we don't know?"

"Uh, no, Bea's cool." His expression was hard to read. "She has some different ideas about stuff—"

"Come *on*, you two." Lou was opening the front door. "That is, if you're done flirtin'," she called back.

Ford grinned at her. I climbed out of the truck and practically flew up the steps after Lou, but she was already inside. "We'll be right back," I yelled to Ford. I started to slam the door behind me, but caught it when Ford called, "What? You guys aren't going to invite me in?"

I stopped and turned. "Oh, I…yeah, you can come in, if you want."

His grin got even wider and he leaned back against the driver's door. "That's okay, Mist. If it'll make you more comfortable, I'll just wait out here."

Ugh. He was teasing. I hated teasing. I rolled my eyes and went inside in search of Lou. She was standing in the middle of Dad's room, looking a little lost.

I hadn't gotten over the flirting comment and I elbowed her. "Dork."

"Nerd," she tossed back. "Well? Where's this legendary bandanna collection?"

In typical, organized Dad style, his bed was made, the covers pulled so taut, you could bounce a coin off the top blanket. His shoes aligned like soldiers under the end of his bed, and his jackets hung on some of the pegs lining the walls. Everything else must have been stowed in the dressers.

"Your Dad's really tidy for a guy."

"Blame the US Navy."

"Ahhh, thus the *FEET ON THE DECK, GIRLS*, we've been getting as our wake-up call every morning. It's all becoming clear."

"Yeah, welcome to my life."

I made for the dresser beside his bed and the first drawer I opened revealed multicolored layers of neatly folded bandannas. "A-ha! Take a look at this."

Lou and I liberated two that didn't look like they'd ever been worn and ran upstairs to change into clean jeans and t-shirts. Next, I used Dad's scanner to copy the picture of Mom in the orchard and left the original on his dresser.

Ford was leaning against his truck when we came back out, staring intently at the screen of his phone.

"C'mon, cowboy," Lou yelled. We jumped down the side steps of the porch and Ford met up with us on the path to the barn.

"Where are we doing this thing?"

I handed him the copied picture. "The orchard's out behind the barn. But we need to bring Rosa in first and feed her."

Lou grabbed the lead rope from a hook hanging on the fence and pushed through the gate into the small pasture where Rosa spent her days. "Hey, sweetie pie," she called. The horse raised her head and slowly ambled toward Lou. Rosa was gentle and seemed to like people. Before long, Lou was leading her into her stall.

While we fed and watered the horse, Ford dug in to the stack of antique farm implements piled against a wall and freed the wood ladder. When we were ready to go, he hoisted it onto a shoulder and followed us out of the barn.

The orchard was on a small rise behind the pasture. Forty or so apple trees had once been planted in neat rows, probably about a hundred years ago. After decades of neglect, their branches were tangled, the rows ragged. Of course, no apples hung from the branches, yet. Lou thought they were too old to bear fruit, but most of the gnarled old trees had new leaves, so at least they were alive.

Sparrows wove between the lacework of branches above our heads, landing lightly and launching into the air. A breeze carrying the warm balsam scent of pine forest swirled around us, rippled tall, green grass against our legs and rustled the fledgling leaves. We wandered through shafts of late-afternoon sunlight, checking Mom's picture and comparing it to what we saw around us.

I stopped. "This is it, I'm sure of it." I held up the picture and pointed to one of the healthier-looking trees—a large one in the center of the orchard. Lou and Ford peeked over my shoulders.

"It's kind of hard to tell," Lou said. "An apple tree's an apple tree, right? But I think it'll work great for the shot."

Ford positioned the ladder against the trunk and tested it.

Lou and I had taken lots of pictures of ourselves and each other. But this time, Ford was behind the camera. It was impossible to relax, at least, impossible for me. My rodeo-queen friend was in her element and hammed it up like the pro that she was.

Ford was a good sport. He even seemed to be enjoying himself. But after a while he lowered the camera, thoughtful.

"What?" Lou asked.

"It *is* Misty's mom in this picture. Maybe we should try one with just her…?"

Lou pretended to pout. She turned and pulled my head close to hers. "I get it. Boy just wants you in his picture." She giggled in my ear. I started to protest, but she hopped down and ran over to Ford. "Smile for the camera, baby," she crooned.

I laughed self-consciously and Ford snapped the picture. He peered at the camera and showed it to Lou.

"Perfect." She motioned me over. "Mist, come see."

I hopped off the ladder and closed the short distance between us. Cupping my hand around the display to get a better look at the picture, I peered at the screen.

And felt that catch in my heart.

I moved my hand to my mouth. My knees felt like jelly. "I look so much like her." I hadn't meant to say it out loud.

Lou put her arm around me, but she was still staring at the screen. "Ford did a great job of framing it—"

Ford interrupted her. "Lou—" I glanced up at him. He was watching me. "Are you okay, Misty?"

Lou was beginning to realize something was wrong, but she was confused. I'd never mentioned my suspicion that it would be easier for Dad to deal with Mom's death if I wasn't around all the time, reminding him of her.

I pulled the camera close again. Maybe I'd imagined it. But I hadn't. *I look just like Mom.* I thought about all the late hours Dad spent at work since she'd died. How it seemed hard for him to look me in the eye. "No wonder Dad has a hard time living with me. I didn't realize how much…" My voice caught. I couldn't finish.

"Aw, Mist." Lou said. "I bet your dad loves that you look like her. Why would it—?"

Our eyes met, and she stopped in mid-sentence.

I handed her the camera and walked away. Why *would* it bother him? But it did, I was sure of it. He'd gotten rid of everything that reminded him too much of Mom. But he was stuck with me.

I could feel my heart slam in my chest, my breath came in short gasps, the dark at the edges of my vision threatened to close in. I couldn't stay there with them. I had to move. I held up my hand, my back to Lou and Ford. Hurrying through the trees, I yelled, "See you guys later," and took off for the woods on the other side of the orchard.

"Misty," Lou called. I could hear the worry in her voice, but I didn't want her to follow me.

I turned, faking a smile. "I'm fine," I yelled. "I need a walk— really. See you later." I jogged away, relieved that Ford and Lou got it, and no one followed me.

Stumbling along the trail, I tried to be angry at Dad. I'd discovered, somewhere along the way, anger is the only thing that brings an immediate end to an anxiety attack. The two must inhabit the same space in a person's soul, and there's only room for one at a time.

But I didn't have the energy for mad. All I felt was sad.

Finally, exhausted, I threw myself down at the base of a large pine. I was shaking, but the running had helped. After a while, the silent calm of the woods invaded my grief. My heartbeat slowed.

I wiped at my face with the bandanna and tried to empty my mind, breathing slowly, in and out, in and out. But Mom was always there, and that wasn't all bad. I wouldn't say time had healed my heart, but I was getting so I could talk about Mom and what happened to her like I was telling a story about someone else. Well, sometimes I could.

I'd come a long way from those first months after Mom's death when I'd spent so many evenings sobbing at Lou and June's kitchen table, completely broken. On the night Dad had announced the project in the Juliets and our impending relocation for the summer, it had all come spilling out, in no particular order. How much I missed mom, how hard it was with Dad.

"I…I feel like screaming," I'd said to June. "But I'm afraid if I start, I won't be able to stop." I wiped my nose with one of the tissues June always had at the ready, grabbed another one and crumpled it in my hand.

"Maybe you should scream," she'd said, massaging my shoulder. "I see you and Paul, both trying to be so brave. But that'll kill you, Misty. You have to let it out. I've been where you are. You have to let it hurt until it doesn't hurt anymore. There's no other way. You're going through some hard stuff. You're supposed to feel sad."

"But it's like Dad doesn't even care!"

"Mist, that's not true—"

"I know." I pounded my fist full of tissue on the table. "But it feels like he wants to get on with life and not think about Mom, not talk about her. He wants to get rid of her stuff and leave our home and act like she was never there."

June held out a wastebasket and I dropped the tissues into it. "Well," she said, "he tried to talk with you about how you're feeling this evening, didn't he?"

"Yeah, right, after telling me we're going to some middle-of-nowhere place for the summer. He didn't even ask me if I wanted to go."

June released my hand and held up both of hers. "Look, I'm not saying your dad should get an award for sensitivity. But you know how hard this is for him. You know how much he loved your mom…"

OF COURSE, HE LOVED her, but I *needed* her. The irony was that no one but my mother could possibly help me get over the loss of my mother. Sometimes, I thought I was getting better, but there was something about seeing that picture of me looking so much like Mom when she was my age.

She would have loved that copycat picture. She would have laughed, and hugged me, and shown the picture to everybody. A chuckle bubbled up from inside me when I imagined her smile. Why couldn't that have been my reaction when I was with Lou and Ford?

Thinking about how weird I'd just been made me squirm, and I clenched my fist around the bandanna. I threw it as hard as I could, but the red cloth expanded like a parachute, floated lazily between some bushes and caught on a branch.

I stared at the bright patch puddled among the leaves, and sure as I left it there, Dad would miss it. Pushing to my feet, I dug the bandanna out of the spiky twigs and looked around. Diffused light through branches scattered dim, lacey shadows around me.

I shouldn't have taken off like that. I shook my head. It was as if I could physically feel my emotions bouncing around my insides like a ping pong ball.

Lou was right—I'd mostly been the easy daughter. The chill kid. But no one who loved me knew the secret that was getting harder to hide: I wasn't that girl anymore.

I never knew what emotion I'd experience next. I was afraid, all the time. I wanted to hide and feel safe and shout and kick and have things back to the way they were—everything, all at once. And in between those bouts of emotion? I felt numb. I felt nothing.

I let out a shaky breath, inhaled deeply. I wasn't about to head home. Not until Ford was gone. I knew where I was, from the map tacked to the wall in Dad's room. Ferguson Creek bordered the ranch's property. The trail where I stood crossed the brook and continued through the woods to the west. I decided to follow the trail up to the top of a ridge behind the ranch. The view was probably amazing, and I'd been meaning to check it out.

Drained, but determined to stay away a little longer, I picked my way along the trail. A log someone had strategically placed over Ferguson Creek allowed me to cross the water. One foot in front of the other, I balanced my way to the other side and scrambled through the underbrush to the trail. I wandered along the path, in no hurry, lost in my own thoughts.

The air smelled piney and clean. There was a hint of the faint, vanilla scent of Ponderosa. As it had the first night we arrived, the scents reminded me of Mom. Again, I had that vision from my childhood of her smiling down at me, taking me in her arms. I tried to picture nothing but that memory, and it helped.

At a curve in the trail, clear space finally opened up between the trees.

The entire valley stretched before me beneath a setting sun that drenched ribbon clouds in pink and orange. Breaking from the dim forest into the light was like entering another dimension.

I wanted to stay and watch the sun go down, but it was getting late. I had no flashlight, no jacket. Nothing. My parents would have been appalled. "Always prepared," was practically the family motto, and I was anything but prepared. Getting stuck on a mountain in the dark and making Dad deploy a search party would be way worse than having to go back home and look my friends in the eye.

A deer trail led from the ridge where I stood, down to the back side of the ranch. *A short-cut, maybe?* I caught sight of movement, an animal weaving through the trees in the orchard. The creature broke out of the scruff of apple trees, but before I could get a good look, it trotted up the deer trail I was about to hike down. The way the animal moved, it wasn't a bear or anything scary, like a cougar. *Probably a deer that will spring away and disappear as soon as it hears me coming.*

Not far from the orchard, the trees thinned, and I could see a horse on the path below me, and not just any horse—it was

Lookout. His big crooked nose and floppy ears were unmistakable, even from a distance. I stopped, and so did he. He eyed me, snorted and pawed the earth.

"Hello," I said.

We each stood our ground, and I wondered if he would come to me like he had before, but he didn't. I ventured a step toward him and the second I moved, he veered off the trail and crashed up the slope. I watched him climb, losing sight of him in the trees. I could hear him plowing up the slope for much longer than I could see him, but eventually, the forest returned to silence.

I couldn't believe it—Lookout, again, and so close to home. Then I remembered the other creature—the cougar that was shadowing him the last time I encountered the wild stallion.

After that, every snapping twig, each rustle in the underbrush, even the wind whispering through the tops of the pines took on an ominous edge. Exhausted or not, I spun around and raced down the trail toward home.

EIGHT

I EMERGED FROM THE orchard as the sun dipped behind the Juliets. A comforting stream of light poured through the window of the barn—Dad, still working in his lab. They must have finished eating already. *What had he and Lou done about dinner? What had Lou told him?*

When I walked into the house, she was huddled in her corner of the couch, staring at her computer. She shoved it onto the coffee table when I came in. "Misty, where have you been? I was about to go out to the barn and tell your Dad we needed to send out a search party."

I stopped in the middle of the room. "Wait. Please say you didn't tell him what happened—"

She gave me a grumpy scowl that lasted a full five seconds, then put me out of my misery with a wave of her hand. "No, of course not. I made some excuse while I was making dinner, about you going for a short hike and I didn't know if you'd be back in time. Your dad's been out in the barn ever since dinner, nose to the grindstone. He probably figures you came back an hour ago."

Relieved, I plopped onto the couch. She pushed one end of her blanket over me. Something about that simple kindness almost undid me, but I swallowed it. "Thanks."

"No problem." She nudged me. "Your dad really trusts you. I can't believe he was like, 'Yeah, whatever,' when I told him you'd taken off. I wish my mom was that way."

I wondered if that was true. Did my father trust me? Or was it his obsession with the latest project, as usual? I knew Dad loved me, but I was pretty sure he found almost anything else in the world more interesting.

I leaned my head back on the couch and stared up at the ceiling. There was a faint smell of warm potatoes. "Stuffed spuds for dinner?"

"Uh-huh. We made one for you to microwave. It's in the fridge."

A log in the stove popped and fell into the cinders with a soft *thump*. "I feel really stupid, Lou. And Ford must think I'm insane."

"No, he doesn't. I explained about your mom. He said Kurt told him she passed away—but he didn't know the details. Or that it was so recent. I hope that was okay?"

I closed my eyes. "It's fine. Means I don't have to tell him."

"He completely understood, by the way."

I didn't respond. I couldn't even imagine what he really thought. I felt Lou squirm beside me.

"Mist?" Her voice was soft. "Do you want to talk about it?"

I pushed myself off the sofa and started toward the stairs with what felt like the last shred of willpower I had left. "I'm so tired, Lou. I just want to go to bed."

"Yeah, okay." She sounded relieved. "G'night."

THE NEXT MORNING, I watched Ford head toward the van to get the last screen. The previous evening was starting to seem like a hazy, melodramatic dream. Hysterics were really not my style. I was furious with myself for being so lame. I resolved to never, ever, let anything like that happen again. I followed him, determined to apologize before I lost my nerve. "Um, Ford?"

He glanced behind him.

"Sorry about yesterday…" I couldn't think of what else to say.

He stopped, his back to me. He'd seemed sort of cautious around me that morning, and I braced myself for some comment along the lines of, "You are some crazy chick." But he pulled the screen out of the van, turned and shrugged. "Nothin' to apologize for."

Then, the grin. I really liked that grin.

He walked away from me, lugging the screen over to the site, and that was it. I figured he probably thought I was crazy, but there were no questions, no pity. He didn't even seem all that concerned, and I wanted to hug him for that reaction. All my friends back home, except Lou, tiptoed around me like the floor had turned to broken glass.

That day was more of the same. Digging, screening, dumping, sorting. Lou and I were exhausted by the time we got home and stumbled in the door. We made scrambled eggs, fried ham and toast for dinner. Dad didn't complain. We showered, rubbed ointment on our blisters and climbed into bed with a moan.

I lay there, listening to the cacophony of tree frogs and crickets that floated in with the breeze through my open window, and started to drift…

"Misty? You asleep?"

Silence, crickets, drifting…

"Mist?"

"Mm-hmm," I responded.

"Oh, okay. Well, goodnight."

"What?" I mumbled.

"Nothing. Go back to sleep."

Yeah, right. I turned over and cracked open an eye. "What?"

No response.

"Whaaat?" I whined. "I'm awake now. Don't make me beg."

Lou rolled over and squinted across the space. "Ford and I were talking—"

"When?" I was suddenly wide awake. "About what?"

"At lunch today. You were helping your Dad bag stuff up, and we were talking…about the pictures. We were wondering if…well, we'd understand if you don't want to do any more."

I'd assumed we'd go ahead with our plan. I hadn't really thought about not continuing, but now she mentioned it? "I'm sorry I freaked out, Lou. I feel bad—"

"No, Mist." She sat up. "It's not that. I told you, we totally understand, and you don't have to keep apologizing."

I sat up, too, and hugged my knees to my chest.

"We don't want you to feel like you have to keep going."

"Do you want to?"

"Do you?"

"*Lou…*" She wasn't usually this sensitive to my feelings, and I wasn't sure how to deal with it. "Sheesh, I really must've freaked you out."

"Okay, I admit I was a little freaked for a minute there. But I got over it, and so did Ford."

I wasn't sure what to say, how to explain what was going on inside me.

Finally, Lou began to talk. "I think it's okay for you to still feel bad, Misty. I really don't think there's any statute of limitations on grieving for a lost parent. Or, even—" Her voice got softer. "Being mad at God for taking her."

I sighed. "Is it that obvious?"

"I don't know. I can't always read your mind. But I would be angry. I never even knew my dad, and I still get mad, I guess, about that. That my life, me and Mom's, had to be the way it is. But how that went down was hardly God's fault. Not like what happened to you guys."

I fell back on my pillow and pulled the covers over my head. "I wish it was that easy."

"What?" Lou climbed over to my bed and pealed the covers back. "I couldn't hear you."

"I said *I wish it was that easy.*" I squeezed my eyes shut. "I wish I could get mad at God and yell at him and get it all out and feel better. But the thing is, I may be mad. I may be going mad, I don't know. But I've never been angry at God for what happened."

Lou raised incredulous brows. "Really? You know, you don't have to be all righteous and Sally Sunshine with me." She nudged my leg. "'Cuz, believe me, I know you're not."

"That's for sure…" I thought back to the night Mom died. Could I tell Lou? "Something happened to me that night, after we left the hospital and went home.

"We walked in the house and it was so quiet, so empty. There was food someone had left for us on the counter, some kind of casserole or something. But we weren't hungry. We went to bed. At least, that's what I did, I don't know about Dad.

"I laid there, thinking over and over, *don't be dead, you can't be dead.* There was a part of me that was sure I'd wake up in the morning and it would all be a bad dream. No way could my brain get that Mom was gone and she was never coming back."

I bit my lip. Lou's eyes were wide, but she was with me. She nodded, so I kept going. "Her death wasn't real to me. I mean, I knew it was real, but I was also sure it couldn't be. This kind of stuff wasn't supposed to happen to our family. You read about tragedy happening to people you don't know.

"I started praying, over and over, *let Mom be okay. I need her, God. You wouldn't take her away. I know you wouldn't. You take care of us. You promised you would take care of us if we loved you.*"

I stopped and tried to gauge how my friend was taking my confession. She wasn't looking at me. She seemed lost in thought. "Lou?"

She shook her head as if to clear it. She was that caught up in my story. "What?"

"Don't think I'm crazy, okay? And don't tell my dad or your mom."

She shook her head slowly back and forth. "I won't. I promise."

"I could feel a…I don't know. A Presence, in my room with me. And there was this…impression. It wasn't a voice out of heaven or a bright light or anything. But it was almost like I *could* hear it, somewhere between my brain and my heart. And it said what I knew, that this was bad. It was like God was there, understanding how much it hurt, unbearably hurt. But also, that…"

I stopped. Lou didn't say anything, but she reached out and took my hand.

"But also, that he *was* keeping us safe. I seemed to hear it over and over. *I've covered this. I have you covered. You'll be okay.* Which I know didn't come out of my brain, because that was the last thing I was thinking at that moment."

"Misty, that's amazing. I don't know what to say."

"I know." I was afraid to look at her. Did she even half believe me?

"What do you think it meant? *I have this covered.*"

I drew in a breath and let it out slowly. She believed me. This was so awesome. My best friend didn't think I was crazy. "I've thought about it a lot since then—"

"I bet."

"Yeah. I'm not sure what it means. All I know is that it was so comforting. Like, everything was out of control, but it wasn't, because…"

Lou smiled. "Because he had it covered."

"But the truth is, it still hurts, and I guess God's okay with me hurting, and Dad hurting. And Mom…what do I *do* with that? All I can do is get up in the morning and take the next step, and sometimes I lose it. I don't know why."

"You're right. It's not easy." She scooted around and flopped next to me on the pillow. "I don't think you're the only one who's confused, Mist."

"You mean Dad? Yeah, that's kind of obvious, huh?"

"When your mom was still here, you guys were the attendance all-stars at church, you know? But since the memorial service…"

"I know. He hasn't suggested we go, not once. But neither have I. After a while, it doesn't seem so strange."

Lou closed her eyes, then opened them. "I used to love to hear your dad pray. He's one of those people who sounds like he's really talking to God when he prays. He's not preaching a sermon or trying to make a point. I couldn't help but picture God stopping whatever he was doing to listen to him. And I loved it when he said he'd pray for me, because I was sure God would hear him. But now—"

"Yeah, I've noticed. I don't know what he's feeling, but I can imagine. Since I was a little kid, when I thought about meeting God, I pictured myself running and throwing myself into his arms. I still want to do that. But, now, I'm not always sure if he'll catch me."

Lou didn't say anything to that. She gave my hand a squeeze and moved back into her own bed. I thought she'd gone to sleep but then, "So, what's the next step?"

"Huh?"

"You said all you can do is get up in the morning and take the next step. What's the next step? Pictures, or no pictures?"

"C'mon, Lou." I squinted, trying to see her eyes across the dim space. "Do you really want to keep going with the picture thing? Is it a dumb idea?"

"No—yeah, I think it's a great idea. I guess, if you're really asking, I want to keep going. And I think Ford does, too. Any chance to spend some more time with us hotties." She giggled.

"What did he really say to you today?"

She stretched out her arms and curled around her pillow. "Strangely, your little episode didn't seem to bother him a bit. He is an interesting piece of work, that boy. He said he was down with it either way."

I still couldn't believe Ford was interested in spending his free time with us. I guessed there wasn't anything else to do for fun in the valley. "I think if you guys are still into it, we should do it." I fell back on my pillow. "I had it all pictured in my head, and I know I'll be bummed later if we don't."

"Oh, good. I was hoping you'd say that."

"I'll try not to freak out again."

"Thank goodness!" Lou rolled over. "Remember, *I'm* the emotional one. *You're* the freakishly balanced one. Got it?"

I yawned. "Got it."

Silence, crickets, drifting…

IT WAS A TYPICAL FRIDAY—we were all tired and cranky, while simultaneously being psyched for the weekend. Far from discovering buried treasure in our test pits, we found a lot of bone and not much else. As the morning heated up and moved into midday, Dad had mercy on the crew and let us return to surveying the woods for Blackwell's homestead site.

Frank and Ford claimed the best toys that day—two metal detectors Dad borrowed from the Ponder Sheriff's Office. "You're looking for stray bits of metal," Dad told us. "Gun or harness parts, spoons or knives. You might get lucky and find some nails or pieces of old tools. Any of that would be evidence we're getting close to the cabin site."

"What about jars of gold?" Frank chuckled. "That qualify?" Everyone groaned and started searching through the trees, scanning the ground at our feet. We pushed aside bushes and bits of forest debris with the soles of our boots. Occasionally someone to my right or left would bend down to examine a promising glint or gleam.

About a half hour into the survey, Ford yelled, "I've got something." That turned out to be an understatement. He kept getting hits in one particular area, and Dad thought it was worth digging a couple of test pits. Soon, Dad confirmed we'd located what we were looking for.

We set up our crews. In no time at all, Dad and I turned up several pieces of china, a spoon, and some shell casings. In the second pit, Ford dug deep and came up with the find of the day—two huge rocks that were the first of many foundation stones we expected to unearth in the next few days.

"This is great, folks," Dad said with a wide smile. "Thanks for all your efforts. I know a few spoons and some rocks may not seem like much, but this is a truly exciting find. A lot of Pacific Northwest archaeologists would give their pinky finger to be able to work on something like this." He looked over at Bea. "And this is definitely something to write home about."

Ford acted like he'd discovered the eighth wonder of the world. He pulled out his phone and started texting. He was talking to himself while his thumbs flew "…so cool." Dad reached over and deftly detached Ford's phone from his whirling fingers.

"Hey, what the…?" He gave Dad a confused look.

"Don't worry. I'm not keeping it. But this brings up a crucial point of archaeological training that I don't think we've covered.

When I said this was something to write home about, I meant it in only the most general terms."

Ford frowned, but I figured that was mostly about being deprived of his phone. He liked Dad. I knew he'd be okay.

Dad handed him the phone while he continued his lecture. "You may not know that a surprising number of nefarious individuals spend their lives robbing sites such as this one. In the archaeology world we call them 'pothunters,' a term that comes out of the Southwest. A thriving market for authentic pioneer and Indian artifacts from the Pacific Northwest also exists, especially in Asia. When archaeologists find a site, we work hard to keep the exact location under wraps, except in official reports. The better the site, the more secret we like to keep it."

Frank frowned. "Isn't that kind of Big Brother? This is public land. Shouldn't this stuff be available for the public to explore?"

"Absolutely." Dad said. "And in a different world, we could trust people to come to sites, enjoy the history, and leave what they see for the next person to experience. Unfortunately, unguarded sites have proven to be too tempting for a lot of folks. So, if people are interested in seeing artifacts, they can visit a museum. It's that, or constantly battling the bad guys out there on the black market."

Ford was smiling again. I knew it wouldn't take him long to regain his enthusiasm. "It's awesome that we get to be here," he said.

"That's the spirit. You should feel lucky, all of you. This is a historian's dream come true, and we've only scratched the surface." Dad touched his lips with an index finger. "But you've heard the phrase: loose lips sink ships? Well, loose lips in archaeology can mean a piece of antiquity, maybe the only piece of information we have about a certain time in history, can be lost forever. It *is* awesome, Ford, that we get to be here. But we want this stuff to be around for future generations, too."

We staked off what Dad guessed was an approximate perimeter of the old cabin, and listened while Ford asked, and Dad answered questions about the site, the history of the area, and the art of archeology.

I watched them, floored once again at how Ford seemed as interested in this stuff as Dad. At one point, Ford caught me watching him. He met my eyes, and for once, I didn't turn away. He grinned and went back to work.

By the end of the day, Dad was treating Ford like a favored son again, and I was a little jealous, but also happy Ford and Dad got along so well. Lou was spot on—I liked Ford, a lot, more every day. I wasn't ready to admit it to her, but it didn't matter. She was my best friend. She knew.

AFTER DINNER, DAD ASKED me to meet him in his lab out in the barn. Lou and I finished the dishes and I left her happily pecking away on her computer at the kitchen table.

The night was still, the air soft and warm. The light wasn't completely gone, but it was dark enough to see a bright sliver of moon hanging low above the stand of pine. I stepped out the back door into the yard lined by the grove of old apple trees.

I started to make my way toward the barn, stepping carefully. What I hadn't thought of was how the tangled trees on the rise would block some of the light, which was dimming by the minute. An owl hooted softly…and something stirred. I stopped to listen. The branches rattled against each other in a breeze that always came up when the sun went down.

The owl hooted several more times, and a raven caw sounded to my ears like a warning. I strained to hear…what? I had a sense there was something else out there other than birds, that I wasn't alone. The wind moved through the branches. Tall grasses rustled against my legs.

I tried to shake off my stupid fear and laughed out loud. But as my laughter died, I was sure I heard a footfall nearby. A twig cracked in front of me. With a sharp intake of breath, I was assaulted by the heavy, musky scent of wild animal. The hairs rose on the back of my neck. I stood stock still, listening. "Is…is somebody there?"

A creature crashed through the bushes behind me and I whirled around. Lookout was coming fast, straight toward me at the same time as a screeching yowl echoed through the orchard. That sound seemed to be coming from every direction.

I screamed and shut my eyes. The ground shook and I could feel the warmth coming off Lookout in a whoosh of air as he thundered past. I turned and caught a glimpse of him weaving through the trees, and he vanished.

A cemetery-like silence settled over the orchard. I was alone…at least, I hoped so. I strained to hear any sound, but all I could hear was my own heart pounding in my ears. I forced my weak legs to move and ran back toward the house, but curiosity won out over my dread of what might be behind me. I couldn't help looking back. I turned my head to see if something was chasing me—and ran straight into Dad's arms.

"Mist, what happened? Are you all right? I heard—"

I buried my head in his shoulder and he hugged me tight. A shudder ran through me, and I couldn't stop shaking. He held on for a minute, pulled back and gave me the Dad once-over, his face tense and filled with worry. "Are you hurt?"

"No," I gasped. "I'm fine. It was Lookout again, and, I don't know, that yowl…"

Dad's expression turned grim.

"Dad, *what* was that cry?"

He stared past me, scanning the orchard, and shook his head. "I can't believe it was that close to you."

"A cougar." Another shudder ran through me. "It was that cougar again, wasn't it?"

"I think so," he said, and turned us toward the lights and safety of the barn. "I'm just glad you're okay."

Inside the barn, we sat for a while on the hay bales, catching our breath. Dad sent Lou a quick text about what had happened, and that she should stay inside.

I was still shaking. "Can you believe I've been that close to a cougar, maybe the same cougar, twice in a couple of weeks? That's really weird, isn't it? What does it have against me? It can't be a coincidence."

"It is strange. I've heard young or very old cougars that can't catch any other prey sometimes stalk people, though it's rare." Dad raked a hand through his hair. "If Kurt's right about that track in the dirt after your first encounter with Lookout, this is the second time that cougar's had you in its sights."

I leaned back…and started to slide off the hay bale before dad grabbed me and pulled me into a side hug. He hadn't hugged me this much since I was little. Right then, I didn't mind at all. I laid my head on his shoulder and it was like being a kid again.

The familiar smell of him, something like soil—but somehow clean—mixed with the spicy-scented soap he'd been using my entire life, was strangely reassuring. He cleared his throat and I lifted my head from his shoulder. His eyes searched mine, eyes permanently blood-shot from too many years hunting for the next big find in sunlit valleys and treeless deserts. His worried expression changed to a wry smile.

"What?" I frowned at him. "If there's something funny about all this, please, let me in on the joke."

He actually laughed. "Much as it grieves me to say this, I guess you're going to have to stick with your dear old dad when you're out at night around here."

It was nice to feel loved, but I wasn't a little girl anymore. "Yeah, right." I gave him a gentle push. "I'll take my chances."

Truth was, sticking close to my father didn't sound like a bad idea. Those two encounters with Lookout left me jittery, but there was also something bugging me. I replayed the two scenarios in my mind again, throwing the cougar into the mix with Lookout, even though I hadn't actually seen the cat.

"I wasn't the only one around both times that cougar showed up."

"You mean Lookout?"

"Maybe it isn't me that cougar is stalking—could be, it's after Lookout."

"You may be on to something." Dad stroked his beard, nodding. "From what Kurt says, Lookout's totally on his own. No other horse has his back, like they would if he belonged to a larger band. He's the sort of prey a lazy, hungry old cougar would find attractive."

I nodded. I thought that made sense.

He lifted his chin, peering down at me. "I can see the wheels turning in there. Any other insights?"

I didn't really know what to say. I'd interacted with the stallion more than once, and every encounter had felt otherworldly. Part of me was crazy scared of Lookout, or the ghost of Lookout…or whatever it was. But the rational side of me knew the horse wasn't a creature from another dimension. He could feel pain and hurt and maybe even loss. Really, he could hardly be held to human standards for the trouble he'd caused. From what I'd learned, he'd been through more than enough trauma for one lifetime. It was tragic to think his life might end in the claws and teeth of a cougar.

That all sounded too emotional to say out loud, especially to my dad. Instead, I changed the subject. "I was actually wondering why you asked me to come out here in the first place."

He held my gaze. He knew I was avoiding the question. "You're really okay? Not hurt? Not too scared to go back out there? After these last few nights, I wouldn't blame you if you wanted to head home to Alton tomorrow."

I wondered if that's what he wanted—me out of the way so he wouldn't have to worry. I sat there beside him on the hay, inhaling all the brown scents of the barn—horse, manure, rotting wood, dirt—I realized I was growing to like those smells and this project. I wasn't ready to leave.

"I'm fine, Dad," I said. "You're right. Considering what's been going on, none of us should be out alone at night until Kurt can figure out what to do about that cougar and Lookout."

I held up a hand. "Not that I'm going to spend the rest of the summer hiding out with my father, though, so don't get any ideas."

He chuckled, but continued to give me the Dad eye. "The question is, *who* are you going to be spending your time with, besides Lou, of course? Maybe a certain seventeen-year-old boy…"

Oh no. Not Dad, too. "Uh-uh," I said, standing and heading toward his workbench. "Don't even start. What ya got? Why'd you want me to come out here tonight, anyway?"

He pushed himself off his hay bale with a grunt and followed me. "Okay, alright. But you know you can talk to me about boy stuff—"

I palmed my face. "Dad, stop! We're not going there tonight."

"Fine with me," he muttered. "I'd be happy if we never had to go there." He pointed at the bones laid out on the table. "Take a look at this, then. I have a quick lesson in faunal analysis for you."

"Oh, goody." I clapped my hands like a toddler. "A bone lesson at the end of a long day. Just what I was hoping for this evening."

He smiled serenely. "Sarcasm will get you nowhere young lady. Besides, you're going to love this in light of recent events."

Dad held up the bone we'd collected the afternoon he'd driven Blackwell and his guests back to the ranch. It was the big bone we'd found on top of the jar of gold-flecked rocks. "You were thinking this was the bone of a…?"

"A deer, maybe? It's pretty big, but it looks too small to be an ox or an elk. Is that wrong?" A sick thought hit me. "It's not human, is it?"

Dad laughed out loud. "Big Foot? Uh, no. Thank God, it's not human. That would certainly change our priorities for the summer, and make this a lot less fun. A deer is actually a good guess."

"But that's not right?"

"Let me show you something." He pointed to an assortment of bones on the workbench. "I've laid these out in their proper anatomical positions."

My turn to smirk. Dad could be such a geek. Ignoring me, he indicated the three bones lined up in front of me, his finger coming to rest on the longest one. "This is called the cannon bone, which is the long bone above the hoof of a horse." He picked up a paint brush-like tool and whisked a bit of dirt from the end of the bone. "First off, this is the right size for a cow or a horse—so we know it's too big to be a deer."

He drew his finger down to two much smaller bones. I started to hum, *Dem Bones.*

Dad didn't miss a beat. "It connects to the first toe bone, which connects to the second toe bone, here." He moved his finger back up to the end of the cannon bone. "This is the crucial bone that distinguishes a horse from a cow. If this was from a deer, an elk, or a cow, you would see a subtle line running down the length of the bone. At the end, where the cannon bone would connect to the toe bone on a deer or cow, you'd see two ridges because they have two toes—split hooves."

He held up two fingers in a "V" sign, then closed his hand so only his index finger pointed up. "A horse has only one, so we see just one ridge. On a horse cannon bone no line runs down the middle—it's one solid piece."

I stared at the bones in front of us. The answer to the question was easy, once you knew what to look for. "This is a horse, then?"

"Yeah, but that's not the most interesting part. Look at this." He pointed to the lower end of the cannon bone near the place where it would connect to the hoof. "You see this flat surface right here? Take a close look. What do you see?"

I bent closer. "There's a bunch of parallel…grooves, or something?"

"Right. Guess what those are."

I put out my hands, palms up. I had no idea.

"Those are the marks left by the saw somebody used to cut the foot off."

"Huh?"

"It looks to me like somebody butchered this horse, like you would butcher a cow."

"Butchered?" I thought about Lookout and felt sick. "That's disgusting. You're telling me this is a horse somebody butchered for food? Was that normal around here in the 1800s?"

"No, it wasn't. Rarely do we find horse remains in somebody's garbage dump. You might have the occasional starving settler or Indian who ate their horse when a winter went on too long." There was a stool next to the workbench, and he sat back on it, shaking his head. "But I don't remember any stories of that kind of desperation around here in the 1800s. Mysterious, right?"

"My dad, actually admitting he doesn't have all the answers."

A smile tugged at one corner of his mouth, but he turned thoughtful again. "Even though we're in the mountains, we're not talking subzero winters with snow piled to the rooftops. This area has mild weather and plentiful game. As far as we know, it's always had a temperate climate. And if a horse was killed because it was sick, or diseased, chances are nobody would have eaten the meat for fear it was tainted."

"Maybe it got injured?"

Dad seemed skeptical. "I guess a horse could break a leg or something and have to be put down, but this leg looks fine."

We both turned back to the bone horse laid out on the table. "In fact," Dad said, "this looks to be the bone of a large, healthy animal." He was silent for a minute, brow furrowed. "I was thinking about what Blackwell said, about the ghost of Gold Creek being Lookout's ancestor, how he was killed by Percival Blackwell…"

"You think maybe we're digging up the horse that started the ghost legend—the one Blackwell's ancestor killed?" I rubbed my thumb along the rough, serrated end of the bone, and I couldn't help but smile. "That is kind of cool."

"I'm glad you think so, because I'd like you and Lou to do a little sleuthing for me this weekend, if you're up for it." He stood, rubbing his hands together. "Several local histories have been written about this area, and we have one good oral historian in Bob Blackwell. I'm hoping the two of you can do some research, possibly, interview Bob, and find some third-party evidence that corroborates our theory the *ghost* horse was eaten after it was killed."

Okay, so maybe I did have Dad's geek genes running through me, because researching literature related to the ghost legend actually sounded fun to me. On the other hand, dealing with Bob Blackwell and his explosive personality made me a little queasy. But I was pretty sure, since it would involve a trip into Ponder, I could convince Lou to help me. It would be something different to do on the weekend.

"Sure, I think we can do that." Dad gave me an 'atta girl pat. I took a last look at the bones. "But Dad, why would they eat that poor horse?"

"Even back in those days, I doubt horsemeat was at the top of anyone's menu." He shrugged. "At the same time, meat's meat, and the pioneers didn't waste anything. I don't know for sure, but it sounds like that horse had caused them a lot of trouble. Stampeding their cattle, running off their horses. Eating its remains might have been their final revenge."

As we left the barn, Dad was still talking about how great it would be to prove that these were the bones of the animal that started the ghost legend. "Connecting a legend to the present could bring history alive for people. It would also provide a whole new angle to the Forest Service efforts to educate visitors about how different people groups and animals use the land and what happens when their interests clash."

I tried to listen. But Kurt had told us Blackwell was out there hunting Lookout—and all I could think was how history might be repeating itself after all.

NINE

LOU DROVE US INTO town Saturday morning. Her usual no fear approach to life carried over to her driving. By the time we pulled into a parking spot at the Ponder Public Library, I wanted to dive out of the car and yell, "Stuck the landing!"

Dad seemed to take it in stride. "I've got a couple of people I need to meet over at headquarters." He handed me cash for lunch at the nearby café and checked his watch. "How about I meet you back here at two this afternoon?"

Before we started our search through the library stacks, Lou talked me into walking up the main street a couple blocks to get a coffee drink at the grocery store kiosk. A few minutes later, we were kicked back at the outdoor tables with our drinks, watching the occasional car cruise slowly by. Lou stared right back at the people staring at us. "What do you wanna bet we're the most exciting thing to happen in this town all year?"

From the way people were looking at us, I was thinking she might be right. Or maybe people in small towns just stare. But before I could respond, a truck stopped at the curb in front of us.

"Oh, look," Lou called, "It's a Ford in a Ford."

"And good morning to you, Lilou Rose," Ford shot back. "Been planning that one for a while, have you?" He turned those dark eyes on me. "Hey, Misty."

"Hi." I was grinning back at him like a moron, but I couldn't help it. He was so shiny and clean and carefree on his day off.

He parked the truck and walked over. "'Sup?"

"We're going to research the legend of the ghost of Gold Creek after this." Lou leaned toward him encouragingly. "Want to help?"

"Absolutely! I'll be right back." He sauntered into the store and reappeared a few minutes later with a twenty-ounce paper coffee cup.

"Sheesh," Lou said, "you know that'll stunt your growth."

Ford pulled himself up to his full height, which I guessed was approaching six feet. "So they say. Hasn't been my experience, though."

Lou craned her neck and squinted up at him towering over her. She turned to me and rolled her eyes.

I laughed at them both. "Ford you're going to love this. Guess what Dad showed me last night…"

A half hour later, the three of us invaded the tiny Ponder Library.

Some librarians actually want people to use their library, others act like their sole purpose in life is to keep people from disturbing them and their books. Fortunately, the Ponder librarian fell into the first category. In between keeping track of teenagers signed up to use the computers for thirty minutes at a time, checking out books to adults, and picking up the toys that kept creeping out of the kid's area with stray toddlers, she pulled local histories from the shelves and helped us set up at a back table.

We spent a couple hours skimming the books and magazines, and found more than one mention of the ghost legend. The accounts of the settlers and their battles with the wild stallion varied a bit in the details, but they all basically boiled down to the story Dad had told us during our Gold Creek camp-out. A huge wild stallion with funny-looking ears had harassed the settlers' horses and cattle. He also stole mares, and his ever-increasing band caused cattle stampedes, knocked down fences, ruined crops, and generally disrupted life in the tiny mountain settlement.

Ford tapped the book he'd been reading. "Not that many people lived here at the time. This says most of them worked for the mining operation. A few settlements were also scattered between Ponder and Gold Creek."

"This book tells what happened with the stallion and lists the men involved," I said. "Only seven men were in the posse, led by Blackwell's great-grandpa, like Bob said. Sounds like it took them a while to corner the horse—that stallion was smart."

I skimmed through the rest of the chapter. "The original plan was to try to capture the horse, but Percival got a lethal shot off at him one night near his cabin. Doesn't sound like the other men were all that pleased about him shooting the horse, for some reason, but it solved their problem. After the band's leader was dead, they didn't have much trouble rounding up the rest of the horses. The men returned the ones that could be identified to their owners, and Blackwell got the rest—"

Lou cut in. "This *Outside* article talks about the legend. It says a couple of years after that shooting, the…" She finger-quoted.

"*Ghost horse* showed up, a stallion that looked like the original, and caused the same kind of havoc. But there haven't been any confirmed sightings since the 1930s, and the legend has kind of died out."

"Until now," Ford said. "What I don't get is why the original stallion could be such a great leader of horses and Lookout seems like the opposite—a loner."

I turned my book around so Lou and Ford, who sat across from me, could see it. "If, like Kurt said, the stallion's ears make communicating with other horses difficult, this answers your question." I pointed to a sketch of the original stallion, drawn by one of the men involved in hunting him down. Despite what Blackwell said, Lookout was *not* a carbon copy of the original.

Ford said, "Yeah, so?"

"I don't get it, Mist." Lou was staring closely at the picture. She had no idea what I was talking about. I remembered I was the only one of us who had actually seen Lookout.

I pointed to the picture again. "Sure, this horse's ears are a little different than your average horse ears. You can tell there's something up with them. But you guys should see Lookout. You could easily mistake him for some undiscovered species. His ears are really low on the sides of his head, much more so than this horse's ears."

"But what is up with the horses around here?" Ford frowned. "Why the ears?"

"Got me," I said. "And we still don't have an answer for Dad about whether or not the horse we're digging up is the original."

The librarian breezed by, deftly redirecting a toddler back to the kids' area. She smiled at us. "The computers are yours— thirty minutes."

At first, we didn't find anything new in our online search. But I hit pay-dirt in an on-line newspaper article about the effects of mining in the area. "Hey," I said to the others who were lined up next to me at their computers. "Look at this."

Lou and Ford rolled their chairs over to my computer, but before I could show them my discovery, the librarian cleared her throat behind us. We all turned.

"Kids." She said apologetically. "Only one person to a computer—library policy—and your time's up."

I quickly printed the article, made copies of the pictures of mom we wanted to use for our project, and paid the librarian. When I met up with Ford and Lou outside the library, she put a hand on her stomach. "I'm starving. Is it lunch yet?"

We found seats in a booth at a café next door to the library and gave our orders to a harried-looking waitress with wiry gray hair and comfortable shoes. Lou, in keeping with her latest diet, ordered the house salad and a large glass of grapefruit juice. Ford and I went with the burgers and fries.

After the waitress left, I showed Ford and Lou the article I'd found on-line about the history of mining in the Gold Creek area. "After the gold ran out in Gold Creek, they discovered silver higher up in the mountains. Apparently, both mining operations produced all kinds of toxins that washed into the streams, and wreaked havoc with the fish and animal populations in the area. The Forest Service has put a lot of time and funds into cleaning the creek, but that's a fairly recent development."

The waitress cruised by and practically threw our plates and drinks in front of us. She rasped, "Need anything else?" and was gone before we could answer.

Lou watched her go, open-mouthed, and turned back to us. "But what does this have to do with the stallion?"

"The reason the article popped up is because it mentions the legend of the ghost of Gold Creek. The theory is that some genetic mutation took place in the horse population from all the sludge in the water, and that's what caused the ears. On top of that, this area has had more than its fair share of stillborn foals."

Lou frowned. "Oh, bummer."

"Right? They're wondering if the mutation has become an inherited trait that gets passed from generation to generation, and that's why the 'ghost' keeps showing up over the years—hey!"

I hadn't eaten much, I'd been so involved in my story. I didn't notice at first that Lou, who'd made short work of her salad, was working her way through my fries.

"Ah, c'mon, Mist," she said, batting her puppy eyes. "Can't you spare a fry?"

I pushed my plate between us. "*Mi fries es tu fries.*"

Ford shook his head at us and took another bite of his hamburger.

While we pooled our funds to pay the check, Lou mentioned that we still didn't have an answer for Dad about the bones we'd dug up.

"I guess we'll just have to go to the source," Ford said. "Or as close as we can get to it, anyway. You guys up for a ride out to the Blackwell ranch?"

I called Dad on my cell, but he didn't pick up. I decided we'd still be doing what he'd asked us to do, and he seemed to like Ford. I left a voice mail about seeing him at home later and figured leaving town would be okay.

About five miles out of town, Ford fish-tailed onto a gravel road and drove under a massive sun-bleached log that had "Double Bar B Ranch" carved into it. "Kurt brought me out here and introduced me around when I first got to town," he yelled over the noise of the washboard road. "I met Mr. and Mrs. Blackwell, but he was busy, distracted. I dunno. That's probably why he didn't remember me the other day at the park."

The truck bumped down the drive, passing grass and cattle and endless barbed wire fences until we encountered an old farm house. The building, once someone's home, seemed forlorn and deserted, falling to ruin and tangling with the native sage and grasslands.

After a few more minutes, the truck vibrated over the metal rungs of a cattle guard in the road, and the barbed wire gave way to a split-log fence. Finally, the ranch house came into view, and *lodge* was actually a better description of the three-story log mansion that rose up before us.

The afternoon sun was hot, and my shirt was stuck to my back from riding in the non-air-conditioned pick-up. As we climbed out of the truck, the house shimmered before us, an oasis in the exhausting heat of midday. Up the steps of a wide, wrap-around porch, guests relaxed in rocking chairs or sat around small tables, sipping refreshing-looking drinks that made me instantly jealous.

Ford opened one of the lodge's double front doors. "I'll go see if I can find the Blackwells. Be right back."

Lou elbowed me and raised her chin toward one of the icy pitchers sitting on the tables. "What do you think the chances are we get in on that action?"

I swallowed past the dry lump in my throat. "My thoughts, exactly."

Wranglers were working horses in the arena off to the side of the lodge. Fans whirled above our heads, keeping the shady porch cool and shooing away the flies that always come with the musky scent of horses.

I passed my hand across the smooth-as-satin pine railing and took in the view of forested hills sheltered by mountain peaks. The view was breathtaking, but I turned back around and leaned against the railing. I surveyed the guests on the porch, trying not to look like I was staring, and shook my head.

This was a professional operation, a resort and a working ranch, which obviously made serious money. I remembered how Blackwell had smiled and tipped his hat that night at Gold Creek. How he'd said bringing the tourists to pan for gold was "all part of the service." I was beginning to think his hick act fell into the same category.

A sound, some movement, made me look to the side. The most beautiful woman I'd ever seen walked from the shadows at the other end of the porch and into the light. "May I help you girls?"

She wasn't tall, but the word "statuesque" still popped into my head. She moved with a grace I recognized from hanging out with Lou—the grace of a dancer. Her make-up was perfect, accentuating her large, dark eyes and full lips. Hair that matched her eyes, shiny chestnut waves, fell halfway down her back.

She reached us at the same time as Ford came out of the lodge.

"Well hello, Ford darlin." Her voice was sultry as the afternoon. She stepped closer to him. "How are you? Have you brought some friends to see our little place?"

Ford grinned down at her. "Hi, Mrs. Blackwell."

I tried to keep my jaw from hitting the floor. Mrs. Blackwell had to be half her husband's age and in a completely different class.

"Ford, hon, please call me Sherrie." She pursed her lips into a charming pout. "And you girls are…?" She turned the full force of her radiant smile on us.

"Oh, sorry." Ford had forgotten we existed. "This is Misty Stevens. Her dad's the archaeologist who heads up our project."

Sherrie and I shook hands. Hers was soft and cool, with perfectly manicured nails. "Nice to meet you, Sherrie," I said. "We met Mr. Blackwell a couple of weeks ago."

"And this is her friend, Lilou Phillips."

"Lou." My friend flashed Ford an irritated look, but smiled as she shook Sherrie's hand. I was pretty sure the smell of her perfume would linger on both of us.

"We were hoping to talk with Mr. Blackwell," I said. "He told my dad to contact him if we had any questions about the old Blackwell homestead site we're working on and, well, something's come up. We thought he might be able to help."

Sherrie lifted an eyebrow. "Really? Bob's not here right—"

We all turned as a truck rolled to a stop in the drive, near the corral. Sherrie said, "Never mind. You're in luck. Here he is now."

Sure enough, Blackwell emerged from the pickup and slammed the door behind him.

One of the cowboys working the horses called out, "Any luck?"

"Nah." Blackwell kicked a boot in the dirt. "First, we can't get rid of the dang critter. Then, when we do go lookin' for him, he vanishes. No one's seen him for days. It's almost enough to make you think he *is* a ghost."

He stalked toward the lodge, scowling, but when he caught sight of us, his steps faltered. His body language loosened, it looked like a conscious effort, and he became the resort host we'd seen at the Gold Creek campout. He grinned and waved at us.

Sherrie called, "Oh, Bob, you haven't been looking for that—"

He lengthened his stride and stomped up the porch steps, interrupting his wife midsentence. "Kids, I see you've met the brains behind this operation. Ain't she somethin'?" He put an arm around Sherrie's waist, pulled her to him, and kissed her full on the mouth.

Sherrie's eyes went wide. I had a feeling this was not common practice for the couple, at least in public, but I suspected it had the effect Bob Blackwell desired—to shut his wife up.

Her cheeks were flushed and she took a breath. "Well, Bob!" She fanned herself, but she didn't really seem embarrassed. He winked and smiled down at her.

I realized my mouth was hanging open and snapped it shut. Out of the corner of my eye, I saw Lou and Ford do the same. There was a titter here and there from the other guests.

"Mr. Blackwell," I said, "Dad wondered if you could answer a couple of questions about the old homestead site."

He turned and seemed to be considering whether or not to help us. But then he smiled that good 'ole boy, toothy grin of his. "Sure. Sit down and fire away." He pulled some chairs around one of the tables, nodding to his guests as he did—the congenial host. "Sherrie, my love. I sure could use something cold and wet. Can you get that boy you hired to bring refreshment?"

Sherrie started for the door. "I'm afraid I have Cody running errands this afternoon. If you'll excuse me, I'll see what I can find."

"Hard to keep Cody on the ranch," he muttered. "Never realized we needed someone to run so many dang errands." He shrugged and sat back, arms crossed, and fixed us with his old guy squint. "How can I help you?"

"We found some bones in the old garbage dump we're digging up," Ford said. "It might even be a dump associated with your great-grandfather's homestead."

Blackwell uncrossed his arms. Ford had his attention.

"The weirdest thing," I said. "The bones turned out to be from a horse. Dad remembered what you said about Percival Blackwell killing the stallion that started the ghost legend…"

I paused when Sherrie reappeared with a frosty bottle of beer for Blackwell and three glasses of cold, yellow lemonade for the rest of us. We thanked her, and Ford offered to pull a chair up to the table for her. She held up a hand and leaned back against the porch railing.

The lemonade tasted fresh-squeezed with plenty of sugar, so cold it almost hurt going down. That didn't stop Ford from tipping back and consuming the entire glass in one chug.

Lou mimed shock, staring at him with her mouth wide open.

He set down his glass and mouthed, *what?*

"Ford, hon," Sherrie asked. "Do you need another drink?"

Ford turned from Lou to Sherrie. "No, Mrs. Bla—I mean, Sherrie." He gave her a sheepish grin and dipped his head toward his glass. "That was just fine."

Blackwell took a drink of his beer and pointed the bottle at me. "Your father is probably wondering if the horse you're digging up is that old rogue stallion." He lifted a shoulder. "No way of knowing for sure, is there?"

"The thing is, these bones have marks on them, like the horse was butchered." I paused, fairly certain I saw a glimmer of recognition in Blackwell's eyes.

He slapped a flat palm on the tabletop, hard enough to make the drinks rattle, and we all jumped. "That confirms it. I know for a fact they butchered that rascal and I have the horsehair sofa in my den to prove it. You kids want to see it?"

TEN

I SAT BACK, SPEECHLESS.

Lou gasped, and I could see from her face she was beyond horrified.

The Blackwells actually had a sofa made out of the hide of the original ghost horse? But I saw something in Blackwell's eyes.

"Bob, don't scare them." Sherrie frowned and turned to us, shaking her head as her husband slapped a knee, chortling at our shocked expressions.

"The only chair on this property that's covered in horsehair of any kind is the one Bob sits down in to take off his boots after he's been riding." With another disapproving look at Mr. Blackwell, Sherrie finished, "No horses have ever been harmed in the building of this ranch, unless you count how hard Bob rides his old Paint."

"Whew! Sorry." The old guy was still chuckling. "Couldn't help myself. I am teasing, but I'll tell you this—you all could be on to something. I remember Grandpa said they ate that stallion after Percival shot it." He shook his head. "That's not something a kid ever forgets. If you're digging up horse bones with butcher marks, chances are, it's the bones of the stallion that started the legend."

Lou wrinkled her nose. "But why would they eat him?"

"They were pioneers and meat's meat." He shrugged, echoing Dad's words from the other night. "Grandpa didn't really say. But back in those days, kids ate what was put on their plates and only spoke when they were spoken to."

"I'm glad I'm not a pioneer," Lou muttered.

Blackwell laughed out loud—a real laugh, not a teasing one, which made us all smile. "Me too, Lou," he said. "Me, too."

After we finished our drinks, Sherrie offered to show us around the ranch house. It was even more impressive inside than out. Stone fireplaces, soaring ceilings, huge windows with more incredible views. A light scent like the combination of clean linen and aromatic woodsmoke lingered in the rooms. There was white pine, colorful rag rugs, Pendleton throws and expensive cotton sheets—high-end rustic, airy and tasteful.

Mr. Blackwell was still relaxing with his beer on the front porch when we came back out, blinking in the sunlight.

"What'd you think?" He pointed the neck of his bottle toward the interior.

"Great!" I answered.

"Very nice," Lou added.

Ford, who'd seen it all before, nodded his agreement.

Blackwell lifted a chin toward Sherrie. "My beautiful wife's brain-child. She designed it, decorated it, everything. Far cry from the old place, I'll tell you that."

Sherrie smiled at the praise, but I was pretty sure I detected a note of wistfulness in Blackwell's mention of his old home.

"I thought I'd show them your arena, Bob," Sherrie said. "Cody tells me Lou is quite the horsewoman."

Lou gave me a quick look and ducked her head. What? Was *Lou* blushing, now? I didn't think she even liked Cody. I thought back, but I couldn't remember Lou telling him she rode when we'd met. How did he know?

We followed Sherrie on a path from the lodge that passed the corral and ran between the stables and the indoor arena. She slid one of the arena doors open and led us onto a huge expanse of hard-packed dirt and sand that stretched at least forty feet across. About a hundred feet in front of us, maybe more, was a fenced-off area with six levels of bleachers rising behind it.

"Sherrie, this is awesome!" Lou gushed. "I'm so jealous you have this."

Sherrie laughed and Lou giggled.

"You sound like you know your way around an arena," Sherrie said. "You can come and use this and the horses anytime you like while you're here this summer."

Lou followed Sherrie like a loyal puppy while she continued the tour. A paddock and a row of stalls ran the long side of the building opposite me, ending near the large viewing area with a glassed-in conference room. That's where Sherrie and Lou seemed to be headed, and Ford and I trailed behind.

"Pretty impressive, huh?" Ford said.

"I'm not really an expert on arenas, but I've seen a few, and I've never seen anything like this."

He nodded. "I've been in larger ones with big horse operations in Montana. But for somebody's private arena, this is pretty cool. Look at Lou and Sherrie. Two peas in a pod, Bea would probably say."

Lou gestured excitedly, and Sherrie threw back her head and laughed.

"Yeah," I said. "They are, aren't they?"

"Oh," he chuckled. "Do I detect a note of jealousy?"

He was teasing, but it hit a little too close to home.

I gave him what I hoped was a withering look and pointed to a partially open door to one side of the conference room, the beginning of a spiral staircase visible through the opening. "I wonder where that goes."

"Oh, that." He lifted his chin like he was an expert. "That's the secret tower where they torture naughty ranch hands."

Before I could think up something suitably sarcastic in response, Sherrie and Lou came out of the conference room and headed our direction.

"You could ask," he said.

"I don't want to seem nosy."

"Hey, Sherrie," Ford called, pointing at the stairs in question, "where do those go?"

"Smooth," I muttered.

He grinned.

"That leads to my loft." She shooed us in the direction of the stairs. "Go on up, if you like. Take a look."

I followed Ford up the winding staircase. When we got to the top, I understood why Sherrie said it was *her* loft. This certainly wasn't any place that would be useful to her husband or the ranch hands.

Ford looked puzzled. "Huh."

Wouldn't you know it? *Two peas in a pod, for sure.* I turned and yelled down the stairs. "Lou, you have to see this."

I heard Lou and Sherrie's steps on the stairs and stepped back. I wanted a good view of Lou's face when she saw the room.

Her eyes widened, the way they had when Ford had swallowed his lemonade in one gulp. This time, though, her shock was for real.

She crossed the gleaming expanse and turned in a slow circle, taking it all in. A row of high windows ran around the three outside walls. Light poured into the room. Across from us, the wall was covered in mirrors and a shiny brass ballet barre was mounted all the way across it.

Lou was speechless.

"So, Sherrie, you dance?" I asked.

"I used to." She was watching Lou, but then turned. "Bob and I did meet in Vegas, you know."

My face must've betrayed me once again, because she touched my arm, shaking her head. "No, I wasn't a show-girl. There are a lot of theatre shows in Vegas. I trained when I was younger and worked as an alternate on some of the Broadway shows that came through town. Now, I dance for fun. It's a great way to stay in shape."

She glanced at Lou, who was still looking around like she'd entered a magical kingdom. "Do you dance, Lou?"

Lou nodded.

"She's been dancing since she could walk," I prompted. "Haven't you Lou—?"

She smiled. "Yep, I have."

"Really?" Ford was staring at Lou, obviously doing some quick reassessment. Oh, man. The jealousy that hijacked me in that moment was more than a twinge. I was used to people being wowed by my overly talented best friend. Most of the time, I felt proud of her…most of the time.

Sherrie was also appraising Lou. "A woman of many talents," she murmured. "Lou, I hope you know my offer to use the arena extends to my little studio here."

Lou clasped her hands together. "Sherrie, that would be so…" Her voice trailed off. Though her eyes shone, she was once again at a loss for words.

"Great," I finished for her. "It would be really great."

My phone buzzed—a text from Dad. He was getting ready to head home and said it was fine for Ford to drive us back.

As we walked from the arena, we passed the corral where the ranch hands had been working horses earlier. I had a moment of déjà vu, like I'd been there before. Something clicked in my brain.

"Wait." I turned toward Ford's truck. "Wait right here!" When I got to the truck, I reached through the open window to grab the box of Mom's pictures. Turning, I saw Sherrie, Ford and Lou frozen at the spot where I'd left them, watching me like I'd lost my mind.

"Sorry," I said when I got closer, "I didn't mean to be so weird. But I'm sure I saw this corral in one of my mom's pictures."

Sherrie frowned. "Your mom…?"

"Misty's mom grew up here," Lou said. "She and Misty's grandpa raised and broke horses in the valley when her mom was a kid."

While Lou filled Sherrie in on my mom's history and our project, I thrust the box into Ford's hands. "Hold that for a sec, can you?"

"Uh, sure, Mist."

Like I'd given him a choice, but I wasn't really worried about the impression I was making on Ford at the moment. I knew I'd seen that picture. "Yes!" I held the photo up triumphantly. At that same moment, the breeze ruffled the other pictures in the box, and one floated toward Sherrie. She grabbed it before it hit the ground.

She glanced at the picture. I held out my hand when I thought she was about to return it, but she pulled the picture back. She stared closely at the image, as if she was looking for something. "This is your mom?"

I moved close so I could see the picture. It was the one of Mom in the same meadow where we'd seen the wild horse band—the photo I'd shown Lou the other night.

"Yeah. Like Lou said, these are all pictures of my mom when she was growing up here."

Sherrie was focused on that picture. "Do you know where this one was taken?"

"I'm not one-hundred percent sure, but I think it might be this meadow where we came across a wild horse band the other day."

"That was the day you met Cody."

It didn't seem like a question, but I answered anyway. "Yeah. I think it's called Opal Creek Canyon?" Why the interrogation? I was trying not to lose patience with all the questions, but I was eager to show them the picture of Mom in the corral.

"Do you know the place, Sherrie?" I asked. "Have you been there?"

She shrugged. "Not that I can remember." She handed the picture back to me, as if she'd lost interest.

I dropped it in the box. I held out the other photo so the three could see the picture of Mom. She was older than in the apple-orchard picture, but still a teen. Standing in a corral with a rope in her hand, she was nose-to-nose with a horse. It was a great battle-of-wills moment in time, and I was sure my mom had won.

"Doesn't this seem familiar?" We all looked from the picture to the corral.

Lou said, "You may be on to something, my friend."

"Yeah," Ford said, pointing around us. "The mountains in the background, those rocks, that stand of pines. They're all the same. The only difference is that the trees are a lot bigger."

"I bet this picture was taken when Mom and Grandpa were breaking horses here." I turned to Sherrie. "Bob says they were the best horse wranglers in the valley. They must have worked with the Blackwells, right?" This was one of the few photos Lou and I hadn't been able to place, until now.

"That barn does look like the old barn. It was over there." Sherrie pointed to a spot opposite the new arena and stable. "But we didn't move the corral—it's where it's always been."

Sherrie's gaze moved past me, and she waved.

"Sherrie, darlin'," Blackwell called, ambling toward us. "Hate to interrupt the tour, but that kid you hired is back and apparently has some pressing information that can't wait. Also, Tiny needs to talk to you about dinner preparations."

Sherrie checked the turquoise-and-silver watch on her wrist. "My goodness, where does the time go? I had no idea it was so late. It was nice to meet you girls—" She smiled as she backed away. "And Ford, always a pleasure." He nodded, complete with cheesy grin.

"Please don't be strangers this summer." She waved and turned toward the lodge. All I could think was, *exit leading lady, stage left.*

Mr. Blackwell startled me when he reached toward the picture in my hand. "What do you got there, Misty?"

"Is this your old barn in the background?" I handed him the picture. "Was it taken here, do you think?"

He pulled the picture close to his face, held it at arm's length, and swore under his breath. Fumbling through his pockets, he finally pulled out a pair of surprisingly modern-looking reading glasses. I wondered if Sherrie had picked them out.

He checked our faces, and I'm sure he didn't find even the slightest smirk on any of them—we were all still wary of Bob Blackwell. "Don't ever get old," he muttered. Glasses perched on the end of his nose, he peered at the picture.

"There it is." His tone this time was definitely wistful. "The old barn. Sherrie had it torn down once we decided on the plan for the new buildings. She was right. It was in bad shape, not really salvageable." He pointed at the picture and smiled at me. "Look at your Mama," he said, his voice full of admiration. "I don't think I ever heard of a horse she and your grandpa couldn't handle. You should be proud to be her daughter."

I stared into the old man's whiskery face. Maybe he was a human being after all. "I am proud."

We locked eyes, and he nodded once, like I'd passed some test. He handed back the picture. We told him about our photo project and got his permission to use his corral to recreate the picture.

But we were all hungry, and I'd told Dad we were on our way home. We decided to come back another day. As we were climbing into Ford's truck, Cody emerged from the lodge and called out, "How're you guys?"

"We're great, Cody." Lou waved at him. "How are you?" She sounded a little too enthusiastic, considering she'd once implied Cody was a huge loser. But I figured maybe she was still riding her Sherrie high.

Cody nodded coolly at me and Ford, but he turned a big smile on Lou. "They're having a treasure hunt, sort of a modified geo-cache thing in town next Friday night. With prizes and stuff…I don't know, might be lame. But it's something to do on Friday night. You want to go?" Lou beamed up at him, and he seemed to take that as a yes. "Cool."

Wait, what? I saw the same questions in Ford's eyes as I had: *Did he just ask her out? And did she just say yes?*

Lou turned to us. "Sounds like, fun, right? We should all go." Her eyes were hopeful, her smile enthusiastic.

Cody, not so much. He shrugged. "Sure, yeah, that's what I meant." He handed Lou his phone. "Give me your number, and I'll send you the details."

I was sure a double date wasn't what Cody'd had in mind. *Double date.* So, if Lou was Cody's date, that meant I was Ford's. But so far, he hadn't said a word.

ELEVEN

DAD AND I WERE no longer church-goers, apparently, but I still woke up early on Sunday mornings out of habit. I'd tossed and turned all night, stressed about my upcoming date with Ford. Or, whatever it was. He'd agreed to go along, but he hadn't seemed particularly enthusiastic about it. I told myself it was the prospect of hanging out with Cody that bothered him, not going out with me. But Ford hadn't given any hints either way.

Finally, I crawled out of bed and into the shower. While the tiny bathroom filled up with steam, I stood under the water and let my mind unravel, back to the drive home the day before, and the unreadable look on Ford's face each time Lou giggled over a message on her phone.

When I asked, "Is that Cody?" she'd ignored me, never tearing her eyes away from the message she was texting back.

While I shaved my legs, I decided Ford's lack of excitement about next weekend was definitely related to his feelings about Cody, not me. I reached for my washcloth. *Please, let it be Cody that bothers him, not me.*

The shower felt heavenly on my achy muscles, sore from all our digging. I tried not to scrape the blisters on my hands, heels and toes with the cloth, but the hot water stung my sores. I whimpered. Aren't blisters supposed to turn into calluses, eventually?

I dried myself, lotioned from head to toe, and pulled on white cut-offs, a thin pink t-shirt, and a brown one over that. For the final touch, I pushed my dreads into a ponytail, rubbed a clear spot in the mirror and decided I was ready to meet the world.

Exiting the bathroom in a cloud of steam and green-apple scented shampoo, I nearly collided with Lou. She brushed groggily past me and shut the door without a word. After a while, I heard the shower and sent up a silent prayer that the hot water would hold out.

LOU SHUFFLED INTO THE kitchen. "That was brisk," she grumbled.

I winced. "Sorry. It was so warm and—"

"Go ahead." She glared at me. "Rub it in."

"I said I was sorry! Sheesh."

"Whatever." She popped a pastry in the toaster and put a cup of water into the microwave. Ignoring me, she sat down at the table and opened her laptop. The pastry popped the same time the microwave pinged. She sighed, got up and poured an envelope of cocoa powder into her cup, slapped some butter on her pastry, and sat back down. Absently stirring her cocoa with one hand, she punched at her computer with the other. Clutching her cup of cocoa with both hands, she hunched behind the screen across from me and continued to act like I didn't exist.

I ducked my head, dug into my bowl of instant oatmeal and waited for her to say something. That didn't happen. "Um, Lou," I finally ventured, "are you mad at me?"

Her eyes moved from her screen to mine, and as I held her gaze, it softened. She shoved her computer aside and ran her hands through her hair. "No, I'm just…" She shifted in her chair and shrugged.

"Hormonal, maybe?"

"Maybe." She grimaced. "I mean, is this all we're going to do this summer?"

She was bored. I was afraid this would happen. "What do you mean?"

"Get up at the crack of dawn, work until we're so tired we can't move, come home, sleep, and do it all again the next day?"

"What about yesterday?" I tried not to sound defensive. Or hurt. We'd spent the entire day with each other. What? I hadn't been fun enough for her? "That was different, hanging out with Ford and going to the Blackwell Ranch. I thought it was kind of fun."

"Yeah, that was cool. But…" Her eyes slid away from mine. "You know, Ford's really into you, and…"

Was that it? Was she jealous? "I don't think so," I said. "Not so I noticed, anyway."

"Oh, right." Her voice dripped with sarcasm. "Like you haven't noticed him watching you, trying to get alone with you, seen him—"

"Yeah, I noticed him. Noticed him enjoying you sitting next to him in the truck, noticed that you two have long conversations when I'm not around, about horses and riding and me being half-crazy—"

"Right, exactly. I'm the one he confides in—guys do that with their buddies. But you're the one he likes."

This was beyond stupid. "Like you haven't been trying to throw us together since the day we got here. Lou…" I stuck my spoon in my oatmeal. "This is ridiculous."

"Misty." She narrowed her dark eyes at me. "Everyone knows you're naïve when it comes to men."

"Everyone?" I stood up. "What do you mean, *everyone?* First of all, Ford's not a man, he's a boy and second…"

She shot out of her chair and put her hands on her hips. "He's more man than, than…"

I put out my hands and raised my eyebrows.

"You are," she finished in a weak voice.

For a second, we glared at each other, then we fell into our chairs, laughing so hard we both started coughing. When she could speak, Lou said, "You know what I mean. He told me he's turning eighteen the first week in October and he'll be a senior next year. And I'm telling you, he likes you."

"So? You're turning seventeen and I'll be sixteen this summer, and we'll be juniors next year. But that's so not the point. I think you've got him wrong, Lou." *Did she?* "Besides, none of us knows each other well enough to be 'into' anyone." I took a breath. "And speaking of being into people, what about you and Cody? What was that about yesterday?"

Her gaze wavered. "He's somebody to hang out with. You've got somebody, so…"

I let out an exasperated sigh and beat my head on the table a couple of times.

Lou giggled at me, or maybe she was laughing at herself.

"Seriously." I sat back and folded my arms. "I don't want to talk about this anymore. I'm not looking to get into a relationship this summer, are you? We're only going to be here a few more weeks."

She shook her head. "Misty, always the sensible one. I won't always be around to keep you company, you know."

"Hey, I'm your forever friend, remember?"

She gave me a crooked smile.

"Go ahead." I picked up my bowl and moved toward the kitchen, giving her an elbow on the way by. "Have your kicks with Cody if you want." She giggled and I shrugged. "You're not wrong. Ford's cool and he's a nice guy."

"Uh-huh."

I could hear the smirk in her voice.

"But I really don't think I'm up for a summer romance." I thought my voice sounded pretty convincing. "The thing is," I muttered, "I've had about all the heartbreak I can handle this year."

I wasn't sure Lou'd heard my last sentence, but she got up and stood beside me. "I'm sorry, Mist."

"I'm just not into drama right now. I want to hang out with my best friend this summer and not have things be complicated. Is that too much to ask?"

She shook her head. "Not too much at all." Her eyes moved to my bowl, still filled with oatmeal. "You're not even done, sit back down." She pulled me out of the kitchen and into a chair next to her. "I didn't mean to scare you off."

We ate our breakfast in silence for a few minutes. Then I got an inspiration. "Hey, I bet we could get Dad to take us back out to the Blackwell Ranch this afternoon, you and me, no guys. We could reproduce that picture of Mom in the corral, and maybe you could try out Sherrie's dance studio."

She tossed her hair back and stretched her arms above her head. "It's been an eternity since I worked out, but I'm so sore from digging."

"C'mon," I pressed, "call it dance therapy for the young, restless, and extremely bored."

I was relieved to see her pout turn into a grin. "I guess I'm in, if your dad is."

I called Dad, who was working in the barn lab. He answered after about ten rings and agreed to my plan. He said he'd be happy to drive us. He wanted to follow up with Bob Blackwell and pick his brain about the old homestead, anyway.

Lou and I ran upstairs to change. She complained about not having the right gear for dancing, while I tried to recreate the boots, jeans, and snap-front shirt Mom had been wearing in the picture. The jeans and boots were easy, but the best I could do on the shirt was a sleeveless denim button-up. I looked in the mirror and decided it would work. There was no way to replicate Mom's short, bobbed haircut, so I left the ponytail and pushed my bangs behind my ear. We were all ready to go by noon.

Before we left, I showed the picture to Dad. He glanced at it, and took a second look. I was never sure what Dad's reaction would be when he saw a picture of Mom, but I understood. If his reactions were anything like mine, sometimes Mom's memory made me smile. Other times, the mention of her would send my heart racing and my eyes swimming. And I had no way to predict when either of us would react badly.

But this time, Dad smiled and we talked about horse-training during the twenty-minute drive to the Blackwells. June had once told me, despite the fact Dad had grown up around horses like Mom had, he'd "never broken a horse in his life." I had a nugget of an idea in my head about Lookout, one that seemed more dream than reality. To see his reaction, I asked Dad how he would go about "breaking" a horse.

"To tell you the truth, Mist, I'm not really an expert on that."

"Dad, seriously?"

He glanced over at me. "Okay, breaking horses was what your mom and Grandpa Ferguson did for a living. Those horses weren't pets—they were tools—your mom and grandpa weren't there to make friends."

"But what about you? I thought you and Mom had that in common—growing up working horses."

"We had a love of horses in common. That's true." He paused, distracted by the road, or maybe just Mom's memory.

"But it was a little different for me. By the time I was born, on my folks' ranch outside Austin—their place was really more stables than a working ranch. We rented out space, mostly to wealthy women, and took care of their horses for them. To most of those women, the horses were one more expensive status toy. The owners would show up every few weeks, if that."

I waited, but he didn't continue. "So?" I said. "What did you do with the horses?"

"To keep the animals from going crazy in between their owners' brief rides, we played with them."

"Some of the clients became interested..." he maneuvered around a slow-moving tractor in front of us. "And we started classes. We taught our clients how to develop a relationship with a horse and become partners, or friends, really, with their horses. It's a completely different way to interact with an animal than your mom was used to."

I thought about that. "How do you, you know, *play* with a horse?"

In the back seat, Lou snorted.

Dad glanced in the rearview mirror. "I get the feeling Lou doesn't think much of my method."

"You let a horse know who's boss—and you're good to go," she said. "There's a relationship there, sure, but I wouldn't call it a *friendship.*"

I crossed my arms. I was getting fed up with Lou's condescending theories on relationships.

"Look, I'm no horse whisperer. But it's the difference between forcing a horse to do what you want, and working with a horse's natural personality, their likes and dislikes— empathizing with them and seeing things from their perspective. It takes time, but in the end, I find it more satisfying. I hear you though, Lou." He half-smiled. "Truth is, Karen actually thought I was kind of a sissy when it came to horses—"

"That's not true," I said. "She thought you..." Dad gave me a questioning look. I felt my throat start to close up. But I was determined. I swallowed over the lump and kept going. "She said you saw things other people missed."

"When did she say that?"

I shrugged, not ready to go there yet. "Anyway, how do you *make friends,*" I emphasized the words for Lou's benefit, "with a horse?"

We pulled into Blackwell's driveway, and Dad brought the Suburban to a stop in front of the corral. He turned to me. "Well, it's mostly about building trust."

That elicited a loud, "Ha!" from the back seat and Dad and I both turned around. Lou returned our looks with a stony stare. "I've been attempting to 'build trust' with Two Tall for most of my life. Still doesn't make him do what I want him to do."

Dad squinted at Lou. I could see he was puzzled, so was I. A snarky tone came pretty naturally to Lou—she used it with her mom a lot and June gave as good as she got. But Lou had always been consistently respectful to my Dad, like everyone else I knew.

"Are we going to take this picture or what?" She climbed out of the car and slammed the door behind her.

Dad raised his eyebrows. "Somebody get up on the wrong side of the bed?"

"I guess." I was as confused as he was.

We followed Lou up to the house and found Mr. Blackwell waiting on the porch. He said again he was happy for us to use the corral. "You'll want Cody's help…" He looked around and cursed under his breath.

My heart sank. This was supposed to be a no-guys kind of day.

"Where is that boy?" He muttered. "He was here a minute ago—"

"Yeah, Mr. B?" The voice came from the shadowy other end of the porch. I could see Cody, leaning a shoulder against the wall, gangly legs crossed at the ankles, hat low.

Mr. Blackwell squinted Cody's direction. "Can you help these girls? They need to get a picture of Misty with one of the horses in the corral."

Cody pushed off lazily and sauntered over. In the meantime, Blackwell ushered Dad inside, mopping his brow with a bandanna as they went. "It's much cooler in here, Doc. C'mon in, and I'll rustle up something to drink."

Lou perked up at the sight of Cody. She grinned at him.

He smiled back. "Hi, Lou, how ya' doing?"

"Great!" She moved a step closer. "And yourself?"

"Better now," he said, and moved way inside her bubble, where Lou seemed more than happy to have him. He glanced toward the door that Blackwell and Dad had entered. I wondered if it was to make sure they were out of earshot.

Had I turned invisible? "Hi, Cody," I said, waving. "Remember me? Misty, the archaeologist's daughter."

Cody gave me the once over and turned back to Lou, like he was reluctant to take his eyes off her. "No Ford today?"

Wow, so we were going there. Straight for the jugular. My heart started pounding and I could feel the heat in my cheeks. I shrugged. "Not today."

Lou smirked. "We gave him the day off." She waved a dismissive hand.

That made me mad, but they didn't wait around to see my reaction. They were already down the steps and headed for the corral. As I moved to catch up, I racked my brain. I couldn't figure out how things between Lou and me had gone so sideways so fast—and I was desperate to figure out how to fix it.

We took the path that led to the stables and arena we'd seen the day before. The stables were designed so horses could be taken either directly into the corral or to the arena. The cooler interior of the stables felt great, and I breathed in the sweet tang of hay, horses and saddle leather.

Cody held out his hand and I reluctantly handed him the picture of Mom in the corral. She was holding a rope, going head to head with a large white horse with black spots—what a horse person would call a "Paint." The Blackwells owned and stabled all kinds of horses, dozens of them. Lou and I waited together while Cody walked down the line of stalls.

Lou whistled softly. "They must clean out the county with all the hay and grain it takes to feed these guys." It didn't take Cody long to find a reasonable clone of the mare in the picture.

He turned her loose and she kicked up her hooves, happy to be out of the dark stable, even if the midday sun was beating down on all of us. Dust billowed behind her as she galloped and pranced around. Cody climbed the corral fence to sit on the top rung, and Lou scrambled up next to him.

I rested my arms on the rails and leaned my forehead against the top one, half-listening to Lou skip from subject to subject with Cody. First, horses, then the project we were working on, how boring small towns were.

In the meantime, I watched that mare gallop around the corral. She kicked another cloud of dust when she passed us. I coughed and tried to picture myself going head to head with her. She was pretty big—not as big as Lookout. But I'd never been trapped in a ring with him.

I could feel the sweat drip down the back of my neck and my stomach started to churn. I really didn't think I was up for this.

My palms were sweating and each breath felt less and less like it was filling my lungs.

Don't get me wrong. I liked horses, I got the attraction—the poetry of their bodies in motion, their personalities. I just didn't get the thrill of riding them. Plus, after the kind of morning this had been, I thought my face would melt if I had to smile for a bunch of pictures. I wanted nothing more than to go home and start over.

"Lou…" I interrupted her mid-sentence. Both she and Cody turned like they'd forgotten I was there.

"I was thinking—these pictures don't all need to be of me. They're supposed to document *our* summer. Why don't you do this one." I tried to keep the desperation out of my voice. "I'll take the picture."

"Aww, get out there." Lou tilted her head at me. "C'mon, you're not scared, are you?"

Cody leaned back so he could see me, and I had two smirking faces pointed in my direction. It was almost enough to make me change my mind. Almost.

I returned their looks, hoping the panic didn't show in my eyes. "I don't feel like it today, okay?" I paused, pressed my lips together. I didn't want to make her mad, or…madder. I did want to get this picture, and I wanted to never have to deal with Cody again. Except, I remembered, I would have to deal with him again next weekend when we all met up in town.

I'd worry about that later.

"Really," I tried to sound encouraging. "You look great today. Get in there."

She smiled at that, finally. Cody climbed down and ceremoniously extended his hand. "M'lady?"

She pushed off the fence, hitting the ground lightly like only a dancer could. "Didn't you see my shirt the other day? I don't need a cowboy to help me into a corral."

Cody's look darkened, but it was brief. He shrugged and grinned. "You go, cowgirl."

I gave her the rope we'd retrieved from the stables, like the one Mom held in the picture. Once Lou got the horse settled down, I shot several great pictures in less than ten minutes. Which was good.

I could feel Cody's eyes on both of us. He didn't say anything or offer to join in or help out, like Ford would have done, even if Lou *had* tried to put him off. Ford would have known she was teasing. Cody just stared at us. I tried not to be weird about it, but it made my skin crawl.

When we were done, he haltered the horse and led her toward the stables. I felt bad we hadn't done more with her. Even though I was beyond thankful I'd managed to avoid having to pose for a close-up with her, she must've wondered why she was being led inside so soon.

Lou climbed over the railing, and I showed her the shots I'd taken. We were debating which one we liked best when Sherrie appeared, looking lithe in form-fitting yoga pants and a leotard.

"I hear I might have a work-out partner today." She graced us with her dazzling smile.

"If it's okay?" Lou tilted her head to the side and laced her fingers together. I couldn't get over how shy she was around Sherrie.

Cody appeared at the stable entrance. He and Sherrie exchanged looks and she called, "I'll take it from here, Cody.

You can go finish that job we were discussing earlier." He turned toward the lodge with a look and nod at Sherrie.

"Thanks for your help, Cody," Lou called.

He waved over his shoulder and called back, "See you next weekend."

Not if I see you first, I thought. But I didn't say it.

Sherrie watched Cody walk away for a second. I was thinking how she seemed to have an interesting effect on some people, when she turned her smile back on Lou. "Of course. I couldn't be more pleased to have you join me." She took in Lou's clothes and raised an eyebrow. "I have some gear you can change into?"

"Oh," Lou said, "I brought some stuff." She spun around and ran to the Suburban.

"I guess I'll go find Dad," I said, to no one in particular, since nobody seemed to care what I was doing.

Sherrie responded to me with an absent, "Mmm," her eyes still on Lou. What was that look on her face? Calculating? Lou slammed the car door and started back to us, and the look was gone before I was sure I'd seen it. Sherrie was, once again, a nice lady who was happy for a dance partner. Lou was probably like the daughter she'd always dreamed of. Except, Lou already had a mom.

"I think your Dad and Bob are about done talking," she said to me. "I told them I'd bring Lou along home in a bit." She smiled as Lou came walking back with her gym bag. "I have a place you can change in the studio." Her tone completely changed when she talked to Lou. She sounded light and enthusiastic. When she signaled Lou to follow her, Lou hurried to her side without a backward glance at me.

I had obviously been dismissed.

Go to https://youtu.be/6r4aZo2Jkxg for a
preview of what's coming up…

HUNCHED IN MY seat next to dad, I stared out the window
as we pulled onto the highway. He cleared his throat. "Uh, Lou
and Sherrie seem to be getting along."

"Yeah," I muttered. "They're getting along great."

We rode for the next five minutes in total silence. I turned
the radio knob through all the channels, found a bunch of static
and one Spanish-language station, and turned it off. Dad
seemed perfectly content with his own thoughts.

I leaned my head against the window and watched the trees
fly by. "What is Sherrie doing out here, anyway? She's a city
girl." I hadn't meant to speak my thoughts out loud, but Dad
answered me.

"While I was talking with Bob this afternoon, he told me
how they met."

"Sherrie said it was in Las Vegas."

Dad nodded. "Kind of an interesting story."

"What story?" I sat up. "She only said that's where they met.
I figured it was where she grew up."

"She grew up outside of Vegas. Her father was a top
executive in one of the big mining corporations. Sounds like he
was well-off. Bob said she was the only child of his second wife,
who was a lot younger than he was, and he'd retired by the time
Sherrie came along. Her mom left not long after."

"It was just her and her dad, then."

Dad glanced at me. "Uh, yeah. According to Bob, he doted on his daughter and she adored him. The two of them liked to go out in the Nevada desert on 'prospecting' adventures."

"Prospecting?"

"It was more like rock hunting. But Bob says she's full of information about geology, rock formations, mining—stuff like that."

Geology? Sherrie didn't exactly radiate "science geek." I was surprised. "Where's her dad now, I wonder?"

"That's the sad part of the story." He braked the Suburban, turning into our drive. "Like I said, he was a lot older than her mom. He died of congestive heart failure a few months before Bob met Sherrie, which wasn't that long ago. They've been married for a little over two years. Bob's first wife died of cancer."

"That's too bad." For reasons I didn't examine too closely, I found it easier to feel sympathy for Mr. Blackwell than I did for Sherrie. "Her dad had money. That must be where all the dollars came from for the ranch renovation."

"I don't think so. After her father died, she discovered he hadn't changed his will after he married her mother. He left everything to his first wife and kids—and Sherrie got nothing. Must be Bob who has the money."

Dinner was still a couple hours away, so Dad retreated to his lab to do some work after we got home. I didn't mind. After dealing with Lou and her moods all day, I was happy for some time to myself. I tried not to think about how much she'd hurt my feelings—or how dismissive she'd been of Ford. But I continued to seethe inside. Hopefully, her dancing away the afternoon, and me having some time off from everyone, would put us both in a better frame of mind.

I grabbed a novel and a blanket and took them outside. The shaded front porch felt gloomy, so I headed toward the late afternoon warmth and light in the backyard. I found a good spot under the shady branches of a black locust tree and spread out my quilt. The gentle-fresh sweetness of a nearby lilac bush heavy with blossom scented the air. The drone of the bees humming around it softened the silence. I closed my eyes and melted into the quiet. I focused on my breathing—*in…out, in…out*—and felt my muscles slowly relax.

Eventually, I rolled over on my stomach and propped the heavy book against the tree trunk. This novel was Lou's recommendation, but we weren't always eye-to-eye on reading material. She tended more toward teen fantasy and doomed romances than I did. But she'd been right about this one. I couldn't put it down.

Over time, the light changed and began to fade. In the back of my mind, I knew I should get up and go inside. Instead, I moved the book closer to my face and kept reading. I barely noticed when the drone of bees slowly faded and the chorus got taken up by tree frogs and crickets.

I was seriously squinting in the dim light to see the letters on the page when something changed. The rustling of small animals and birds in the orchard was like white noise I hadn't even noticed, until it all went silent. Something big came crackling through the branches and undergrowth—a large, shadowy figure emerging from the trees, too far away for me to make out. I drew in a breath and froze. Before I could jump up and yell for Dad, the creature moved again, triggering the motion sensor on the outside light.

It was Lookout.

He stopped when the light came on, sniffed at the air and snorted. He tilted his head toward me. The breeze ruffled his mane and sent his tail hairs flying. I held my breath, afraid I'd scare him away if I moved even one muscle. He took a step in my direction.

TWELVE

I STARED, MOTIONLESS, STRUCK again by how massive the stallion was, but I felt vulnerable on the ground. I couldn't help it—I rose to meet Lookout when he moved toward me, and it startled him. He pawed the ground and bobbed his head, ears pointed toward me, eyes focused on me. Snorting, he spun, tail high, and trotted into the trees, disappearing from sight. For a big, strong wild stallion, he could be shy as a sparrow.

I resisted the urge to follow him. The sun was low above the ridge and I hadn't forgotten the creepiness of being alone in the orchard the other night. Nothing would ever make me forget the scream of that cougar. I shook my head, bent down and gathered my book and blanket.

I walked around to the front door and up onto the porch, giving myself a few more minutes in the perfect evening air. When I entered the house, there was Lou, curled in a corner of the sofa, head bent over her laptop. I stopped in mid-step for a second, halfway in and halfway out. I probably appeared as skittish as Lookout, but Lou didn't see it. She didn't even look up when I shut the door behind me.

I plopped into the other corner of the sofa, hugging the blanket and book to my chest. "Wow, I didn't even hear you come home."

Without looking at me, she held out a small, white snack bag. "Peanut cluster?"

I tried to keep from smiling at the peace offering, not ready to let her off that easy. But I reached into the bag. "What's in them?"

She muttered, "Peanuts and…peanuts and stuff," absorbed by whatever was on the screen in front of her.

The clusters were sweet, caramelly and crunchy. "Not bad."

Still pecking at her keyboard, she mumbled, "I know, right?"

I sat there for a minute, waiting to see if there would be something more. An apology, perhaps? But that was too much to ask, apparently. "Talking to somebody?"

She glanced at me and shrugged. "You know, the usual." She jabbed a few more keys and closed the computer. As if nothing bad had happened between us, she leaned against the arm of the couch, crossed her arms and watched me serenely.

I stared back and decided not to tell her about my most recent encounter with Lookout.

Finally, her eyes faltered from mine. She twisted her hair around her finger, which is what she did when she was stressed. "Sorry I was such a dork earlier. You were right. I needed to get out for a while."

I smiled. An actual apology. "You had fun, then?"

She gave me a happy nod, set her computer aside and scooted closer. "Dancing was a blast. Sherrie's really great, but I am *so* out of shape."

I wanted to bombard her with questions about her afternoon and about Cody. But I restrained myself in an attempt to avoid the morning's landmines. I asked, like I barely cared, "And dinner? Was it good?"

"What I tasted of it." She chuckled. "They ended up having more guests stay in for dinner than they expected. Some of the other help had gone into Ponder to catch the movie, so Sherrie was shorthanded. I helped Cody serve. We grabbed a few bites between courses."

"They invited you for dinner and they made you work for it?"

"Well, yeah." Lou drew back and frowned. "But it was still kind of fun. Besides, they didn't make me. I volunteered."

"Okay." I put up a hand. "I can see where that might be fun, I guess…really, I'm glad you had a good time and you're feeling better."

"I am, Mist. Thanks."

I made fat deli sandwiches and chips for dinner, which included Lou because she really hadn't eaten much at the Blackwells. We sat around the little Formica table, and Lou told us all about the guests at the ranch. With the exception of the researchers from Japan, the guests sounded like they were about the same age and attitude as Frank, Donna, and Bea.

I laughed at Lou's impressions, ate my sandwich and felt relieved the tension between us had dissolved.

I fell asleep that night to the sounds of Lou's peaceful, soft snores in the bed across from me, thankful I would never have to repeat that day again.

DAD'S PHONE RANG MONDAY morning on our way to the project site. I was too far back in the van to hear what he said over the roar of the diesel engine and all the talking around me. He seemed preoccupied while we unloaded the equipment, and then he called us all together.

"I have some good news and some bad news. Which do you want first?"

Bea piped up without hesitation. "The good news."

"I got a call this morning from the assayer's office where I sent those rocks from the jar we found. He confirmed that those rocks were, indeed, gold."

"Cool!" Ford said. And everyone started talking at once.

Bea clapped her hands together, face beaming. "How exciting."

"See," Frank turned to his wife, "I told you this would be our best adventure yet."

She shook her head at him affectionately.

Dad caught my eye and winked. The news of buried treasure had definitely renewed the crew's enthusiasm. But I had all kinds of questions, the biggest one being…

"What's the bad news?"

The chatter abruptly stopped, and everyone turned to Dad.

"Good question," he responded. "Based on the chemical fingerprint of the rock, the guys in the lab were able to determine that the gold is definitely from this area—"

After a second, the other adults started nodding. Lou glanced at me, a question in her eyes, and back at Dad. "I don't get it, Dr. Stevens," she said. "Why is that bad news?"

"It's not really bad news, *per se*. But it means we need to be very cautious about talking to people when it comes to the particulars of this project. We don't want to start another gold rush in these mountains, at least not until we finish studying the site and determine the best way to protect it."

"What do you think it means?" Ford asked. "Is there anything that jar of gold can tell us about the past that we don't already know?"

Dad gave him an approving nod. "The right question for an archaeologist to ask."

Ford attempted, and failed, to remain straight-faced after Dad's compliment. A smile caught the corner of his mouth, and soon he was beaming from ear to ear.

"I don't know that it can tell us anything" Dad continued, "other than someone had a jar of gold they wanted to hide. It's a safe bet to assume the someone was a Blackwell, but a lot of this is speculation. We'll have to see what else the site turns up."

He rubbed his hands together. "So, we have two pieces of information we've discovered over the weekend. Somebody used this garbage dump for something more than garbage, and the horse buried here might be the original who started the ghost legend."

Lou banged her shovel on the ground a couple of times. "Let's get digging!"

It made me happy to see her so enthusiastic about the project for a change, and she wasn't the only one. We all attacked the old garbage dump that morning with renewed fervor, visions of buried treasure and bone horses dancing in our heads.

Lou, Ford and I were mostly focused on the horse aspect of the project. Every time a new bone showed up in a screen or a shovel, we would call Dad in for an on-the-spot analysis to see if it was from the horse, and more than once, it was.

Donna and Bea, while excited about the gold discovery, seemed turned off by our grisly delight concerning the consumed horse. At lunch, Bea lowered herself wearily to the ground and fixed Lou and me with a solemn look. "You kids seem happier than fleas on a tick's back, but I'm not so sure about all the joy you seem to derive from digging up this dead horse's spirit."

I swallowed my bite of granola bar. "What do you mean, Bea? You don't think it's cool to find the actual source of a legend? One that's been around for over a hundred years? This is about the closest archaeologists around here get to searching for the Holy Grail."

"Ugh." Donna shuddered. "I'm with you, Mom. It's creepy."

Lou frowned. "What's creepy about it?"

Bea actually glared at Lou. "I'm old enough to believe that some things in life are still sacred. This was once a magnificent animal. I believe every being, animal and plant has a spiritual essence. What happens after that being dies?" Without giving us a chance to answer, she wagged a finger at us and continued. "Its spirit remains, and if you don't treat it with respect, it can come back to haunt you, so to speak. People do say they've seen spirits around here."

"But Bea," I cut in, "we've explained that. Lookout's as real as any of us."

"You're sure?" Donna said. "After that one encounter?"

I opened my mouth to protest. I'd encountered Lookout more than once. But something stopped me. I wasn't ready to reveal my secrets, even to win an argument. I clamped my mouth shut and shrugged.

"Anyway," Donna continued. "You *think* you've explained it, Misty. There's more to life than you kids know. Than you can find on the Internet." Her condescension set my teeth on edge. "I've heard of Indian burials where their horses were buried with them, as transportation to the afterlife."

She looked to Dad for confirmation.

He gave a non-committal shrug. He never divulged any information about digs that involved human remains.

"What do you think, Ford?"

Ford startled when she turned to him. "Uhhh…"

"Your family's Native American, right? You understand what I'm saying?"

The look on Ford's face was difficult to read, but his tone of voice was not. "I'm Catholic. Most of us aren't into animal worship."

Donna raised her eyebrows. I don't think that was the response she'd expected. But Bea didn't miss a beat.

A beatific smile spread across her face. "I'm glad to hear spirituality is a part of your life."

"I said I was Catholic," Ford muttered. "I didn't say I was spiritual."

Bea either didn't hear him or pretended not to. She turned a questioning gaze on Lou and me. "And what about you girls?"

I didn't know what to say, especially in light of my most recent "spiritual" experiences.

Lou was beginning to squirm like a bug under a magnifying glass. "We're Protestant." She swallowed. "Misty and I go to the same church back home."

"Ahhh…" Bea nodded. "What kind of Protestant?"

Lou looked confused and widened her eyes at me. I turned to Bea. "The, uh, Jesus-following…kind." I wished I sounded more confident. I turned to Dad, hoping for a rescue.

He was doing his anthropologist thing, studying the interaction between all of us in an objective, observational kind of way.

Frank, who'd returned from the direction of the latrine about halfway through the discussion, followed my gaze. "I suppose, you think bones are just bones, Dr. Stevens. You do this kind of thing every day, right?"

Dad didn't say anything at first. Our eyes met. I was pretty sure I knew what he was thinking. This was a typical discussion for mid-way through an archaeological project. You spend a bunch of time in close quarters with people who value history and the environment, the conversation always gets around to religion and politics at some point. We'd both heard discussions like this countless times before. But what came out of his mouth surprised even me.

"I think Misty's right, and I don't blame the kids for being excited. Finding the source of a legend, understanding more deeply how the past influences the present? That's what archeology is all about." He gave us an encouraging smile. Then he turned a serious look on the three adults. "But I also agree with you, Bea. I do believe there is more to life than what we see with our eyes. Sometimes, we need to see with our hearts."

Bea seemed satisfied with that answer, nodding at Dad.

Ford, seated on the ground across from me, gave me a knowing look. I remembered what he'd said when Lou and I were talking about wanting to be like Bea when we were her age. *Bea's cool, but she has some different ideas about stuff.*

I had a memory of Bea's face, that far-off dreamy look in her eyes when Lou was talking about her mom's rebellious stage and coming back from Europe unmarried but pregnant. Bea thought June's adventure sounded bohemian, romantic. I'm sure parts of it were. I was glad my best friend had been born, but I also knew a life of single parenthood hadn't been a cakewalk for June, especially at first. June was a great mom, but growing up without a dad had been hard for Lou. She'd told me that more than once.

We all stood, stretched and picked up our tools and shovels to head back to work. Ford brushed my shoulder as he passed me. He murmured, "Told you."

I gave him a wavery smile, mostly because he'd brushed my shoulder, which sent an electric shock sliding all the way down to my fingertips.

The rest of the afternoon, the members of our group seemed in a quieter, more thoughtful frame of mind. But that wasn't the end of the discussion, at least as far as I was concerned. I knew Dad really didn't agree with Bea at all, and I wanted to hear what he hadn't said.

I managed to wait until we'd dropped the others off to launch my attack from the back seat. "Dad, how do you do that?"

"Do what? Make my job look so easy? Let me tell you, it's not as simple as it looks. It takes time, education, practice—"

He could be so annoying. "No. How do you pretend to agree with someone who I know you totally don't agree with?"

He pressed his lips together, as if he was trying not to smile. He knew what I was talking about, even seemed like he'd been waiting for me to bring it up. "You mean Donna and Bea today."

"Yeah, Donna and Bea today. I know where you stand on all that new-age crap."

Dad's smile vanished. "I'm not sure what you mean by 'all that new-age crap', as you so charmingly put it, but I meant every word I said to them."

"*What?*" My voice was reaching decibels only dogs could hear. "Don't tell me you buy all that make-it-up as you go along—" I finger-quoted the word, "*spirituality*. We're all one with the universe and god is in the trees and the animals and in you and you're god *and* the tree—"

Dad started laughing. Lou and I were sitting in back, and she was watching us volley back and forth. I was hoping for a little support, but she gave me nothing. Mostly, she seemed interested in what Dad was going to say next.

I crossed my arms and glared at the back of Dad's head. "I don't see what's so funny."

"Mist, calm down." He was completely unruffled by my tirade. "Think about what they really said and what I said. I didn't agree with everything Bea put out there. You know I don't." He glanced in the rearview mirror. "And I admit, there was a time I would've reacted as negatively to someone I didn't agree with as you are."

"Isn't it easier to nod, smile and move on?" Lou asked. "You have to pick your battles, right?"

"Sometimes," Dad said. "Look, I would never suggest that you sacrifice your beliefs on an altar of peace. Our beliefs are a major part of who we are."

Dad shifted in his seat. "But here's the thing—and Misty, your mom was an expert at this—if you work at it, you can almost always find something in another person to connect with. Sometimes it's only a thread, but you need to find it, and grab it. Because that thread will make it possible to begin to understand who a person is, where they're coming from, what's important to them, and maybe, someday, how to love them. Your mom also would have said, that's why we're here."

Lou started to say something, then shut her mouth. She lifted a shoulder and stuck her earbuds in.

He'd invoked Mom's memory. In fact, that was the first time I could remember him mentioning her without someone else's prompting since she'd died. How could I disagree?

Instead, I changed the subject. "I was wondering about what you said earlier, about breaking—or training—horses. You said it's mostly about gaining their trust. What'd you mean by that?"

We rolled to a stop at a crossroads. Instead of moving forward, Dad turned around, arm on the back of the seat, and stared at me. "Why the sudden interest? I didn't think horses were your thing."

"I don't know…with all the horses around and, I guess, thinking about Mom growing up here…" I watched the landscape outside my window, avoiding his eyes. "I'm curious." I hadn't admitted to myself the why or how of my growing relationship with a wild stallion. But I'd never had a big secret that was all my own before. Wasn't that what growing up was supposed to be about? Making things yours?

I glanced at Lou, hoping this wasn't going to turn into another debate about horsemanship. But she was zoned out, head on the seat, eyes closed. I could hear the tinny beat of whatever music was blasting into her brain.

I met Dad's gaze. "Say you had a horse that had never been broken. How would you start from scratch, gain their trust?"

He faced the road again, and we rolled through the intersection. I breathed a quiet sigh of relief.

"You have to remember," he said. "Horses are prey animals, and we're not. We smell like predators to them. The best thing you can do initially is be there with them and not eat them."

"Dad, seriously?"

"I know it sounds funny." I could see him smiling in the rearview. "But look at the situation from their point of view. They're very sensitive to everything around them—noises, smells, movement. They have to be, because for a prey animal, being hyper-aware is the difference between life and death. At the same time, they can be like children. They have an innate drive to play, and they're very curious. If you can put yourself into their world without forcing them or pressuring them, curiosity will win out. They'll come to you."

We turned off the highway down the long drive to the ranch house. He made it sound so easy, but I knew from my previous encounters with Lookout that connecting with a wild horse was anything but simple. *Connecting with a wild horse?* What was I thinking? "How do you put yourself 'into their world' without scaring them off?"

He stopped the car in front of the house, pulled on the brake, and turned to me. "What I used to do, when I was your age, was to take a good book, something that held my attention. I'd hang out in the round pen with the horse I was trying to gentle. Then I would ignore it."

"Ignore it? What would that do?"

"Sometimes it would take a couple hours. Sometimes—" He grimaced. "Several days. Depends on the horse. But like I said, at some point, curiosity would win out over their fear and they'd come to me." The corners of his mouth turned up. "And I knew I had 'em."

Lou opened her eyes and pushed out the door, yelling, "Dibs on the shower."

"Lou, a little help here," Dad called, climbing out of the Suburban. But it was pointless. The only response was the screen door slapping behind her.

After we'd lugged all the gear to the barn, I left Dad in his lab and sat alone on the porch, waiting for Lou to get out of the shower. I thought about my encounter with Lookout the day before. I was on the right track. I had the book, and I thought I had the patience.

Something else was nagging at me, though. Dad's description of how he interacted with horses—it all sounded sort of familiar. My whole life, up until the day Mom died, I'd really believed he wasn't that interested in me. But what if he hadn't *just* been ignoring me? What if all these years, he'd been patiently waiting, hoping that curiosity would win out, and I'd come to him?

MY INTERACTIONS WITH FORD for the rest of the week were less than relaxed. I didn't know what he was thinking, but the closer we got to the weekend and our double date with Cody and Lou, the more awkward I felt. We didn't talk about the impending event, other than his wave when we dropped him off at the campground Friday afternoon to pick up his truck.

He threw us a quick backward glance as he climbed out of the van, and said, "I'll see you guys in a couple hours."

Two hours later, Lou posed behind me, surveying us both in the full-length mirror on the back of the bathroom door. She looked amazing, as usual, from her dark hair, which was twisted into a casual bun, and her lined azure eyes—to her cowboy boots, torn white jeans and a cool blue-and-white striped t-shirt.

I let out a breath and tried to shake the tension from my shoulders. Over the past hour I'd tried on every piece of clothing I'd brought with me, and a bunch of Lou's shirts, shoes and jewelry. I'd ended up in a denim shirt tied at my waist, one of Lou's maxi skirts and a pair of her macramé sandals. At some point, Lou had hung a bunch of sparkly chains around my neck.

I sighed at our reflections. "You don't think the skirt's too much?"

"We're going to be in town, right?" She gave me a nudge, an encouraging smile. "Cheer up, my little camper. Seriously, you are such a goof-ball. You know how naturally adorable you are, right? I mean, your parents?" She gave me a look. "You inherited some great genes, girl. Work it." She opened the bathroom door. "C'mon. Let's go outside and wait for your date on the porch."

Was I really going to do this? A double date with Ford, Lou and—I winced—Cody. I took one last peek in that mirror and decided I looked…awful. And anxious. But Lou said I looked great. I shrugged. What difference did it make? This was Lou and Cody's date, really. Ford and me tagging along was an afterthought. I'm sure Ford didn't think of it as a date. Before I left the bathroom, I pulled Lou's chains from around my neck and hung them on the hook behind the door. They would drive me crazy all night. One more peek in the mirror. *Better.*

We'd decided Ford would pick us up and we'd meet Cody in the grocery store parking lot. I followed Lou out to the porch and watched Ford's truck come into view. Dad was nowhere in sight. He'd given up on us an hour ago and headed out to the barn, with a parting warning not to forget our phones.

When he pulled to a stop in front of the house, Ford did a double take. Because, of course, Lou was beautiful. Then he met my eyes and smiled. He was definitely looking at me and liking what he saw. *That's a good sign, right?* Lou grabbed my hand and pulled me behind her down the porch steps.

She opened the passenger door and pushed me ahead of her into the middle.

Next to Ford.

"Hey, handsome," she cooed and climbed in beside me. "Don't you two make a good-looking couple?"

Ford laughed and nudged me. "Of course. Was there ever any doubt?"

My friend arched an eyebrow, and I shook my head, but I wanted to laugh out loud.

I'd never met anyone as comfortable in their skin as Ford Tomaka.

I loved his confidence. It radiated off him like heat, and it gave me confidence, too. I relaxed and we all yelled when he put the truck into gear and peeled out. Maybe this was a date, after all. And maybe it was going to be great.

THIRTEEN

WHEN WE ARRIVED, DOZENS of teenagers and younger kids, with parents who were trying and mostly failing to keep them corralled, milled around the parking lot. Ford parked the truck and sat for a moment, watching the crowd. "Does the whole town turn out for stuff like this?"

It seemed like it, with all the couples and families wandering in and out of the store and the Ponder City Hall next to it. We climbed out of the truck, and Lou spotted Cody with a bunch of locals, including Matt and Becca.

"'Sup?" Matt said when he saw us. Becca waived, and it was nice to see someone familiar, friendly. She made it seem like we belonged there, even though the six other kids with them gave us a cold once-over. They were all in shorts, flip flops, baseball caps.

I felt overdressed.

But Lou owned it. She walked straight up to Cody and gave him a full body hug. He looked smug, and put his arms around her. "That's what I'm talking about. How you doin,' darlin'?"

Lou smiled up at him. "I'm fabulous, as always."

She didn't linger in the hug, at least there was that. But he kept a territorial arm around her shoulder, and threw Ford and me a triumphant look, like he'd made a conquest.

"Everybody," Cody said, waving a hand toward Ford and me. "This is Ford and Misty. They're working on the dig up near Gold Creek." That sparked a few interested looks. "And this gorgeous girl," Cody continued, "is my friend, Lou."

A couple of the other kids said hello. One guy said they'd heard a lot about us, and I wondered what Cody had told them. But mostly, I was thinking *his friend?* Really. So that's how it was. All that secret texting and emailing wasn't so mysterious anymore. In fact, Lou and Cody seemed extremely comfortable with each other. I wondered how friendly they'd gotten the night Lou had stayed at the ranch for dinner.

Cody waved a hand around the group. "Misty and Ford, this is everybody."

"So," Lou said, never one to stand around, "what's next?"

Becca grabbed Lou's hand and pulled her away from Cody. *Go Becca!* "Come with me and we'll get the coordinates of the first clue. It's sort of a modified geocache thing. Who does geocaching anymore, right? But they're offering a bunch of prizes for the people who find it, including a drawing for a new iPhone, so I'm in."

Her voice faded as they walked into the front door of the City Hall. Cody turned to his other friends, completely ignoring Ford and me, but Matt made his way over to us. "Good to see you guys again. How's the dig going?"

Ford answered before I could. "Ah, it's all good, you know. A lot of dirt, some bones, stuff like that." Dad's lectures about keeping our finds a secret had paid off. "How're things at the ranch?" Ford asked. While the guys talked about horses and cattle, I stood there, impressed at how easily and quickly Ford had steered the subject to safer ground.

By the time Lou and Becca returned with the coordinates of the first clue, the sun was just beginning to dip behind the Juliet Range. We pulled up the GPS apps on our phones to get some idea of where to start.

After less than a minute, Cody pointed at the highway. "I think we need to head toward the park, the one with the baseball fields and the stage… Hey, that would be a perfect place to hide it, right? I bet that's where it is." He started for the shoulder along the highway. "Lou, C'mon."

While Lou stood there, looking uncertain, Ford frowned, squinting at the park we could barely see from the store parking lot. "That's at least a mile-and-a-half away. What if that's not the right place? We'll waste a lot of time."

"We could drive over." I was searching for a compromise. I could see where this was headed, and I didn't want to get separated from Lou.

Ford shook his head.

"Yeah, Misty," Lou said, waving a piece of paper. "The rules say we have to hunt on foot, or we're disqualified."

"No guts, no glory, dude." Cody gave Ford a hard stare. "Look, it'll be a bigger waste of time to follow all those clues they created for the little kids, when chances are it's somewhere around the theater. But if you guys want to follow all the rules, be my guest."

He turned as if to head across the parking lot toward the highway. Lou stayed where she was and Cody faced her, still backing away. "You coming?"

She took one tentative step in his direction, throwing me a look. I shook my head, willing her with my eyes to stay.

"You could stick with us, Lou," Ford said, looking from Cody to her. "It'll be more fun to stay together…"

Cody was getting farther and farther away. Which was fine with me, and Lou wasn't making a move. I closed the distance between us, so only she could hear me. "C'mon," I said. "The guy's a jerk. Let him go."

Her eyes hardened. "It doesn't mean he's a jerk. Just because he has a different way of doing stuff. Everything's always so black and white with you. You don't always have to follow the rules."

Cody yelled her name again, and she turned and ran toward him without a backward glance. He put an arm around her and they ambled off along the shoulder of the highway.

"Stupid," I breathed.

"Yeah." Ford had come up to stand beside me. We watched Cody walk away with my best friend. "He's not the brightest bulb in the socket."

I'd meant me, how I'd said exactly the wrong thing to Lou. Again. I should have known better. But Ford made me smile. I noticed we were the only ones left in the parking lot of the group of kids we'd met.

"We do need to head that direction." He checked the GPS coordinates again. "I think if we walk behind the store and across those hills, we'll be closer to the place we're supposed to find the first clue. It's basically the same direction they're going. We'd be coming at it from the back instead of going around to the front of the park. I think it'll be a shortcut."

He shielded his eyes to see the hills, their tops illumined in the last rays of the sun. "It looks like it might be a hike. You up for that?"

He took in my long skirt, my sandals. I squared my shoulders and set off toward the back alley of the grocery store and the foothills beyond. "I can hike in anything." I glanced back at him, and he was still standing there. "Let's go. I so want to find that cache before Cody does."

Ford caught up as I rounded the corner. The sun was almost gone, and no light filtered into the narrow space between the stores and the cinder block retaining wall keeping the sage-covered hills from encroaching on the town.

The alleyway was dark and scattered with shadowy shapes.

"Whoa." I stopped. "I can't see two steps in front of me."

Ford directed the light from his phone ahead of us, and we waited a few seconds, giving our eyes a chance to adjust. If we could get through the alley, past the back side of City Hall, the variety store and the library, we would be in the park foothills. But it was going to take some time. The few feet we could see in front of us revealed a narrow corridor littered with discarded display shelves, appliances, over-flowing dumpsters and other miscellaneous garbage.

I tripped over a board and Ford put out a hand to steady me.

"This could be perilous," I said.

"Nice word." He looked down at me, nodding. "SAT word."

"I have to take that test next year, huh?" I shuddered.

"Something tells me you're gonna ace it."

Before I could answer, a pallet tipped over and crashed against a dumpster. I screamed and jumped back. Ford swung the light's beam toward the sound, and yellow eyes glowed back at us from a narrow space between the dumpster and the wall.

My mouth went dry. "Uh…raccoon?" My voice cracked on the last syllable.

I could just make out Ford's expression in the dim light. He licked his lips and nodded, eyes on the animal. "Yeah, I think so. Let's try not to make him any more bothered. Raccoons can be territorial."

He held out his hand. "It's dark, and I have light. Really, I'd feel better if we stick together."

I had my phone, too, which I could've used. We both ignored that fact, or pretended not to remember. Hand-in-hand, we moved carefully, threading our way through all the junk. His palm was warm and dry. I wondered if anything ever shook him.

Just as we could, literally, see light at the end of the tunnel, my skirt caught on the corner of a splintered crate. I let go of Ford's hand to free myself, but turned too fast. When I landed on the side of my foot, a sharp, burning pain shot through my ankle and up my leg.

I yelled, and Ford grabbed my arm as I went down, easing my descent to the dirty, crumbling concrete. I was faintly aware of the sound of Lou's skirt ripping.

"Misty?" He dropped to one knee. "Are you okay?"

He sounded really concerned, which I kind of loved, even while I tried to blink away tears. I refused to be a total wuss, but the pain was intense.

"Yeah," I gasped, rocking back and forth. "I twisted my ankle. I'll be okay. Give me a minute."

He reached toward my ankle. "This one?"

"No!" I cried, then pressed my lips together. He drew his hand back like he'd been stung. "Sorry." I gave him an apologetic look, and realized he probably couldn't read my expression in the dark. "Just, please, don't touch it."

He held up his hands. "Man, it must really hurt."

"It does, but…" I moved it a little bit. "But I think I can walk." I was determined I would. I put my hand on his shoulder to push myself up. "You mind?"

"Be my guest, Misty. Whatever you need. All I can think about right now is getting you back to your dad in one piece."

Dad. I had to get through this without letting on I'd hurt myself. He'd never let me go anywhere with a guy again. I tried to stand up without putting pressure on my ankle, and managed to rise to a standing position. So far, so good. I slowly put my foot down, toe first. I could live with the ache…until, that is, I tried to put my whole weight on that ankle.

The pain knifed through my leg and I broke out in a cold sweat. "Whoa. That's not going to work. Ford, I don't think I can do this." I hoped he couldn't hear the sob I was trying hard to hold back. I was shaking, and there was nothing I could do about that. "Do you think you could get your truck back here?"

He didn't say anything for a few seconds, then he stood and put an arm firmly around my waist. "Put your arm over my shoulder, and let's see if we can get you to that doorway over there." He practically carried me the few steps across the alley and deposited me on the low step in the entryway.

Placing his lit-up phone on the step, he knelt in front of me. I could see his face in the faint glow the light cast around us. "Mist, I know your ankle really hurts and you don't want me to touch it. But I am a volunteer EMT back home…"

"You can EMT at seventeen in Montana?" I sat up straighter. "Lou and I wanted to do that, but we have to wait until we're eighteen in Washington State."

"That's cool…" But there was doubt in his voice.

"What?" I said. "You don't think we could do it?"

"No, I'm sure you'd be fine. It's not something I pictured you two being interested in."

"Us two girls, you mean?"

Ford shook his head. "That's not what I meant…"

I let it go and shrugged. "It was Lou's idea. She's always looking for something new to try, which is what's cool about her, and I'm actually really good in an emergency.

"But when everything's all over, I don't know."

I slumped. "I don't really want to do it anymore…" *After mom.* I stopped, at a loss. I'd stumbled into the subject of my mom, and I was in too much pain and way too bothered with Ford kneeling that close to me to be able to figure out what to say next.

"Misty, Lou told me about what happened to your mom. I'm sorry. I can't even imagine what that must have been like."

I swallowed and thought for the millionth time how impossible it was to respond appropriately to people's sympathy. "Thanks," I finally said. We sat there for a few seconds, staring at each other. I turned my head away, and Ford took a breath.

"So, yeah, you have to be eighteen in Montana, too. But my dad got me into the wilderness EMT basic course last fall. So, I'm not official, but I think I can tell the difference between a broken ankle and a twisted one."

I was so grateful he'd changed the subject and moved on. "Well, okay, as long as you're trained, I'm sure it will be fine."

He grinned. "You're being sarcastic, right? That's you, doing sarcasm?"

I made a sound that was halfway between a sob and a laugh.

"Yeah, well, no guarantees. But if I can tell that you're okay to walk, it'll be better than spending the night in this alley, I guarantee you."

If he was with me, I didn't think that would be so bad.

He looked up at me, eyebrows raised.

I gritted my teeth, shut my eyes, and nodded.

Nothing happened.

I peeked open one eye.

"You have to chill, Misty. I promise, this will be okay." He bent his head toward my leg and I was so glad I'd shaved them, twice. He gingerly lifted my ankle onto his knee. "Keep your eyes open. If you know what's coming, you won't get so stressed."

He was right. It wasn't that bad. My ankle hurt like crazy when he squeezed the side in certain places. But he was able to move my foot around without too much pain. Ford touching me didn't feel awkward. He was business-like, clinical. Sitting there, in the dark, with this amazing guy—who'd suddenly gone from being my date to my doctor.

Finally, he gently lowered my foot onto the concrete and sat back. "Yeah, I'd bet my future as an EMT, your ankle isn't broken, or even sprained. I think you twisted it. I'm no doctor, but go ahead and take two aspirin and call me in the morning, anyway." He gave my shoulder a doctorly pat. "I think you're going to be okay."

Now that he mentioned it, the pain was less than a few minutes ago. "Let me try standing again."

"You sure? I think you're good, but that doesn't mean you're ready to go hiking in the hills." He assessed the space around us. "I might be able to get the truck back here…"

"Let me try this Ford." I held out my hand. "If I can at least make it to the end of the alley, you can get the truck and pick me up there."

He stood and grabbed my hand.

"Easy," I warned, but I should have known he'd be careful. He put his other hand under my elbow and slowly helped me rise to a standing position. I put the foot with the injured ankle down, and it hurt, but it held my weight.

He backed up and I took a few hopping steps toward him. "Brave," he said.

Was he making fun of me? I took a step closer and saw honest admiration on his face. It was ridiculous how happy that made me.

THIRTY MINUTES LATER, THE pain in my ankle had calmed to a dull throb and Ford was winding the truck through the park, on the hunt for Lou and Cody.

We cruised through the entrance and past a baseball field, a play structure, and a basketball court. Farther on, we found ourselves among gently rolling hills dotted with picnic tables. Ford had his brights on, and he was scanning the areas reflected in the truck's lights. "I know I've seen that amphitheater Cody was talking about—"

"Over there!" I pointed to a concrete half-shell at the base of the hill we were cresting. One bright spotlight lit up the area, and I could see silhouettes of people in the light's glow.

Ford braked and put his arm on the back of the seat. Leaning across me, he squinted at the scene out my window. "There's got to be some way to drive closer to that place if they do performances down there."

I opened my door. "Can't you park the truck here? We can hike down. It's not that far." For some reason, I felt an urgent need to find Lou. She'd been alone for a couple hours with Cody, and the better I got to know him, the creepier he made me feel.

Ford put a hand on my shoulder before I managed to exit the truck. "Are you sure? How's that ankle?"

I slid from under his hand and hopped out of the truck. I'd forgotten all about my ankle…until my foot hit the pavement. I winced, but I wasn't about to let it stop me. "It's fine."

Ford looked skeptical.

"Okay, I've felt better. But like you said, I'm not really hurt."

"I didn't say you weren't hurt. I know it hurts. Been there, done that."

I shrugged off his concern. "Really, I'm fine. You can stay here with the truck. I'll go get Lou."

"Hang on," he said. "Wait a minute. I'm coming." He pulled off the road and locked up the truck. I could hardly wait for him to join me before I started limping down the hill, toward the light and the sounds of music and laughter.

The closer we got to the little stage, the more laughter and shouts we could hear. The sound traveled—I guess that was the idea of the half-shell. A bunch of people were down there—a lot more than Lou, Cody, Becca and Matt. The night smelled like sage and dust and, the closer we got to the stage, alcohol and weed.

Ford stopped. "Misty…"

"Come *on*." I grabbed his arm and tugged him toward the kids. "We have to find Lou."

He swallowed and nodded, but stayed where he was. "Yeah, yeah we do. But I'm wondering if I could get you to wait here while I go get her."

"What? Wait, why?"

"I don't think your dad…"

Was he kidding me? "Seriously? Why didn't we just bring him along?"

He laughed. "What do you mean by that?"

I wished he'd quit bringing up my dad. But before I could put my irritation into words, we heard Cody's voice calling us. At least, I thought it was Cody. He sounded a little thick.

"Who's out there?" Yep, definitely Cody.

Then Lou's voice, as we made our way into the circle of light. "Is that you Mist?" She was sitting on the concrete floor of the stage, her booted feet dangling over the edge. Cody sat next to her, goofy-grinned and pasted to her shoulder, clutching a beer.

Lou ignored my wide-eyed look of disbelief. "Come on in and join the party." She giggled, but she was on edge, which was not a normal state for Lou.

"Hey, Lou," I called, from the edge of the crowd.

"Don't be shy, you two." Cody waved us over with the bottle in his hand. In the same moment, a truck careened around the stage from the parking lot. Ford and I dashed toward Lou and Cody to avoid getting hit.

A ground-shaking beat was pounding from the truck's speakers as the driver, who turned out to be Matt, stumbled out of the truck. "Whoa, sorry you guys." He offered us a heavy-lidded but apologetic look. "I didn't see you there." A bunch of people whooped and started dancing in the truck's headlights. Several others hopped into the truck bed.

I hoisted myself up on the stage next to Lou and leaned close. "Did you guys find the cache?"

"No." She giggled. "We have no idea where it is. I don't think anybody really searched for it that long. Everyone just kind of ended up here." She waved her hand vaguely around the group as if, unconscious and sort of against their will, they'd been transported there by aliens.

"What about you guys?" Her forehead wrinkled. "Were you limping?"

"She twisted her ankle pretty bad." Ford had stopped to talk to Matt for a second, but now he stood in front of us. "You ready to go, Lou?"

"Oh, no. Misty," she looked stricken, "are you okay?"

At least she still cared.

"Bro," Cody broke in, "party's just starting. You can't take Lou away from us, yet."

Ford acted like he hadn't heard, and continued to stare at Lou, waiting for her to answer.

"It looks like fun, right?" Lou said. "It's not that late. Let's stay for a while."

Ford answered her with a nod that acknowledged what she'd said, but hardly communicated enthusiasm. He came over and leaned against the stage next to me, silent, unmoving. We sat there, the kids dancing and drinking in front of us. The music vibrated around the little amphitheater along with the wafting scent of marijuana.

I swatted at a mosquito on my cheek and tried to figure out what to say to Lou that wouldn't sound so completely lame I would lose her to this crowd for the night. It wasn't like it was the first time I'd seen Lou drinking at a party. No matter how protective her mother was, she'd spent her life on the rodeo circuit—people partied hard all week, went to cowboy church Sunday morning and prayed for forgiveness.

In the past, though, she'd always been around friends we all trusted. I knew she was a big girl. I knew she could handle herself. I simply couldn't bring myself to leave Lou's fate in the hands of a drunk Cody.

After a few minutes, Ford tilted his head toward the party. "I feel like I'm in a scene from Footloose." He said it loud enough for me to hear, maybe Lou, although she didn't acknowledge him. I was sure Cody didn't hear, because he was dancing and shouting, "Woohoo," at the top of his lungs, while swinging the bottle over his head.

"Original?" I asked. "Or, the remake?"

"Original, of course. Although, Kevin Bacon's way too good for this group."

I laughed and a smile tugged at the edges of Lou's mouth. She'd only been pretending not to hear him. She lost that battle and shook her head at us. "You guys, give 'em a break. They're just having fun." She'd barely finished that sentence when Cody let loose with another *Woohoo*, and we all burst out laughing.

"Okay, okay." Lou slid down off the stage. "Let's go."

I started to follow her, putting careful weight on my ankle. But we weren't escaping that easily. Cody jumped down in front of us, his face about two inches from Lou's. "Aww, don't go yet. I wanted to talk to you guys 'bout that project you're workin' on. You know, they say there's buried treasure in these mountains."

We looked at each other and immediately looked away. I tried to assume an uninterested expression, as if Cody was talking about his sock drawer. If Ford and Lou's faces were any indication, though, none of us were very good actors.

Ford raised an eyebrow. "Who says there's buried treasure?"

"All the local kids." Cody yelled over our heads at Matt. "Matt, buddy, come over here and tell these guys what you told me the other night."

Matt was slow-dancing in the bed of his truck with Becca. At least, I think that was the idea. I was pretty sure he'd actually fallen asleep on her shoulder and she was kind of stumbling around underneath him, trying to stay upright.

"Matt!" Cody yelled again, and Matt's head popped up so fast Becca fell backwards. Everyone who saw them doubled over in laughter. Matt turned around to see who they were laughing at, and their laughter turned into howls.

Cody grabbed Lou's hand and towed her to the other kids at the truck, Ford and I trailing behind. I wanted to get out of there, but I was also curious about what Matt had told Cody.

"Waddya say?" Matt dropped onto the truck's gate with a heavy thud that caused the truck to squeak and bounce. I flinched. He was a big guy, but fortunately, he owned a Matt-sized truck. The gate held.

Cody shook his arm. "Tell them what you told me about buried treasure in the mountains."

Matt blinked his groggy eyes and slowly nodded. "Oh, yeah, there are legends about some of the miners from gold rush days skimming off the top, you know, and hiding their cache up there in the caves and hollows. People say the gold is still there, and that ghost horse'll lead you to it, if you can catch him."

I looked at Ford out of the corner of my eye, but he shook his head. "You guys are high. Ghost horse. What a joke."

"People been telling that story up here for generations, though," Matt responded. "And there's always been that horse—"

Cody took a threatening step toward Ford. They were nose-to-nose. "Yeah, Tomaka." He sneered Ford's name like it was an insult. "What do you know? You got here, like, yesterday."

"We did find that one jar of gold—"

It was as if I heard Lou say it in slow motion and the world stopped moving. I couldn't believe those words had come out of her mouth. Had she just revealed exactly what Dad had warned us not to tell anybody? Here, in the middle of a bunch of drunk locals? The news would be all over the internet in about five minutes. Everyone within hearing distance turned toward us.

"Lou!" Ford and I said her name at the same time. I moved toward her. I don't know why, except I was so desperate to shut her up I might have clamped my hand over her big mouth to do it.

The blinding, red lights that started flashing all around us at that moment perfectly matched the adrenaline already coursing through me. Somebody screamed and all the kids scattered. Ford grabbed our hands and dragged Lou and me up the slope, away from the lighted lot where everyone else was parked, including the sheriff's cruiser. We got halfway up the hill and he shoved us down into the tall grass.

"What the…?" Lou tried to struggle back to her feet, but he held her down.

"Stay there," he whispered through clenched teeth. "Don't move. They won't see us here, it's too dark. They'll go after the easy pickings in the parking lot. If we're lucky, they won't see my truck parked on the road."

Why were we hiding from the cops? "Can't we tell them we were looking for the geocache? We haven't done anything wrong."

Ford turned on me, eyes wide like I'd lost my mind.

Lou snickered and I could practically hear her rolling her eyes. "She's homeschooled," she whispered to Ford, and started to giggle.

He shushed her and turned to me. "Trust me, Mist. We're not from around here. We don't want to get caught in the middle of this."

We lay on our stomachs in the grass, faces in the dirt, afraid to even breathe for what seemed like an eternity. After maybe an hour, things quieted down, and Ford whispered, "Let's go." He nudged me. "Stay low."

Lou started giggling. "From Footloose to Rambo…"

"Quiet, Lou," I begged. But she couldn't stop snickering. Ford pulled her up the hill and shoved her into the passenger side of the truck. I came limping up from behind and he practically picked me up and threw me in beside her.

"Chill out," Lou snapped when I landed on top of her. But Ford wasn't listening. A missile focused on its target, he was only about getting us out of there.

Winding our way without lights along the narrow road was hair-raising, but at least the park appeared to be completely empty. No kids. No cops. Ford flipped on his headlights when we neared the exit.

I sighed. That beautiful strip of highway in our headlights meant freedom.

He leaned around Lou and caught my eye. "Dodged that bullet."

Something like the sound of an air horn made us all jump, and a brilliant floodlight illuminated the truck an instant before we pulled onto the highway. We squinted into lights pointed at us from the shadow of a massive pine at one side of the park exit.

Ford braked and we all froze in the glare.

Red and white lights on top of the sheriff's cruiser flashed, and Ford had no choice. He groaned, put the truck in park and rolled down his window.

At the same time, the image of Dad's face, his eyes narrowed in one of his stoniest glares, flashed through my mind. How would we explain getting stopped by the cops or, *please God, no,* getting hauled into the local station?

Ford sighed and I figured he was thinking the same thing I was. He also must've gotten the same lecture as Lou and me about traffic stops in Driver's Ed. *Turn off your engine and your radio. Wait with your hands on the wheel.*

Lou closed her eyes and put her head in her hands. "Are you kidding me? This can't be happening."

I nudged her leg and gave her a look that I hoped translated into *be cool.* This was no time for hysterics. The last thing we needed was the sheriff to notice she'd been drinking. I may have been homeschooled, but I wasn't stupid.

"Shhh, Lou, it'll be okay." I kept my voice low. "Ford will probably just get a ticket or something…"

Ford gave me an exasperated look, his mouth set in a grim line.

I tried for a save. "Not that getting a ticket would be a good thing…"

He shook his head. I closed my mouth and looked toward the sheriff's cruiser. *What was taking him so long? Do they take their time to make people crazy?*

I realized the officer was no longer in his car about the same time he appeared at the back end of the truck. He was talking into the radio mic attached to his shoulder. He said some numbers and something about the north entrance to the park.

He peered into Ford's window and a blindingly bright flashlight swept across the three of us. By the time I could see again, his attention was focused on Ford. "Good evening. I'm Sheriff Friesen. I stopped you because you're leaving the park well after closing. Did you know this park closes at dusk?" His voice was crisp, professional.

"I'm sorry, Sheriff. We didn't know." Ford cleared his throat. "We're from out of town."

The sheriff didn't acknowledge Ford's response, but his eyes swept over the three of us again. "May I see your driver's license and proof of insurance?"

Ford pulled his license from his wallet. "My insurance is in my glove compartment." He handed his license to the officer. "Is it okay if I get it?" *Yep, definitely the same driver's ed course.*

The sheriff nodded and Ford reached across Lou and me. Lou scrunched her dirt-covered knees over so Ford could get to his insurance. Smoothing my torn skirt, I realized how smudged and scruffy we all were, which I'm sure wasn't helping our case with Sheriff Friesen. After a few seconds of fumbling, Ford found his insurance card and handed it to the officer.

"Please stay where you are." The sheriff returned to his cruiser and sat down in his car with the door open. I could see one leg sticking out, the heel of his black, shiny boot resting on the ground.

Lou elbowed Ford. "You don't have any wants or warrants, do you?"

Ford whipped his head around and the look on his face was so fierce, I shrank back against the door. Lou stiffened against me. "Lou, seriously…" He sucked in a ragged breath and blew it out slowly. "I need you to be quiet now, okay?"

"Okay, jeez!" She crossed her arms and stared straight ahead.

Sheriff Friesen appeared at Ford's window and handed him his license and insurance card. "What brought you to the park tonight?"

"We…" Ford hesitated. "We were participating in the geocache event they were doing in Ponder. We thought the cache might be here in the park."

"We've been having some trouble with underage drinking and vandalism in this park." The sheriff's gaze took us all in. "Do you have anything that proves you were involved in the geocaching event?"

Ford's shoulders sagged, and he started to shake his head.

"Wait." Something clicked in my brain. "What about that piece of paper we got from City Hall? With the directions and the first coordinates?"

Ford threw me a look of gratitude. He reached into his pocket, drew out the creased paper and handed it to the sheriff.

He stepped back and used a flashlight to scan the page before he handed it back to Ford. "It looks like you have a clean driving record." There was a *but* coming, I knew it. My heart was beating time to the flashing lights on the cruiser.

"Since you're not from around here," he paused. "I'm going to let you go with a warning. But like I said, we've been having trouble after hours here lately. Do yourselves a favor and stick to the posted closing times."

Yes! I wanted to hug Lou, Ford and, what the heck, Sheriff Friesen. Ford nodded, thanked the officer, and promised to obey the posted signs.

The sheriff started to turn away, but in the middle of our collective sighs of relief, he stopped and swiveled back toward the truck.

"Out of curiosity, what brings you to Ponder?"

"We're part of a Passports in Time volunteer crew with the Forest Service," Ford said, with a glance at Lou and I. "We're working on a dig in the wilderness area near Gold Creek."

He couldn't have said we were tourists? This was a small town. It wouldn't be long before my dad got the news about his wayward daughter, and friends.

Sheriff Friesen's whole demeanor changed. He was human after all. "I heard about that dig." He smiled. "You guys find any gold yet?"

WHEN WE PULLED UP to the ranch house, we were still arguing about what had happened.

"What was I supposed to do, lie to the sheriff?" Ford didn't exactly yell it, but we were all on edge, voices raised. It was past midnight. I was scanning the house, trying to see what lights were on where, unable to shake that vision of my dad's glare.

As soon as Ford stopped the truck, Lou reached past me, popped the door handle and shoved me out of the truck. She shot out of her seat and vaulted toward the front steps. Her parting words, yelled loud enough we could hear her from the porch: "Worst. Date. Ever."

I closed my eyes and shook my head. Dad would hear that.

I watched her go and slowly, head down, shut the passenger door with both hands. Still leaning against the door, I risked a glance at Ford through the open window.

"It *was* pretty much the worst date ever," he said. "Sorry."

I shrugged. "It wasn't your fault, and…" I glanced toward the house. Still no sign of Dad.

"It had its moments," Ford said, finishing my sentence. I looked back at him and he was grinning. "You want me to stay and tell your Dad—?"

"No!" I interrupted, before he could finish.

He laughed and put the truck in gear. "Okay." He flashed me a peace sign. "I'm out. See you Monday."

I stepped back from the truck and watched him drive off. When I turned toward the house, the front door opened. Dad stepped onto the porch.

FOURTEEN

I CLIMBED THOSE STEPS like nobility heading for the guillotine—head held high, but slowly and with resignation. Gritting my teeth, I did everything I could to hide my limp.

Dad's hair was all spiky on one side, like he'd fallen asleep on the couch waiting for us. He checked his watch. "I know I didn't give you a curfew, but a call would have been nice."

I stopped in front of him. "I know, Dad, sorry. We should have called. Stuff just kept happening…"

He peered at me, stepped closer. "Are you all right?"

I imagined what I must look like—sweaty, tired, torn skirt.

"I'm fine." I dropped into the porch swing and instantly regretted it. It wobbled, I instinctively steadied it with my foot and winced at the pain. "I twisted my ankle and it took a while to get back to the truck. Then we couldn't find Lou and Cody."

Dad leaned against the railing, facing me. "Sounds like quite a night. Are you sure your ankle isn't seriously injured?"

"Yeah, it started feeling better after a few minutes. Ford…uh…checked it out. Did you know he went through EMT training this spring?"

He scanned my face, nodded. "I saw that on his Passports app. It's one of the reasons I feel comfortable about you three wandering around alone."

"Thanks for not making a big deal out of us being so late."

I thought he was going to say something, but he didn't. In the end, he cranked his head back and forth like he was trying to loosen up his neck—or, maybe, denying himself a lecture was about to make his head explode.

"As long as you're really okay, you're welcome. But call next time, yes?" He held out his hand to help me out of the swing.

"Yes," I said. He pushed the front door open and I limped past him to the stairs. When I got to the top step, I could hear Lou snoring.

Something made me look back. Dad was still down there, illuminated by the light from the porch, watching me. I whispered, "Night, Dad."

His reply was soft, but distinct. "Night, Sweetness."

I untangled from my clothes and fell into bed. *Sweetness.* Dad hadn't called me that for years. Maybe I wasn't the only one who had misgivings about me growing up. But when I closed my eyes, what I saw was Ford's smile. My last thought before I fell asleep? *Growing up might have its moments.*

I WAS SORTING THROUGH a screen on Wednesday when Kurt's forest service truck pulled into the site. He'd come by every day, as excited by our finds as we were. But each time he appeared, my heart did double time, sure he'd heard about our run-in with the sheriff over the weekend. Every time, I was sure he'd come to bring news of our wayward ways to my father.

We were working under a hot sun, finishing up the test pits at the garbage dump site. When Dad called a break for lunch, everyone happily headed for the shade of the trees. I couldn't stand the suspense and wandered nearer to where Dad and Kurt were talking. The dig seemed to be their only topic of conversation.

They were more and more convinced we'd discovered the old Blackwell site, which meant we were working on one of the oldest homestead sites in Oregon. "With the discovery of what appears to be the ghost legend bones," Kurt said, "this site has the makings of a very cool historical monument. I think we could come up with funds for an interpretive sign, at the very least."

Since our run-in with the law seemed to have passed without repercussions, I took advantage of a lull in their conversation to find out about the search for Lookout.

"Misty," Kurt said, "if I didn't know better, I'd almost believe that animal really is a ghost. The crew hasn't seen any sign of him in his usual haunts. I'm sure he'll turn up eventually, though. He always does." He had talked with Bob Blackwell earlier in the week, and although the rancher was still steaming, the volunteers doing the wild horse count had put in extra hours to gather his horses.

"That helped calm him down. I'm sure he was being honest with me about not seeing Lookout himself. In fact, he sounded like he might give up on his search and leave it to us. I hope he does."

"As far as I know," Kurt continued, "there haven't been any cougar or Lookout sightings for a couple of weeks—not since your close call in the orchard, Misty. Unless you've seen something?"

Dad shook his head. "Nothing around our place, or the site."

I said nothing. The fact was, despite my visits to the orchard almost every evening, Lookout hadn't made any recent appearances to me, either.

Kurt pulled off his cap and ran a hand through his hair. "I wish I had time to deal with all of this, but I don't, and now that the volunteers have all gone home…" He had the tight look of someone who was tired and more than a little stressed. "Several of them will return in a couple of weeks to finish up the count. They spent so much time helping Blackwell look for his horses, they weren't able to do everything they'd originally hoped."

"Maybe they'll run across Lookout when they go back out," Dad ventured.

"Maybe. They often do."

After a minute of staring at the test pits in front of us, Kurt said, "Maybe more."

Dad and I turned to him with what I imagined were matching puzzled expressions.

Kurt smiled. "Maybe we could do more than a sign. We actually received a fairly sizable chunk of funds for facilities improvements last year that never got used and, miracle of miracles, we were able to get it reallocated this year."

Dad became even more puzzled. "You've got money that you're having trouble spending?" Federal budgets were tight.

"The director before me landed the money with the idea of remodeling and upgrading the Gold Creek Station," Kurt shook his head. "It's the usual—we have this money to improve facilities this year, but the way budgets are looking, I don't know if we'll have the funds to staff the station next year." He lowered his voice. "They're talking about consolidating offices and housing everybody at the Pendleton facility."

"Whoa." Dad shook his head.

"This area is getting more and more use," Kurt continued, "which means more and more run-ins between campers, hikers, horses and other wildlife, plus cattle, ranchers and farmers. Don't even get me started on the ATVs. How they expect us to manage all that from Pendleton…"

He talked about his increased reliance on volunteers, like the riders searching for Lookout and counting the horses. "Thank God for them. We have an active *Friends* volunteer organization out here, too, among the older locals."

He rubbed his hands together. "I'm picturing an interpretive structure that could be manned by volunteers in the summer. Something that would teach people about the history of the area—and help us keep an eye on all the campers. Blackwell's wife is active in the Friends of Gold Creek Wilderness, and the Blackwells certainly bring their guests out a lot.

"With the family connection, I'd think they would be interested in being involved with this project. Be good for their operation and the forest." Kurt seemed to loosen up the more he thought about this latest idea. "I'm not seeing a down side at this point."

THAT EVENING, I headed out to the orchard with my book, as usual, leaving Lou crouched over her computer, engrossed in an online conversation she obviously didn't want to tell me about.

I stopped in at the barn on my way by. Dad was focused on organizing the day's finds. After the cougar sightings, we'd decided to bring Rosa in at night, even though the nights were beautiful. This was Lou's night to bring her in, which she'd already done, and my turn to feed her.

I threw some hay in her stall, and Rosa's nicker seemed like gratitude. I rubbed a hand across her side, and her hide rippled in response. I even scratched behind her ears and gave her an air kiss. She hadn't been getting much attention, lately, and I felt I owed her at least that.

"Do horses understand kisses?" I whispered in her ear. She lifted her head at me like a nod, which made me laugh. She stuck her nose in her feed. I may not have been my father's girl when it came to horses, but Rosa was growing on me.

I took a deep breath as I headed out back, trying to shake the perpetual, low-lying anxiety I had about meeting the cougar again—or even Lookout. After our first few encounters, I quit being afraid of him, but horses, especially wild ones, were unpredictable. Fear that I would mess up and cause Lookout to do something dangerous was always on my mind.

At the same time, most people were upset with my new friend, and I wasn't sure what might happen to him if he was found. It seemed like, if that cougar was tracking anyone, it was Lookout, and my presence might've scared it off both times. I kind of liked the idea that I was protecting him.

I settled into my usual spot, back against a tree, and opened my book. I tried to read but I couldn't focus on the story.

I had no fully-formed plan when it came to Lookout. I'd felt wonder verging on awe each time we met. He was beautiful— wild, free—but not hostile. And, for some reason, he was interested in me. Trying to reach him, to connect with whatever motivated him, took more courage and creativity than anything I had ever tried to do. I couldn't wait to experience it again.

When I heard the rustling of brush, the heavy footfalls that were the unmistakable sounds of a horse's approach, I scanned the trees, searching for him, holding my breath.

But Dad had said to do the opposite of what my instinct told me. I exhaled slowly, shifted my gaze back to the pages of my book, and attempted the impossible task of ignoring the wild stallion moving closer and closer to me.

But I couldn't help sneaking a few glances. He munched the grass growing between the rows of apple trees while his skin twitched and his tail swished at the flies circling his body. Once, he rubbed against one of the bumpy old tree trunks. He stopped and dug into the soft ground with one hoof, as if finding something particularly sweet and much more interesting than I was.

He was calm, his movement circumspect, but with every step he was working his way, almost imperceptibly, closer and closer to where I sat. And then, there he was, standing above me.

I tried not to tense up when he shoved his nose in my hair and sniffed, like he had the first time we met at the site. *Why was he so intensely interested in my hair?*

Sitting in that apple orchard, an obvious stop on Lookout's foraging route, it hit me. This horse, like all horses I'd ever known, must love apples. And what was my favorite shampoo? Apple-pectin. The words from the back of the bottle floated through my head: ...*derives its unique fragrance from real apple pectin, a complex carbohydrate found in real apples. The shampoo also contains apple extract...* I'd have to write the manufacturer and let them know they could add, *the shampoo also attracts authentic wild stallions.* The thought, along with his big, crooked nose tickling and snuffling in my ear, made me giggle.

At the sound, the stallion stepped back and eyed me. He didn't seem startled, only puzzled by my response.

"Oh, Lookout," I ventured softly, "it's okay. You make me happy. That's a good thing, big guy."

He tilted his head to the side, as if considering whether or not I was too silly to be his friend. I wasn't sure what he decided, but he didn't approach me again. Yet, he didn't leave right away, either. Instead, he continued to weave through the trees, pulling up grasses, lifting his head and pulling his lips back—tasting the breeze. He moved away from me the same way he'd come, gradually distancing himself, until he was gone.

And none too soon, it turned out. As I stood and picked up my blanket, I heard Dad calling my name from the barn's back door. When I reached him, he didn't look happy.

"What is it?" I asked, certain what the answer would be.

"Come inside the house, please. I've had a call from Kurt. I need to talk with you and Lou."

I followed him, the condemned heading for the gallows. Kurt had heard about our run-in with the law. Dad wouldn't let us get together with Ford and the kids in town after this.

"Anything you want to tell me about what happened last weekend?"

Lou, sitting across from me at the table, flushed. I could feel my face doing the same thing. I opened my mouth to plead for mercy, but she cut in, eyes convincingly wide and innocent. "Why? Did someone say something?"

Dad was leaning against the wall, arms crossed. He gave her a look over his glasses that said he wasn't buying the innocent act.

"Well, some…some of the kids got together in the park," she stammered, "and I guess we weren't supposed to be there. But we didn't know, and we didn't get in trouble."

"That's what Kurt said. But he also said some of the kids were picked up for drinking and using, including Cody. You know anything about that?"

"We haven't seen Cody since we left that night," I said. "I didn't know he'd gotten picked up. What happened to the kids they caught?"

Across from me, Lou seemed very interested in exploring a crease in the table's cracked Formica with her fingernail, which was better than having to meet Dad's eyes. I felt pinned by his gaze.

"Bob Blackwell bailed him out, and chewed him out, apparently, right there in the police station. According to Sheriff Friesen, who I've also talked with, Sherrie appears to have smoothed things over between Bob and Cody. He's back at work on the ranch. However," Dad paused and caught Lou's eye. "I've already talked with your mom and she agrees with me. We don't want you to go out alone with Cody after this."

Lou's eyes widened. "But, anybody can make a mistake."

"Yes, but it sounds like this isn't the first time Cody's been in trouble. I know you're friends, and if he wants to come here while I'm home, that's fine. But for now, neither your mother nor I feel comfortable about you being out alone with him."

Lou's hands curled into fists, and she clenched her jaw. Her face was bright red. But she knew better than to argue with Dad, especially if he'd already teamed with June. Even though she hadn't mentioned Cody since that night, I could tell she was biting her tongue. Lou had a volatile personality, but this was a different level of seething than I'd ever seen.

The picture flashed in my mind of all the time she'd been spending, head bent over her phone or computer, her long hair conveniently screening whoever she was talking to. Of course. She'd been talking to Cody.

FIFTEEN

I STARED AT LOU, feeling betrayed, stupid. She'd always told me everything. At least, that's what I'd believed until now.

She jumped to her feet, shoved her chair away and stomped across the room. "Fine. Whatever. I'm going for a walk."

I flinched when the screen crashed shut on her way out, but I noticed she had her phone with her. What kind of texts about the horrible injustices she'd suffered were streaming to Cody's phone right then?

"Mist?" Dad said.

I turned to him with a sigh. *Now what?* "Dad," I interrupted whatever he was about to say, "don't ask me about Lou and Cody. Really, I have no idea what's going on."

"I wasn't going to. You're not responsible for whatever Lou is doing behind both our backs. You can't protect her from the consequences of the friends she chooses to keep." He gave me a wry smile. "That's my job, sort of. As far as that's possible. I was actually going to ask you about Ford."

Oh.

"What about him?"

"He should have told me what happened the other night. He is the oldest of the three of you, and I had the impression he felt responsible for you two. Maybe that's expecting too much of a 17-year-old…"

"He did ask me if I wanted him to talk to you. I told him, no."

"Huh. I bet he was relieved."

I smiled, remembering the way he hadn't given me time to think twice about my response. "Yeah, he was."

FORD LED THE CHARGE at the cabin site for the next few days, along with Frank and Dad. They worked methodically with long metal probes to find the rest of the foundation stones, mapping the perimeter of the cabin that had once rested there.

Lou and I, Bea and Donna, worked in teams, digging small test pits in and around the cabin, collecting jagged pieces of pottery, flatware, cooking utensils, parts of old bits and harnesses, various kinds of metal and bone.

At one point, Lou and I extracted flakes of interesting-looking stone. When we showed Dad, his eyes lit up. He hunched down next to Lou at her screen and took the sharp-edged piece of rock out of her hand. It didn't look like anything special. It was smooth and creamy-coffee-colored. Smiling, he turned the flakes over and over in his hand.

Lou said, "You look more excited about this than you were about that jar of gold."

"I am." Dad nodded eagerly. "This stuff was used in early flint-lock rifles, which, among other things, can date this site to very early in the settlement's history."

Kurt stopped by the site every day, and he and Dad spent a lot of time discussing the logistics of an interpretive site in a wild and remote area. They decided the installment should go nearer to the road, closer to the new toilets, for obvious reasons, and also to protect the location of the actual site for future research.

In the van and headed home for the weekend, Dad informed the group that we had more hot, sweaty work near the dusty road coming up the next week.

"Oh, goody," Lou said, a sour look on her face. "I can't wait to get back out into the blazing hot sun."

I was as grateful as everyone else that the cabin site was mostly in shade. I tried not to think about the upcoming hot, dirty work next week and focused on the weekend, instead.

When we arrived at our drop-off point at the Gold Creek campground, everyone piled out except for me and Lou, who asked Dad if she could meet up with Sherrie that afternoon. "She texted me and said she'd like a work-out partner."

He turned and leveled a lethal gaze at Lou. "*Sherrie* texted you?"

"You can call and ask her if you want." Lou's voice was innocent, as if Dad hadn't just made it clear he no longer trusted her. She started scrolling through information on her phone. "Do you have her number?"

Dad picked up his phone from the dash, climbed out of the van and walked away. I watched him dial and put the phone to his ear. Lou's expression betrayed nothing. I hoped she wasn't bluffing, because if she was lying to Dad, he'd send her home in a heartbeat. I was sweating on the seat, and I was too antsy to sit there, waiting for whatever would come next. I climbed out of the van. Lou followed me.

"Sherrie really texted you?"

She gaped at me. "I wouldn't lie to your dad, Misty."

I shrugged, too tired to argue.

Ford drove by in his truck and caught sight of us standing there. He rolled to a stop and leaned out his window. "Everything okay?"

Dad nodded and I breathed a sigh of relief. Apparently, Lou wasn't lying about Sherrie.

"Could you do me a favor?" he asked Ford. "I've got a bunch of equipment to take back to the Sheriff's office and F.S. headquarters. Sherrie invited Lou over for the evening—would you be up for driving her?"

"Sure," Ford said, and his eyes moved to mine. "You coming, too? I can drop you off at home after Lou."

I turned to Dad. "Can I—" my voice was high and squeaky, like a little kid asking for candy. I coughed to cover and lowered my voice. "Okay with you?" I asked him.

One corner of his mouth twitched. "Okay. I'll see you in a bit. Be careful." Those last two words were pointed, and directed straight at me.

LOU SEEMED UNUSUALLY ANXIOUS on the drive to the Blackwells. Her thumbs were moving across the screen of her phone so fast they were a blur. When she wasn't texting, she was running her fingers through her hair and sighing, like she couldn't wait to get to the ranch.

"Not too tired to work out?" I asked her. "I'm exhausted."

She shrugged, and I could swear she was avoiding my eyes. "It's a different kind of movement. It'll feel good to stretch out."

I wouldn't have admitted it, but I was glad Lou would be gone for the evening. I'd been distracted all day planning my own moves for our days off, ready to take the next steps in my delicate dance with Lookout—assuming he showed up. With Lou occupied, that was one less detail I had to arrange.

Ford brought the truck to a stop near the corral at the Blackwell ranch, and the first thing I noticed was Cody, leaning against his trashed Honda Civic. When he saw us, he pushed off the car, which looked like he'd spray-painted it black, and sauntered our direction.

I rolled my eyes at Lou and said, "I wonder what *he* wants?"

But she was already halfway out the door. She climbed from the truck with a big smile on her face and waved at Cody.

I slid out after her. "Lou?"

Ford came around the truck and stood next to me. When she glanced back at us, her smile faded. She giggled nervously. "It's no big deal. We're just going to see the movie in town…"

Cody stopped in front of her—really close. "You ready? We should get going." He didn't even acknowledge Ford and me.

Lou tilted her face up to Cody's and melted like ice cream. She took a breath and sighed. "Okay."

Something clenched inside me. "*Lou?*"

"Cody, give me a minute, okay?" Lou's smile tightened, but she hung onto it. "I'll be right there."

He hesitated, grunted and stalked to his car. Arms folded, he leaned against the hood and glared at the three of us.

For a few seconds, no one said anything. It was so quiet, I was aware of the pines creaking in the wind, the horses nickering in the corral, the thud of their hooves on the packed dirt. I was afraid to say anything, because I knew it was impossible to say the right thing.

Sherrie appeared on the lodge porch and came down the steps. She put up a hand to shade her eyes and waved our direction. I didn't bother to respond. I knew she wasn't waving at me.

"Lou," I said, "tell me you are not going somewhere with Cody tonight. Tell me you didn't get Sherrie to lie for you so you could do exactly what Dad told you not to do. Do you want him to send you home?" I shot a glance over at Cody's increasingly impatient stance and lowered my voice. "Besides, he's like, old. He's in college."

Lou's eyes flashed. "He's only eighteen, Misty. He graduated a year early, so he can't be as much of a loser as your dad thinks he is. And Sherrie didn't lie, exactly. She and I *are* going to work out after Cody and I get back and she *is* going to take me home."

"So." I folded my arms. "He's the one you've been texting all week." I was being accusing, judgmental, all that. But I couldn't believe Lou would keep all this from me.

"Quit making a federal case out of it. I told him I'd do this before your dad laid down the law, and I didn't want to cancel at the last minute. Becca and Matt were coming, but they ended up having to work tonight—"

"Yeah, I bet. Lou, this is so stupid."

"Just because you've kissed dating goodbye," she glanced at Ford, "doesn't mean the rest of us have to. And your dad will only send me home if he finds out. Your call."

Lou slammed her bag over her shoulder. "I'm outta here." She marched toward Cody without a backward glance.

"Lou!" I yelled, following her, but Ford grabbed my arm.

"Misty, let her go."

When I jerked away and turned on him, he threw up his hands. "Whoa," he said. "I come in peace."

I stood there, staring at Ford, experiencing complete brain lock. Car doors thudded shut behind me. Cody's car growled past us, followed by a cloud of dust. Lou was gone.

I slumped against Ford's truck. He leaned back next to me and crossed his arms. The lowering sun was hot on the back of my head, and I could feel angry tears of betrayal gathering at the corners of my eyes. *I would not cry in front of Ford.* I rubbed at my eyes like I had an itch.

Ford cleared his throat. "Look…" He paused, like he was searching for exactly the right word to say next. I wondered what his response was going to be to Lou's "kissed dating goodbye" comment. Amazing how someone you love can also make you feel completely humiliated. "Unless I'm wrong about you two," he continued, "I mean, you guys aren't planning on starting a family after high school or anything, are you?"

Seriously? I gave him what I hoped was an extremely withering side-long glance. "Don't be stupid."

"Only checking. I'm just saying, I know you and Lou are close and all, but at some point, you're going to have to let some other people in."

"People?" I pushed off the truck and whirled to face him. "What *people?*"

He looked past me. "Well—"

"He's *so* not right for her, and you know it."

"Okay, I admit I think the guy's a jerk." His mouth set in a line. "But Lou's not nine—she's almost seventeen and he's not some forty-three-year-old pervert. He's not that much older than I am…"

"He's an adult—even though he doesn't act like it—and she's not…we're…not." Visions of past summers flickered in my head like old home movies, me and Lou and our friends, running around, playing hide-and-seek in the fields and hazy woods of Alton. It wasn't that long ago.

I saw something in Ford's eyes.

"What?" I asked.

"She'll be okay. Lou's led a different life than you, Misty."

"What do you mean?"

"Stuff happens on the rodeo circuit. Cowgirl's been around."

My mouth dropped open and I took a step toward him. We would have been nose-to-nose, except I had to crane my neck because Ford was about four inches taller than me. "She is not like that. Lou's a flirt, but she's not…" I stopped. I didn't want to admit that Ford was actually echoing my thoughts in the park the other night about Lou and her rodeo background.

He put up his hands. "I think she's stupid to sneak around behind your dad's back. Pretty sure she can take care of herself, though. Besides, what are you gonna do? Tell your dad?"

What would I tell my dad?

Ford said, "So much for best friends for life."

He was right. She would never forgive me if I ratted her out. And yet, what are friends for? Was I supposed to keep her secrets, even when she was doing something I knew was bad for her? I met Ford's eyes.

"But friends don't let friends drive off with jerks?"

Great. Now Ford was reading my mind. I really was the most transparent person on the planet. I sighed and flopped against the truck.

He said nothing, just scuffed the heel of his boot in the gravel. Finally, he nudged me with his elbow. I attempted a smile. The poor guy had endured more than enough girl drama for an afternoon.

"She'll be okay, Mist," he said, again, and it sounded like an apology. "When she comes back, talk to her. You know, the way you guys do. She's not stupid. She's bored."

I knew he was trying to help. But I was so sad and confused, and it didn't help to think that I was boring her. Lou was changing before my eyes, and I didn't get it. Why was she taking these crazy chances?

"How come you're not bored?" I asked abruptly. Even to my own ears, I sounded grumpy. I tried to lighten up, failed. "Your family lives near Missoula, right? You've got to be used to more excitement than this."

I thought he was going to answer me, but he didn't. Instead, he smiled at me, like he was about to tell the best secret in the world, and that smile—it made me feel shivery, warm and wanted, in a way I never had before. After feeling rejected by Lou, all I wanted was to close my eyes and wrap that feeling around me.

Still, when he reached out, I instinctively pulled back a little. But he just nudged me out of the way to open the passenger door of the truck. "C'mon," he said. "I better get you home."

WE WERE NEARING THE turn-off to the house when Ford said, "What are you going to tell your dad?"

He asked the question as if we'd been having a normal conversation during the trip home, instead of the reality—me, slouched in silence the entire drive. I thought hiding Lou's activities from Dad would be wrong. At the same time, I wanted to give her the chance to do the right thing. A world champion at second guessing, I also thought I might be making a big deal out of nothing.

Ford glanced at me.

"Sorry," I said, straightening up. "I don't know. Maybe if she's not too late, I'll…" I slumped back down. "I'm not a very good liar."

Ford shifted in his seat. "I don't think I heard Lou ask you to lie for her."

Kurt's truck was parked behind our Suburban when we pulled up to the house. We walked through the front door and were immediately engulfed in the aroma of pepperoni pizza. Dad and Kurt were at the kitchen table, laughing around mouthfuls of food.

"Hey, you two." Kurt waved us over. "Thought you'd never get here, so we started without you." Half the pizza was gone already. Dad had a big smile on his face, kicked back in his chair, totally relaxed.

I stood there for a minute and watched my dad, amazed at his transformation. He'd been having a great time with Kurt, and the thought hit me—Mom had been Dad's best friend. Now that she was gone, who did Dad have to talk to? At least I had Lou. Or, I used to have her.

"Since Lou is taking the night off from cooking," Dad said around a bite of pizza, "I figured you deserve a break, too. What took you so long?" His question sounded innocent, but it was directed at Ford, not me.

I answered quickly, before Ford had a chance to respond. "We stopped to talk with some of those kids we met the other day." I figured that was kind of the truth.

Ford said, "Cool!" grabbed a plate, tossed three huge slices of pizza on it, and pulled up a chair. He started filling Kurt in on his latest finds at the site.

Not quite ready to meet Dad's eyes, I placed my bag on the coffee table, took a deep breath, and headed for the fridge. "How about a salad, guys?"

Dad blocked my way with his leg and pulled me into the chair next to Ford. "Misty, take the night off, for Pete's sake." He shook his head. "We'll survive one evening without antioxidants."

The others laughed, and Kurt held out a plate in front of Ford. "Help me out, here."

Ford slapped a greasy slice on the plate and set it in front of me. I sat there, cheeks burning under the expectant gaze of three pairs of male eyes.

"Eat!" they said in unison.

I ate.

Kurt and Ford joked back and forth with Dad, which made it easier for me to pretend I wasn't worried about Lou. I could barely get a word in, even if I'd wanted to say something about where she was, which I didn't.

After dinner, Kurt and Dad cleaned up by tossing the paper plates in the trash, and the guys decided to follow Dad out to the barn to see how much of the "bone horse" he'd reconstructed. I knew Dad would go into Professor Stevens mode, and I was more than aware of Ford's growing infatuation with archaeology.

He asked, "You're coming, too, aren't you?"

I shook my head and shooed him toward Kurt and Dad. "I've already seen everything." I hesitated. "You could come see me when you're done, though." I pointed toward the back yard and shrugged a shoulder. "You know, if you wanted."

His eyes lit up and he said, "I'll see you out there." He backed away from me, then turned and eagerly followed the other men into the barn.

I settled in my usual spot against the gnarled tree trunk and prepared to wait. About thirty minutes later, I'd finished one chapter and was well into the next. I glanced up from my page. The light was fading. Shadows and tree lines smudged together. I hadn't seen Lookout for a while, so I wasn't that disappointed he hadn't shown himself. It was why I'd felt comfortable inviting Ford to join me, and I was confident he would.

But I completely forgot about Ford when I heard the familiar sounds I'd been hoping to hear for days—muffled hoof-fall through decades of accumulated leaf litter.

This time, Lookout stepped toward me without hesitation, dropped his head and pushed his big nose through my hair. The whiskers on his chin tickled my ear, and I was engulfed in the musky scent of wild horse.

I held my breath and slowly laid down the book. He met my gaze when I looked up—no hint of shyness. Mustering my most soothing tone, I murmured, "Hello. How are you, my smelly friend?" At the same time, I reached up and rubbed the back of my hand along the side of his jaw. His hide quivered and the eye I could see rolled with the movement of my hand. That was all. No startling, no sound. He stood his ground, waiting to see what would happen next.

I could barely suppress an urge to stand up and release the victory yell bubbling up inside me. Lookout tolerated my touch—he even seemed to enjoy it.

The horse was so near I could sense when something changed for him. His muscles clenched before I heard the source of his tension. His ears swiveled toward the sound of crackling twigs and shifting underbrush. He bobbed his head up, pivoted a few steps away and snorted. His nostrils flared.

But he didn't leave. He stayed with me, stamping one hoof, completely focused on who or what was coming at us.

I was scrambling to my feet, ready to run, when Ford shoved his way through the tangled branches. He stopped in mid-step, staring from Lookout to me. My relief that Ford wasn't the cougar was quickly replaced by panic. How would I explain this? I sank back down to the base of the tree and wished with all my heart I could become invisible.

SIXTEEN

I PRESSED MY HANDS against the ground and my back against the tree. Ford's gaze moved from the horse to me, and then back again.

Lookout returned the stare. He sniffed the air and seemed more curious than alarmed. After a few seconds, he flung up his head, snorted and wheeled around.

Weaving deftly between the trees, he vanished from sight.

Ford threw me a guarded look, as if he wasn't sure who I was anymore. While he approached me, I ran story options through my head.

I could pretend my connection with Lookout was a chance encounter. But I hadn't been kidding when I'd told Ford I wasn't good at lying. My poker face was the worst. Besides, the fact was, I really wanted Ford to know about Lookout.

He squatted down so we were face-to-face. I returned his gaze, my calmness revealing the truth to him. I watched his expression go from surprise to understanding. "This becoming a thing for you two?"

I bit my lip and shook my head. "I've been trying to…" What was I trying to do? "He doesn't seem threatening—"

"What are you thinking?" Ford cut in. "He's a wild animal. One with a history of violence. If you've suddenly decided to get into horses, you picked the wrong one."

He sounded almost angry and that surprised me. I pulled back. "I know," I said, fiddling with the pages of my book. But I hated how defensive I sounded, how weak. I was proud of the progress I'd made with Lookout.

I took a breath and met his gaze straight on. "I thought that if he's friendly with people, and he doesn't seem so wild, they won't kill him. He doesn't deserve to die. He's damaged by what's happened to him and he's trying to survive the only way he knows how. He just needs a chance."

Ford stared back at me and I tried to read the emotions passing across his face. The slam of a car door echoed from the front of the house. Ford stood up. "Kurt and I are takin' off."

"Are you going to tell him?"

Ford drew in a breath and blew it out. "I had a feeling Lou wasn't the only one with secrets."

Enough secrets. I made the decision fast, before I had time to be scared by all the implications. I stood up and faced him. "You can tell Kurt. I won't be mad."

I sounded braver than I felt. A lot of people had been looking for the stallion, and I knew they wouldn't be happy that I could've told them weeks ago where to find him. I thought about how angry Dad would be, but I pushed my fear aside. "Really, it'll be okay. Or I can tell Kurt, if you want."

Head down, he stood there, not a word. Now it was his turn to run scenarios through his head. Whether he liked it or not, Ford had learned some things about Lou and me this evening that he probably wished he didn't know. This could be a turning point for all of us, for Lookout, and for every relationship in my life that currently meant the most to me.

We both listened to the rumble of Kurt's truck moving toward the highway. Even after silence returned to the orchard, Ford didn't move. Finally, he said, "You should be careful."

I let out a sigh of relief…although, he hadn't actually said he wouldn't tell anyone.

He squinted down at me. "Have you really kissed dating goodbye?"

My mouth dropped open. This? Right now? "I…well…" My shoulders sagged, and all my newly acquired confidence evaporated. "It's complicated."

He chuckled—one of those laughs like he couldn't believe what he'd just heard. He reached out and took the tips of my fingers in his. His skin was rough and warm. "Mist?" he said.

I tilted my head up—our faces were so close. I wasn't sure what he was going to do next, but I hoped he worked fast, because *my* hands were going to be sweaty in seconds. "Ford?"

"You are…interesting."

"Wow," I said. "*Interesting*. Awesome."

He grinned that slow, easy grin, dropped my hand and gave me a little shove. "*Be careful*," he said again. "See ya later."

I watched him stride out of the orchard, weaving through the trees, reminding me of Lookout. Except, Ford was walking in the opposite direction.

WHEN I FINISHED MY shower and emerged from the bathroom, I found Lou sitting on the couch, staring into the fire. She didn't look up. I felt smug, at first, that she was home so early. Her date hadn't gone well, that was obvious from the forlorn set of her mouth, and her unwillingness to meet my eyes.

But in minutes, guilt kicked in. I hoped things hadn't gone horribly wrong with her and Cody. She was hurting, I could see that. I sat down beside her.

"Everything okay?" I ventured.

"Fine."

I waited for more, but she didn't offer any further explanation, and I spent the rest of the weekend wavering between extreme curiosity and a desire to pretend like our fight and her date with Cody had never happened.

All day Saturday, her laptop sat on the coffee table, untouched. Her phone was strangely silent. It seemed like whatever she'd been doing with Cody had come to a mysteriously abrupt end.

MONDAY MORNING'S SUNRISE motivated nothing inside me but a desire to sleep forever. When I heard Dad grinding the coffee downstairs, I forced my eyes open and rolled onto my back. I squinted up at the beam above my bed where Mom's initials were carved, and allowed myself a brief fantasy in which she was downstairs, making breakfast with Dad. She would know what to do about Lou and Lookout…and Ford. I wouldn't have to worry about Dad anymore.

Snapping back to reality, I crawled out of bed. Lou trailed behind me, wordless, down the stairs. She looked even less enthusiastic about the day than I felt.

When we arrived at the campground to pick up the crew, Ford slid into the front passenger seat of the van and threw a

"Good morning!" back to Lou and me like nothing had happened over the weekend. The others piled in one-by-one. I felt jangly and out of sorts.

I stole a glance at Lou. She had a far-off look and was tearing at her fingernails, which she'd already worked down to the pink. I knew she had stuff going on in her head she might never share with me, and I felt like a bad friend because I wasn't sure I wanted to know what she'd been doing with Cody.

Last weekend had seemed *almost* like old times. We'd eaten junk food, watched a couple chick flicks on the computer, hiked the ridge for hours and shot dozens of pictures. But she practically oozed melancholy and often seemed distracted, like she was listening to something I couldn't quite hear.

Bea, Frank and Donna were sitting in front of us. I viewed the backs of their heads and wondered if their lives were as complicated as ours. They had their own little senior-adult club. They were cool old people, though. All this thinking about Mom when she was young, sorting through her pictures, listening to Dad and Ford go on and on about the history of the area and the Blackwell site—I began to wonder what my older co-workers' stories were.

I knew Frank had served in wars—he wore his U.S. Marines cap proudly—and yet he was one of the most peaceful people I'd ever met. Donna was an Idaho earth-mother to the core, but she was childless. There was Bea, who'd been on this earth so much longer than any of us. I could only imagine all the changes in the world she must have seen. I tried to grasp the fact that they were young once, like me. They'd known tragedy, success, failure, starting and starting again.

There they sat in front of me—gray hair, creaky bones, crinkly wrinkles, gloved fingers wrapped around travel mugs filled with strong coffee. They talked about their weekend, the site, and reminisced about other journeys they'd traveled together. They always seemed so steady.

In the front seats sat the two males who made my life so perplexing. Ford, who could cause me to wheel between happiness, comfort, anger and painful embarrassment, all in the space of five minutes. And there was Dad. Dad…*without Mom.*

It was as if I could see the words materialize in the air in front of me. That's who he was now. This new person, this *Dad-without-Mom*—in which state he was pretty much like everyone else in the vehicle—someone I was only now learning to love and barely beginning to understand.

When we pulled into the site, I climbed out of the van and drew in a gulp of fresh air. Grabbing a trowel-filled bucket, I wandered into the trees toward the cabin site. I wanted to see all we'd accomplished the week before to help fortify me for the work we had cut out for us along the road.

When I arrived at the stakes and flagging tape we had used to mark off the site with meticulous care the previous week, I gasped and dropped everything. For a few seconds, I couldn't move or make a sound.

I took a breath and yelled, "Dad!" as loud as I could.

Within seconds, he burst from the trees. "Misty, are you okay?" Running my direction, his eyes moved from me, scanning the area for wild animals or bad guys. He saw the mess in front of me and stopped cold.

He stood at the edge of our disastrously mangled test pits and swore under his breath, while digging his phone from one of the many pockets on his vest.

Ford was the first one after Dad to join us. He sucked in a breath and stopped beside me. "Mist, who would do this?" Everyone else piled up behind and around him, their questions turning into groans of disappointment and anger.

The neat, square test pits we'd dug on the grid Dad created had been replaced by dozens of deep, haphazard gashes in the earth. I knew Dad would feel every one of those gashes like a cut to his own skin. There were hills of fine dust everywhere— fresh dirt that had been run through a screen.

Phone to his ear, Dad muttered, "Somebody was at this most of the night." His tone shifted. "Yeah, Kurt, I need you out here… No, not more animal sightings. This time we've got human trouble." He listened for a few seconds, hung up with a terse, "Okay," and began picking his way through the piles of dirt and debris.

Ford asked again, "Who would trash the site like this?"

I met Dad's eyes.

"Pothunters," I said.

Lou's scrunched face smoothed and her eyes widened. "Wait. Dr. Stevens, you mean those people you talked about when we found the cabin site?"

Kurt arrived while Dad was explaining again how much cash people could get—especially internationally—for historic and pre-historic artifacts.

Frank pulled off his cap. "Recklessly destroy a site like this?" He gave his knee an angry whip with his hat. "I know you talked about this, but I guess I'm still surprised. Hard to believe there's that much demand."

"No, dear." Bea put a hand on his arm. "I've read about this. It's sort of a crisis in the world of archaeology, isn't it Dr. Stevens?"

"This is what I was trying to tell you," Dad said, nodding at Bea's comment. "The problem is significant. Collectors all over the world are fascinated by anything that has to do with Native Americans or the Old West. And there are plenty of unscrupulous collectors who don't ask questions about how the artifacts are obtained. The sale of artifacts has even been used to launder drug money internationally."

"But we haven't found anything that valuable yet," I said. It made no sense to me. "It's interesting to us and adds to the history of the area, be we haven't discovered anything that would attract someone to take this kind of risk—"

I caught the look of anguish in Lou's eye. I'd almost forgotten. Ford turned from me to Lou, who was biting her lower lip. The gold. And who had Lou blabbed our gold discovery to? Practically every kid in town, that night at the park. But no one else in the crew knew what had happened that night.

"You got here fast," Dad said, turning to Kurt. He sounded surprised.

"I was checking fences nearby. I was already on my way when you called." He gave a low whistle. "I knew this was a possibility but as long as we kept the gold find to ourselves, I was hoping…"

Dad's head shot up. "You knew this was a possibility?"

"No point in keeping it a secret, now. Word's obviously gotten out." He gave Dad an apologetic look. "I should have told you the minute you found this site, and that jar of rocks. But in my defense, all the locals—all the ones with any sense, anyway—truly believe it's just a story, one they don't generally share with outsiders."

"What, exactly, *are* you talking about, Kurt?" I watched the muscles in Dad's jaw clench. His voice was tinged with suppressed anger and impatience, a tone that usually caused people to snap to and carry out his requests without hesitation. Even I never pushed him when I heard that tone.

Kurt stuffed his hands in his pockets and scowled. He scanned the site and turned back to the crew. "What we have here, folks, is another gold rush."

For a beat, we were quiet. Then we all started asking questions at the same time.

"Hold on." He threw up his hands. "Locals tell a story that may partly explain the gold you found, and there are many versions of it. Now that we know the rocks in that jar actually contain gold, I'll tell you the version I was planning to share with Dr. Stevens. It makes the most sense and has the ring of truth. But I think the first thing we need to do is clean this mess up."

Dad agreed, and we spent the rest of the day screening all the dirt the weekend's vandals had disturbed. The adrenaline shot we'd received when we saw the vandalized site, mixed with our anger, seemed to energize the group. We bagged and tagged without a lot of extra talk. At the end of the day, we refilled the holes as best we could.

As we were finishing, Kurt straightened, put a hand on his lower back and stretched.

"You have people who can plant a poison oak screen?" Dad asked him. "That would be a good deterrent to intruders. It would at least keep the curious away until we come up with a better way to protect the site."

"I have some Service Corps interns that can handle it. I'll move this task to the top of their list." Kurt looked over at Ford. "Interested in joining me for a stake-out tonight? The vandals probably won't be back. But it's worth sleeping on the ground one night, on the chance they return to the scene of the crime."

Ford said, "Heck, yeah, I'm in."

But the crew was frustrated. You could see it in the set of Dad's jaw. Bea's determined movements, Frank's somber face. Even with all that, Lou seemed unusually quiet. The entire afternoon, she'd moved like a furtive animal trying to avoid notice.

Shuffling to the van, screen between us, my curiosity finally won out. She was pale, with an exhausted droop to her shoulders, struggling more than usual under the weight of the screen.

"You okay?" I peered at her, trying to see her eyes, eyes she'd kept averted from me all day. When she lifted her head, the fear and guilt on her face were unmistakable. I dropped my end of the screen and moved closer. "Lou, what's wrong. Please, *please* tell me."

She glanced around, as if she was afraid someone might hear us. I thought she would say what was wrong, but she gave her head a stubborn shake and continued trudging toward the van, the screen dragging behind her. I hoisted my end, and we moved along in strained silence.

"I feel sick." Lou's voice was barely audible. "I want to go home."

After we'd stowed the gear, she crawled into the van, laid her head back on the seat and closed her eyes.

I gave her hand a quick squeeze. "We'll be home, soon."

But I was wrong. The group decided to meet at the campground to hear Kurt's story about the site. Lou trailed behind everyone else as we walked to Bea's campsite. She threw herself into a camp chair near Frank and Donna's tent with a shaky sigh.

Kurt sat for a minute at the picnic table where the others had gathered. After everyone settled in, he cleared his throat. "I guess I'll start from the beginning. Like I said, the locals don't believe anything sinister happened in the early days of the Gold Creek settlement. Stories get blown out of proportion over time. But this one has persisted for generations." He paused, shrugged. "After today and your gold find, I'm starting to think it might not be so far-fetched, parts of it, anyway."

"It all started back East, in New York City."

SEVENTEEN

I GRABBED TWO BOTTLES of water and handed one to Lou as I dropped into a chair beside her, across from the picnic table where Kurt was telling his story.

"When gold was discovered in California, a syndicate of East Coast investors hired a young man named Percival Blackwell, a minerals engineer, to prospect along the West Coast and report back to them. He carried a copy of a contract that stipulated he'd receive ten percent of the proceeds from any discoveries he made. Roughing it for a while in the squalid, rough-and-tumble mining camps of California, he staked a few claims, and heard rumors about the Juliet Mountains. Eventually, he made his way here.

"Percival was the one who discovered the gold in Gold Creek and reported his find to investors. After receiving their go-ahead, he staked a claim on the syndicate's behalf for the mineral rights in the area of Gold Creek—and Opal Creek, too, for good measure.

"The syndicate hired him to oversee their operations, and he built the cabin at Gold Creek to be near the mining works—"

Frank cut in. "So, other sites along Gold Creek are associated with the mining operation?"

"Yes," Dad said, "and most of those sites have already been recorded. Except Blackwell's cabin, until now."

"Over time," Kurt continued, "more settlers moved into the valley. One of them, a man named Nelson Downing, was a farmer with a daughter of marriageable age, Sarah.

"According to the Old Church register, it wasn't long before Blackwell married Sarah. In time, she gave birth to a son, Robert."

"Bob Blackwell's grandfather?" Ford asked.

Kurt nodded. "All of the information I've shared with you is well-established and verifiable fact. However, after the birth entry in the church register, the story moves into the realm of myth and legend.

"Percival Blackwell was an intelligent, resourceful individual. He was not, however, a friendly man. The Downings were, by all accounts, well-liked and pillars of the community. But Blackwell and Sarah kept to themselves."

"Poor Sarah." Lou echoed my thoughts. I thought of Cody, and wondered if Lou could somehow relate to Sarah's story. I hoped not. I wanted few things more than to pretend Cody had never happened into our lives. I hoped Lou felt the same.

"Yeah," Kurt said, "but there's more. The other settlers would have found their behavior strange, to say the least. In a remote settlement like this one, your neighbors were your world and often your lifeline. Bartering with each other and the Native bands who traveled through would have been their means of survival.

"Hard to imagine, today, how tight-knit the community would have been. They helped build each other's houses and barns, worked together to plow and harvest. Church socials were special events that all the settlers attended with enthusiasm. They wouldn't have dreamed of doing otherwise, nor wanted to. They all supported each other every step of the way from welcoming new life to memorializing and burying the dead, except the Blackwells.

"The legend says Percival made it crystal clear: He was not in these mountains to stay, and he tended to be disdainful toward anyone who was. With his share of the proceeds from the gold operation, he was well-off and neither asked for nor offered assistance. He fiercely guarded his family's privacy, to the point of not allowing Sarah to have any visitors, including her family. This, along with the fact that many people resented that all the profits from the mining operation were going back East, did not make Percival a popular individual.

"That animosity may be the source of some of the more vicious rumors about Percival, but it's hard to separate fact from drama, here."

Ford fished a potato chip from the bag Bea placed on the table and shoved it in his mouth. Between crunches he asked, "Like, what kind of rumors?"

"Some said he…" Kurt paused, and his look turned sour. "Well, they said he beat Sarah and their child in fits of rage, for one."

"Oh, no," Bea murmured.

"But it's the rumor I'm about to tell you that may have led to Percival's ultimate demise. According to the Downings and despite Percival's growing wealth, over time he came to believe the syndicate was cheating him. Percival believed he should have received more than the share originally agreed upon. After all, he'd discovered the gold, and he was handling the management of the operation.

"He became more and more angry and withdrawn, and then, folks started noticing that he would be gone for days at a time, leaving Sarah alone and the mine in the hands of his second-in-command. Locals swore they saw him in the little shanty town the gold boom had created, sneaking to and from the gold trader's office late at night, long after closing.

"Since Percival had an assistant, an accountant of sorts, who handled the trading part of the operation, folks wondered why Percival needed to visit the assayer so frequently. The gold trader swore that people were mistaken about Percival's midnight visits, but they were sure he'd bought the trader's silence.

"The Downings were convinced Percival had found his own gold vein, maybe in Opal Creek Canyon, was mining it by himself—and keeping all the profits. Problem was, since he never staked a claim, and appeared to be trying to keep it a secret, the settlers suspected that Percival was mining somewhere within the syndicate's claim."

"He was robbing his associates," Dad said.

"Sounds like it. That was what people were whispering. They suspected he'd found a rich vein somewhere nearby and was secretly amassing his own substantial fortune. Things went along like that for months, people becoming more and more convinced Percival was up to no good.

"The incident with the first wild stallion, where Percival killed the horse, happened about this time. Not long after he shot the horse, the story comes to an abrupt end—with Percival's death."

Kurt paused.

"Don't keep us on pins and needles," Bea exclaimed. "Tell us what happened."

"Simple answer? He got thrown from his horse and broke his neck." Kurt took a swig from his water bottle and shrugged. "He left one morning, on another of his secret expeditions, and the next day his horse showed up at the cabin without him. Despite his lack of popularity in the community, Sarah's family was well-liked and respected. As soon as she put out the alarm, a search party was formed. They soon found Percival at the bottom of a ravine near here, neck broken.

"The thing is, Percival was an expert horseman. He'd been wandering around in rugged terrain on horseback for decades, and he knew this area—its dangers and pitfalls—intimately. The locals weren't inclined to accept his death as a tragic accident. Most figured his associates back East had somehow gotten the word that he was robbing them, and they sent someone to get rid of him."

Kurt waited while we took that in. "But that's not all," he continued. "This is really when the ghost horse legend began."

I straightened up. "How so?"

"The other theory about his death was that the angry specter of the stallion Blackwell shot got his revenge."

"Sweet," Ford said.

Donna shuddered. "Creepy. What happened to Sarah?"

"She and Robert moved back to her folks' farm. That was Bob Blackwell's childhood home, and he inherited it. It's now the current Blackwell Ranch. But Sarah swore she knew nothing about a gold stash, and she certainly never appeared wealthy. The settlers searched all around the old cabin, much like our vandals this weekend, and never found so much as a fleck of gold. The little jar that you all found is the first solid evidence to give any credence to the legend. If Percival had a fortune in gold hidden somewhere, he took the secret of its location with him when he died."

"I'll be thumped down and shot at," Bea exclaimed. "Buried treasure!"

Frank chuckled. "This gets better and better."

Kurt smiled, but I saw him catch the grim look on Dad's face, and his smile faded. "It's just a local legend," he said defensively. "The people around here keep a pretty tight lid on it, and for good reason—same reason the Forest Service doesn't put it in any of our literature. If word got out a chest of gold might be buried in this area, this little episode of pot hunting would look like child's play, which it very well might be. The kids in these parts tell stories about the gold and the ghost horse around bonfires at night. Some tourist may have heard, and here we are."

Kurt took in Ford, Lou and me. "The local teens like the ghost story aspect of it. I think adults around here tell the story because it's about an unpopular outsider who got his, in the end. Percival was not a nice man, and he suffered an accident that most people believe was divine justice."

Lou squirmed in the chair next to me.

"Still," Dad said, "I wish I'd known."

Kurt nodded. "I do, too, in hindsight. But it's policy at this office to withhold information about Percival and the legend unless it's necessary to reveal it. No evidence exists to substantiate the speculations. I didn't think it would impact our plans for this project…" He trailed off.

"Kurt," I said, "the Opal Creek Canyon, where the wild horse band hangs out? That's where Percival shot the original stallion, right? It said so in some of those articles we read. Is that why they think he was mining there?"

"Yep. Actually, some people believe that's the real reason he shot the horse. He was afraid if people searched for the stallion, they'd discover his hidden mine. But again, no one's ever seen any evidence of mining in the Opal Creek drainage."

Kurt stood up and stretched. "Not long after Percival's death, the U.S. economy went belly-up in one of the many financial crashes of the late 1800s. The syndicate, which had mined everything of worth gold-wise out of Gold Creek, abandoned the works and moved their interests closer to home. The bad economy, combined with a number of very harsh winters, resulted in many failed farms. People gave up and moved to greener pastures, literally. Not many folks remained after that, and those who stayed, tried to help each other survive."

"Makes sense," Frank said. "Still, if there was any chance of there being buried treasure around here, I wouldn't think people would ever stop looking for it."

Kurt responded with a non-committal nod. "The harshness of their lives may have kept whispered rumors of buried treasure alive in their dreams. For instance, the Downings purchased the mineral rights to the area, and Sarah inherited them. But it seems more practical concerns kept people like the Downings on their land, planting and harvesting, scraping out an existence in the hope that if they held on, better times would come. And for some, it worked out. Look at the Blackwell Ranch now."

LOU WENT STRAIGHT FOR the shower and bed when we got home. I was sure she was scared about something, and I was also certain the thing that troubled her was bigger than her slip about the gold at the park the other night. But I didn't follow her up the stairs to our loft. Pushing Lou to tell me what was wrong would be worse than useless. I knew my friend. Confiding in me would have to be her idea.

After dinner, I took my quilt and book and headed for the barn. I dumped my stuff on a hay bale, grabbed the lead for Rosa and headed outside. Since there had been no cougar sightings for weeks, we'd resumed leaving her in the pasture during the day. She came to me easily, and I rubbed her neck as I hooked the lead to her halter.

"How have you been today, Beautiful?" I whispered in her ear. "Have you been lonely, or does Lookout come visit you, too?"

She whinnied and rolled an eye at me, like she was answering. "I wish I spoke horse."

"It takes time."

I jumped at the sound of Dad's voice behind me. "But it looks like you're learning her language." He was leaning against the door frame, watching us. He stepped back, and I led Rosa into the barn.

"I don't think I'll ever understand what goes on in their minds. But at least they're starting to feel less…alien."

Dad lifted an eyebrow. "They?" He made a show of looking around. "There other horses here I don't know about?"

I shrugged it off. "You know what I mean. Getting to know Rosa makes me feel like maybe I could be more comfortable with horses in general."

Dad seemed to accept my explanation, but I gave myself a mental forehead slap. *I had to be more careful.*

He helped me herd Rosa into her stall and we fed and watered her together. We stepped back and watched her over the gate.

"Is Lou okay?" Dad asked.

"I think so. She said she feels sick, though." I looked at him out of the corner of my eye, but he was watching Rosa. "Hopefully, she'll be better after a good night's sleep."

"I hope so." He turned to me. "How about you? How are you doing?"

I avoided his eyes and grabbed my quilt and book. "I'm okay. I'm going to go read for a while."

I slipped past him and through the door. I had a feeling he was watching me, and I sighed with relief when the house came between me and his field of vision. The sun had yet to work its way down behind the mountains, but the evening was settling into pleasantly warm. The insect buzz halted as I walked among them and started up again behind me. I settled into my usual spot in the dappled shade under the tree, every sense tuned behind me to any hint Dad was coming. When he didn't make an appearance, I relaxed and opened my book.

I hadn't seen a sign of Lookout since Friday night, and had no reason to believe I would. Even if he did decide to grace me with his presence, I couldn't expect him until dusk, so I had plenty of time. I moved my head to a less bumpy spot against the tree trunk and closed my eyes. A cool breeze under the orchard's canopy caressed my skin. The insect buzz created white noise that shut out the world, and I could feel myself dozing off.

A gentle bump against my head woke me. I stretched out my hand, brushed a velvety nose and breathed in the pungent odor of wild stallion. Without opening my eyes, I smiled. "Hello, Lookout."

When I did look up, he took a step back from me. I tried to think what I should do next with the stallion, but it was hard because he kept nudging my head, and despite how comfortable I was beginning to feel around horses, he was still huge and smelly, with giant hooves that kept clomping perilously close to where I was sitting.

"Stop, Lookout," I whined, pushing his nose away as gently, but firmly, as I dared. I stood up slowly, but the book I'd forgotten in my lap thudded to the ground. He startled at that and took a hop to the side.

The sun was setting and we didn't have much time. For obvious, cougar-related reasons, I didn't think either of us should be in the orchard much after dark. I stepped toward him. "It's okay, baby boy."

He took another step back. I stopped, and so did he. I took a step forward, and again he moved back. It reminded me of the night we first met at Gold Creek, when he had seemed to mirror each move I made. *What was he thinking?*

I took one step back. Lookout took a step toward me. I took another step back and again he followed me. I moved to the side, and so did he. We moved like that, forward and back, side to side, Lookout mimicking each of my moves. It was comical—the orchard two-step.

"Do you waltz?" I asked, curtseying.

He swiveled his ears toward me and snorted.

I laughed. "I'll take that as a *no*."

Lookout tensed and swung his head to the side. After a few seconds, the stallion trotted away from me and stopped, several rows of trees between us.

I took a quick breath when a man's form appeared in the trees—and breathed it out when I saw the man was not my father, but Ford.

"Over here," I called, waving, and he headed in my direction. I felt giddy coming off my dance with Lookout, and I couldn't wait to tell Ford.

He grinned down at me. "Hi. I thought Lookout might be here…" His voice trailed off when he caught sight of the mustang.

The horse turned and took another step into the trees.

"It's okay, Lookout," I called.

But he was gone, smooth as dusk.

Ford stared after him. "Has he ever come closer to you than that?"

"Couldn't get much closer." His eyes got bigger and bigger while I described our recent dance lesson and Lookout's fascination with my hair. I hoped he wouldn't lecture me about the dangers of wild animals, but we seemed to be past that. It made me happy that he seemed as excited as I felt.

"I've played those kinds of games with Grandpa's horse, but he was born in captivity and raised messing around like that.

The fact that a wild mustang would do that with you," he shook his head. "That's incredible."

"Right? It's cool, huh?"

He turned toward the last place we'd seen Lookout. "He really is different, isn't he?"

"I don't think he's that weird-looking." I jumped to Lookout's defense. "Not like everyone makes out—"

Ford touched my arm. "I didn't mean that—I saw the ears, and you're right, he's kind of awesome. I mean, it's crazy the way he *is*. The way he is with you, anyway."

I reached down to pick up my stuff, and Ford took my novel, looked it over and handed it back without comment. "Horses can be like that, though," he said. "They have unique personalities, like people. The reasons we like someone don't always make sense."

"I wish I knew what to do next."

We hiked through the tall grass in the dimming light, parting and coming back together around apple trees, in a silence that was surprisingly not awkward. When we broke into the open, Ford made an abrupt swerve around the last tree and stopped in front of me. "I know!" he said. "Hide-and-seek."

I stared at him, puzzled.

"When I was a little kid, I used to play hide-and-seek with my grandpa's horse. Grandpa would give me a horse treat, like a piece of apple, and he'd hang onto the horse, or distract him. I would hide somewhere in the pasture—behind a horse shed or," he pointed toward the orchard, "up a tree—then Grandpa'd let the horse come find me."

I fantasized for a few seconds about playing a game like that with Lookout. But, would I get the chance? "Yeah, actually, I meant I was wondering what to do concerning Lookout's ultimate…"

"Destiny?"

"Sooner or later, I have to tell Kurt or Dad or somebody, or let things play out. And who knows what will happen to Lookout?"

The floodlights flashed on when we neared the porch. I dropped my book at the step on the way to Ford's truck, but kept the quilt wrapped around me. Only a trace of sunset remained. My eyes had become accustomed to the fading light, and I hadn't realized how late it was.

"Probably sooner than later," Ford said. "Kurt says the volunteers are coming back next week, to work with the researchers from Japan and finish the herd count." He leaned against the truck. "Sorry, but they sound determined to capture Lookout, or do whatever they have to do to stop him. Kurt's promised Bob Blackwell they'll get rid of the horse, one way or another."

I stomped my foot. "I'm getting so close to…something."

"Sorry to be the bearer of bad news." He really did look sympathetic.

"It's not your fault. Hey, are you leaving already? Did you see Dad?"

He shook his head. "I'm going out to the site to keep Kurt company—no way I'm missing a stakeout. Do you think those pothunters will show up, again?" His body was practically vibrating, he was so excited. "I hope they do."

"Whoa, Indiana. Be careful out there." But he hadn't answered my question. "Did you need something from Dad?"

He looked down at me, then up at the house. "I…just…stopped on my way out. I knocked at the house, but no one answered, so…" he tilted his head toward the orchard.

"Lou's in bed, I think."

"That's weird. I pictured Lou as sort of nocturnal."

"She is, usually. She said she felt sick, so she crashed early."

He shoved his hands in his pockets. "She didn't look so good today."

As usual, the temperature had dipped as soon as the sun dropped behind the mountains. I was glad for the quilt around my shoulders.

Ford asked, "Do you really think her reveal about the gold the other night is what caused someone to vandalize the site?"

I lifted a shoulder. "I hope not. If Kurt and Dad connect that trashed site to her, poop and fans come to mind."

He was puzzled, then started snickering. "*Poop?* Seriously?" He was laughing at me.

"What?" I grabbed his hand and pretended to pull him toward the barn. "Let me introduce you to my father, the man who raised me and would as soon wash my mouth out with soap as hear naughty words come out of his daughter's mouth." I stopped. "Oh, wait, I think you met him."

"Yeah. He never actually washed your mouth out with soap, though, did he?"

"I've never given him the chance."

Ford ran a hand through his hair—the hand that wasn't holding mine, which he wasn't letting go. I clutched the edges of the quilt around me with my free hand.

"Anyway," Ford said, "I wasn't looking for Lou."

"Oh…well…Dad's out in his lab…"

He nodded. "I figured."

"Oh." I got it. Finally. He'd come to see me. I felt myself blushing. A minute ago, I'd had a normal heartbeat, one you don't notice, instead of this thing slamming against my ribs.

He reached a hand toward my face.

I blinked and drew in a breath. He pulled his arm back and showed me the long piece of hay he'd pulled out of my tangled hair. Chuckling, he opened his fingers and let it float to the ground.

"Don't worry, Mist." He brushed his thumb over mine, and I shivered. He smiled. "I'm not like the guys in those books you read. I don't bite."

He let go of me then. I stepped back as he opened the door, climbed in and started the engine. He leaned an arm out the window. For a few seconds he searched my face, intently, like he wanted something.

I couldn't think of anything to say, and I wasn't sure any sound would come out if I tried. He was playing with me, a little bit, and I kind of liked that he cared enough to tease, and I kind of didn't—the conflicting sensations felt like biting into sour apple candy.

Finally, he put the truck in gear and called, "See you tomorrow."

The truck disappeared almost as soon as it left our circle of light. I stood in the driveway, hugging the quilt around me, and listened to the hum of the motor fade into the distance.

SOMETHING WAS PULLING ME from my dream, and I didn't want to leave, because it wasn't the usual. Like sticky cobwebs, fragments of the dream—me, Lookout and Ford, dancing a waltz in a formal ballroom, Mom onstage playing a violin—held me back. I couldn't see Mom onstage, but I knew it was her, and I wanted to find her. I willed my mind to return to the ballroom. I had to see her—"

"Misty!"

I pulled my shoulder away from the hand that was shaking it and opened my eyes. It was dark, but someone was climbing under my quilt at the foot of my bed.

"Mist? Wake up." Lou nudged my leg with her foot.

I groaned.

"I need to talk to you." Her voice was insistent and she was wiggling my foot. She obviously wasn't going away. "Wake up— please, Misty."

I rubbed my eyes. "I'm awake. What?"

Crickets.

I sighed and turned over. "Lou," I mumbled, "if you don't start talking, I'm going back to sleep."

"I think I know who trashed our site."

I listened to the echo of that sentence in my mind and wondered if I'd heard her right, or if it was part of my dream.

"You *what?*"

EIGHTEEN

I FUMBLED WITH THE lamp and switched it on.

Lou's face was pale and blotchy. She'd been crying. "I'm so stupid," she whispered. "I wanted…I don't know. I guess I was excited that somebody like him would be interested in me."

She swallowed, kneading the quilt between anxious fingers. "But he wasn't, really. He was using me to find out about the site."

"Cody?" I sat up. "You're talking about Cody, right?"

That elicited zero response. She stared past me, seeing something—memories, maybe—that I couldn't see.

"Besides," I said, trying a different angle, "how do you know he was only interested in the site? I mean, *Cody*? A pot hunter? He doesn't seem like the type to go to all the trouble."

"I'm not imagining this, Mist." She shook her head back and forth. "I finally called him on it the other night when we were driving to town for the movie. I guess I was already grumpy because of my…thing…with you, and I didn't care what he thought.

"He kept asking me all these questions—what'd we done during the week, had we found anything valuable—stuff like that. I finally asked him what was up with the third degree? I told him I was really sick of it and could we talk about something else."

"What'd he say?"

Tears pooled in her eyes. "He got all weird. He was quiet for a long time. Like, scary quiet. I tried to make a joke of it. But he whipped the car around and brought me home. That's why I was here so early." A tear rolled down her cheek and she rubbed it away. "He said he didn't feel like going out after all and," she finger-quoted, "*everybody* thought I was too young for him, anyway, so maybe we should cool it. I told him to have a nice life.

"And that was it. I haven't heard anything from him since. No texts. No calls. Nothing."

I wasn't sure what to say. How do you tell your best friend that maybe she was imagining something, so it would seem less painful that she'd gotten dumped? I tried for a sympathetic look. "Good riddance."

"Mist," she said, "I know it sounds like I'm trying to make excuses for the fact I got dumped."

What? Were my thoughts written on my forehead?

Lou squinted at me like she was willing me to believe her. It reminded me of the other night, when I'd told Lou about feeling that presence after Mom died. I'd so needed her to believe me, and she had.

She scooted closer. "Don't you think that's a little too much of a coincidence? Really, it's *all* he wanted to talk about, and when I call him on it, he freaks out. When I saw the site today, I knew it was him."

I decided she had a point. Beyond the fact she was sneaking around behind Dad's back, the whole thing with her and Cody had felt off from the start. Her theory was plausible, anyway.

"What do you want to do?" I asked her. "Should we tell Dad? Or Kurt?

"I don't know, Mist." She gave me a searching look. "That's really what I should do. But I'd have to explain about me and Cody. I already feel so stupid. What would your dad think? I'd feel even worse if your dad found out everything." She raked her fingers through her hair, pressed her palms against her temples. "And what if it is all my imagination? I get in trouble and so does Cody—for nothing, really."

I didn't want Lou to get in trouble, which I was pretty sure would mean Dad would send her home. But there was a part of me that felt positively gleeful at the prospect of messing up Cody.

I glanced at the clock. Almost eleven-thirty. "How late does Cody usually stay up? I seem to remember you two texting pretty late a couple of nights."

"I think he's kind of a night owl." Her eyes narrowed. "What are you scheming?"

I climbed out of bed, grabbed her phone off the floor next to her bed and tossed it to her. "What if we test your theory? See what happens if you tempt him with some great artifact, or more gold that we supposedly found? If he gets excited and starts asking questions, maybe you're on to something. If it's your imagination run wild, he probably won't even respond and," I yawned and stretched an arm, "we can go back to sleep."

We decided to try a teaser text—offer a little information, but nothing too specific. Lou held her phone in her hand, took a breath and started to type. I watched over her shoulder.

U there?

sorry bout Friday

found cool stuff today

 wanna hear?

Barely breathing, we waited for a response. It didn't take long.

S ok

wasn't really mad

cool stuff?

We turned to each other, mouths open. "Told you so," Lou said. "What should I say?"

"I don't know." I suddenly wasn't sure this was a great idea.

Lou rolled her eyes at me and started to type.

I caught her hand. "Don't go overboard. Keep it casual."

She bit her lower lip, thought for a few seconds, then her thumbs started to fly.

Not spposed to tell—but beautiful & worth $$$$

someone messed with the cabin site

getting all the good stuff tomorrow & shipping it off

then back to boring bone & pottery, proly

can't wait, haha.

The response came back lightning fast.

cool

gotta go

take care

Lou blew out a breath. "Do you think…?"

"He's headed for the site. He has to go now if he wants to find anything good." I launched myself off the bed and started for the door. "We have to tell Dad so he can warn Kurt and Ford."

I didn't get more than a step before Lou grabbed my arm in the kind of grip that leaves a mark. "Misty, we still don't know for sure. Please don't. If he shows up, Kurt will get him. If he doesn't…" She folded her hands in front of her like she was praying. "Please?"

What was I supposed to do? "Lou, I hate this." I stood there, rubbing the spot on my arm she'd just released from her death grip.

"I know. I do, too, and I'm really sorry." She started to cry. "I'll never do anything like this again. I've been so dumb."

"I guess we don't need to tell anyone tonight. But listen, if it does turn out it's Cody, everything will come out. That jerk won't keep you out of this. Get ready for Dad and Kurt—and your mom—to find out. Really, you've got to psych yourself up for that."

"And you'll get it, too, because of me." She plopped onto her bed. "It's all my fault. I'm so sorry, Misty."

I sat next to her. "You keep saying that."

She started to say something, but I interrupted. "It's okay. We'll figure it out and face the wrath of our parents together." I elbowed her. "I've got you covered."

She laid her head on my shoulder. "Thanks, Mist."

About an hour later, we heard the Beethoven ring of Dad's cell downstairs. We both shot up from where we were drowsing, propped against each other. The clock said two a.m.

We strained to catch Dad's words, but all we could hear was the muffled sound of his voice below us. The conversation lasted for about five minutes, then all was quiet. We waited, but after a while it was obvious he'd gone back to bed. Anti-climax doesn't begin to describe the moment.

Lou finally whispered, "What do you think happened?"

I was so tired I could barely shake my head. That call could have been anything, maybe nothing to do with us. I couldn't dredge up the will for any further speculation.

"Search me," I said, climbing back into my own bed. "I'm sure we'll find out in the morning. Enjoy the reprieve."

"I can't wait that long."

"No choice," I mumbled. "G'night." I turned over and shut my eyes. If Lou said something else, I didn't hear it. But the ballroom in my dreams had gone dark. The only things I saw for the rest of the night were the insides of my eyelids.

MORNING LIGHT WOKE ME way too soon. I pried open my eyes and, squinting, turned my head. Lou was awake, sitting with a blanket wrapped around her, in the same spot I'd left her the night before. She had dark smudges under her eyes. The clock said six a.m.

"I don't know how you could possibly sleep." She squirmed. "I'm about to crawl out of my skin."

I struggled to a sitting position. This was not a day I looked forward to.

"I heard your dad get up and make coffee an hour ago. I think he's down there, waiting for us."

I forced myself out of bed and sat next to her, shoulder to shoulder. "Lou, it'll be okay." My words sounded hollow.

She clenched a fist. "All the sneaking around. And Misty, stuff happened with Cody. We didn't exactly hook up, but—"

This was more information than I could handle at six in the morning. With *Cody*? I blurted the first thing that came into my head. "What if we pray?"

She blinked. "Uh, okay." She nodded. "Yeah, that would be great Mist, thanks."

Wait. I couldn't believe she'd gone for it. We'd attended church and youth group together for years. We'd both prayed in groups, Lou more than I ever did.

But just the two of us? Never.

Praying for starving children in Africa or something—that's one thing. But with someone who knows everything about you, every bad thing you've done for the last four years, every mean thing you've said about other people? *Pray, like you deserve to be heard, yes. But with someone who knows what a hypocrite you are?*

We sat cross-legged on the bed, facing each other. Lou grabbed my hand like it was a lifeline and I was her only hope for survival. We bowed our heads and sat there in silence for a few seconds that felt like an eternity. Finally, I realized when I'd said, "What if we pray?" what Lou had heard was, "How about *I* pray for *you*?"

But there was no going back. I took a deep breath and let it out. "God," I started, "We're really…scared…" I don't remember what I said after that. I'm sure it wasn't eloquent. But at some point, Lou stopped shaking. When I finished, she didn't seem so upset, and my weird combination of numb and anxious seemed better.

I gave her hand a squeeze as I finished and she managed a tremulous smile. "Okay," she said, but she had the look of someone during their last days on death row. "Let's go."

Dad was standing in the kitchen when we walked in.

We stopped, unsure what move to make next. I imagined we both had that deer in headlights expression.

He took a swig of coffee and gestured his cup at us. "Morning. Lou, your mom wants you to call her."

Lou glanced at me out of the corner of her eye. "Uh, okay. Did she say why?"

"I think she said something about a couple of birthdays next weekend."

Next weekend! I would turn sixteen next week, and Lou would turn seventeen two days later. With everything going on, I'd lost track of the date. I couldn't believe I'd forgotten my sixteenth birthday. We'd planned that Lou's mom, June, would come down to celebrate with us.

We each pulled out a chair and sat at the table across from Dad, our weight barely on our seats, as if they might collapse beneath us. But he gave no indication he was upset.

The suspense was killing me. "Um, Dad. I thought I heard the phone ring late last night. Was that June?"

"No," he shook his head. "June texted me, because she wasn't getting any response from Lou."

"Dang!" Lou said. "My phone must be out of power. I think it needs a new battery." She got up from the table and pulled the orange juice out of the fridge.

"Anyway," Dad leaned forward, "it was Kurt who called. They caught the vandal at the site. Guess who it was?"

Lou stood at the counter, back to us, reaching for a glass with the cautious movements of someone working with live explosives.

"Who?" I was surprised by how natural my voice sounded.

"That kid from the Blackwell ranch you were hanging out with…what was his name? Cody?"

The glass clattered onto the counter.

Dad turned. "Lou, you okay?"

She nodded, righting the glass with a less than steady hand.

"No way." My voice was squeaky.

He scrunched his eyebrows as he scanned my face. "Yeah, I had a hunch he was a troubled kid. And Kurt's pretty sure he has an accomplice. At one point, the kid said *we,* but so far, they haven't been able to get any information out of him as to who that person might be."

He stood. "You two better get some breakfast and into some clothes." He punched at his phone, told us the time, and rose from the table. "It's getting late."

"Um, Dad?" I said.

Lou turned, her eyes pleading.

"No kidding? Cody? Was he on a search for Blackwell's gold? Did he actually believe that story?"

"Apparently. The lure of easy money can make people stupid. He had no idea how much trouble he'd get into—or that tampering with an archaeological site is a federal offense. He's lucky he wasn't armed with anything but a shovel last night, because Kurt *was* armed and someone could've ended up hurt— or dead."

My stomach started to roil. I hadn't stopped to consider we'd sent Cody into mortal danger last night. Kurt was a law enforcement officer. I should have known. When I got up to walk across the kitchen to Lou, my legs were shaking. I stood next to her, our backs to Dad, and whispered, "You should tell."

But that stubborn set had returned to her mouth. She shook her head a fraction of an inch, the movement barely discernable.

"I'm going to load the van," Dad said. He scooped up his keys and turned for the door. "I need you girls outside in fifteen minutes."

Lou collapsed into a chair as soon as he was gone. She swiped a hand across her forehead. "Whew! That was a close one."

"Lou!" I thought my head was going to explode. I knew I was bright red. "Are you out of your mind? How long do you think Cody is going to keep you out of this?"

"Shhh, Misty. Keep your voice down, would you?" She huffed a clipped growl of laughter. "Don't you see? Cody's not talking about me. He has some other accomplice who's in on this. He must, because he wouldn't hesitate to give me up for a second.

"Believe me, he wasn't in love with me," her eyes watered up, and she took a breath, "even though he said he was. He was *using* me. There must be somebody else. Maybe it's Becca…or Matt, or both of them. They all seem pretty tight. I'm probably the last person on his mind right now."

I opened my mouth to disagree, but I could see her logic. She was probably right. Cody'd obviously just been using Lou for information. He wasn't the type to protect her identity, if he was thinking about her at all. He was more like the kind to throw her under the bus. Either way, I couldn't stand the uncertainty hanging over our heads. How could she?

"You've got to tell Dad what you did, Lou. I can't take this."

She bit the side of her cheek and dropped her head. "I *know* I should, and when you were praying, I was sure that I could."

I took a step toward her. "You can—"

She shook her head. "Not right now. What will your Dad think of me? I need some time."

I rolled my eyes. That was her biggest fear? What Dad would think of her? "How much time?"

She slapped a hand on the table and pushed back her chair. "Don't be so dramatic, Misty. I had a couple secret dates. I made out with some guy I shouldn't have. I regret it, believe me—but it's not that huge. It's in the past. Let it go."

"Seriously? That's your Disney solution?" I threw out my arms. "*Let it go?*"

She made a face at me, stood up and headed for the stairs. "I'm getting dressed. We now have ten minutes before your dad starts honking the horn at us."

The peace I'd felt less than an hour ago was a distant memory. I sat there for another five minutes, paralyzed by anxiety, guilt and uncertainty, until I heard the sound of Dad's footsteps on the front porch.

WE GATHERED AROUND FORD at the site, who replayed, scene by scene, how he and Kurt had captured Cody the night before.

"We left our cars near the highway and hiked in. We were camped out in our sleeping bags over there." He pointed to a spot near the cabin site. "Behind those bushes. A little after midnight, I was dozing off, and Kurt shook me awake. When I opened my eyes, I saw this light bobbing toward us. Then someone marches right up to the site, not even trying to be quiet, sticks his shovel in the dirt and starts digging."

"Unbelievable." Frank rubbed a hand across his jaw. "I wish I'd been there. What'd you guys do?"

"We were stunned." Ford took a deep breath, as he and Kurt must have the night before. "We slid out of our sleeping bags and for a few seconds, we crouched there, watching him dig and dump, like it was something he did every day. When I saw who it was, I was like, *whaat?*"

His smile faded. "Then, Kurt told me to stay down, and he actually drew his gun—which was surreal, considering I personally know the guy he was aiming at. And he shines this big flashlight on Cody and yells at him to drop his shovel and put his hands behind his head.

"You should have seen Cody's face. He whipped around, eyes huge, dropped his shovel, and—" Ford threw up his arms in a comical impression of a criminal caught in the act, "yells, *don't shoot.* I swear, I thought he was going to pee his pants!"

Ford was still high on adrenaline from the night before. Typical guy, he wasn't dwelling on how close Kurt came to shooting Cody. I couldn't get the idea of Cody losing his life over something this stupid out of my head. Lou looked like she was about to throw up. I figured she was thinking the same thing I was—we'd sent Cody into that danger, and we'd done it on purpose.

I caught Dad watching me, and saw him glance at Lou before I turned away. He knew something was up, he just hadn't figured it out, yet. But he would, I was sure of that. He patted Ford on the back. "Thanks for the recap. Kurt told me what happened when he called last night, but he was pretty upset, so I didn't ask him for details."

"Yeah," Ford nodded. "He was really mad at Cody. I've never seen him like that."

"His anger probably had more to do with how close he came to shooting that boy." Frank's mouth was set in a grim line. "You don't ever get over something like that."

"I'm sure you're right," Dad said. "I'm thankful things turned out as well as they did, for Kurt *and* Cody. Hopefully, this will be a wake-up call for that young man."

Dad turned toward the site and rubbed his hands together. "We need to get this mess cleaned up, again, and figure out our next steps at the pit toilet site—so let's get to it."

Lou didn't waste any time. She grabbed a screen and set to work.

I'M SIXTEEN.

That was my first thought, even before I opened my eyes.

The room was silent, except for the soft flap of the curtain at my open window. I tried to hang on to that moment of floating bliss where nothing mattered but the cool pillow under my cheek and the sun-kissed breeze caressing the back of my neck.

But it didn't take long for that smothering weight to settle over me, that feeling like a fist clenching my heart.

My first birthday without mom. In fact, it was the first celebration of any kind that Dad and I would share since we'd lost her. I wondered if the idea of celebrating without her was as unappealing to him as it was to me. At least we weren't having a party. Lou and I would do that together when her mom arrived on Sunday.

I rolled toward Lou and opened one eye, wondering how she felt about her mom's imminent arrival. In the same instant that I realized Lou was gone, she burst through the door.

It was like an entire party entered my room. "Wake up, birthday girl!" she yelled, clapping her hands. "Breakfast is ready."

I managed a half-grin, sat up and pushed my bangs out of my eyes.

Lou surveyed me, tapping a finger against her chin.

I yawned.

"Oh, dear," she said. "Looking a bit rumpled." She dashed over and smoothed my bangs with her fingers in a surprising mom-like gesture. With her other hand, she fumbled blindly for a barrette on the crate between our beds. Grasping one, she twisted my bangs and clipped them back with a firm snap.

"Ow!" I shoved her hands away. "What are you doing? Do I smell bacon?"

Her mouth curved up in a mischievous smile. "I know you didn't want to make a big deal out of your birthday, but if you must know, a little birthday breakfast awaits you downstairs…and a guest."

"Bacon, good. Guest, bad." I fell back on my pillow. "Unless it's your mom, I exercise my birthday princess prerogative to have the bacon brought up to me on a silver platter." I waved an imaginary scepter. "And the guest banished from my kingdom."

Lou giggled and headed for the door. "Don't be such a party pooper. Everything's ready." She glanced back. "And, um, put on a bra before you come down, okay?"

I sat up. "What?"

She gave me a wink and clattered back down the stairs.

Go to https://youtu.be/UJ3tBFnljdA for a peek at what's coming up…

NINETEEN

I APPRECIATED THE BRA tip when I walked into the kitchen and was greeted by a platter of pancakes and bacon, and the excited faces of Lou and Ford. Dad was standing at the counter with his back to me.

When Lou and Ford yelled "Happy Birthday!" Dad turned. He gave me a wistful smile when our eyes met. He crossed the room and enveloped me in a hug. "Happy Sixteenth, Misty."

The tears started then, and threatened to turn into sobs. I buried my face in his shirt for a few seconds, pulled away and turned toward the bathroom. "Thanks, guys." I cleared my throat. "I'll be right back. I have to...wash up."

I closed the bathroom door, shutting out the uncomfortable silence that settled on the room behind me. If I'd been Lou, I would have stood in the middle of the room and blubbered away. But that's not how I rolled.

Seated on the closed toilet lid, I silently sobbed, stuffing the little garbage can under the sink with wads of soggy toilet paper. As my tears slowed, I took some deep, shaky breaths and tried to psych up for going back out there.

A shiny black beetle half the size of my thumb struggled across the slippery linoleum floor in front of my bare feet. Poor thing. It was the season for the insects to be on the move. We saw them everywhere, and they were all headed in the same direction. I wondered how the little bug had ended up here, trapped in my bathroom, and the thought made me start to cry again. *Sheesh.*

I jimmied the empty toilet paper roll off of the holder and gently scooped up the bug, pulled open the window and shook him onto the outside sill. "There you go, buddy. At least one of us can escape."

I stood at the open window watching him crawl away, and breathed in the clean, morning air. Finally, I stepped back and, placing a hand on either side of the sink, leaned toward the girl in the mirror. The red-eyed, raw-nosed, anxious version of me whispered, "Another year older and looking good." I had no alternative but to wash my face and brush my teeth, plaster a smile on my face and open that bathroom door.

Three worried expressions met mine when I walked back into the kitchen. I widened my grin until I thought my face would crack open. "Sorry that took so long. Did somebody mention pancakes?" Their worry resolved into relieved smiles and I sat down at the table.

Ford and Lou piled on the pancakes and bacon, and Dad scooted the peanut butter and maple syrup next to my plate. I forced myself to dig in. After the first few bites, my stomach muscles relaxed and I started to enjoy the food, complete with an eye roll at the first bite of bacon. "Mmm," I murmured, "bacon my love, it's been so long." Everybody's laugh may have been louder than my comment warranted, but that was okay.

Dad placed a manly-wrapped box in front of me—brown paper, tied with a hiking boot lace. I pushed my plate aside and tore into it. I knew how hard this day was for him, and I wanted to show him I appreciated the effort.

When I saw the outside of the box, my feigned enthusiasm turned into the real thing. I shrieked, jumped up and threw my arms around him. "Thank you so much."

He patted my back. "Do you like it?"

"It's exactly what I wanted." I couldn't believe it. I'd asked Mom for it months ago. She must have told him, or had she gotten it before…?

I sat down, opened the box and pulled out my new Nikon camera.

Lou's mouth dropped open. "Ohhh, that's gorgeous."

I held it up like a prize and Dad laughed.

Ford nodded. "Nice."

"There's so much I can do with this." I was more excited than a geek at a comic-con. "It's pretty much a no-boundaries camera—sharp pictures of moving objects, video, low-light, special effects—this camera is supposed to handle anything."

Lou placed a little drawstring velvet bag on the table in front of me. "Before you head off to play with your new hardware, Happy Birthday."

I pulled the bag open and dug out some cool 80s-style Wayfarer sunglasses with tiger stripe frames. "Very cool. Lou, where did you find these?'

"You know that little thrift store in town? Amazing all the crazy stuff they have in there."

I leaned over and hugged her. "I love them."

"I knew you would."

I put on the glasses and put my head next to hers while Lou took a picture of the two of us with her phone.

Ford dangled something between his fingers and I pulled down the sunglasses to see it better.

"Sorry, I didn't have time to wrap it," he said. "I just found out it was your birthday, so…"

I held out my hand and he dropped the gift into my palm. It was a thin bracelet, woven of green and purple threads.

"A friendship bracelet," Lou said, reaching for it. "That's so retro. Let me see."

Ford shrugged. "Well, Misty's sort of a retro girl."

I loved that he called me that, *how* he said it, gentle and matter-of-fact. As if he really got me. Of all the surprises that day, the most startling was the relief I felt at being known by Ford Tomaka. No heat in my cheeks. No anxiety. Only relief.

Lou pinched the bracelet between her fingers and held it in front of her face. "*Retro girl.* True that. Did you make this?"

"Yeah, my mom makes all kinds of jewelry. She taught me how when I was a little kid."

Lou held it out and I gave her my wrist.

I raised my eyes to Ford's and smiled. "Thanks, really. It's great."

He grinned back. "You're welcome." He ducked his head. He hadn't known I'd like it? So even Ford could have an awkward moment—another revelation.

Lou finished with the bracelet and noticed me watching Ford. She looked at him and back at me. "Hmmm, yeah, great. Anyway, the festivities have only begun. Clever of you to have your birthday on a Saturday, because guess what your dad says we can do next?"

She grabbed my wrist and pulled me toward the front door. I gave a "what's up?" look to Dad and Ford, following behind us, but Lou didn't stop for explanations. A few minutes later, we were at the corral, surrounding a saddled-and-bridled Rosa.

Despite what Lou had said, Dad's voice held a less-than-enthusiastic note. "Kurt said it's fine for you to ride her—" He rubbed his hand down the little horse's neck. "I'm not sure he got permission from Rosa's owner, and this horse is shy."

My friends had planned everything. Ford would ride Rosa on one of the longer trails through the woods around Lookout Mountain and meet up with us at the meadow in the Opal Creek drainage, where we'd first seen the wild horse band. Lou and I would hike in, and we'd all eat the lunch she'd already packed and loaded into Rosa's saddle bag.

"I wish your new camera was charged." Lou ran her fingers absently through Rosa's mane. "I thought with you and Rosa, we could recreate the picture of your Mom in the meadow. But we can use a phone. Then—" She grinned. "Ford and I will give you some riding lessons. After that, I'll ride Rosa home, and you two can hike back."

"Really?" I was laughing at them. "And this is a birthday present for *me*?" I crossed my arms and peered over my new Wayfarers. "You shouldn't have."

The last few weeks had probably been the longest my two friends had gone without riding a horse since they were old enough to hang onto a saddle horn. They smiled back at me, bright-eyed and a little giddy. Rosa pawed the ground and snorted. She was obviously as ready to gallop out of that corral as they were.

Dad was the only one who didn't look excited. "I wonder if you guys shouldn't go for a hike. How about you give me another week to work with Rosa if you really want to start riding her."

"Ah, c'mon Dr. Stevens," Lou pleaded. "It might be the last chance we get all summer to do this together. Look at her. She's gentle as a lamb. We'll be careful, and she'll be fine."

He turned to Ford. "What do you think?"

"No problem." Ford ran a hand across Rosa's side. "I think she's good to go."

I was pretty sure it wouldn't have mattered if Rosa had started to buck and kick at that point. Nothing would keep my friends from climbing onto that horse.

In the end, after he checked with Kurt one more time by phone, Dad gave his permission. He made sure we all had powered phones and back-up walkies, then Ford and Rosa trotted away. They were out of sight in minutes.

The morning was still cool, but the air had warmed at least five degrees since we'd left the ranch house a half hour before, and the clear blue skies stretched over us like a promise. Lou chattered away, excited about her mom's visit. "She said she might make it in tonight or tomorrow morning, depending on when she gets out of Alton."

I shook my head with memories, still fresh in my mind, of how happy she'd been to leave her mom a few weeks before. "You're actually excited she's coming, aren't you?"

"Don't you dare tell her." She gave me a warning look, cracked a smile. "But I've missed her, a lot more than I thought I would."

I held up a hand and tried for casual, but it came out shaky. "Really, I get it."

Lou's smile faded. "I know you do." She gave my hand a squeeze. "I'm sorry, Misty. I wish your mom was coming with her."

"It's okay. But it wouldn't hurt to let your mom know you still kind of like having her around."

"Maybe—" Lou chuckled. "But I'm not giving her that kind of ammo."

The trail narrowed and steepened. We walked for a few minutes in silence, single file. Lou came up beside me as the path widened. "So, I was thinking about what you said, about that night your mom died. Is it okay if we talk about it?"

"Sure," I said, "I guess."

"What you said…or heard. What you felt like God said to you. *I've got this covered.* It sounds so normal. Don't you kind of picture God being bigger? Awe-inspiring?"

I nodded. "I've thought that, too."

She fell silent, but I could tell she wasn't done talking.

"What?" I asked her.

She glanced at me. "I feel like I need to apologize again and try to explain why I was so weird about the Cody thing. And everything lately. But it sounds so dumb and I'm afraid I'll make you mad. Or sad."

What was this? "I promise I won't get mad, but you don't need to apologize again. I get it. I think you should come clean with Dad and your mom, though."

"I don't know if you do get it, Mist. Cuz, I wasn't just bored or being rebellious. And I wasn't in love with Cody or anything." She shuddered dramatically. "The thing is, I think I was jealous. And it's hard for me to say this…"

"Jealous? Of what? You're not talking about the Ford thing again, are you? Because I swear—"

"I know, I know." She waved my protest off. "You're friends." She said it like she wasn't buying my story for a second. "No, it's not about Ford. But I've thought a lot about how I was acting, and I realized I was jealous…of you…and everything you have."

Lou laughed at the shocked expression I turned on her. We'd made our way onto a small bridge that spanned a deeper part of the creek and she stopped there, eyes on the water. Popping the top on her water bottle, she took a swig, and replaced the lid slowly. "Misty, I loved your mom, and I miss her so much, so I can only begin to imagine how hard this is for you. But I love your dad, too. I know you guys have your stuff, but I don't even know who my dad is, *where* he is, if he's even alive."

She clenched a fist at her side, then opened it, letting something free. "If I had a father, I'd want him to be like your dad. Unfailingly faithful. Always fair. You haven't been at the other end when he thinks you're in danger—that night we were camping, the other day at the site.

"You called for him and there wasn't a second of hesitation. He flew. He would never, *never* let anything bad happen to you. And the three of you together, you were part of the best family I've ever seen. You had that gift for fifteen whole years, and truth is, I've *always* been a little jealous of that."

What could I say? Lou was on the edge of tears, and she was right. I knew she was right, but that didn't make it any easier. What I couldn't say to her, to anyone, is that Dad might not *want* to let anything bad happen, but he did. He let Mom go, before I could even say goodbye. I know it was stupid to blame him for that, but still. I couldn't look at Lou. I just nodded.

Out of the corner of my eye, I saw her shrug. "Okay, there was the Ford thing." She put a hand on my arm and I turned. "And, you know, it's okay for you to like him. You're allowed."

My eyes slid back to the creek gurgling beneath our feet. I wanted to believe her.

"And then," she continued, "you told me about the night your mom died, where you felt so close to God. Misty, I've never felt that presence the way you have, ever. I'd give anything to have an experience like that, to really know God was there."

Give anything? A rough laugh escaped from between my lips and I shook my head once.

She sighed and pulled her fingers through her hair again. "Okay, yeah, maybe not anything, I guess I'm not there. But when you told me about that night, I thought, wow, Misty has the dad I always wanted, and Ford's like, infatuated with her, and now she has God talking to her—"

"It wasn't like that, Lou."

"I know. But I thought, I need that kind of comfort, too. I want a family like Misty's. I want to know God actually listens and hears my prayers. It made me mad." She shook her head. "I can't explain it, and I can't believe I felt that way. I don't anymore. When you prayed for me, I realized how much I have, too. I have you, and Mom, and your dad's so cool to me. And I know I should come clean with him, but can't you see what that would do? I couldn't handle the look on his face. To have him disappointed in me that way."

I had no idea how to respond. My life was so messed up. My relationship with my dad was anything but enviable, and I missed Mom like crazy. Literally, I felt like I was going crazy. And God?

The conflicted feelings I had about God and his willingness to leave me here, a motherless child with a father who seemed perfectly content to let me work through my grief all on my own. I didn't let those thoughts wander any further than that. If I did, I was afraid I might start yelling, and never stop.

That anyone, especially Lou, could be jealous of me was a thing I never would have imagined—not in a million years of imagining. Finally, I said, "Thanks for telling me. But Dad would forgive you. He'd still love you. *Unfailingly faithful and fair*, remember?"

Her mouth turned up in a reluctant smile. "Maybe."

From the footbridge at the creek, we struggled up a steep hill and, after a thirty-minute walk through the dappled shade of a copse of pines, finally arrived at the Opal Creek meadow. Ford was already there, in the midst of hobbling Rosa. When he stood, he saw us coming and waved. "Perfect timing," he called.

I called, "How was she?"

Lou walked over to Rosa and gave her a pat. The horse looked none the worse for her ride. She seemed content, happy to munch the sweet grass and wildflowers near the creek.

"She was great, really responsive." He shrugged. "I'm not sure what your Dad was worried about."

"Don't look at me. I never know what's going on in his head."

"You..." Ford's smile faltered. "You and your Dad seem sort of—"

"C'mon, you guys. I'm starved!" Lou was sitting on a blanket, unloading the picnic food. My stomach rumbled.

I spun away from Ford, happy to escape whatever he was going to say about my inability to understand my father. "After that breakfast we had—I can't believe I'm saying this, but I'm hungry, too."

We dove into our sandwiches and chips with as much relish as Rosa with her nose in sweet grass. After we finished, we stowed everything away in the saddle bags and explored the meadow. Across Opal Creek there was another copse of feathery juniper, pine, and mountain birch. A narrow deer track led us on a meandering path through the woods to a drop-off where the creek trickled down between rock and pine.

It wasn't far to the forest floor below us, and the wall was steep but not sheer. Ford pointed to where the falls pooled among some large boulders. "That looks like fun."

"It does." The day had warmed, and my shirt stuck to my sweaty back. "But, Rosa." Thoughts of the cougar were never far from my mind, even though we'd seen no sign of the cat for weeks. Still…

Lou nodded. "Misty's right. We should get back. Besides," she rubbed her hands together and raised an eyebrow at me. "There are riding lessons to begin."

We turned, jumped the creek, and hiked the way we'd come on the meadow side. The canyon was similar to others I'd seen since coming to the Juliets. From the drop-off, the ravine expanded into flat meadow with Opal Creek trickling through the middle, a few ponderosas scattered here and there. I could see the tops of mountain peaks above the rock walls and I knew, even if we climbed to the tops of those, there would be more, even taller mountains above them.

Rosa seemed happy and satisfied when we returned to the meadow. She lazily lifted her head as we approached and went back to her grazing. You'd never know she was a rescue horse who'd once been abused. She was so relaxed, I found it hard to believe anything in the world could ruffle her.

My worries about Rosa seemed unfounded, and I wished then we'd explored the drop-off. But Lou threw out her arms and yelled, "It is so great to not be breaking our backs and eating dirt in a ditch. Man, what a perfect day!" She kicked off her shoes.

"Uh, Lou, this isn't a studio," I warned, but I was smiling. I knew what was coming. "Meadows have rocks and holes and trees."

She winked at us, struck a ballerina pose, then executed a modified pirouette away from where we were standing.

Ford shook his head. "Is she really going to do that here?"

He knew Lou danced, but he'd never actually seen her. After a couple minutes of watching her twirl across the meadow, he whistled long and low. "Whoa, rodeo girl. What is this?"

"Rodeo girl has a gift," I said. My smile felt stiff, and I hated myself for that. Out of the corner of my eye, I watched Ford watch Lou.

In front of us, she twisted and turned her willowy body. After rippling like the knee-deep grasses she was spinning through, she stood up tall, mimicking the trees ringing the meadow. Her arms waved softly like branches in a breeze and spread apart. She glided away from us, a hawk catching the perfect current of air. Her dark hair floated around her, her whole body radiated joy. She was beautiful.

"No kidding she's got a gift," Ford said. "I don't know anything about dancing, but she's really good, isn't she?"

I managed to unclench my jaw enough to say, "Yeah."

Ever since I'd known Lou, I couldn't wait to watch her dance. It was the coolest thing to see that party-girl image peel away and be replaced by an innocence and joy and playfulness that, to me, felt like the real Lou.

But in this moment, all I could think was, *this is it. This is where Ford realizes he's picked the wrong girl.* I determined then and there, I couldn't care less. I would *choose* not to care. I'd said all along that I only wanted Ford's friendship. *Be careful what you wish for.*

By the time Lou whirled her way back to us, I was sure I had my feelings firmly under control. I applauded with as much enthusiasm as I could muster.

"Bravo!" Ford chuckled. "Aren't you full of surprises, Lilou Rose?"

Lou curtseyed at him in a way that managed to come off as graceful and a little flirty, instead of cheesy, and I knew it was all over but the crying.

Except, no way would I let some boy make me cry.

Ford turned to me then, and smiled. I looked into his eyes— and realized nothing had changed. His face, when he'd been watching Lou, held amazement, admiration. When she winked at him, I saw affection.

But these searching eyes, this smile directed at me was different. It was like being discovered, and what he'd found was surprising, and exciting and beautiful. And I could see it—he wanted more. But how could he? I was just me. As much as I wanted to believe Ford liked me, I still questioned it.

"What about you, Mist?" He gave my shoulder a little shove. "What aren't you telling me? Concert pianist? Math genius?" He took a step closer and murmured, "Horse whisperer, maybe?"

I gave him a warning look and shook my head. "Sorry. I'm afraid with me, what you see is what you get."

"Yeah, right."

Lou snorted. "Horse whisperer? Ha!"

Now who was jealous?

The back of her hand alongside her mouth, she stage whispered to Ford, "Let me tell you about the last time I managed to get Misty on a horse.

"I finally got her up on Too Tall, my barrel-racing horse, a while ago, but…" She started to giggle so hard she couldn't get the words out. So, I took over. I could feel my cheeks blazing. I figured my version might be slightly less embarrassing.

"The minute we left the corral," I said, "he took off like he'd been stung. I was holding onto the reins for dear life and I could hear Lou yelling—"

"Yeah," Lou interrupted. "I was yelling, *pull back on the reins, pull back on the reins.* But she and Too Tall kept going, and vanished over the horizon." She held a hand over her brow like she was viewing a distant shore.

I rolled my eyes. "As if I wasn't yanking those reins as hard as I could. But Lou's voice got fainter and fainter and Too Tall didn't stop until he found the creek and came to a screeching halt. He almost threw me off, but I managed to stay in the saddle and there we sat, parked in the deepest part of the water, my feet dangling in the water and him slurping away—what could I do? I couldn't get him to move and I didn't want to climb off him into the creek."

Lou started giggling again. "And that's where…"

I held up my hand. "And that's where Lou found us. I thought she was going to die laughing at Too Tall doing exactly what he felt like doing and me stranded on his back." I started laughing, too. This was one of Lou's favorite embarrassing stories to tell about me, and normally it annoyed me so much.

But this time it didn't matter, because I knew Ford wouldn't care, and he didn't. He shook his head and gave me a wink Lou couldn't see because, at that moment, she was bent over double, laughing at me. Ford knew what Lou didn't—the Too Tall catastrophe wasn't my last horse relationship, and the one I was in now was straight out of a fantasy novel.

Not that I wasn't nervous about riding Rosa. I had almost zero experience with horses, because Mom and Dad moved too often to keep them. Couples on a career track with the Forest Service had to work hard to stay married. Adding kids to the equation was even more challenging. And horses?

June and Lou occasionally talked Mom into riding with them, but between part-time contract work with the NFS and homeschooling me, she didn't have much time to ride. I actually had the impression she'd gotten enough of the horse thing by the time she left the ranch where she grew up. Mom hadn't pushed me to learn to ride after my experience with Too Tall, and I'd truly had no desire to ever try again, until now.

Lou rode Rosa first, letting her explore the meadow. They trotted up and down hills and ridges, in and out of shadows, back and forth across the stream. When Lou thought the horse was comfortable enough in her surroundings, she brought her over and slid off.

"She's ready for you. Ford's right, she's very responsive to the reins. Way more compliant than Too Tall. You won't have any trouble."

I licked my lips and wiped my suddenly sweaty palms on my jeans. Ford held Rosa and watched me climb on. Once I was settled, he looked up at me. "You'll have the best control if you sit up straight—"

I made my back ramrod straight and he chuckled. "But relax. You can be gentle on the reins with Rosa. You know how to direct her, right?"

I nodded.

"Good," he said. "Feel her rhythm. Let her rock you from side to side without resisting. But don't watch her—" He smiled and smoothed a hand down her flank. "As beautiful as she is. Look at where you're going, and enjoy the movement. If the fastest you two ever go is a walk today, that's fine."

I nodded again and he stepped back. "We'll be right here."

As soon as I flicked the reins and Rosa moved forward, I could tell she was tense. So was I. My heart was racing. I figured I was the problem. Horses are sensitive to human emotions, that much I'd learned over the summer. I took a slow breath, willed my heart to calm, and prepared to follow the same path that Lou had taken with the horse.

We'd only moved forward a few steps when, with no warning, Rosa froze. I felt her muscles bunch beneath me.

I gasped and grabbed the saddle horn seconds before she started to buck.

TWENTY

EACH TIME I CRASHED back into the saddle, I was sure my spine wouldn't survive another hit. I held on and tried to keep my seat—the last thing I should have done. A few explosive bucks, and Rosa burst into a full gallop.

We careened across as I tried to yell, "Whoa, Rosa. Whoa! Stop," but it came out in breathless gasps. I couldn't believe the little horse could take strides that long. Even with my hands clamped to the saddle horn, I felt myself slipping to the side.

Through watery eyes, I could see a grove of trees looming in front of us—low branches, fallen logs, rocks and bushes. I wouldn't survive it. Rosa showed no signs of slowing, and I knew I had to get off of her before we hit those trees.

After she jumped the creek it would be too late, but my panicked brain couldn't work out how to fling myself off a racing horse. It felt physically impossible to unclench my fingers from that saddle horn. But Rosa solved my problem for me.

She came to an abrupt halt at the edge of the creek and I kept going. I hit the ground with a thud and a splash, half in the creek, half on the ground. I'd flipped over her neck and landed on my back. Unable to breath or move, I stared up at her chin hairs, praying I wasn't paralyzed for life.

Rosa stood stock still above me, a statue horse. Maybe I'd died and this was that pause before you see the white light. A high pitch rang in my ears, but it didn't sound like angels.

A horse screamed from the other side of the creek and I flipped to my stomach. That movement made my head spin, but I recognized that horse's cry. Lookout!

The stallion burst from the trees screeching like a banshee, and the ground trembled beneath me. He reared and Rosa's head snapped up. She took one look at the stallion, snorted, spun around and galloped away.

Lookout cleared the creek and me in one graceful leap and turned.

I tried to sit up, but as soon as I started to rise, I saw stars. The last thing I felt before everything went dark was Lookout's nose nudging my head.

SOMEONE WAS CALLING MY name. I opened my eyes and two worried faces came into focus above me.

"Misty!" Lou grabbed my arm. "Thank God you're alive. Where does it hurt? Please be okay."

She had tears in her eyes.

Ford sat back and wiped his hand across his face.

I managed to get one elbow underneath me and used it to lever up my other side. Propped up on my elbows, I took a shaky breath and wiggled my toes.

Ford stopped me with a hand on my shoulder. "Don't move too fast. I don't think I can handle you passing out again. Are you having any trouble breathing? Did you hit your head? On a scale of one to ten, what's your pain level?"

He was going into EMT mode.

"I don't think I hit my head. I just got the breath knocked out of me." I sat up with help from them both. "Did he take off with Rosa?"

Ford's forehead wrinkled. He turned to Lou. "It could be a concussion."

They exchanged a worried glance, and Lou said, slowly, as if to a small child, "Did *who* take off with Rosa, honey?"

I scanned the meadow. Neither horse was anywhere to be seen. "Lookout."

Lou took in a quick breath. "Lookout was here?"

"We didn't see the stallion." Ford tilted his head back toward where I'd started my ride. "All we saw was Rosa, bucking and galloping away with you hanging on for dear life. When you guys hit that rise back there, we lost sight of you. We were running—

"And screaming," Lou cut in. "The next thing we see is Rosa trotting back, no rider. When we came over the ridge and saw you, lying on the ground…" Her face went white. "I nearly passed out on the ground right next to you." She hugged me. "I'm so glad you're okay."

Ford stood up and walked around me, head down. "I see the stallion's hoof prints now. I wonder if he's what spooked Rosa?"

I held out my hand and Ford helped me to my feet. He didn't let go of my hand until he was sure I was steady. "I don't think Lookout spooked her. She couldn't have even seen him from where she started to buck. I think, maybe, Lookout was trying to help me. He may not have spooked her, but he definitely stopped her."

We stood there, dazed. I moved my neck around, stretched my back. Everything seemed to be moving fine. "What now? I'm supposed to get back on the horse that threw me, right?"

Lou's mouths dropped open. "The idea was to teach you to ride," she said, "not take a plunge into extreme horsemanship."

Ford was shaking his head. "Misty, I mean, I admire your courage. But I don't think anybody could ride Rosa right now, assuming we can find her. I think we should walk her back." He shrugged. "I guess your dad was right."

"Sheesh," Lou said. "If Rosa shows up at the ranch without us, your Dad is going to freak."

Ford scanned the meadow, face scrunched and worried-looking. "He's gonna kill me," he mumbled. "I don't want to rush you, Mist. But we need to find Rosa. You could stay here…"

I felt alright, and I couldn't stop wondering what had spooked Rosa. I was sure it hadn't been Lookout. It may have been a snake or something else none of us had seen, but we couldn't completely discount the cougar, either. I really didn't want to be by myself. There was no guarantee my guardian-angel horse would be there for me next time.

"I feel fine," I said. "Let's find Rosa."

We trudged away from the creek and breathed simultaneous sighs of relief when we topped the ridge and found Rosa, nose in the grass. She was skittish, but with some patient, gentle coaxing, Ford was able to grab her reins.

I gave her nose a rub, to let her know there were no hard feelings. She returned my gesture, an apology nudge with her nose, so we were still friends. Cautious friends.

No one seemed to be seriously injured, except when I thought about what I'd just been through, the world began to buzz and waver again. I dropped onto the nearest log, and Lou followed me.

"You okay, Mist?" she asked.

I nodded, slowly, but Ford squatted down in front of me and I could see he was about to run through his EMT checklist again. Before he could start, I put a hand on his arm. "I'm fine. I guess I need a little more time to recover."

Actually, I knew exactly what was happening. It was my usual reaction to danger—calm in the moment followed by complete and total collapse.

Lou patted my hand and stood up. "Take your time."

She grabbed Rosa's reins and led her several feet away from us, all the while talking in a soothing tone. "You're okay, aren't you girl? We all have crazy moments sometimes, huh?" To my surprise, she put one hiking-booted foot into Rosa's stirrup and swung onto her.

Rosa went still, an imitation of her body language before trying to buck me off. I sucked in a breath. Lou placed her hand on the horse's neck and spoke in a firm voice. "You're okay. Come on. You're fine. That's a good girl."

Then, Rosa seemed to come unstuck. She snorted softly and stepped to the side. Ford visibly relaxed along with me. Rosa allowed Lou to urge her a few more steps away. They turned to face us. I didn't know horses well enough to understand Rosa's little head shake, but Lou's expression was triumphant.

"Ha!" she smiled. "Look at us."

"Lou." Ford stood up. "Are you sure about this? We still don't know what spooked her."

"You know horses. They're flighty as sparrows. Could have been anything. I really think she'll be fine. I want to ride her back. You got your chance."

"Yeah," he nodded, "and it was fun. But, I—"

"As long as Misty is feeling semi-decent?" She sounded so hopeful and ready to ride.

I waved at her while guzzling most of the contents of my water bottle. I finished and took a breath. "I actually think I may have been a little dehydrated. I'll be fine."

"Good," Lou said. "Load us up with picnic stuff and I'll see you two back at the ranch." Ford started to say something, but she didn't give him the chance. "I'll be fine, Ford. I have the phone and a walkie. If anything even remotely weird happens, I'll call you or Dr. Stevens." She raised her eyebrows at him. "You need to chill. Load me up."

Ford looked from me to Lou, and gave in with a resigned shrug. "You're a big girl. But if something happens, Dr. Stevens will be mad at me."

"Oh, please," Lou said. "I'll take all the responsibility, okay?"

"It's not about wanting to take the heat, it's about who's actually going to get burned." But he loaded the leftover picnic bags and blanket into Rosa's saddlebags. The last thing he said before we waved her off was, "Be careful."

So like my dad. And like him, Ford was taking responsibility for all of us, whether or not he needed to. He dropped onto the grass beside me and fell back. He closed his eyes against the sun and raked both hands through his hair.

And I thought of Dad again. Weighed down. Is that what Dad was? He'd lost the person who carried half of our family's cares—probably more than half—that's how Mom was.

Despite the buzzing of the heat bugs, the meadow seemed quiet after the two-beat thud of Rosa's trot faded into the distance. The heat felt oppressive, which made the beckoning gurgle of the creek irresistible.

I bent over and untied my boots.

Ford propped himself up on his elbows, watching me. Several seconds went by before he said anything. "Mist? Whatcha doin'?"

I tilted my head toward the sound of the water. "It's calling to me."

A slow grin spread across his face and he kicked off his boots. "Yessss. Race you."

We ran full out for the creek and jumped in. I flinched at the icy sting.

Ford yelled, "Whoa, yeah!" He dipped both hands in the water and sent it flying everywhere, splashing us both with icy drops.

Even at its deepest, it only came to the middle of my calves. But it didn't take long for my feet and ankles to numb and the coolness to seep up to my core. Splashing through the creek under a canopy of pines, we slipped and slid over the mossy rocks, trying to stay upright and failing. One time, I grabbed Ford to keep from falling and we both went down. It had been months since I'd laughed that hard.

Eventually, we encountered the falls we'd seen earlier, and peered over the edge.

"It doesn't look so bad." Ford glanced at me and back to the forest floor below. "What do you think?"

The drop-off wasn't a sheer one, the bottom maybe twenty feet below us. I smiled. "I'm in."

Ford didn't give me time to change my mind. He leaped down the bank next to the waterfall in a barely controlled fall.

I squished my toes through moist moss and into the damp, loamy dirt at the edge of the waterfall. Resting a hand against the bark of the nearest pine, I started down, moving from tree to tree, grasping at low-hanging branches. I went into a side-slide as I neared the bottom. One more leap and thud landed me at the water's edge.

Maybe it was the jolt up my spine when I touched down, maybe it was residual terror from the run-away horse. But something about hitting the ground shook loose my dream image of Mom landing on the ledge where she died. I felt the air knocked out of my lungs for the second time that day. The edge of my vision clouded, my ears buzzed. My muscles tensed, then turned to rubber. Weak-kneed, I dropped and pulled my knees up to my chin. I breathed in the sweet-dusty smell of leaf litter decay and held it—*one…two…three…four*, then released it, *one…two…three…four.*

Ford squatted in front of me and put a hand on one knee. "You okay, Mist?" He leaned in so I could hear his voice over the sound of the waterfall. "Maybe we shouldn't have done this. It's possible you have a concussion or—"

I shook my head. "Ford, stop. I didn't hit my head. It's not that. I get…shaky, sometimes." I took another deep breath, counted silently to four, and let it out. Not now. Please, God, not now. "I'll be okay," I said, more to convince myself, than reassure Ford.

"More water?" he asked.

I gave him a maybe nod, and he unscrewed the top from his water bottle and handed it to me. I tipped the bottle toward him like a "Cheers," and took a drink.

"Better?" His look was hopeful.

Not really. "Mm-hmm." I nodded and smiled.

After a concerned glance, Ford stood and faced the waterfall. I needed every little piece of my shredded self-control not to reach out and stop him, to keep him from leaving my side.

Instead, I continued to focus on my breathing. The glade where I sat was an idyllic little oasis, its own ecosystem. Lacy ferns grew from the rocks, the pines hung with wispy moss. Everything, including Ford and me, glistened in the spray from the falls, and the peace and beauty slowly calmed my racing heart.

At this time of year, the run-off was more a veil of spray than a waterfall, but I liked what I could see of the falls above the boulder that loomed next to us, blocking the way between us and the shower of creek water.

Ford sat next to me. "You sure you're okay?"

No. "Yeah," I said. "Why?"

He peered up at the boulder, like he was judging something. "Because I want to go stand under that waterfall."

"Sounds like fun, but, uh, whatcha gonna do about that boulder, Superman?"

Ford grinned. He left my side and, within moments, he'd scaled the rock. He stood on top of it, hands on his hips, laughing at my shocked expression from about twelve feet up. All he needed was a cape.

I yelled up to him, "Check you out. How did you do that?" I couldn't quite believe my eyes.

He said something inaudible over the cascading water, which ended with a gurgle beside me at the base of the boulder.

He turned and descended the rock about halfway, pushed off and dropped to the ground. Feeling stronger, I rose to meet him.

"My dad does a lot of search and rescue," he said, "and being able to climb is sort of a requirement. I've been rock climbing with him since I was in preschool."

He put a hand on each of my shoulders and scanned my face. I felt my cheeks warm. I took a breath and tried to look cool and confidant. I'm sure I didn't. I know my smile was shaky. But I held his gaze, and whatever he saw in my eyes seemed to satisfy him.

"You look pretty steady, now." He pointed at the rock. "You want to try it? If you look close, you can see hand and footholds all the way up." He started up again, showing me the way.

"I think you may be overestimating my upper body strength," I called up to him. *Not to mention, my nerve.*

He smiled down at me. "You can do it. This rock has so many great places to get a hold and, heck, even if you fell, the ground is so soft, it wouldn't hurt. Do what I do, and keep at least three points—like two hands and a foot—on the rock at all times."

"Do what he does," I muttered, getting a toe and some fingers into the lowest indentations. "But you're Superman."

"What?" he yelled down.

"Nothing. Don't make me talk." I'd grown up exploring forests and wilderness areas. It wasn't like I'd never climbed a rock before, and this wasn't El Capitan. But rock climbing had never been my favorite thing. And especially, not since Mom…

Crouched at the top, Ford yelled encouragement and advice at each advance as I slowly worked my way up the boulder. When I got close enough to reach him, he leaned down and dragged me the rest of the way. By that time, I was sweating, one knee, one elbow, and a good part of my stomach were all scraped.

But I felt like Wonder Woman when I conquered that rock, and I wasn't scared or wobbly anymore. Ford yelled, "You did it!" and gave me an exuberant congratulatory hug, as if we'd just summited Everest. Standing on top of that boulder with Ford, I felt like I could take on the universe.

Still, I was thankful that on the other side, rocks and gravel descended gradually into a dip, where the veil of mountain run-off collected in a crystal-clear pool.

Ford grabbed my hand. We slithered down the rocks and plunged beneath the shower, where I gasped, Ford yelled, and we immediately splashed back onto rock. The water was glacial. My soaking hair streamed into my eyes. Ford turned his head back and forth and droplets flew everywhere.

He smiled, reached out and pushed my bangs from my eyes. "You look like a wet puppy."

"Hmm, attractive, I'm sure."

He cupped my face in one hand and wiped a drip from my cheek with his thumb.

I felt exultant, free like I hadn't in, maybe, forever. Still, I wasn't sure I was ready for where Ford was taking us. I shivered, not from the cold, but I used it. I turned away and said, "My whole body is numb. Let's go find some sun."

We were still damp and shivering after we got to the meadow. I was surprised to see the sun resting near the top of the canyon wall. I pulled my phone out of our pile of boots and socks to check the time. Six-thirty. We threw ourselves on the ground in the last rays of sun, soaking up what warmth we could.

Ford said. "This has been a good day."

I nodded, my arm over my eyes. It had been a great day, despite the occasional moments of sheer terror. I still felt happy and confident as I had on top of that rock.

I turned on my side to face him. "I hope Lou made it home, but I guess no news is good news." Still, I lifted my phone and sent her a text. I hoped it would make it through the hills to wherever she was. "I guess we should get going."

He stood up and put out his hand, and there was a time when I would have paused, maybe pretended not to see, and pushed myself up. There were other times I would have taken his hand awkwardly, embarrassed by how much I wanted to be close to him.

This time, I didn't give it a second thought. At that moment, there was nothing I feared, least of all, Ford's touch. I grasped his hand and he pulled me up, but he didn't let go. Instead, he pulled me in, the question in his eyes.

TWENTY-ONE

I NODDED AND CLOSED my eyes when his lips met mine. That first kiss was tender and sweet, a gentleman's kiss. He stopped, and I opened my eyes. He was smiling softly, and he smelled like rain-washed cotton, and horse, and sun and earth.

I gathered his shirt in my fists and the next kiss wasn't as gentle. I stood on my toes and kissed him back like we belonged to each other, as if I was revealing all my secrets, until I could only feel him and me and how good it was to be that close.

For the last few months, I'd felt so anxious and sad—restless, and not like me at all. When I looked in the mirror, it was as if someone else was looking back. There'd been moments when I would've done almost anything to feel something different. I wondered if Ford was my answer, my solution. For a few minutes, wrapped in his arms, I thought he might be.

Somewhere in the back of my mind came muffled voices, like the sound of talking behind a closed door. I tried to ignore the voices, but they were persistent.

"Stuff happens on the rodeo circuit…" Ford had said it about Lou's past. What about his? How did he know? *"Cowgirl's been*

around, Misty." Been around. Would Ford put me in that category, too, after today? And what about him? This may have been my first real kiss, but his lips were working their way past my jaw line and down my neck, and I was pretty sure this wasn't his first rodeo.

And then Dad's voice, *"Whoa, Sweetness."* As if on cue, the phone in my back pocket dinged a text.

I didn't push Ford away out of any sense of virtue—virtue barely entered my mind. I was really just trying to push away those voices. I still had one hand on his chest and I could feel his heart pounding.

His eyes were wide. "I didn't mean…that was…whoa."

I stood there, hand on his chest, trying to catch my breath. After a few seconds, I dropped my arm to my side and the rest of the world came back into focus. The light was changing. The sun had continued to dip behind the mountains, and it was past time to start home, or be caught out in the dark.

I slid my phone out of my pocket. It was a text from Dad. "Lou's back. You two on your way?"

I sighed. I couldn't believe that text had gotten through. The coverage in the mountains that evening was near-miraculous.

"Your dad?" Ford asked.

I nodded and texted back. "On our way."

"W…we should get going." My voice sounded husky and breathless. I headed for my shoes.

Ford sat down next to me, and he was still for a moment. Finally, he took a breath and said, "Mist, I'm sorry." He pulled his boots toward him. "I didn't mean to, uh—" He ran his hands through his hair. "Well, I *did* mean to, but…"

I tied one boot and slipped a foot into the other one. Did he think I was mad? "It's okay. Really." I smiled, and he looked relieved. "It's all good. Just, I told Dad we're on our way."

He nodded, and I think it was thoughts of my father that caused us to focus on our boots as if they were the most fascinating things in the universe.

We weaved our way back through the trees and caught the trail home. After a while, somehow, my fingers were threaded in his, and things didn't feel so awkward.

We talked about all the places we'd lived with our gypsy, Forest Service parents. Ford mentioned again being half Native American because of his mom, and half Polish because of his dad.

"And the Japanese last name comes from…?"

"Ha, ha." He rolled his eyes. "Yeah, nobody ever gets that Tomaka is Polish. Drives my mom crazy."

"It's just you and your mom and dad?" I couldn't believe I'd never asked that question, and Ford was shaking his head.

"I have a little sister—"

"What? You never said."

"What's to tell?" But he was smiling affectionately. "Anna's fourteen—and *she* drives *me* crazy."

"She's a pill, but she's okay." He bumped me. "You know, for a girl."

"This is so weird." I shook my head. "You're rocking my world. I thought you were an only child, like Lou and me. No wonder you're so good at handling her."

He threw back his head and laughed. "Yeah, maybe. I do have practice with annoying girls who think they're all that."

"I always wanted a sister—and then I got Lou. I do love her."

"It's cool you guys are so close."

We walked for a while in silence. The breeze shifted and moved against us, whispered through the pines. My curiosity finally got the better of me. "So, that day we met you. Kurt said you have some family near here—on your mom's side, right? And you seemed sort of like you didn't want to talk about it?"

"So you're going to make me talk about it?"

Talk about annoying girls. I tried to back-track. "N-no. It's okay."

Ford chuckled. "I'm just messin' with you." We'd made the footbridge and he stopped. He leaned against the railing. "Grandma and Grandpa—my mom's parents—met in college. The state colleges had programs that would pretty much pay for tribal members' educations, but my grandparents were the only Native Americans at the school. So, I guess that drew them together, even though they were from two different tribes." He paused. "Tribes that don't…how do I explain? Not a lot of love, there."

"Really." I was trying to keep it neutral.

"What? You think being Indian means one big, unbroken hoop of Native peace?"

"W-Well—"

"Mist, you know what it's like. You've grown up in small towns. Everybody knows everybody, like in the Forest Service." He sighed. "Everybody knows everyone's business, there are no secrets, all your mistakes are hanging out there for everyone to judge—nobody ever forgets an insult or a grudge."

"Yeah," I said, "I know, but—"

He turned and I followed him off the bridge. After a few more steps down the trail, he stopped. "Yeah, well, on the Rez, you can meet somebody you've never seen before in your life, and as soon as they figure out who your people are, you're either their cousin or the great-grandson of the person who shot their grandpa and kidnapped their grandma."

I laughed.

Ford didn't. "Except, with that side of my family," he said, "the grudges go back to like, the beginning of time. Or, in Grandma and Grandpa's case, to when one tribe's chief supposedly betrayed the other tribe's chief in some army ambush."

"Wow." This was an intense side of Ford I'd never seen before, and I liked it.

"Or something," he continued. "I never got the whole story. All I know was that Grandma's family wouldn't even acknowledge her after she married Grandpa. They went to live with his family, but she was never really accepted, and neither was Mom. She left the Rez as soon as she could. Ended up going to the same college as my grandparents and that's where she met Dad, who grew up in Jersey, came west, and never looked back."

"And the circle was complete?" I couldn't help it.

He shot me a stormy look, but then, the grin. "Yeah, sorry about the overshare." He took my hand and we started walking again. "But you asked. Anyway, you can see where I wouldn't be all that excited about meeting the relatives."

"Yeah," I said. "But…no, yeah, I guess."

Ford stopped. "*I guess*, she says. What? You'd drop by?"

Why couldn't I keep my big mouth shut? Should I change the subject? It seemed like Ford wanted to talk about this, but didn't guys want girls to be fun and positive? Inwardly, I shrugged. I was who I was, and part of that meant being an anthropologist's daughter with a firm grasp of history and its consequences. I'd thought about this a lot.

"Well, yeah, people were really mean to each other. And we have to live with the consequences of their actions. But we're not them, and when are we going to move past all this hurt that doesn't belong to us, that isn't who *we* are?"

He was staring at me. I couldn't tell if he thought I was crazy or just weird. "The world's a mighty small place," I said, "and as far as we can tell, all we have in the universe is each other."

He didn't say anything.

"Never mind. I'm a dork."

"Yeah, but you sorta make sense."

"Oh, so I am a dork, but a sensible one?"

He smiled. "I get what you're saying. But if I'm being completely honest…"

"What?" I asked, as we started walking again.

"A part of me feels like that's easy for you to say. You've seen the ranchers out here flying confederate flags in their yards, right?"

I nodded.

"They're not flying those because they don't want *you* for a neighbor, Misty. Nobody mutters, 'Go back to the rez,' behind your back when you're in town. And that's happening right now, today."

Whoa. "People have said that to you, here?"

"Not to me, exactly. Cowards don't say it to your face, usually."

That made me so sad and angry, it took my breath away. But while I was struggling to respond, Ford shrugged. "One of Grandma's sisters wrote to her a while back, wanting to mend bridges, I guess. She and Gram have been writing and talking on the phone, mostly about old times. When Grandma told her I'd be here, she invited me to visit."

I was still stuck on the run-ins he'd had in Ponder. "Those people in town… Ford, I hate that you have to deal with that."

"It is what it is." He sounded more resigned than bitter, and for a second, I hated the whole world. But then he said, "What do you think? Go see the relatives, or not?"

"You should go," I urged. That, I was confident about. "Family is important."

"That's what Grandma says," he stopped and faced me. "But enough about me, what's up with you and your dad?"

"Wh…what do you mean?" An hour ago, I'd wanted to tell him all my secrets. But now, even to my ears, my voice sounded defensive. I was ready for sharing time to be over. I could feel my palms dampen, so I dropped his hand and moved ahead of him.

He caught up with me and tried to catch my eye. I ignored the attempt.

"You seem a little…your dad's cool, you know. But you two seem…"

"Uncomfortable," I finished for him.

"Maybe."

We walked in silence for a while. A mourning dove lamented the fading light, or maybe it was an owl. Dad would have known.

The breeze carried the familiar scent of dry sage and grass, and I knew we were getting close to home. The light was fading fast when we broke through the trees and hiked through the orchard. I could see a light in the barn, and I led us to the front porch, to get as far away from that lighted window as possible.

It was quiet. Lou was probably in bed and Dad was still out in the barn. I knew Dad wouldn't be happy with us coming back so late, and I didn't want Ford to have to face him. I was getting ready to send him on his way, when I remembered one of the reasons we'd wanted to go to the meadow.

I turned at the door and snapped a finger. "We forgot all about redoing the picture of Mom at Opal Creek. I really wanted to get that shot."

"There is that picture of you and me at Opal Creek." Ford moved in front of me, but I took a step back. "Remember? Lou took it the first day we were on site, with the horses in the background." He smiled down at me. "I like that one."

"Me, too." Before he could say, or do, anything else, I said, "Well, 'night. See you on Monday." Returning his puzzled look with a bright smile and wave, I slipped through the door and shut it behind me. I felt bad about leaving him standing there, but really, I was doing him a favor. Whether he knew it or not, he did not want to meet up with my dad at that moment.

I took the loft stairs two at a time. Lou was sitting up in bed, eyes wide. She started to say, "Where have…?"

I waved frantically and put my finger to my lips, shushing her. Our windows were open and Ford was still down there. I knew how easy it would be for him to hear every word we said. I breathed a sigh of relief when I heard him start down the porch steps.

Then I heard the words I'd been dreading.

"Oh. Hi, Dr. Stevens."

TWENTY-TWO

I EASED ONTO MY bed, grabbed my pillow and buried my face in it.

"Ford," was all Dad said.

"I was just dropping off Misty. I guess Lilou got back a while ago."

"She and Rosa made it in around six. I imagine she's gone to bed by now." Dad's tone of voice would have sounded mild, to the untrained ear. I knew a lecture was coming.

"Uh, yeah. She probably told you." Ford sounded really apologetic. "You were right about Rosa."

I lifted my head. Telling my dad he was right was a stroke of genius! I could imagine Ford inching his way backward, off the porch, ready to make a break for his truck.

Lou nodded with a glint in her eye and mouthed, "Oh, he's good."

"Have a seat, Ford." There was the sound of chairs scraping, boards squeaking, and a resigned sigh from Ford.

Silence. Crickets.

Finally, Dad's voice. "Ford, I don't have a lot of rules. I've always believed the more rules there are, the more creative people will become about breaking them."

Oh, Lord, not his professor voice, please.

"But the Stevens family does have a certain way of doing things. I'm not saying it's right for every family—it's just what we do. You understand?"

"Uhhh," was all he got from Ford.

Lou eased off her bed and inched her way to mine, expertly avoiding all the squeaky floor boards.

"Ford—" Dad sounded stern. "In the Stevens family, we do not date—"

Lou snicker-whispered, "What, are you Amish? Because I have some novels you should read when we get back home. You're not doing it right."

I shook my head and murmured, "Wait for it."

She whispered, "What?"

I plopped my face back into the pillow.

"Dr. Stevens," Ford said, "kids don't really date anymore."

Dad ignored him. "We, sort of…court, but we don't date."

"You *court?*" Ford sounded confused. I could imagine the look on his face. "As in, preparing to ask someone's hand in marriage? That kind of court?"

Lou buried her head in my shoulder. She was laughing so hard my whole body shook, but at least she was doing it quietly.

"Well," Dad mumbled, "not in a creepy, Christian Taliban kind of way. The fact is, Misty's been through a rough time."

Dad was actually having trouble with this. I'd rarely heard him fumble over the, "no exclusive dating" talk. He'd never had to have this conversation with a guy he knew as well as he knew Ford. It made me feel a tiny bit better.

"Don't you think—" Ford sounded like he was choosing his words very carefully. "Don't you think Misty and I are a little young to be thinkin' about marriage?"

Dad pounced on that like a cougar on a baby deer. "Exactly!"

Lou threw herself backward on the bed, turned and buried her head in the quilt to cover her laughter.

"I have to say, this summer has been crazy different than I thought it would be." Ford's voice sounded so normal. I lifted my head from the pillow.

"But, it's been great," he said, "and I think I get what you're saying."

I couldn't believe it. Was Ford actually sitting down there, calmly talking with Dad like this made sense?

"Ford, you seem like a good kid." A chair creaked. I pictured Dad leaning toward him. "So, I'm going to tell you something I wouldn't normally admit."

"Okay."

Lou sat up and leaned closer to the window.

"I have to confess, I haven't always been able to walk the line I've set for myself in life. Who does? But—" he paused. The breeze ruffled the curtains. I stared at the window, unblinking, like somehow that would help me hear better. "It's not the occasional misstep that concerns me, so much as the general direction you're headed. You understand what I'm saying?"

"Uh, yeah. I think so."

Chairs creaked. Boots moved across the porch. "Good night, then," Dad said.

"Good night, Dr. Stevens. See you Monday."

Lou and I sat motionless, listening to the sound of Ford's boots crunch down the drive. His truck fired up and the sound faded in the distance.

She turned to me and opened her mouth, but I put my hand over it, willing her with my eyes to stay quiet. Dad was still down there. Finally, after what seemed like forever, we heard him move across the porch to the door. The screen squeaked open, but before it slapped shut, his voice drifted up to us.

"Goodnight, girls."

WE WOKE EARLY SUNDAY morning to a knock at the door. Lou pushed past Dad as soon as she saw who it was, and with a happy whoop, threw herself into her mom's arms.

June wrapped her in a warm embrace and smiled at me as I stumbled down the steps from the loft behind Lou. I was moving slow, still sore from the day before.

"I made it to Ponder late last night and checked into the motel," she explained. "I was going to call, but I thought a surprise would be fun."

Lou stepped away from her. "Surprises are good." She laughed, and she looked so happy.

We spent the cool morning on the porch, sipping cups of steaming coffee and hot chocolate. Dad and I occupied the porch chairs, and June and Lou took over the swing. The two of them rocked gently back and forth, catching up on Alton gossip. Lou updated her mom about Rosa, and all the intrigue and "treasure" surrounding the Passports in Time project.

She focused more on the treasure and the legend of the Ghost of Gold Creek, skimming quickly over the pothunting incident, even though that should have been the most exciting part. A couple times, I forgot I was supposed to be keeping all that happened between her and Cody a secret. Then it would hit me, and I'd do an anxious reassessment of my interactions with Dad to be sure I hadn't given anything away. It was exhausting.

But I laughed as hard as anyone at Lou's descriptions, in vivid and hilarious detail, of Bob and Sherrie Blackwell and their ranch, and Kurt, Frank, Donna, and Bea. It seemed like she'd memorized every quirky thing Bea had said all summer, and she had everyone's voices and gestures down perfectly. When she mimicked Bea saying she'd, "be thumped down and shot at," June choked on her coffee.

"And then," Lou threw me a mischievous glance, "there's Misty's boyfriend, Ford Tomaka."

Good thing she wasn't close enough for me to reach her. Dad shot me a look.

"Yeah, what Lou means," I said, glaring at her, "is that he's a boy, and he's a friend—my friend *and* Lou's friend." I was still wearing the friendship bracelet he'd given me. I didn't realize I was moving it nervously around and around my wrist until Dad's eyes started following the motion. I stopped and put my hands under my legs. "Actually," I said, staring Dad down, "Ford's sorta like the son Dad never had."

I was hoping for a defensive denial, something that would take his attention off of me and Ford. But Dad didn't take the bait. Instead, he echoed what he'd said last night. "Ford seems like a good kid. I'm glad the three of them became *friends* this summer. Everyone on the passports team gets along great."

June smiled at Dad, and her gaze quickly returned to her daughter. She reached out her hand and pushed Lou's hair from her face, but one lock of dark hair escaped. She gently wound it behind Lou's ear, and my friend turned and smiled into her mom's eyes.

It was such a normal, everyday, wordless exchange between a mom and daughter, and it brought tears to my eyes. I managed to wipe them away before anyone noticed, but I was relieved when they decided to drive into Pendleton, the nearest city of any size, for some birthday shopping and dinner.

June invited both of us, but Dad laughed at the idea of spending his Sunday shopping with three women. Lou and I had already talked about how this time with her mom might be a chance for her to come clean about Cody. Then June could break the news to Dad. I pleaded exhaustion from the day before, so they could have some time alone.

Before they left, though, June insisted that the two of us take a walk together. "Show me this orchard I've heard so much about."

The moment we had the house between us and the others, she nudged me. "How you doing?"

"Okay." I shrugged. "You know."

She nodded, like she knew, and didn't fill the silence.

When we reached the middle of the orchard, she stopped me and turned my body to face her. "Misty."

That's all she said, but it was clear she really wanted to know what was going on with me, and more than that, wasn't about to leave until she did.

So I told her about Dad. How sometimes I thought maybe we were connecting, and other times I was sure that we didn't get each other and never would. How I worried so much about him that it made me cry, left me sleepless. And how, sometimes, he was so infuriating, I wanted to leave him to himself and never come back.

I finally stopped and looked at June, but she was looking past me with a little smile. "What?"

"I want to tell you something. But I need to work up to it. Bear with me, okay?"

I nodded.

"Do you remember that day a few winters ago," she continued, "after we'd been snowed in for weeks? Liberty Bell managed to get their team bus up the hill and we were actually going to get to have the biggest game of the year after all?"

"Yeah."

"And I came to pick you up…"

"And Dad said I couldn't go because I hadn't finished shoveling the driveway before dinner like he asked me to."

June chuckled. "You were so mad…"

"Yeah, ha, ha."

She gave my hand a sympathetic squeeze. "Your Dad was gone—some emergency conference call he couldn't get out of—and you started storming around, slamming doors, yelling at your mom about how mean your Dad was. And, oh, by the way, hadn't he ever heard of a snow blower, and what on earth ever attracted her to such a grumpy kill-joy?"

I puffed a laugh. "I didn't know you were there for all of that."

"I was hiding from the storm in the kitchen, where your mother and I were having a perfectly great conversation until you exploded. I sat in there listening to your mom handle you." June shook her head. "Lord almighty, she was patient. I would have yelled right back at you, but not your mom. Do you remember what she did?"

I remembered. She had raised her voice at me, and that's when I knew I'd really crossed the line.

"Misty, sit!" she'd said.

And I sat.

She threw herself down on the couch beside me. I dared an eye roll, but I was prepared for a lecture, or worse. She was silent, eyes closed, and I suspected she was counting to ten in her head.

Then, she started telling me a story about her and Dad.

It was about an outdoor concert she and Dad attended a few years before, on a trip to celebrate their twentieth anniversary. They were sitting up on a hill, apart from the rest of the crowd, waiting for the show to start.

"It was getting pretty dark," Mom said, "and I heard your dad murmur, 'Here it comes.' I thought he was talking about the band, but he was looking the opposite direction. He pointed at the top of the hills. I didn't see anything out of the ordinary." She paused, her eyes distant. "The next second, this brilliant white light spilled over the hillside, and the round edge of a huge, glowing full moon appeared."

"We held hands and watched it come up." Her smile widened. "But Mist, a part of me wanted to stand up and yell at everybody staring at that stage, *look, there's the real show. You're missing it.* So, in answer to your question, that's what attracted me to your dad, among other things. He notices things that other people miss."

June was watching me remember. "He sees stuff that everyone else misses. I heard her tell you that. And she put her arms around you, and what did she tell you next?"

I whispered it. "She said, 'And you're just like him.'"

"And the people we are most like…" June took my hand in hers. "Those are the people we tend to clash with the most. But they're also the ones who can understand us the best, if we just give each other the chance."

I sniffed and wiped at the tears gathering in the corners of my eyes. "I know. But we don't even know how to talk to each other. She was like the ambassador between our two countries."

June laughed at that. "You may have something, there."

"Mom would have wanted us to do this better. But I don't know how."

"Neither does your Dad," she said softly. Then she smiled. "But you two love each other, I know that, and I also know you'll figure this out. Don't give up on him, Misty. He is trying."

I STOOD NEXT TO Dad and watched Lou and June climb into their truck. Lou was wearing the cool black T with a white dancer silhouette I'd given her for her birthday, skinny white jeans and flip flops. She looked awesome, as always, but also happy like a little kid on a day out with her Mom. At that moment, that's exactly what she was.

June called through the open window, "You're sure we can't tempt you?"

I shook my head and waved her off.

"Okay, then," she said. "But don't wait up. We're going to shop 'til we drop and do dinner and a movie."

The truck started off, then abruptly halted. Lou hopped out and ran back while I walked away from Dad and met her halfway. "Mist," she said, "are you sure you don't want to come? I can have the whole Cody conversation with Mom later…"

"Later? Like, when?" I gave her a look. "Your Mom's leaving first thing in the morning." I turned her with a little shove toward their truck. "Go. You've been looking forward to your mom coming all week. Have a good time and, you know, sort of, weave in what happened with Cody. The way you do."

She was backstepping away from me, and she giggled. I started toward the barn. "Have a good time," I called back to her, "and hey, good luck."

I watched until they were out of sight before I went inside the barn. Dad was already at his workbench, mending the screens we used to sift dirt at the site. I led a grateful-looking Rosa out to the pasture and mucked out her stall, dumped the wheelbarrow load behind the barn and threw some feed and fresh hay into the area I'd cleaned out.

I grabbed a couple water bottles from the garage fridge and handed one to Dad, before leaning against the door frame and enjoying the feel of the breeze on my sweaty face. Rosa noticed me and clopped my direction. Her enthusiasm for my presence made me smile. "I know you only love me for the horse cookies I give you."

Dad walked up beside me, twisting the cap off his bottle. "Rosa looks like she ran through some rough stuff yesterday."

I didn't know how much Lou had told Dad about our adventures with Rosa. I took a sip of my water. "Her mane and tail are covered in burs. Is there any way to get those out, short of scissors?"

"Go get her, and I'll show you my secret weapon."

What was he up to now? I grabbed the lead and climbed through the fence into the pasture. Rosa came right to me, which was gratifying. Maybe horses and I really could coexist peacefully after all. "Hey pretty girl. I think Dad might have a makeover in mind."

Inside the barn, he was standing near Rosa's stall with a can of something in his hand. As I got closer, the bold letters and numbers on the side came into focus: WD40.

"You're kidding."

He raised an eyebrow and waved us past him into the stall. "Never any confidence in your old man. Come and be amazed."

Dad handed me the can and a brush and pointed at the first cocklebur. I wasn't sure how Rosa was going to react to the hiss of the aerosol, but she took it all in stride.

He gave an approving nod. "I think Rosa may have been through this routine before."

The oil was, in fact, a miracle worker. With only a small amount of the magical liquid, the burs slid right out. Dad helped me get the burs from her legs and chest, then returned to his screens while I tackled her mane. I soon fell into a rhythm— spray a little oil, brush, brush, brush and work out the small burs and pieces left behind with my fingers. The most difficult part was avoiding the sharp poke and prod of the prickly burs.

The only sounds, other than the spray of the aerosol and the brush scraping through her mane, were Rosa's snuffles, and an occasional pling or squeak from whatever Dad was doing to the screens. Every once in a while, the breeze through the open barn door swirled the dirt and hay on the floor with a soft swish.

After about thirty minutes Dad stopped what he was doing and looked up. "Those fumes getting to you? Why don't you wander outside and get some air? Horses are like little kids," he said. "They have short attention spans, especially when it comes to standing still." He rubbed a hand across Rosa's side as we walked by. "She's behaving so well, but you should reward the good behavior before she gets antsy."

After we returned to her stall, even with the WD40 magic, I worked for over an hour to remove the cockleburs from Rosa's mane. Next, I tackled her forelock, and that was an even greater challenge. The sensitive space between her ears, made worse by those pesky cockleburs, was an area she did not want me to touch. She kept shying away.

Dad suggested I spend a little time petting her face, her neck and ears. I'd work at a couple burs, by hand, since she would have nothing to do with me brushing her forelock, and I'd pet her face…

Back and forth, and back and forth, pet, pull out a bur, pet, pull out a bur.

Of course, this sensitive area also had the most burs, and it took me another hour to work them free. More than a little pleased with myself, I stepped back to look at my handiwork. The lack of cockleburs was definitely an improvement, but she didn't look quite right yet.

The burs had left long tendrils of dead hair in her mane, which made it frizz. I began brushing through it again and, when that still wasn't quite enough, Dad handed me his pocketknife. I ran it down the ends of her hair, like I was performing a razor cut at the hair salon, through the weak tendrils that were already dead, and brushed all the excess out.

Three hours after I'd started, I was tired, sweaty and finger-sore, but Rosa was restored to all her former glory, maybe better than I'd ever seen her.

Dad came next to me and looked her over. "She looks good, Misty. Nice work." He tilted his head toward the workbench. "Come on over. I want to show you something." I was proud of my work and reluctant to leave Rosa. But Dad had just given me what, for him, was a huge compliment. I tried not to be greedy. After I put Rosa in her stall, I joined him at the workbench.

I wondered if he'd come up with some new insight from the artifacts we'd gathered at the site that week. Which reminded me. "Have you heard any more about what happened with Cody?"

Dad shook his head. "Kurt said they scared him with jail time if he ever came near another archaeological site, but they only charged him with vandalism. His parents showed up and bailed him out, pending a trial. Kurt's still sure Cody had an accomplice, but the kid wasn't talking," he paused. "Anyway, this isn't about the project."

He missed my relieved sigh when he turned to grab something I couldn't see from a low shelf. Facing me, he held whatever it was behind him. "I have one more birthday present for you. But I wanted to give it to you when we were alone."

He laid a book with a soft leather cover in my hands. "I've been looking through it, and I thought you should have it."

"Mom's Bible." I stared at him, stunned.

"I know she seemed fearless. But she didn't muster all that courage on her own."

My eyes started to tear up, and Dad was ready with some tissue.

"Wow, you thought of everything."

He lifted a shoulder, half-grinning. "After yesterday morning…"

"You catch on quick." I was being ironic, but he didn't notice, and I was actually glad he didn't. I took the tissue from him and dabbed at my eyes, plopped down on the barn floor and started paging through the Bible. There were notes and highlights on almost every page—everything that Mom thought was important or wanted to remember. "She's still telling me things I forgot to ask."

Dad lowered himself next to me and leaned back against a hay bale. "What'd you say?"

I shook my head.

"Misty, you can talk to me. You know that, right? I do want to know what's going on in your head, but I can't, if you don't tell me."

"Why don't we go to church anymore?" I blurted it out and continued to page through the Bible, not looking at him.

He didn't answer me. When I looked up, he'd leaned back his head and closed his eyes. "We'll go back," he finally said, "when we get home, okay? Every time I got near that building, it reminded me of her memorial service."

"Are you mad at God for taking her?"

He sat up. "Wow."

"You wanted to know what I'm thinking."

He laughed once. "And I do…" He took a breath. "I don't think of Him as being the one who took her—God isn't the one in this world who steals our joy. I think of Him as the one who comforts me, now she's gone. I'm not mad. I'm…sad."

"Me, too."

He brushed my bangs off my forehead and ducked his head to see my eyes. "I know," he said. "And I'm glad you've had friends around this summer to help with that."

I nodded. He was right, maybe not in the way he thought. But as frustrating and confusing as my relationships could be with Lou and Ford, they did keep my mind from constantly circling back to Mom, except at night.

Then there was Lookout.

"And about that," Dad said, like he'd read my mind.

"About what?"

"When you and Ford didn't come back until late last night…" He let that hang, as if waiting for an explanation.

Here it was, the Ford talk. Just when I was starting to feel like maybe I could connect with Dad. I stared, unseeing, as the pages in my lap blurred and the silence between us expanded, pushing us apart.

He cleared his throat. "When Lou came back alone, and it got so late, I got to thinking. I like Ford, I do. But we don't really know that much about him, his background."

"Dad, we lost track of time, that's all. Ford's a good guy." I sounded defensive, like I'd done something wrong. *Great.*

"I think you're right, Misty, but even good guys can be really stupid when they're young. And around girls. Lou's friend Cody would be a case in point. Girls have to be careful."

Oh, man, he had no idea. And I was so tired of being careful. "I'm not Lou. You have enough to handle. You don't need to worry about me."

"And yet," Dad said softly, "I do."

At least when it came to Ford. I sighed and pushed myself up. I didn't know what to say to him. If it had been Mom I could have maybe...*maybe*...told her what happened with Ford yesterday and how confused I was. But Dad? So, I wasn't that different from Lou, after all. I couldn't bear his disappointment.

He was watching me. "Leaving?"

I started for the door of the barn and the path to the orchard, while waving the Bible I held in one hand. "I'm going to take this and look through it for a while, okay? I'll be back in time to make dinner."

"Misty," he called.

I pretended not to hear.

SLIDING DOWN TO THE base of my tree in the orchard, I let the Bible open in my lap and hoped Lookout would make an appearance. The Bible opened to Psalms, where mom had marked lots of phrases.

The Lord is my rock, my fortress and my deliverer... Even though I walk through the darkest valley, I will fear no evil, for you are with me... For in the day of trouble he will keep me safe in his dwelling; he will shelter me and set me high upon a rock...

I wondered, *is that where you are? With the God you loved so much, safe and beautiful? I'm happy for you, but we need you.*

I heard rustling in the orchard, but there was no stallion in sight. Breeze ruffled the tissue-thin pages of the Bible and they turned. More highlights, and the words were familiar to me, verses Mom had taught me to memorize over the years, but ones I hadn't thought about in a while.

The Lord is close to the brokenhearted and saves those who are crushed in spirit…God is our refuge and strength, an ever-present help in trouble. Therefore, we will not fear, though the earth gives way and the mountains fall into the heart of the sea…

Words to comfort in a time of trouble—all that memorization wasn't just an educational exercise. Mom had been trying to prepare me for a time she hoped I'd never have to face. But she knew how hard the world could be.

I felt broken-hearted, that was for sure.

She used to tell me, "When God doesn't make sense to you, look at Jesus."

I turned to the New Testament and found more markings…*Blessed are those who mourn, for they will be comforted…Do not let your hearts be troubled. You believe in God, believe also in Me…Where, O death, is your victory? Where, O death, is your sting?*

To hope, maybe believe, my future didn't depend on me being strong and doing everything right *was* comforting. I wanted to believe that there was a God who had my mess covered and somehow it would all work out. Dad and I would figure out how to love each other. Lou would be okay. Ford would…I didn't even know what I wanted to happen with Ford. All I knew was that I wanted to believe in happy endings, for everybody.

But I still felt stung—bruised, battered—by her death.

Twigs crackled in the orchard, but not Lookout's heavy-footfalls. Some small animal was hidden in the tangled bushes and underbrush. High above me, I heard a screech and searched what I could see of the sky between my tree's branches. A hawk wheeled in cloudless blue, and the small birds flitting through the orchard went silent. They'd learned how to survive in this beautiful, tragic world we inhabited together.

I stared at the spot where the woods had begun to encroach on the orchard—the last place I'd seen Lookout before my wild ride with Rosa. I didn't really know what I was trying to accomplish with the stallion. Never once did I consider attempting to ride him. I might as well have hopped on an elk, or a moose. We'd become companions of a sort—friends, maybe. But I knew Lookout was a wild animal, and I was always surprised to see him, half expecting each of our encounters to be the last.

I thought I might never see him again, but that night, I wanted him to come so much. With Lookout, I could be who I was becoming, instead of who I'd been. Ford had a similar effect on me, but Lookout was the only one in my life who didn't seem to demand more than I felt prepared to give. I couldn't fake it with the stallion and he still accepted me, the real me. The present me.

"Lookout," I whispered, "where are you?"

TWENTY-THREE

I WAITED AT THE edge of the orchard until darkness fell, but Lookout never came. I'd forgotten about dinner. Dad didn't mention it when I came in. He'd made himself a sandwich and I did the same. All that had happened over the weekend had left me bone-tired and soul weary. I left the dishes in the sink and took my sandwich up to my bed.

LOU'S MATTRESS CREAKED AND I opened one eye. The first thing I saw was my half-eaten sandwich on the crate between our beds. I'd thought Lou was just getting home, but I must have completely missed that part of the night. Sunlight filtered through the curtain at my window.

Lou cooed, "Morning sleepyhead. Man, you were out." She pointed toward the porch. "Mom's leaving. I came up to see if you wanted to say goodbye."

I pushed myself halfway up. "So, she's letting you stay?" I mumbled.

"What?"

I pushed my hair out of my face and rubbed my eyes. "She's letting you stay? Even after hearing about the thing with Cody?"

Her eyes slid away from mine. "Umm…"

"Lou," I shook my head. "You didn't tell her."

She ignored me, lifted the curtain at her window, and her eyes widened.

I twisted around to catch a glimpse of June before she left and was greeted by the sight of Dad and June sharing a lingering embrace beside her truck.

My jaw dropped as I watched them hold each other.

Dad gave June's shoulder a final, gentle squeeze as he stepped back and opened the truck's door. She climbed in and, with a cheerful wave, drove away.

I blinked, my sleepy brain dancing drunkenly around the implications of that embrace—*we don't date, we court.*

Lou and I turned and locked eyes for a few seconds. Her mouth curled into a mischievous smile. "Well, it wouldn't be so bad, would it, Mist? To really be sisters?"

I couldn't believe what I had seen—what she was saying. I loved June, but she could never be my mother, and Dad wasn't Lou's father. My fist tightened around my pillow, and I imagined launching it as hard as I could, right at her stupid, smiling face.

Instead, I plopped back into bed with my back to her and pulled the quilt over my head.

It didn't seem to dampen her spirits in the least. "Anyway, I guess it's time to get up. Dibs on the bathroom." I heard her feet, light on the stairs, then the thumping of the old plumbing when she turned on the shower.

I stayed curled in the safety of my cocoon, eyes tight against anything else the world might throw at me. It felt impossible, facing Dad this morning…or Ford…or Lou. The band tightened around my heart and pain started to radiate up my neck and into my head.

Lou came, got dressed, and left again. When Dad yelled up the stairs for the third time, "Mist, feet on the deck! Let's go," I knew I couldn't hide any longer.

"God, Mom, somebody," I whispered, "help. I can't do this. I can't."

I'd only read the words last night, but I'd once had them memorized, and there they were. *The Lord is close to the brokenhearted and saves those who are crushed in spirit…God is our refuge and strength, an ever-present help in trouble. Therefore, we will not fear, though the earth gives way and the mountains fall into the heart of the sea…*

I took a deep breath, but it caught in my throat. My chest still felt tight, my heart pounded. I sat up, rolled my shoulders and cracked my neck. That was better. I took another breath and the tightness in my chest loosened.

As usual, I had no choice but to keep moving, to take the next step. I threw on some clothes and marched down the stairs.

WE WERE RUNNING LATE, so there was barely time to talk. The three of us hurried through breakfast and packed the van in silence, avoiding each other's eyes. When we met up with Ford and the others at the campground, I was surprised at how casual Ford was, until I realized he had no idea Lou and I had overheard his and Dad's entire conversation Saturday night.

The day was overcast but warm and humid. The sun and the sky felt like weights on my head. By mid-morning, we were all caked in dust and sweat. We'd found nothing interesting in the ground or the screens, and the crew was grumpy. Everyone seemed exhausted and we were getting careless. At one point, Ford missed the middle of Frank's screen with a bucketful of dirt, and the whole mess tipped and poured back into the test pit.

Frank immediately launched into a lecture about how "You kids today don't understand hard work and responsibility," how he'd been in boot camp and then the jungles and deserts of battle when he was about Ford's age, how Ford needed to decide what he wanted out of life.

Ford set his jaw and ignored him, which seemed to make Frank even angrier. That was when Dad, thankfully, called a break. Lou and I threw ourselves down in the meager shade of some scrawny juniper, a little way from the others.

"I'd pretty much rather be anywhere than here, right now," Lou said. "Stick a fork in me, I'm done."

I was ecstatic not to be digging and dumping pails of dirt. "You sound like Bea," I said, and wiped my gritty lips on my sleeve. "I feel like I've eaten a bowl full of dirt this morning."

"No kidding."

Ford wandered over, pulled off his work gloves and sat next to me.

I nudged him. "Sorry about Dad the other night."

He grinned. "So, you heard about that?"

Lou elbowed me, hard, which pushed me into Ford. "Heard about it?" She cackled. "We heard the whole thing. You know those windows above the porch?"

Ford's smile faded and he moved away from me, so our shoulders no longer touched.

"I can't believe Dad gave you that talk," I said. "You handled it really well, though." I was trying to sound encouraging. I should've kept my mouth shut. I racked my brain, frantic for a way to change the subject.

His head dropped. "Jeez," he mumbled.

Lou smirked. "I can't believe you actually used the words, 'hand in marriage.' I was laughing so hard."

I put a warning hand on Lou's arm, but it was too late. The rest of the crew threw us some curious looks, but I was fairly sure they were too far away to hear what we were talking about.

Ford's head shot up and he glared at Lou. "Oh, yeah, cowgirl. Like you could've handled that situation any better."

"Lou," I pleaded. "Ford."

They both turned on me. "What?"

"I don't know. It's not a big deal. Don't be stupid."

"Too late for that." Ford looked hurt. "And maybe what happened on Saturday wasn't a big deal to you—"

"Ugh." I put my face in my hands. "That's not what I meant."

He pushed himself up and took a couple steps, then turned around. "You know what I told your Dad Saturday night?" His voice was so cold it gave me goose bumps. "About this summer being pretty great? You just changed my mind."

We watched him stalk off without a backward glance. I fell back onto the hard, prickly ground.

Lou collapsed beside me. "I'm an idiot."

I couldn't muster a response. We were both lying there, watching the thunderheads stack over the mountains, when Dad called us back to work.

The three of us spent the rest of the day in mostly sullen silence, communicating only enough to get the job done. The adults gave us a few puzzled looks, but left us alone. By the time we dropped off the others at the campground, I didn't want to do anything but drink a gallon of water, shower, and sleep.

"I'm really sorry, you guys." Lou said after the adults exited the van at the campground. She glanced at Dad, and I knew she was hoping he couldn't hear her.

Ford was already halfway out the door. "Yeah, *no big deal,*" he muttered, without looking at either one of us. He marched to his truck, hopped in and peeled away in a cloud of dust.

"I can't imagine how lame he must think I am," Lou whispered.

"Never mind, Lou." I sighed. "I shouldn't have brought it up. Besides, you know Ford. He'll get over it." I hoped he would. I sounded more confident than I felt.

I caught Dad watching us in the rearview mirror, but he didn't say anything. We'd had a long day and finished up late. He was tired, like us. On our way through town, he stopped off at the taco truck, and we ate dinner on the way home.

At the house, we unloaded and hauled the equipment into the barn. Lou and I were headed for the shower when Dad called me from inside the barn. Lou continued into the house while I backtracked to Dad.

"Yeah?" I sighed and dropped onto a hay bale. Walls of the stuff rose up all around me. I leaned my head against the hay. It felt scratchy, but it smelled sweet and clean after the dusty day.

Dad was looking in one of the notebooks we used to record information. "You all right?"

I nodded, but he wasn't looking at me, so I added, "Uh-huh. What's up?"

"I met with Kurt the other day while you guys were at the library. He says the archaeologist for this district is retiring this year, so the position will be open."

I closed my eyes and whispered, "No, Dad. Please."

He was walking away. He didn't hear me.

He knew I would hate the idea, not to mention that he'd promised me we weren't moving, that this was only for a summer. Four years in one place was like an eternity for our family, and Alton was home, *my* home. He was giving me the bad news the way you'd rip off a bandage. And I knew there was nothing I could do to change his mind.

The day before, I'd left the brushes I'd been using with Rosa on the workbench. Dad picked them up, carried them across the barn and placed them on a shelf beside her stall. "I know a move isn't what we talked about."

His back was to me, but I could see his hand shifting a brush back and forth, as if he couldn't quite find the right spot for it. "I've thought about this job a lot, and I think it's the right move for us." He looked over, like he was trying to gauge my reaction, but I gave him nothing. I felt drained, empty, and it was a familiar feeling. I was in shock.

Rosa shifted nervously and snorted. She knew something was up. Dad reached over and rubbed her shoulder. "I've already applied for the position and I think I have a good shot at it."

I got up and walked out of the barn while he was still talking. I didn't need to hear the rest. Of course, he would get the job. He never failed to get a position he applied for—he had a great reputation in the Forest Service, and he was good at what he did. It wasn't as if there were an excess of PhD archaeologists in the world.

He believed I'd get used to the idea, and why wouldn't he? We had moved so many times before. "Home" was wherever we were together. While I hadn't been wild about some of our past moves, somehow, Mom always turned exploring a new place into a grand adventure, and her enthusiasm was infectious.

But this time she wasn't here. This time, her absence didn't make me sad, it made me mad. As I stumbled toward the house, it was like I could feel all my grief and sadness compress into a tiny searing nugget in my chest. Then it exploded.

I was mad at Lou for so many things, and at Ford for not being more understanding this afternoon. I was mad at Lookout for disappearing, and I was mad at myself.

If I were a better person, I would have been able to fix the awkwardness between Dad and me. But I was mad at Dad for making the decision to move us again without even asking me, and now I catch him hugging June? Mom was barely gone and he was hugging another woman.

My chest and throat burned hot as I ran through the front door, past the bathroom where Lou was showering and up the stairs to the loft.

Truth was, I was mad at Mom most of all. Why hadn't she watched her step? How could she have been so careless? How could she have raised me to believe life was beautiful, and leave me in a nightmare world I didn't know how to navigate without her?

And then there was God—where was He? He'd taken my mother from me and now I felt nothing but alone. What? Wasn't I brokenhearted enough, yet?

I stood in the middle of the loft and spun around, gasping for breath, feeling trapped. I heard thunder in the distance, so I grabbed the first jacket my hands touched—Mom's orange sweater. I tore out of the house, sprinted past the orchard and into the woods. My lungs felt like they would burst, but I ran hard and fast, just so I could feel something different than the anger and grief that felt like it was searing my heart to cinders.

I DIDN'T THINK, OR NOTICE where I was going. The saplings and brush beside the trail snagged my clothes as I tripped and stumbled past. I didn't care. Everything was a blur, except my anger, which was clear, sharp and excruciating.

Finally, completely spent, I doubled over, coughing and struggling for breath. I wasn't exactly sure where I was, but I didn't think I could have gone too far. I wasn't concerned about being lost, and I wasn't ready to go home. Right then, I didn't think I'd ever be ready to face Dad again.

I hiked forward on a narrow, brushy trail, more cautious than I'd been before. I had a sense of heading the general direction Lou and I had hiked on Saturday, but it wasn't the same trail. As the light started to fade, the shadows lengthened, and the forest took on an eerie, unfamiliar feel. I turned back, but the trail became harder and harder to make out, until all I could see ahead of me was dense brush and juniper.

I had no choice. I turned around again and tried to pick my way along the trail in the other direction, pretty sure I was headed away from the ranch, hoping I could find the main trail and circle back.

Because of the heavy cloud cover, I was wandering through an early dusk. The trees creaked in the rising wind. A twig snapped behind me. I whipped around and scanned the trees and underbrush. Nothing seemed alarming, but I had a sense of not being alone. If Lookout was following me, he would have shown himself by now. I jumped when a flock of small birds burst from the bushes, whirled into the clouds and disappeared.

I kept moving as fast as I could to distance myself from the sounds behind me. I had no trail to follow, only dense undergrowth to push through. It became darker and darker. My breath came in gasps.

I scanned the skies above me, but the thick cloud afforded no hope of stars or moonlight. Thunder rolled in the distance, and each explosion sounded closer.

There came a point where the sky was so dark, I had to feel my way from tree to tree, then came the lightening. Using the strobe-like light, I continued to make my way in a direction I prayed would take me home. If something was following me, I was making too much noise to hear it. I hoped the noise and the weather had scared it off.

In between bursts of light, I inched forward, feeling my way in the total darkness as if I was at the edge of a cliff. For all I knew, I was.

The gentle incline I'd been stumbling up became steeper, and the bushes and dirt gave way to crumbly rock. Brush no longer tore at my clothes and hair, but my relief was short-lived when the hillside became so sheer and the rock so loose, I was forced to drop to my hands and knees. The thunder rolled in, crashing closer and closer.

Instinctively, I ducked and turned my head as another flash illuminated the pitch-black hillside. That flash gave me a brief snapshot of where I was, and the picture was this: me, on a slippery slope, framed by impenetrable darkness.

And below me, a huge cat with glowing eyes.

The thunder roared up the canyon like a fighter jet and boomed above my head. Its echo reverberated against the canyon walls and died, leaving a gloomy silence behind. I hugged the hill in the darkness. My heart pounded in my ears and I took a ragged breath.

I knew how fast a cougar could move. Yet, I was rooted to the spot where I'd crouched. Muscles tensed, I listened for the deadly sound of that cat scrambling up the rocky slope.

Another bolt of lightning tore the sky wide open. Thunder crashed and rain slashed over me in sheets. Adrenaline shot up my spine and kicked me into motion. I clawed my way through the mud streaming down the hillside. It was nearly impossible to get any traction. Raindrops plastered hair to my face and sent shivery fingers down the back of my neck. Water mixed with sweat, and I could taste my own panic.

I squinted through stinging eyes into the pitch-black night, frantic and searching desperately for something, anything, I could use as a weapon.

I was trembling violently, so it took a minute to realize that the ground under my hands had begun a sickening shudder of its own. I'd thought the thunder was loud, but the sound of the hill ripping open was deafening.

Trees swayed like reeling giants and the world collapsed. A yowling screech echoed off the hills, mingling with my own cries of terror. Out of control, I hurtled through a dark hole of rain and mud and pain.

TWENTY-FOUR

I EXPECTED TO LAND in the dagger claws and piercing teeth of the cougar.

Instead, the hill swallowed me whole. I tumbled downward at breath-sucking speed. Branches tore at my hair and sharp rocks gouged me to the bone. With a sickening thud and a crack that I heard *and* felt, I hit rock and finally stopped.

Later, I'm not sure how much later, I woke in darkness. I prepared to move, but my first deep breath caused nauseating pain to lance through my middle. I couldn't budge from where I slumped, legs splayed like a rag doll, leaning against something hard and cold.

I listened to the sound of the storm, but I could no longer feel wind or rain pelting my skin. I was in a sheltered spot. My hand brushed rock beneath me, but the thing at my back didn't feel natural. Behind me, trickling water plinked through what I supposed was the hole I'd fallen into.

I opened my eyes as wide as I could, trying to penetrate the inky void around me. *Where was that cougar?*

My eyes kept slamming shut, my head lolled forward, and I was unbelievably thirsty. My tongue felt thick and swollen and it hurt to swallow—when I did, I tasted blood. I wanted nothing but to end the pain.

I opened and closed one hand, then the other. They both felt like refrigerated meat. Sometime during my wild descent, Mom's sweater had been ripped from my body. It was gone forever, buried somewhere on that hillside in rain and muck, and for some reason, that's what made me cry.

I WAS BACK IN my usual dream, but unusually aware of mom's pain in every bone of my own broken body. This was new, and so was what came next. This time, Mom no longer suffered alone, cold and shivering on that mountainside, waiting for a rescue that came too late. This time, Lookout, my sure-footed wild miracle of a stallion, appeared above us. He picked his way down the side of that sheer cliff, slowed, stopped and nudged Mom gently with his nose. As he lowered himself next to her, she curled into the warmth of his body.

I watched, awe-struck, as they both began to transform. He became smaller and smaller, until he was no bigger than a newborn colt. She shape shifted and expanded until she was a beautiful, healthy mare. She licked him and loved him, and I was him, and she was my mom and his mom.

Despite the pain, I smiled. I opened my eyes and I could make out my surroundings—dawn was breaking. Filtered light revealed rock walls on every side, and I realized I had fallen into a large cave.

The ceiling was maybe fifteen feet above me. I'd come to rest on a mound of rocky earth and forest debris. Below and in front of me, about ten feet away, was the cave's opening, although the view beyond it was obscured by brushy growth. Most of the light was coming from above, shining through the hole that had swallowed me.

I could no longer hear the slash of rain outside. The storm must have come and gone, as it often did in the mountains, crashing through like a transient vandal in the night and continuing on its way. Though the rain had stopped, I could hear the sound of rushing water nearby. Some Gold Creek tributary tumbled past, not far from the cave's opening. My thirst returned with a vengeance.

The normal sounds of an early morning in the mountains sifted into my cave. Bird calls joined with the stream's burble. It was comforting, and I started to convince myself I'd imagined the cougar last night in the storm.

Something came pushing through the brush at the mouth of the cave.

I drew in a sharp breath. Fiery pain lanced through my gut and shot down my spine. Everything inside me screamed, *move!* But even turning my head caused the darkness to gather in the edges of my vision. *Maybe passing out was the lesser of evils.* I wanted to turn away, but I couldn't even do that. I squeezed my eyes tight, and waited, shivering from the cold and the fear.

As I listened to the approaching creature get closer and closer, time slowed. Other than whatever was creeping toward me, I was alone in that cave, I was sure of it. Yet, I felt something like two arms wrap around me, and I heard a voice, that wasn't really a voice but like the echo of one.

Do not let your heart be troubled… God is our refuge and strength, an ever-present help in trouble. Therefore, we will not fear, though the earth gives way and the mountains fall…

Warmth and comfort I hadn't felt since the last time my mother's arms were around me flooded over and through me, replacing the pain. I let my conscious mind go to the place I'd kept locked away, the mountainside that haunted my dreams at night—to those last moments of Mom's life.

I imagined her lying there in the snow, broken beyond repair and alone—and yet, maybe not so alone after all. This comfort, this warmth. She *must* have felt it, too. The terror drained out of me and took all my anger with it. Finally, peace.

The footfalls coming toward me were too heavy for a cougar, and I opened my eyes at the same time as something soft and warm nuzzled my neck, enveloping me in his familiar musky scent. I reached out a shaky hand and rubbed the yielding neck of my friend—*Lookout.* Ford's idea about playing hide-and-seek with Lookout flashed through my mind.

"You win," I whispered.

He nickered in response, but his head abruptly swung away and he stepped back.

I whimpered. *Don't leave me.*

It was *then* I saw the cougar. He pushed through the brush and limped into the cave with a low, ominous growl. He was injured and bloodied, but still deadly, still stalking us, still rumbling threats. The cougar's snarl swelled into a roar that reverberated off the cave walls as he leaped up the mound toward us.

Oh, God, I whispered. Perched in full sight above the big cat, paralyzed by pain, there was nothing I could do but wait for death and hope it would be quick.

In one fluid motion, with a scream, Lookout turned, reared and struck the cougar in mid-air with his front hooves, flinging the cat onto its back. The cougar rolled through the cave opening, and I lost sight of him. Moments later, I heard the sharp report of a rifle.

Relief flooded through me. We were saved.

Lookout trotted toward the cave entrance and started to step through the vines that covered the opening. Another shot rang out and the stallion's head twisted back.

I could see Lookout in profile, completely still, one blank eye wide, as if in shock. My brain couldn't comprehend what had just happened. I was so dizzy, I wasn't sure I could trust my own eyes and ears.

His front legs buckled beneath him, and I thought he was about to collapse. Instead, he recovered and charged out of the cave. I thought I heard another shot, but also, hoofbeats pounding away from me.

Someone shoved through the brush and into the cave, rifle in hand, and pulled up short when she saw me. I didn't recognize her at first. She was not her usual cool self. Her hair waved wildly around her face, her eyes darted from place to place and, like me, she was soaking wet.

My relief at seeing another human being melted into dismay as I stared at Sherrie Blackwell and that rifle. Had *she* shot Lookout? But why? Had I been wrong about Mr. Blackwell, after all? Had he and Sherrie continued to hunt Lookout behind Kurt's back?

I tried to say something, but all that came out was a barely audible murmur.

Sherrie stood there, those crazy eyes locked with mine. She was surprised, I could see that. But she offered no expressions of concern, no move to help. She seemed to be sizing me up, trying to come to some decision. "So, this is where you've gotten off to, Misty Stevens." She shook her head, as if I was a naughty child. "A lot of people are searching for you, girl."

Really? Someone was looking for me? Maybe I would survive this.

"You're in bad shape," she said, as if I was an extreme inconvenience. "I can tell that just by looking." Then, talking more to herself than to me, "And you've gotten between me and my gold—and that, I cannot have." She sat down on a rock, not far from where I lay. Rifle resting on her knee, she scanned me up and down with an intensity that made me shudder.

Gold? My brain might not have been working right, but I was pretty sure she'd said gold. I slowly stretched an arm behind me. The pain was savage, but I could feel the thing my back was resting against.

The smooth, flat surface was cold—colder than I was. I pictured a metal box. Maybe my pain caused a moment of clarity, but for whatever reason, the truth was suddenly obvious. The legend about Percival Blackwell wasn't a legend after all. He had hidden his gold in these mountains. I might even be lying in his secret mine, and Sherrie had found it.

Her chuckle bounced off the cave walls. "She understands." She said it like grudging praise. "You're too smart, hon, for your own good. You know that, don't you?"

I don't know anything. I tried to shout the words, but the pain took my breath away. The cold dread I felt now was completely different than my panic of the hours before. Despite the charm—the warmth and hospitality—she projected to those around her, I'd never felt comfortable around Sherrie. I'd thought it was me.

But the woman who stood before me was practically unrecognizable. This Sherrie made no attempt to disguise the malevolence in her cold eyes. This woman's voice was dull, her face was hard, and she nervously fingered the trigger of her rifle.

"Finding it was so easy once I started looking. Daddy taught me well. He turned me into a minerals expert." Her lips set in a disgusted line, "And the locals here are dumb as posts. I knew the first time Bob told me that story the night we met, that if the gold was here, I could find it. I bet my life on it."

She snickered. "And it's not as if I'm stealing, really. The Blackwell family owns the mineral rights here, and what's Bob's is mine. Of course, he doesn't need to know about the gold. You can't miss what you never knew you had."

I was a goner, I was sure of that. She'd never let me live. But, strangely, the most powerful emotion I felt was sadness for Mr. Blackwell. He was a crusty old guy, but I'd grown fond of him. He probably loved Sherrie, and he believed she loved him.

As my disgust at her deception crossed my face, Sherrie gave a defensive shrug. "You think I'm staying in this backwoods hole the rest of my life? Not a chance." She pointed the rifle at the metal box I leaned against. "And that's my ticket out. Despite what you may have heard about diamonds, gold is definitely a girl's best friend in this economy. The only one she needs."

She lifted her chin, adding in a petulant voice, "I've treated him well. He's enjoyed himself, and I'm leaving him with a great operation. He can have the ranch. I don't need it."

Without explanation, she turned and walked out of the cave. I thought I caught the sound of voices filtering down through the opening above me. I strained to hear, but Sherrie reentered the cave, drowning out any other sounds.

Two docile horses loaded with saddle bags clopped behind her. She left them several feet away and walked toward me, stopped, and crouched so we were face-to-face.

"A girl has to look out for herself," she said, continuing our one-sided conversation, as if we were chatting over coffee. "Bob's not getting any younger, you know, and he'll eventually leave me, like Daddy did." She raised one beautifully arched eyebrow. "They always leave, honey, and don't let them tell you otherwise."

Her expression changed abruptly from petulant to smug. "You got rid of Cody for me, and for that, I am grateful. The fact is, my flirtation with that boy worked a little too well. He followed me around like a love-sick puppy, and he was completely ineffective when it came to pumping you girls for information." She shrugged. "Men. Always disappointing."

Sherrie was manic, bouncing from thought to thought, and each time, her demeanor changed. In my dazed state, I was having trouble keeping up. But I blinked at the mention of Cody, and she smiled. "Oh, he told me you girls sent him out there that night. You should have heard the blue streak that came out that boy's mouth. The *names* he called you two and your boyfriend, Ford." She shook her head and whistled. "I assured him I'd get revenge for the both of us, but," she flicked a hand. "Good riddance to that kid. He could've blown this thing for me, and he still might, if he decides to talk."

"So, you present a problem, Misty." She squinted her eyes at me. "I'm thinking you're about to drop off into a permanent sleep." She brightened. "Which would solve my problem. But they're looking for you, and I need to get what's in that box and be on my way before they get to this side of the mountain. I know I hit that horse. They'll find him dead somewhere, which will end all the searching around here for him."

Relief that my friends were looking for me tangled with the sad certainty that Lookout was dying out there, and I couldn't ease his suffering, or say goodbye. Another stallion sacrificed to Blackwell's mine. A tear rolled down my cheek, but Sherrie didn't seem to notice.

"Knowing your Dad and your friends, they won't stop looking until they find you." Her expression became indignant. "Why, if they find you here, they might figure out why I up and left without a word." She put a hand on her hip. "I might even get blamed for your death."

She tilted her head, as if considering her options.

I watched as her eyes darkened. "I'm going to have to move you, darlin', and it's gonna hurt. But, hey, that's life."

She stuck the rifle in a holder on one of the saddle horses— I was obviously no threat—and climbed up the slope to me. I was helpless. I couldn't even take a deep breath and steel myself for the shock.

But when Sherrie grasped my shoulders and lifted me, pain knifed through my body and I found my voice. A scream ripped from my throat and reverberated through the cave.

I'd been almost completely silent up to that point. Startled, Sherrie dropped me flat on my back. My head smacked the rock beneath me with a crack that jarred every nerve and bone in my body. Stars burst in front of my eyes. Death would be a relief.

When my vision cleared, I found myself looking at the hole above me. Ford's face appeared in the opening, and just as quickly disappeared. Had I imagined him? But then a foot came through. Dirt rained down and pebbles ricocheted off the cave wall, crackling like gunfire in the cavern. I turned my head, closed my eyes and somehow managed to roll onto my side.

It sounded like something bounced off the cave wall, and dropped beside me. I opened my eyes as Ford knelt between Sherrie and me, a hand on my shoulder. He was breathing hard and he looked scared, but mostly furious and ready to fight like I'd never seen him. His other hand clenched into a fist.

I was just beginning to grasp that Ford was really there, when Bob Blackwell burst through the cave entrance. Sherrie dove for her rifle, grabbed it from the saddle holster and pointed it at Blackwell, then swung around and pointed it at Ford and me.

Her eyes were wild. I had no idea what she would do next, but I was sure it wouldn't be good. I swallowed over the thickness in my throat.

For a few heartbeats, all was quiet. Then, I heard shouts above us, and sounds of people scrambling toward the cave mouth.

Blackwell had raised his rifle, probably out of instinct, when Sherrie pointed her gun at him. "Sherrie," Mr. Blackwell pleaded, lowering the rifle as if it had become too heavy for him. "What are you doing? Put down the gun."

Sherrie stuck out her chin and shook her head back and forth, her rifle still pointed at us.

"I don't know what's going on, honey, but we'll work it out," he said. "It'll be okay."

Sherrie wavered for only a second. The steel returned to her eyes. "Look, darlin'," she called to him over her shoulder, her voice smooth and sweet, so impossibly opposite of the expression on her face. "I found Grandpa Percival's gold. Now we can have everything we ever wanted."

At first, Blackwell said nothing. His eyes were sad above a tight jaw, yet he raised his rifle and pointed it at his wife's back. He took a resolute stance. "Sherrie, hon," he said, "I was darn near satisfied before you came into my life. I'll miss you, but I don't need gold to make me happy." He swallowed and took a firm grip on the barrel of his gun. "Now, I don't think I can shoot you because, Lord knows, I have loved you. Please, honey, put that gun down, and we'll talk it out. I don't want to shoot you. You know I don't."

Sherrie's mouth spread into a slow smile, and she straightened her shoulders. She thought she'd won. She couldn't see Blackwell's face, or who was coming up behind him.

Shadows danced over the cave walls. Exclamations of shock and surprise at the scene in front of those entering the cave bounced around the cavern. Sherrie's smile faltered, but she didn't turn around and her rifle never wavered. I had an impossible urge to duck, but I couldn't move and there was nowhere to go.

As the faces of the people now standing with Blackwell came into view, I felt the tiniest twinge of hope. They were beautiful, wonderful, fierce faces.

"However," Mr. Blackwell continued, his voice sad but firm, "Kurt is right behind me. While I believe he has always liked you, he's a law enforcement officer, and this mine is on Forest Service land. And there's Dr. Stevens, right here next to me, also heavily armed this morning. He is not taking kindly to you pointin' a rifle at his daughter."

I wasn't looking at Sherrie anymore, just Dad, standing beside Blackwell. He held my gaze and his eyes said it all—no way would he let Sherrie hurt me again.

A horrible shrieking—which I think was Sherrie—felt like it would split my pounding head in half. I squeezed my eyes shut. Shouts and the sounds of struggle rolled round and round the cavern, jumbling one on top of the other. Metal thumped against rock. Horses clopped and whinnied.

But I didn't see what happened, or at least I don't remember. When I realized my dad was coming to get me, I stopped struggling against the darkness and the pain. The last thing I saw was Ford's face in front of me. The last thing I heard was Dad saying my name, "Misty!" he called. "Misty, stay with us!"

I tried, but I couldn't. The cave and everything in it shimmered, faded, and went black.

TWENTY-FIVE

MY ARMS CIRCLED DAD'S waist and we rode effortlessly on Lookout's back through a whirlwind of rainbow colors and flashing shadows. It felt like flying. Out of the corner of my eye, I could see Rosa beside us, and I knew Mom was riding her. I could hear the smile in her voice when she called out the familiar words, "You're just like him."

I understood, somehow, that Dad was terribly concerned for me. I told him, "I'll be okay, now. You don't need to worry about me.

He turned his head back and our eyes locked. He said, "But I do."

TWENTY-SIX

I WAS ALIVE, BUT I had no desire to move or open my eyes. I lay still, enjoying the cool air of the room, the smoothness of the sheets against my skin.

Later, the same sensations, but also the scent of antiseptic, and voices outside my room. I realized I was not in my own bed, but in a hospital. I became aware of something taped to the inside of one wrist.

The events of the days before began to drift back in disjointed slow motion. My cloudy brain kept trying to put the memories in order. I replayed running from the house, the storm, the cougar, falling, Sherrie. I remembered thirst and the sound of a rifle and Lookout's head reeling back. I knew it had all happened, but I remembered the reality of the last hours as if it was another one of my nightmares. Only the dream I'd had at the end felt authentic.

The next time my brain rose lazily to the surface of consciousness, I was aware of others in my room.

"She's going to be okay." Lou's voice. "She's just sleeping now, I guess. That's what they said."

Then Ford. "But she still hasn't opened her eyes? Said anything?"

I was glad my friends were on speaking terms again, talking barely above whispers to each other.

"No, but Dr. Stevens says it's a matter of time. I heard the doctor tell him something about a 'simple rib fracture' and 'minor liver laceration'."

"Doesn't look simple to me."

"Yeah, she looks bad, huh?"

Fantastic. Served me right for not telling them I was awake.

"All those cuts and bruises. She lost a lot of blood and the doctor said she was hypothermic. Her body went into shock. That's what almost—"

"I know." Ford interrupted her. "Don't say it."

Silence.

"I wish she'd wake up," Lou said.

"You been here all day?"

"Me and Dr. Stevens. We're taking turns watching her. He's downstairs getting us something to eat right now, not that I'm hungry."

They fell into silence, and I started to slip back to sleep.

Ford said, "That life flight was pretty dramatic, I bet. Your first time in a helicopter?"

"I really don't remember much about it. I was so focused on Misty and whether she was going to be okay. Dr. Stevens, he was crazy with worry."

Lou's voice caught and Ford said, "It doesn't look like he's the only one. She'll be okay, Lilou."

"She's my best friend." Lou sniffed

"I know," Ford paused, "but you guys are really different from each other."

I pictured Lou nodding. "I'm the 'fun girl,' you know? People like to have me around because I keep the party or the conversation or whatever, I keep it rolling—right?"

"Mm-hmm."

"The flip side of that is, as you well know," her voice became apologetic, "I cannot keep my mouth shut."

"Yeah, well," Ford said, "we've all said things we regret."

"Me more than most." She sighed. "Misty always gives me the benefit of the doubt. She's there for me, no matter what, and I sort of took advantage of that this summer."

Silence.

"Also," she added, and she was laughing, "we make a good team, because being around us makes for a 'pretty great' summer, wouldn't you say, hero?"

"So you keep saying."

She shot back, "But I wasn't the first one to say it, now, was I?"

I fell back to sleep to the sound of them teasing each other. To this day, I'm not sure if that conversation was real, or if I dreamt it, because I've never asked.

What I do know, is that when I woke up the next time, I was wide awake, ravenously hungry and thirsty, and we were all friends again.

I was still exhausted, and everything hurt. I spent the next few days in the hospital, asleep more than awake. One evening, I opened my eyes to moonlight casting shafts of light and shadow across my bed. Dad was sitting in the same chair he'd sat in for days, it seemed, watching me.

"Hey, there she is." He reached over and placed a gentle hand on my arm. "How are you feeling? Do you need anything?"

"No, I'm good."

I'd told my story to him and law enforcement officials of various types earlier in the day. It was the first time Dad had allowed anyone to ask me questions, thankfully, because the interrogation had worn me out. I'd tried to impress on all of them the importance of finding Lookout, how he'd saved my life, right before Ford and Mr. Blackwell had saved me again. I hadn't asked what happened to Sherrie, and nobody offered the information. But I was very concerned about Lookout.

"Any sign of him, Dad?"

He shook his head. He knew who I was talking about. "Everyone's keeping their eyes open, Sweetness, but there's no sign of him, which could be a good thing. Sometimes, no news is good news."

I must have looked doubtful. I remembered the last time I had used that phrase—*no news is good news*—about hoping Lou had made it home from our hike with Rosa. So much had happened since then. So much had changed.

"Misty, I don't want you to worry about that horse." His voice was verging on anger. "I know he's important to you, even though the last thing I thought you'd fall in love with this summer was a horse. But there's nothing a worried mind will do for him. You need to put your energy into getting better."

I knew he was right, and I knew he wasn't mad at me. He was mad at what had happened to me. I also knew I'd seen Lookout get shot. I didn't hold out much hope I'd ever see the stallion again.

"Dad?" I prepared to ask a question I'd had since waking up after that night, one I wasn't sure I wanted to know the answer to.

He leaned in. "What, Mist? What is it?"

"I sort of blacked out when Sherrie went down. I was wondering who got her gun away from her—who took her down?"

Dad sat back and his eyes slid away from mine.

"Dad, it was you, wasn't it? What were you thinking? She was crazy, and she was armed."

"Yeah, she was, and her rifle was pointed at you." He met my eyes, and I could see his were haunted with that memory. "I more…shoved her aside, on my way to you."

That made me smile.

"Water?" Dad was holding out the water bottle with the plastic straw pointed toward me.

I pushed myself up, took the bottle and dutifully had a few sips. We sat for a minute in silence, until I started to fall asleep. I felt my hand jerk and opened my eyes.

Dad scooped the water bottle away before I dropped it, and I slipped back down onto my pillows.

"They're talking about springing you tomorrow, Mist." He sounded concerned. "What do you think about that? Do you think you're ready?"

"Yeah, I feel pretty good, and I'd like to go home." I yawned. "I feel so lazy, lying here." I stopped fighting the urge to sleep and closed my eyes.

"Takes a lot of energy to recover from injuries like yours. I don't think laziness is something you need to be concerned about at this point. Just rest."

"It's been so long since I slept well." I opened my eyes. "There have been times, the last few months, I've been afraid to close my eyes at night. Afraid of my dreams. But until we came here, it was also hard to get excited about anything but sleeping."

He nodded. "I know. This summer's changed a lot of things."

"True that. The last few days," I closed my eyes again. "Sleep feels so good, so peaceful, I kind of wish I was awake to enjoy it."

Dad chuckled. "You wish you were awake enough to enjoy being at rest?"

"Mm-hmm."

"Well, that would be what heaven's like, Sweetness."

"You think?"

"Yeah, I really do."

He sounded so sure, I believed him.

I WAS SNUGGLED ON the porch swing, propped up with pillows, surrounded by the people I loved and cared about, and I felt like Dorothy returning from Oz.

Everyone was there—Bea, Frank and Donna, Kurt and Ford, Lou and Dad. Bob Blackwell and June were there, too, which was a surprise. Lou's mom had driven all the way back up the mountain when Lou called to tell her what had happened to me.

Dad, Lou and I arrived around dinner time and discovered the women had been cooking all afternoon. They presented us with homemade chicken soup, salad, and fresh-from-the-oven bread that smelled heavenly, especially after the so-called food at the hospital. Dad said a prayer before we ate, a real prayer. He thanked God for the meal, for each person there, for bringing me home safe.

After dinner, Lou handed me an honest-to-goodness paper and cardboard-covered scrapbook filled with all our pictures from the summer, combined with the pictures of Mom we'd been reproducing. I flipped through it, smiling at all the memories. "I didn't even know they made scrapbooks like this anymore."

"Mom found it," was all she said.

As the late afternoon wore into evening, we gathered on the front porch, each person recounting his or her perspective on the night that had almost been my last.

Lou said she'd gone to sleep, thinking I was still out with Dad. She'd awakened in the middle of the night and realized I'd never come to bed. "I searched everywhere in the house for you, Mist—in the kitchen, out on the porch. I even stuck my feet in my boots and went up to the orchard with a flashlight. The weather was insane—wind rattling the windows, rain, thunder, lightning. That was when I decided I had no choice. I woke up your dad."

Dad, sitting in the swing next to me, made a frustrated sound. "At first, I couldn't understand what she was saying to me. I'd gone to bed thinking you were both already asleep."

Lou caught the expression on his face and frowned. "I shouldn't have waited so long. I thought maybe she'd gone for a walk or something and I didn't want to…" Her voice trailed off.

She sat on the porch floor, near enough for me to reach with a foot, and I gave her a nudge with my toe. Raising her head, she returned my smile. We both knew she'd been trying to keep me from getting into trouble.

"I really was taking a walk," I said. "You couldn't have known I was lost. It's not like I've ever done anything that stupid before."

Kurt said, "The fact that such behavior wasn't like you, made it easier to get volunteers out of bed in the middle of the night to start a search. They helped us cover a lot of ground."

"Still," he shook his head, "when that storm hit with full force, a lot of the horses couldn't take the thunder and lightning, and most of the volunteers on horseback had to head for home."

Remembering that night still made me squirm. I swallowed and willed my heart to stay calm.

"In the end," Kurt said, "we only had those of us on foot. Frank, Donna, and a couple of my seasonal employees searching around Gold Creek Canyon—"

"And the rest of us searching in Opal Creek Canyon," Ford said. "Bea stayed here at the house in case you came back."

"I confess, Misty," Bea cut in, "I was prayin' like a saint on Sunday that you would come sauntering through that door. Been years since I've prayed, but I prayed that night."

"I think we were all praying hard," Lou said softly. Everyone nodded and I tried to come up with words that would express the gratitude I felt for all of them.

"Thank you," was all I managed.

"And thank goodness for that old orange sweater of your mom's," Dad said. "Because that's what saved you. Those first gun shots led us in the right direction, and I caught sight of that muddy sweater hanging on the edge of the cave-in.”

Of course, it was Dad who saw the sweater. *He sees things other people miss.*

“It was weird,” Ford said, “to hear voices underneath us, inside the hillside. We could hear Sherrie’s voice, but we couldn’t figure out where it was coming from at first. And then I heard you scream—”

“I was freaking out,” Lou interrupted. “Ford disappeared down that hole trying to get to you, but I didn’t know what he was doing. He just vanished!”

“I sort of can’t believe I did that.” He caught my eye. “Instinct, I guess.” He looked around the group. “Don’t anybody tell my mom.”

“Too late,” Kurt said.

Ford groaned. “What’d she say?”

“The first words she said,” Kurt cleared his throat. “I’m not going to repeat—”

Ford rubbed the back of his neck. “Great.”

“Nah, it’s all good.” Kurt patted his shoulder. “She’s proud of you, Ford.”

“I’m glad you did what you did, kid,” Mr. Blackwell said. “You distracted Sherrie long enough for me to get inside that cave.”

Blackwell’s face had aged about ten years, it seemed, in the last few days. Deeper lines were etched in his forehead and around his mouth. The sparkle had left his eyes, which made me sad. “You saved my life, Mr. Blackwell. I don’t know how I can ever thank you.”

He dipped his head. "I knew Sherrie'd been sneaking off, but I had no idea…"

Bea put her hand on Blackwell's arm, and he gave her a wan smile.

Kurt said, "I know a few more pieces of the story. I think you'll especially find this interesting, Misty."

All eyes turned to Kurt, but he turned to Blackwell. "You want to tell 'em, Bob?"

As Mr. Blackwell prepared to speak, a tiny hint of that old sparkle returned to his eyes. "I was feeling real low after what Sherrie did." He slumped, but recovered and straightened his shoulders.

"Kurt told me how that horse saved your life, Misty, and I began to feel sorry for the bad feelings I'd had toward the animal. I had a hunch where Lookout might have gone if he was hurt. It's a clearing on the ridge above the old cabin site where I often see wild horses. There's good grass up there, and they can see danger coming from every side. So, I called Kurt and we headed over."

"Good thing he did," Kurt added. "That cougar and Lookout had evidently taken up where they'd left off—"

"Wait." I frowned. "The cougar? I thought Sherrie killed it."

Blackwell and Kurt shook their heads. "They were so torn up, I don't know which one would've come out on top," Blackwell said. "But they were both still alive."

I sat up straighter. "You saw Lookout? He was alive?"

Simultaneous smiles spread across the men's faces, and Kurt said, "*Is* alive, Misty. Lookout *is* alive."

I couldn't believe it. "You know where he is? Is he okay?"

"We took him to our holding pen in Ponder," Kurt said. "It took us a while to find the bullet that hit him. We had to tranquilize him to catch him and while he was out, Doc searched and searched and finally found the bullet lodged in his big fat tongue. Pulled it out, and I'm sure he'll be his old ornery self in no time.

"We do have a problem, though." Kurt looked from Dad to me. "We can't let him continue to wander free around here. Even before this happened, he was scheduled to be removed. The question is, what do I do with him now?"

I turned to Dad, but he was one step ahead of me. "I think we might be able to help you out with that."

Kurt grinned at him. "I thought you might."

I was speechless. Lookout was okay, and Dad had offered to adopt him. He actually seemed happy about it. I was suddenly the owner of a wild, rogue stallion. I had no idea what to do with him, but Dad would help me. Ready or not, Lookout was alive and well, and he was mine.

"What happened to the cougar?" Ford asked.

Blackwell closed one eye and pulled an imaginary trigger. "No one has to worry about that old cat, ever again."

He pushed off the railing he'd been leaning against and held out a hand, which I took. "Misty, you're looking real good." He smiled. "I'm glad you're recovering so well. And I apologize, for everything."

"No worries." I gave his gnarly knuckles a squeeze. "Thank you so much for saving Lookout, and me."

Blackwell straightened and some of his old swagger was back. He flashed me a toothy grin and tipped his hat. "All part of the service, darlin', all part of the service."

He turned at that, climbed down the porch steps and headed for his truck.

Frank stood up out of one of the low chairs and stretched as Blackwell drove off. "I think we'll be heading back to camp. Your dad says you can take notes for us, Misty, so I guess we'll be seeing you at the site, after you've had a few more days to recover."

This was news to me. Dad looked encouraging, so I shrugged at Frank. "Guess I'll be seeing you."

"Bob Blackwell is a rough old guy," Kurt said, after the others had gone. "But I've always liked him, and he certainly showed his character on this one. He visited Sherrie every day at the jail in town, before the federal marshals moved her to Portland—not that she seemed grateful."

I wasn't inclined to make excuses for Sherrie, but there was a part of me that could relate. "She wasn't in her right mind," I said to Kurt. "Losing her dad did something to her, I think."

He acknowledged that with a nod and stood up. "One thing Sherrie was right about—the Blackwell family still holds the mineral rights to this area. I don't know what the government will work out with Bob in that regard, but he's already said he's going to start an endowment with the gold Sherrie found. He wants to support the work the Forest Service does here with the wild horses, and promote the area for conservation and tourism."

"Your budget troubles may be history, then?" Dad asked.

"Every bit helps. Speaking of the work I do," he checked his watch, "I've got to get going. You coming, Ford? Morning'll be here before you know it."

Ford nodded. "In a bit."

The light started to fade, and the sky turned gold.

"Dr. Stevens," Lou said, "remember that day Lookout, or the cougar, scared off Mr. Blackwell's horses? He said these horses had been left behind here. Where did they come from, anyway?"

I smiled at Dad and he smiled back. A chance for him to talk about history—Lou had no idea how happy she'd made him.

He thought for a few seconds. "Most scientists would say that at the end of the last ice age, all of the wild American horses died. This was at the same time as the last of the wooly mammoths, the last of the mastodons, the last of the ice. In some places, it looks like people may have hunted some of these animals to extinction, but no one knows for sure. It wasn't until the 1500s that horses returned to the Americas with Spanish explorers.

"By the early 1700s, according to the stories of the oldest of the elders, tribes in the Pacific Northwest started to ride horses. But these horses here now are remnants of horses the US military brought during the late 1800s, when they were at war with local tribes. After the military was done with them, it was cheaper to turn the horses out than ship them back east."

"So, Mr. Blackwell was right," Lou said. "These horses aren't native to this area."

"I don't know." Ford stood up. He caught my eye. "I think what matters is that we're all here now. And the question is, what are we gonna do with each other?"

"Good question, that," Dad said. "You headed out?"

"Yeah, unlike some people lounging on this porch, I have to get going at the crack of dawn tomorrow."

I struggled out of the swing. "I'll walk you to your car."

Ford held up a hand. "You don't have to do that, Mist."

Dad said, "You're looking kind of tired."

"Misty," Lou was laughing. "You could have a lot of fun with this."

"Right?" I stood up, carefully. The bandages around my middle made it hard to bend, or breath. I was stiff and sore, but I managed to suppress a groan as I climbed out of the swing. "You saved my life," I said to Ford. "The least I can do is walk you to your car."

Dad helped me down the two steps to the ground. When we got to Ford's truck, we went around to the driver's side, which gave us a little bit of privacy.

I wasn't sure what to say, and I guess Ford felt the same way. We leaned against the truck, our arms touching, watching the last of the light make the mountaintops glow.

Finally, I looked up at him. He was still looking at the mountains and I watched him, his face in profile. I'd missed that face while I was in the hospital. "Dad said you went to see your Grandma's sister."

He nodded.

"How was that?" I wondered.

He was quiet. Then, "It was kind of weird. And kind of good…she reminded me a lot of Grandma." He paused, shrugged. "It was a start."

"Were you glad you went? Or, no?" I was the one who'd encouraged him to go, and it seemed like he had mixed feelings about the visit, at the very least.

To my relief, he looked down at me and grinned. "Yeah, Mist. It was the right thing to do. I'm glad I went."

I stepped around and stood in front of him. "I feel like I should at least give you a hug for saving my life, but the doctor's told me hugging is forbidden for the next few weeks."

The grin turned into a wry smile. "Bet your dad loved that."

How much to heart had he taken that conversation with Dad? And what did it mean for Ford and me?

With a quick breath, I stepped closer. "My lips aren't injured."

His eyes went wide and he glanced back through the truck's window at Dad. He seemed occupied in a conversation with June and Lou, but I had a feeling, and I'm sure Ford did, too, that he was aware of our every move. I didn't really expect Ford to take me up on my offer, but I wanted to know what he was thinking. His eyes met mine and he said, "It's *my* mouth getting injured that concerns me, if your Dad sees me kissing you."

I laughed and held out my hand. "Shake, then?" I was only half kidding, hoping for some kind of connection before he left.

He took the hand I offered and held it. He pulled me closer and raised my fingers to his lips. "There," he said, giving my hand a squeeze. "That's *courtly*. Let's see what your dad does with that."

He turned and pulled open his door while I stepped back.

The truck sputtered and roared to life. Ford drove off with a quick wave to the others on the porch.

I stood, rooted to that spot and confused. Part of me felt like something had ended. Was he letting me down easy, because we still had to work together? I wasn't shocked, after all the drama and secrets, his conversation with Dad, and how angry and betrayed he'd seemed that last day at the site. Besides, soon, we'd all be going home.

Just like I was sure of Lou, somehow, I knew Ford and I would always be friends. But I'd given him pieces of my heart that I'd barely known existed before we met, and when he drove away, he took those pieces with him. Only as the distance lengthened between us did I realize how much that would hurt.

I trudged slowly toward the porch, blinking back tears. *He finally made me cry. At least he'd never know.*

Dad rose to help me up the stairs, in the same moment, I heard the sound of Ford's truck returning.

It rolled to a stop at the porch and Ford leaned out. "Misty," he called, "I forgot to tell you something."

I dashed away the tear on my cheek and stood close enough to his open window that those on the porch might not hear our every word. "Yeah?"

He looked me up and down, and his eyes softened at the tears shining in the edges of mine, but all he said was, "I forgot to tell you, cool hair."

My hopelessly tangled, dirty, blood-soaked dreads had been cut off by the emergency room staff so they could clean and staple my head wounds. Appearances were obviously not a priority for whoever made short work of my hairstyle. The remains were short and spiky, pointing every direction. I was almost bald in spots. It was a disaster.

I smiled and shook my head, but he managed to keep a straight face. "I'll be seeing you, Misty Stevens."

"Really?" I asked.

"Wild horses couldn't keep me away."

He was grinning, and so was I, as he drove past me and circled toward the road.

After he was gone, I was ready to float up the porch steps, until I turned and met the eyes-over-the-glasses look on my father's face. He didn't say anything, though, so neither did I as he helped me up.

June, however, "He's a cute one, isn't he?" She winked at me, so like Lou.

There was a warning in Dad's voice when he said, "June."

"Oh, Paul, don't be such an old curmudgeon." She held out her hand to Lou. "You ready for bed, roomie? Despite the fact I get to 'lounge' around here tomorrow with Misty, I am beat tonight."

Lou yawned and allowed her mom to pull her up. "Me, too."

It was nearly impossible for me to get up the stairs in my current condition. June and Lou were taking over the upstairs, and I was sleeping in the downstairs bedroom. Dad was on the couch.

Lou hugged me, carefully, and so did June. "So glad you're out of the hospital, sweets," June said, with a kiss on my cheek. "Sleep good."

She turned to Dad. "Sure hope you'll be okay on that couch, Paul. Doesn't look very comfortable."

"Believe me," Dad said. "I've slept on much worse. Goodnight."

"Goodnight, you two." I gave them a wave. "Love you."

I WAS BEYOND THANKFUL for cool, fresh air after days in my climate-controlled hospital room, and I breathed it in as the sky darkened. Nighthawks materialized like shadow spirits, and their tiny dark bodies swooped through the air, dove and skimmed the tips of the grasses. The sounds of Lou and June climbing into bed faded until all I could hear were Lou's familiar snuffling snores.

Voice low, Dad said, "Lou, June and I had quite a talk while you were recovering in the hospital. Actually, it's difficult to get Lou to stop talking once you get that girl started."

"Tell me about it. But, you know, that's part of her charm—she talks, and I don't have to. What did she say?"

"She told us about Cody."

"Really. How did that go?"

Dad chuckled. "June is a force to be reckoned with, I'll tell you that. You'll notice there's been no phone or computer anywhere near Lou since you got back?"

Now that he mentioned it—no wonder Lou had created an old-school scrapbook instead of an on-line album.

"June said something about returning her devices when Lou's thirty." He became serious. "I don't want to lecture you, Misty, now of all times. But if you'd been honest with me about Lou and Cody, that knowledge may have given Kurt some leverage. He might've been able to get Cody to tell him who his accomplice was. It's possible none of this had to happen."

"Then there was what was going on between you and Lookout."

"Maybe. But I didn't feel like the thing with Cody was my secret to tell, and I knew Lou would 'fess up eventually. And I was planning to tell you and Kurt about Lookout. I was wrong to wait so long."

"Hindsight. I wish you could trust me, though."

"I do trust you, Dad. It's just hard to know what the right thing is sometimes."

After a couple minutes, he took a breath. "I'm sorry for not talking with you about moving, Misty. I realize now that it's only the two of us…" He stopped. "Without your mom, well, I've been thinking I need to make these decisions alone. But you're getting old enough…" He shifted in his seat, and shook his head.

I couldn't stand how hard this was for him. "It's okay, Dad. Really."

"Lou said…" Dad's voice trailed off again.

This was getting awkward. What had Lou told him?

He began again. "You know, Misty, it really doesn't bother me how much you look like your mom."

My jaw dropped.

"I will admit this." His voice sounded wistful, but there was also a smile in it. "Sometimes when you walk in the room, especially now that you're getting older, the resemblance takes my breath away, but it's not a bad thing. Your mom was beautiful—and so are you."

"Aw, Dad," I mumbled, "you're makin' me blush."

"Mist, there's nothing you can do, or not do, that makes missing your mom any better or worse for me. Her loss is slowly filling the space where her life once was. But that takes time, and I don't know how it will end. And I'm pretty sure you understand that."

I nodded. Of course I did.

"I hope you haven't been thinking I expect you to try to fill that hole in my life…in our lives."

I couldn't look at him. Is that what I'd been trying to do the last few months?

His voice was soft. "You're not your mom, Mist."

I hung my head and tears pricked the corners of my eyes. "That's for sure." One tear escaped and ran down my cheek.

"Misty look at me." He gently turned my chin toward him and wiped away the tear with his thumb. "I know *you're* still figuring all this out," he said. "But I do know who you are, my sensitive, insightful, intrepid daughter, and I wouldn't want you to be anyone else. I thought you were the most incredible miracle the minute I laid eyes on you, and sixteen years with you haven't changed my mind."

He put an arm around my shoulders and slowly pulled me to him. "I love *you*, Misty. You must've felt like there wasn't a lot you could count on, lately, but no matter what, you can count on that."

"I think that's a line from a novel," I said, but I couldn't help smiling.

He laughed, nodding. "It might be. Books are where I get some of my best lines—doesn't make it any less true. And about June."

I froze. *Here it comes.*

"Lou told me what you two saw—or thought you saw. I'll tell you the same thing I told her."

I closed my eyes and waited. For a few seconds, there was only the rustling sounds of the grasses in the field, the creak of our swaying swing.

"What you need to understand," Dad finally said, "is that June and I, we're friends. She was close to your mom—their friendship was very deep—and talking with her comforts me. But Misty, that's all. We're two friends comforting each other. June knows that. Now Lou knows, and I hope you understand."

I pulled away and scanned his face. I could see it was hard for him to talk about this. He was a little red, and he was jiggling his knee, which made the swing bounce. I was pretty sure his feelings for June, and hers for him, could easily grow beyond friendship in the future. For some reason, that thought didn't sting like it had a few days ago. But I could also tell Dad was being as honest with me as he could right then. I nodded, relieved.

He brushed at my bangs—not like a mom would—just so he could see my eyes. But it felt like love. "From here on out," he said, "I'll try to remember that the decisions I make affect you, too. You're old enough to have a say in this family's future. We'll decide together what to do and where to go from here."

My pain medication must have been wearing off at about that point, because every muscle, every bone, every nerve in my body was beginning to hurt—except my heart. In the deepest part of me, I felt light and open to possibility.

And there came those words again.

Do not let your heart be troubled…not tonight. So, I leaned back on Dad's shoulder, and found a place to rest.

Acknowledgements

On one level, this is a book about searching for treasure, and readers won't have to dig too deep to find homage to many of the teen books and authors I've loved over the years. Enjoy spotting them, and thank you so much for reading my book. To Madeleine L'Engle, wherever you are, thank you for *A Wrinkle In Time*, which, when I read it, made me say for the first time, "I want to be a writer." The seeds of this story were planted during a conversation with Debbie Driesner, sitting on the front porch of her Double D Mustangs ranch in Oregon. We were talking about Debbie's famous search and rescue mustang, Eeyore (RIP), and how all those horse and girl adventure books helped us through our early teen highs and lows. I'm thankful for Debbie, her Eeyore, and that day. (Read Eeyore's story, on whom Lookout is based, at mustangsandmohr.org). To my first readers and critique groupies, Becky, Valerie, Kathy, Michelle, Marguerite, Laurie and Amber—thanks for keeping me laughing and for rolling with my perpetual revisions—this is a better novel because of you. To my pre-release reader/authors Heather, Peter, Hilarey, and Patrick, and to all the authors and writers at Idahope Christian Writers—I respect you all immensely, and your encouragement has meant the world to me. To the staff and my students at Boise Classical Academy, getting to spend my days with you while I completed the final edit on this novel kept me firmly grounded in a teen world—thanks for that, and for always being so awesome. To my bookseller friends here in Boise, thanks for keeping the fire burning. To my sister-friends, Gina, Robin and Karen, my sweet friends Michelle L., Niccole, Michelle D. and her daughter Malena, and my nieces Melissa, Katherine and Erika, who waded through earlier versions of this novel as it evolved and offered advice and encouragement—labor of love doesn't begin to describe it. To my actors Katherine Boord, Daniel Pearson, Kaila Ho, and Paul Zimmerman, and all the crew who worked on the trailer and cutscenes for this book: Jake Hess and Samara Attridge, for grip and production assistance, Isaiah Zimmerman's direction, and David Rhoades with Giant Killer Media for photography and editing, what a blast you all are. It was a pleasure and a joy working with you. To all my nieces and niece-like peoples, thank you for allowing me into your lives while you navigated the exciting waves and treacherous waters of teen girl-hood, especially Melissa, Erika and Sierra—you three were my first muses. In addition, Erika and Melissa, you are the high priestesses of the mysteries of horse-love and knowledge. Thank you for always being there to patiently answer my bajillion questions and for ensuring I honored these creatures you know and love so passionately. To my editor and mentor, Rebecca Carey Lyles, my eyes are welling up just thinking about you—one of my life goals is to be the kind of mentor you are to so many. To my family, Mom and Dad, both gone too soon, who always believed in and encouraged my compulsion to write, and my siblings, Nancy, Mike and Paul—

I don't know how I would live in this world without you. To my sons, Jake and Joe, you make every day better. To my husband and favorite person in the world, Sean Hess, thank you for always believing in me, encouraging me, never allowing me to give up—and for liking my hair. I'm a better person, and writer, with you. Finally, thank God, for life, love, mercy, compassion, inspiration, beauty, comfort, joy and rest. It's all for You.

The good stuff in this novel is the result of my relationships with the aforementioned. The mistakes are all mine. And speaking of mistakes, you don't need to write and let me know when you find one—it's okay. Forgiving each other's mistakes is the hallmark of every great friendship.

And now that we're friends, I'd love to get to know you better! Find me on Facebook and at www.lisamichellehess.com.

Lisa Michelle Hess has lived in every state on the West Coast of the U.S. and loved all of them. Over the years, she's been a journalist, non-profit consultant, and bookseller, which were all her favorite jobs while she had them. Her current favorite career is teaching high school literature in Boise, Idaho, where she lives with one husband, two sons, two dogs, and two turtles. You can find some of Lisa's other stories in *Passageways: A Short Story Collection. The Ghost of Gold Creek* is her first full-length novel. Find out more about Lisa at lisamichellehess.com.